A Dawn of Onyx

OF
Onyx

KATE GOLDEN

BERKLEY ROMANCE
NEW YORK

T0037138

BERKLEY ROMANCE
Published by Berkley
An imprint of Penguin Random House LLC
penguinrandomhouse.com

Original map design by Jack Johnson

Library of Congress Cataloging-in-Publication Data

Names: Golden, Kate, author.
Title: A dawn of onyx / Kate Golden.
Description: Berkley Romance trade paperback edition |
New York : Berkley Romance, 2023. | Series: The sacred stones |
A Dawn of Onyx was originally self-published, in different form, in 2022.
Identifiers: LCCN 2023022558 (print) | LCCN 2023022559 (ebook) |
ISBN 9780593641903 (trade paperback) | ISBN 9780593641910 (ebook)
Subjects: LCGFT: Fantasy fiction. | Romance fiction. | Novels.
Classification: LCC PS3607.O4523 D39 2023 (print) |
LCC PS3607.O4523 (ebook) | DDC 813/.6—dc23/eng/20230512
LC record available at https://lccn.loc.gov/2023022558
LC ebook record available at https://lccn.loc.gov/2023022559

Berkley Romance trade paperback edition / October 2023

A Dawn of Onyx was originally self-published, in different form, in 2022

Printed in the United States of America
2nd Printing

Book design by Daniel Brount
Interior art: Flower background © sokolova_sv/Shutterstock.com

For Jack.
Thank you for being my real-life MMC.
You taught me what the truest love looks like.

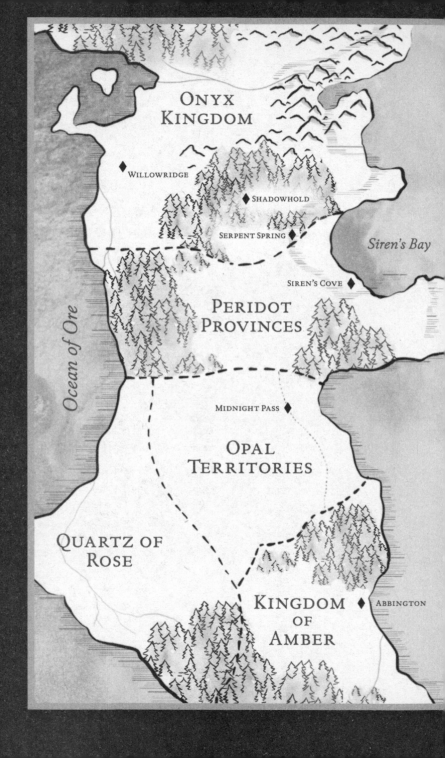

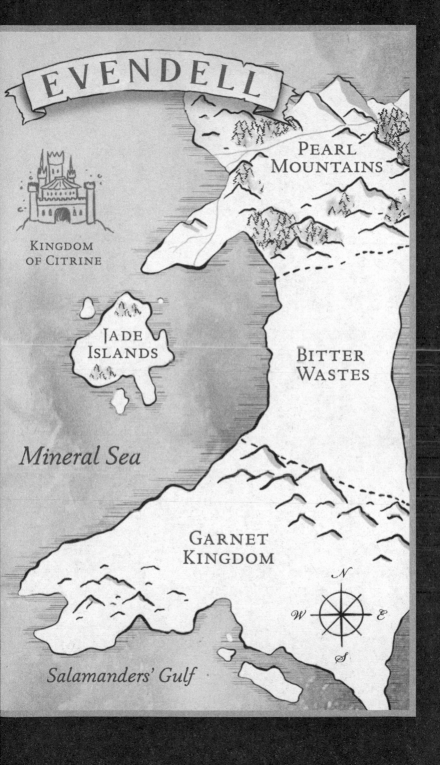

1

RYDER AND HALDEN WERE PROBABLY DEAD.

I wasn't sure what was making me feel sicker, finally admitting that truth to myself or my aching, burning lungs. The misery of the latter was, admittedly, self-induced—this section of my morning run was always the most brutal—but today marked one year since the letters had stopped coming, and while I'd sworn not to think the worst until there was reason to, the epistolary silence was hard to argue with.

My heart gave a miserable thump.

Attempting to slip the unpleasant thoughts under the floorboards of my mind, I focused on making it to the edge of the clearing without vomiting. I pumped my legs, swung my elbows back, and felt my braid land between my shoulder blades, as rhythmic as a drumbeat. Just a few more feet—

Finally reaching the expanse of cool grass, I staggered to a halt, bracing my hands on my knees and inhaling deeply. It smelled like the Kingdom of Amber always did—of morning dew, woodfire from a nearby hearth, and the crisp, earthy notes of slowly decaying leaves.

But deep breaths weren't enough to keep my vision from blurring, and I collapsed backward onto the ground, the weight of my body crushing the leaves beneath me with a satisfying crunch. The clearing was littered with them—the last remnants of winter.

Eighteen months ago, the night before all the men in our town were conscripted to fight for our kingdom, my family had gathered on the grassy knoll just behind our home. We had watched the pink-hued sunset fade like a bruise behind our town of Abbington all together, one last time. Then, Halden and I had snuck away to this very glade and pretended he and my brother, Ryder, weren't leaving.

That they'd be back one day.

The bells chimed in the town square, distant but clear enough to jar me from the melancholy memory. I eased up to sitting, my tangled hair now littered with leaves and twigs. I was going to be late. Again.

Bleeding Stones.

Or—*shit.* I winced as I stood. I was trying to swear less on the nine Holy Gemstones that made up the continent's core. I didn't care so much about damning the divinity of Evendell's creation, but I hated the force of habit that came from growing up in Amber, the kingdom that worshipped the Stones most devoutly.

I jogged back through the glade, down the path behind our cottage, and toward a town just waking up. As I hurried through alleyways that could barely accommodate two people heading in opposite directions, a depressing thought filtered in. *Abbington really used to have more charm.*

At least it was charming in my memories. Cobblestone streets once swept clean and sprinkled with street musicians and idle merchants were now strewn with garbage and abandoned. Mismatched brick buildings covered with vines and warmed by flickering lanterns had been reduced to crumbling decay—abandoned, burned, or broken down, if not all three. It was like watching an apple core rot, slowly turning less and less vibrant over time until, one day, it was just gone.

I shivered, both at the thoughts and the weather. Hopefully, the chilly air had dried some of the dampness from my forehead; Nora did not like a sweaty apprentice. As I pushed the creaky door open, ethanol and astringent mint assaulted my nostrils. My favorite scent.

"Arwen, is that you?" Nora called, her voice echoing through the infirmary's hallway. "You're late. Mr. Doyle's gangrene is getting worse. He might lose the finger."

"Lose my *what*?" a male voice squawked from behind a curtain.

I shot Nora a withering look and slipped inside the makeshift room separated by cotton sheets.

Bleeding Stones.

Mr. Doyle, an elderly bald man who was all forehead and earlobes, was in his bed, cradling his damaged hand like a stolen dessert that someone aimed to take from him.

"Nora's only kidding," I said, pulling up a chair. "That's her fun and very professional sense of humor. I'll make sure all fingers remain attached, I promise."

With a skeptical huff, Mr. Doyle relinquished his hand, and I got to work carefully peeling away the layers of rotting skin.

My ability twitched at my fingertips, eager to help. I wasn't sure I needed it today; I liked the meticulous work, and gangrene was fairly routine.

But I would never forgive myself if I broke my promise to cranky Mr. Doyle.

I covered one hand with the other, as if I didn't want him to see how gruesome his injury was—I had gotten very good at finding ways to sneak my powers into patients. Mr. Doyle closed his eyes and leaned his head back, and I allowed a flicker of pure light to seep from my fingers like juice from a lemon.

The decaying flesh warmed and blushed pink once more, healing before my eyes.

I was a good healer. I had a steady hand, was calm under pressure, and never got squeamish at the sight of someone's insides. But I could also heal in ways that couldn't be taught. My power was a pulsing, erratic light that poured out of my hands and seeped into others, spreading through their veins and vessels. I could fuse a broken bone, give color back to a flu-ravaged face, or stitch a gash closed with no needle.

But it wasn't common witchcraft. I had no witches or warlocks in my family heritage, and even if I had, when I used my powers, there was no uttered spell followed by a flurry of wind and static. Instead, my gift seeped from my body, draining my energy and mind each time. Witches could do endless magic with the right grimoires and tutelage. My abilities would fizzle out if worked too hard, leaving me depleted. Sometimes it could even take days for the power to come back fully.

The first time I exhausted myself on a particularly brutal burn victim, I thought my gift was actually gone for good, leaving me with an inexplicable mix of relief and horror. When it finally returned, I told myself I was grateful. Grateful that when I was growing up and was covered in welts or had limbs cracked at odd angles, I could heal myself before my mother or siblings could notice what my stepfather had done. Grateful that I could help those around me who were suffering. And grateful that I could make a decent amount of coin doing it when times were as tough as they were now.

"All right, Mr. Doyle, good as new."

The older man shot me a toothless grin. "Thank you," he said, before leaning in conspiratorially. "I didn't think you'd be able to save it."

"The lack of faith hurts," I joked.

He moved gingerly out of the room, and I followed him into the hall. Once he was through the front doors, Nora shook her head at me.

"What?"

"Too chipper," she said, but her mouth lifted in a smile.

"It's a relief to have a patient who isn't on death's door." I cringed. Mr. Doyle was actually quite old.

Nora just snorted and refocused on the gauze in her hands. I slunk back over to the cots and busied myself sanitizing some surgical tools. I should have been thrilled with how few patients we had today, but the quiet was making my stomach twist.

Healing took my mind off of my brother and Halden. Helped to quell the misery that churned in my gut at their absence. Like running, there was a meditative quality to healing people that calmed my chattering brain.

Silence did the opposite.

I'd never expected to be thrilled about a case of gangrene, but it seemed like anything that wasn't certain death was a win these days. Most of our patients were soldiers—bloody, bruised, and broken from battle—or neighbors I'd known my entire life, shriveling away from parasites found in the meager food scraps they could get their hands on. That, at least, was a better fate than starvation. Parasites could be healed in the infirmary. Endless hunger, not so much.

And through all this pain and suffering, loved ones lost, homes destroyed—it was still a mystery why the Onyx Kingdom had started a war with us in the first place. Our King Gareth was not one for the historical tomes, and Amber land was not known for anything but its harvest. Meanwhile, kingdoms like Garnet were rich with coin and jewels. The Pearl Mountains had their ancient scrolls and the continent's most sought-after scholars. Even the Opal Territories, with their distilleries and untouched land, or the Peridot Provinces, with their glittering coves filled with hidden treasure, would all have been better places to begin the gradual crawl toward power over all of Evendell. But so far, every other kingdom had been left unscathed, and lone Amber was trying to keep it that way.

Still, no other kingdom fought beside us.

Meanwhile, Onyx was dripping in riches, jewels, and gold. They had the most land, the most stunning cities—or so I had heard—and the biggest army. Even that wasn't enough for them. Onyx's king, Kane Ravenwood, was both imperialistic and insatiable. Worst of all, he was senselessly cruel. Our generals were often found strung up by their limbs, sometimes flayed or crucified. He took and took and took until our meager kingdom had little left to fight with, and then inflicted pain for the sport of it. Cutting us off at the knees, then the elbows, then the ears just for fun.

The only option was to keep looking on the bright side. Even if it was a dim, blurry kind of bright side that you had to bribe and coax to come out. That, Nora had claimed, was why she kept me around. *"You have a knack for this, you're optimistic to a fault, and your tits entice the local boys to donate blood."*

Thank you, Nora. You're a peach.

I peered up at her, putting away a basket filled with bandages and ointments.

She wasn't the warmest associate, but Nora was one of my mother's closest friends, and despite her prickly exterior, she'd been thoughtful enough to give me this job so I could take care of our family once Ryder left. She even helped with my sister, Leigh, when Mother was too sick to take her to classes.

My smile at Nora's kindness faded as I thought of my mother—she had been too frail to even open her eyes this morning. The irony that I worked as a healer and my mother was slowly dying from an ailment none of us could identify was not lost on me.

Even worse—and maybe more ironic—my abilities had never worked on her. Not even if all she had was a paper cut. Yet another sign that my powers were not that of a common witch, but something far stranger.

My mother had been sick since I was old enough to talk, but it had worsened these past few years. The only things that helped were the little remedies Nora and I put together—concoctions made of the white canna lilies and rhodanthe flowers native to Amber, blended with Ravensara oil and sandalwood. But the relief was temporary, and her pain grew worse each day.

I physically shook my head to rattle the unpleasantness away.

I couldn't focus on that now. The only thing that mattered was taking care of her and my sister as best I could, now that Ryder was gone.

And might never be coming back.

~⚓~

"NO, YOU DIDN'T HEAR ME RIGHT! I DIDN'T SAY HE WAS *CUTE*, I said he was *astute*. Like, smart or worldly," Leigh said, throwing a log on the dwindling hearth fire. I bit back a laugh and pulled three small bowls from the cupboard.

"Mhm, right. I just think you have a little crush, that's all."

Leigh rolled her pale blue eyes as she turned around our tiny kitchen gathering cutlery and mugs. Our house was small and rickety, but I loved it with my whole heart. It smelled like Ryder's tobacco, the vanilla we used for baking, and fragrant white lilies. Leigh's sketches hung on almost every wall. Every time I walked in our front door, a smile tugged at my lips. Perched on a little hill overlooking most of Abbington and with three well-insulated, cozy rooms, it was one of the nicer houses in our village. My stepfather, Powell, had built it for my mother and me before my siblings were born. The kitchen was my favorite place to sit, the wooden table put together by Powell and Ryder one summer back when we were all young and Mother was healthier.

It was uncanny, the warm memories tied to the bones of our home in such contrast to those that swam in my head, in my stomach, when I thought of Powell's stern face and clenched jaw. The scars on my back from his belt.

I shuddered.

Leigh squeezed in beside me, jarring me from cobwebbed memories and handing over a bundle of roots and herbs for Mother's medication.

"Here. We don't have any rosemary left."

I peered down at her blonde head and a warmth bloomed in me—she was always radiant, even with the misery of wartime that surrounded us. Joyful, funny, bold.

"What?" she asked, narrowing her eyes at me.

"Nothing," I said, biting back a smile. She was just starting to see herself as a grown-up and no longer tolerated being treated like a kid. Loving stares of adoration from her older sister were clearly not allowed. She liked it even less when I tried to protect her.

I swallowed hard, throwing the herbs into the bubbling pot over our hearth.

Recently, rumors had been swirling in the taverns, schools, and markets. The men were all gone now—Ryder and Halden had likely given their lives—and we were still losing to the wicked kingdom in the north.

The women would have to be next.

It wasn't that we couldn't do what the men could. I had heard the Onyx Kingdom's army was filled with strong, ruthless women who fought alongside the men. *I* just couldn't do it. Couldn't take someone's life for my kingdom, couldn't fight for my own. The thought of leaving Abbington at all raised the hair on the back of my neck.

It was Leigh I worried about. She was too fearless.

Her youth made her think she was invincible, and her hunger for attention made her loud, risky, and brave to the point of recklessness. The thought of her golden curls bouncing onto the front lines made my stomach twist.

If that wasn't bad enough, both of us being carted off to fight against Onyx meant Mother would be left alone. Too old and frail to fight, she might avoid the draft but wouldn't be able to take care of herself. With all three of her children gone, she wouldn't last a week.

How was I supposed to protect either of them then?

"You couldn't be more wrong about Jace," Leigh said, pointing a fork at me with faux assuredness. "I've never had a crush in my life. Especially not on him."

"Fine," I said, searching through a cupboard for carrots. I

wondered if Leigh had purposely distracted me—if she could tell I was worrying.

"Honestly," she continued, plopping down at our kitchen table and folding her feet underneath her. "I don't care what you think. Look at your taste! You're in love with Halden Brownfield." Leigh made a disgusted face.

My pulse rose at his name, remembering the date and my anxiety from this morning. I shook my head at Leigh's accusation.

"I am not *in love* with him. I like him. As a person. We're just friends, actually."

"Mhm, right," she said, mocking my earlier sentiments about her and Jace.

I popped the carrots in a separate pot for dinner, beside Mother's medication. Multitasking had become one of my strong suits since Ryder left. I opened the window above the hearth, letting some of the heat from both pots billow outside. The cool evening breeze washed over my sticky face.

"What's wrong with Halden anyway?" I asked, curiosity getting to me.

"Nothing, really. He was just boring. And fussy. And he wasn't silly at all."

"Stop saying 'was,'" I said, with more bite than I intended. "He's all right. They both are."

Not a lie. Just that same bright-side thinking that could occasionally border on denial. Leigh stood to set the table, gathering mismatched mugs for our cider.

"And Halden is silly and interesting . . . and fussy," I conceded. "I'll give you that one. He's a little tightly wound." Leigh smiled, knowing she'd gotten me.

I considered my sister. She had grown up so much in so little time that I wasn't sure what information I was protecting her from anymore.

"Fine," I said, stirring the two pots simultaneously. "We were seeing each other."

Leigh raised her brows suggestively.

"But truthfully, there was no 'in love' to speak of. By the Stones."

"Why not? Because you knew he would have to leave?"

My gaze landed on the hearth, watching the meager flames flicker as I thought about her question in earnest.

It was shallow, but the first thing that came to mind when I heard his name was Halden's hair. Sometimes, especially in the moonlight, his blond curls looked so pale they nearly glowed. It was actually what first drew me to him—he was the only boy in our town with fair hair. Amber mainly produced chocolatey brunettes like me or dirty blonds like Leigh and Ryder.

I had fallen for that ice-blond hair at the determined age of seven. He and Ryder had become inseparable right around then. Certain I was going to marry him, I didn't mind trailing their every adventure and clinging to their scraped-knee-inducing games. Halden had a smile that made me feel safe. I would have followed it anywhere. The day word of conscription came to Abbington was the only time I ever saw his smile falter.

That, and the day he first saw my scars.

But if I'd been enamored with Halden since I was little, why didn't it feel like love when he finally saw in me what I had seen in him for so long?

I didn't have a good answer, and certainly not one fit for a ten-year-old. Had I not loved him because I'd never seen it go well for anyone, namely our mother? Or because sometimes I'd ask him what he thought of Onyx's expansion of their already sprawling land and his dismissive responses would make me feel prickly for some reason I couldn't quite place? Maybe the answer was far worse. The one I hoped wasn't true but feared the most—that I wasn't capable of such a feeling.

There was nobody more deserving of it than Halden. Nobody else whom Mother, Ryder, or Powell would have wished me to be with.

"I don't know, Leigh."

I swept my attention back to the dinner preparation and sliced vegetables in silence. Leigh, sensing I was finished with that particular line of questioning, returned to setting the table. When Mother's medicine was done boiling, I moved it to the counter to steep. Once it cooled, I would fill a new vial and place it in the pouch by the cupboard as always.

Maybe I could do this—take care of them all on my own.

The savory aroma of stewing vegetables mixed with the medicinal notes of Mother's medication drifted through the home. It was a familiar scent. A comfortable one. Amber was surrounded by mountains, which meant the valley we were nestled in always had chilly mornings, crisp days, and cold nights. Every tree wilted brown leaves year-round. Every dinner was always corn, squash, pumpkin, carrots. Even the harshest of winters brought only rain and bare branches, and the hottest summer I could remember had a mere two trees of green. For the most part, it was brown and blustery here every day of the year.

And after twenty of them, there were days when it felt like I'd had enough corn and squash for a lifetime. I tried to imagine my life filled with other flavors, landscapes, people . . . But I'd seen so little, the fantasies were blurred and vague—a cluttered constellation of books I'd read and stories I'd heard over the years.

"It smells divine in here."

My eyes found my mother as she hobbled in. A bit worse for wear today, her hair was tied back in a damp braid at the nape of her neck. She was only forty, but her thin body and sallow cheeks aged her.

"Here, let me help you," I said, walking to her.

Leigh hopped off the table, leaving one candle unlit, to come to her other side.

"I'm fine, I promise." She clucked at us. But we ignored her. It had become a well-choreographed dance at this point.

"Roses and thorns?" she said, once we had seated her at the table.

My sweet mother, who, despite her chronic fatigue, pain, and suffering, always genuinely cared about what happened in our days. Whose love of flowers had made its way into our nightly routine.

My mother had come to Abbington with me when I was nearly one. I never knew my father, but Powell was willing to wed her and take me in as his own. They had Ryder less than a year later, and Leigh seven after that. It was rare in our traditional town to be a woman with three children, one with a different father than the rest. But she never let unkind words cloud the sunshine she radiated daily. She worked tirelessly her whole life to give us a home with a roof, food in our bellies, and more laughter and love each day than most children get in a lifetime.

"My rose was saving Mr. Doyle's finger from being amputated," I offered. Leigh made a retching sound. I left my thorn out. If they hadn't realized it yet, I was not going to be the one to share that our brother hadn't written to us in a year.

"Mine was when Jace told me—"

"Jace is the boy Leigh thinks is cute," I interrupted, and gave my mother a conspiratorial nod. She shot back a dramatic wink, and Leigh's eyes became slits aimed at both of us.

"His cousin is a messenger in the army, delivering plans directly from King Gareth to his generals where even ravens can't reach them," Leigh said. "The cousin told him that she saw a man with wings in the Onyx capital." Her eyes went big and blue as the sea.

I looked to my mother at the absurdity, but she just nodded politely at Leigh. I tried to do the same. We shouldn't poke so much fun at her.

"How curious. Do you believe him?" Mother asked, resting her head on her hand in thought.

Leigh contemplated this as I sipped my stew.

"No, I don't," she said after deliberating. "I guess still-living Fae are a possibility, but I think it was more likely some kind of witchcraft. Right?"

"Right," I agreed, even though I knew better. The Fae had been completely extinct for years—if they had ever been real at all. But I didn't want to burst her imaginative bubble.

I smiled at Leigh. "I see why you're so in love with Jace. He's got all the good intel."

My mother bit back a smile. So much for not poking fun. Force of habit.

Leigh frowned and launched into a tirade about how she *obviously* didn't have *any* romantic feelings for this boy. I grinned, knowing that song and dance all too well.

Stories like Jace's cousin's were always floating around. Especially in relation to Willowridge, Onyx's mysterious capital city. The night before Halden left, he had told me it was rumored to be filled with all kinds of monstrous creatures. Dragons, goblins, ogres—I could tell he was trying to spook me, hoping I might nestle myself into the safety of his embrace and allow him to protect me from whatever was beyond our kingdom's barriers.

But it hadn't frightened me at all. I knew how those tales went. Men, built up in story after story, twisted by retellings into some horrific beasts, wielding unknown powers and capable of untold torment. In reality, they were just . . . men. Evil, power-hungry, corrupt, debauched *men*. Nothing more, nothing less, and none worse than the one who had lived in my own home. My stepfather was more vicious and cruel than any monster from a story.

I didn't know if that truth would have brought Halden more or less fear on the day he and Ryder were sent off to war. It definitely wouldn't help me if Leigh and I were forced into battle next.

Truth was, our King Gareth was doing the best he could, but Onyx had a far superior army, better weapons, stronger allies, and I'm sure countless other advantages I knew nothing about. I could promise that Onyx wasn't winning this war because of some big bad that went bump in the night.

My mother's sigh brought my thoughts back from wicked, winged creatures to our warm, wooden kitchen. The last dregs of daylight were slipping across the room, leaving the dancing flames of the hearth to cast her sallow face in shadow.

"My rose is this stew, and my two beautiful girls sitting in front of me. My kind, responsible Arwen." She turned to Leigh. "My bold, brave Leigh."

Ice ran through my veins. I knew what was coming next.

"And my thorn is my son, who I miss so, so dearly. But it's been a year since we've heard from him. I think . . ." She breathed. "I think it's time we accepted that he—"

"Is fine," I interrupted her. "Ryder is fine. I can't imagine how hard it must be to get a letter out in the conditions he could be in."

"Arwen," my mother started, her voice warm and comforting and making my skin itch with its gentleness.

I babbled over her. "Can you imagine trying to send a letter to a small town like ours from a jungle? Or, or . . . a forest? From the middle of an ocean? Who knows where he is?" I was starting to sound hysterical.

"It makes me so sad, too, Arwen." Leigh's little voice was even harder to bear. "But I think Mother may be right."

"It's healthy to talk about it," Mother said, taking my hand in hers. "How much we miss him, how hard it will be to continue on without him."

I bit my lip; their serious faces were cleaving me in two. I knew they were right. But saying it out loud . . .

As soothing as her touch was, I pulled my hand away and turned to face the window, letting the evening breeze whisper over my face and closing my eyes to the cool sensation.

My lungs filled with dusk air.

I couldn't be the one to make this harder for them.

Wrapping my hands around my bowl to quell their shaking, I turned back to face my only remaining family.

"You're right. It's unlikely he's—"

The deafening sound of our front door slamming open caused the bowl I was holding to jump from my hands and shatter on the floor. Bright orange splattered everywhere like fresh blood. I spun and saw my mother's face go slack with shock. In front of us, breathing heavily, face bloodied, and leaning into the doorframe to support a twisted arm, stood my brother, Ryder.

2

For a moment, nobody moved. Then, we all moved at once.

I shot to my feet, heart in my throat, pulse pounding in my ears. Ryder's pain was clear across his face, and my mother lunged for him, tears welling in her eyes. Leigh scrambled to shut the door behind us as I helped them both to the table.

Relief, profound and overwhelming, coursed through me. I could barely stand at the onslaught of emotion.

He was alive.

I swallowed a deep inhale and considered my brother. His cropped, sandy hair; bright blue eyes like stars; his wiry, lanky frame. He looked so foreign in our small home now—too dirty and thin.

Leigh pushed our bowls from the table to the side, and climbed directly on top of it, sitting right in front of him. Ryder's eyes shone bright with joy but flickered with something else, too. Something darker.

I waited for the dust of shock to settle, but my heart continued to beat so fast that it felt like my rib cage was rattling.

"Look how big you are!" Ryder said to Leigh, one hand still pressed to his other arm.

Bandages. He needed bandages.

I flung through our drawers until I found some, then grabbed a blanket and water for him, too.

"Here," I said, wrapping the knitted fabric around him roughly and kissing the top of his head, careful to avoid his shoulder.

"What's wrong with you? Why are you back early?" Leigh asked, frantic. "Arwen, what's wrong with him? What's happening? Mother?"

Our mother said nothing as silent tears fell down her face. Ryder took her hand in his.

But Leigh was right. As wonderful as it was to have him back—something was wrong. For him to be home so soon, and with no battalion, no procession . . .

Not to mention the dripping wound.

He must have deserted.

"Calm down," Ryder rasped. "And keep your voice down."

"Leigh has a point," I forced out. "How are you back? What happened to you?"

When he didn't answer, I ripped the bloodstained fabric from his tunic and used it as a tourniquet above the wound in his arm. It was a deep, jagged gash—crimson oozing down in rivulets. As soon as my hands touched his skin, a familiar tingle spread through my palms and trickled out to seal the ripped flesh.

Closing the wound helped us both. It slowed my heartbeat and calmed me down. After I wrapped his arm tightly in bandages, I got to work trying to fit his shoulder back into the socket it was dislodged from.

Ryder closed his eyes, wincing. "I'm fine. I'm with my family again. That's all that matters."

He leaned in to kiss Leigh and our mother on their foreheads. Leigh at least had the wherewithal to feign disgust and wipe the kiss away.

Mother still held his good hand in hers, but her knuckles had gone white with force.

"Ry," I said, losing patience. "That is not all that matters. Where are the other soldiers? And why are you bleeding?"

Ryder swallowed thickly, his eyes connecting with mine.

"A few weeks back," he said, voice low, "our convoy happened upon an Onyx battalion in Amber land. We heard they had lost men and assumed it would be an easy conquest. We approached their camp carefully but still . . ." He trailed off, his voice rough. "It was a trap. They knew we were coming. All my friends were killed, and I barely escaped with my life."

Something horrific dawned on me, and I felt sick that it had taken me so long to put the thought together.

"Halden?" I asked, barely audible. My stomach had turned to lead.

"No! No, Arwen." His eyes were pained. "He wasn't in our convoy. I— To be honest, I haven't seen or heard from him in months." Ryder looked down, his brow furrowed. "I didn't think I'd make it out—" With one final *pop*, I pushed his shoulder back in.

"*Gah!* Shit!" he yelped, grabbing at his shoulder.

"Language," Mother said out of habit, though she was still too shocked to be truly angry.

Ryder moved his arm in tentative circles, feeling it out. Enjoying the sensation of a working shoulder again, he stood up, gangly and tall in our small home, and paced in front of us. I slouched into a chair, slightly weakened.

"I hid behind an oak tree. I thought they were the last few moments of my life, that at any second they'd stumble onto me and tear my limbs off. I'd lost my men. I was wounded. It was all over . . . And then I realized, while I was singing my swan song, the entire Onyx crew had left. They hadn't even seen me."

I studied him closely. There was too much glee in his eyes. Not just joy at making it home again, but something else. A sinking feeling found its way into my stomach.

"So I started to back away, and I quite literally tumbled over a sack of coin bigger than my head. *Onyx* coin." He paused to look at us, but I didn't think anyone was even breathing. My daring, reckless brother.

I prayed he hadn't done what I feared.

"They must have lost it after the fight. So, I took the thing and ran all the way here. I've been running for the last day and a half."

Bleeding Stones.

"Ryder, you didn't," I breathed. The flames of the hearth, only embers now, shrouded the room in dancing shadows.

"The king will have you killed," my mother whispered. "For abandoning your battalion."

"Well, it doesn't matter."

"Why not?" I could hardly get the words out.

He sighed. "I had made it mere hours from Abbington when I caught the eye of another band of Onyx men. They must have seen the Onyx colors, or found me suspicious or something, but they followed me. And—"

"You led them right back to us?" Leigh said, voice ratcheting up an octave.

"Shh," he whispered. "Keep your voices down, remember? They won't find us if you do what I'm asking, and quickly."

I spun around to peer out the window. I wasn't even sure who—or what—I was looking for. "Why not?" I asked. "Where will we be?"

Ryder's eyes lit up. "In the Garnet Kingdom."

I sank deeper into the chair. I was going to be sick.

Ryder must have beheld the horror on all our faces, because he sat back down and tried again, more earnestly. "I've seen what's out there. It's worse than we thought. Our kingdom is falling apart in this battle. We won't win." His jaw ticked as he inhaled. "The rumors are true. We are terribly outnumbered. The women will be drafted next, and soon. Arwen . . . you and Leigh . . . you won't be able to escape." He turned to our mother and took her hand once more. "And, Mam, you'll be left here. I don't want to think about what Abbington will look like then. Between rioters and your health . . ." His voice drifted off as he looked at me. I knew what he was implying.

I bit down on the roiling in my stomach.

"Garnet is far away enough to be out of the fray, and close enough for us to make it by boat. We can start a new life there." He looked at our mother pointedly, then Leigh, then me. "Together, somewhere safe from a war that will only get worse."

"But we don't have a boat." Mother's tentative voice surprised me. I would have gone with *You're out of your damn mind*.

"There's enough Onyx coin to buy the four of us safe passage on one this evening. We need to leave right now and head for the harbor. We'll make it to Garnet in just a few days. But, Mam, we have to move swiftly."

"Why?" whispered Leigh.

"Because the Onyx men won't be far behind me. We aren't safe here anymore."

With that, the room fell into silence, save for the wind rustling in the tree branches outside the open window behind me. I couldn't look at my mother or Leigh as my thoughts churned along with my stomach.

The options were pretty clear: stay put and watch Ryder be beaten and killed in our own home by incensed soldiers, who would then likely kill the rest of us, or pack everything we owned and travel by sea to an unknown land and start anew. There was no guarantee of safety or survival either way.

But hope was a tricky thing.

Even just the spark of an idea that our lives could be more than they were here in Abbington—that Leigh and I could avoid the draft, continue to take care of Mother, maybe even get her more help, better medicine—it was enough to force me to my feet.

I didn't want to leave Abbington. The world beyond this town was so unknown—so vast.

But I couldn't let them see the terror spinning inside me.

It was all I had been striving for—to take care of them. To be strong enough to protect them. This was my chance.

"We have to go."

Leigh, Ryder, and Mother all looked at me with the same surprised expression, as if choreographed.

Ryder composed himself first. "Thank you, Arwen." Then, he turned to Leigh and Mother. "She's right and we need to move right now."

"Are you sure?" Mother asked Ryder, her voice barely more than a whisper.

"Yes," I said for him, though I wasn't.

It was enough to get Mother and Leigh haphazardly throwing tunics and books into cases two sizes too small. Ryder followed after them, his sore arm hardly holding him back from grabbing everything he could get his hands on.

It was a luxury, I told myself. A blessing. If anyone left in Abbington could have afforded the journey, or had somewhere to go, they would have left years ago.

I ran outside to gather some food from our small garden for the journey and say goodbye to our animals. Leigh was already out there, weeping against our cow, Bells, and our horse, Hooves, both of whom she'd named when she was three. She was incredibly close to them, feeding the animals every morning and night. Bells, especially, had a bond with the girl we couldn't imagine breaking, not even out of desperate hunger.

Leigh's stifled sobs rang through the pen, and my heart began to truly ache. I even felt a surprising weight in my own chest when I approached the speckled cow and caramel steed—their loving faces had been a stalwart presence in my life, too, that suddenly I couldn't imagine waking up without. I nuzzled them both, and felt their warm breath on my face in contrast to the cool night air.

"We have to go," I said to Leigh, lifting my face from Hooves's warm back. "Go grab the pouch with Mother's medicine. I'll tie up the animals. Nora will take care of them, I promise."

Leigh nodded and wiped her nose with a pale cotton sleeve.

I thought of Nora. Would she need me at the infirmary? She was a harsh woman, but I would miss her. In some ways, she was my only friend.

Tears prickled in my eyes, for my animals, for my work, for the humble life that I had lived here in Abbington. For all my offhanded thoughts of new experiences, now that I had a chance at something more, I was nothing but afraid.

I realized with another thorough pang of sadness that I probably wouldn't ever see Halden again, either. If he were to return home safely, how would he ever find us in the Garnet Kingdom?

I couldn't even leave Halden a note alerting him to our choice, as the Onyx soldiers might find it.

I'd never know what could have happened between us, and if I might have grown to love him. That thought made my heart break all over again. I was so grateful Ryder was home and alive, but I'd had no idea I'd be saying so many goodbyes tonight because of it.

I didn't want to leave. I couldn't help it—it was too much change.

As we filed outside, I peered into our cottage one last time. It looked exceedingly bare. How wild to think that just two hours ago we were having stew for dinner like every other night. Now we were fleeing for a foreign kingdom.

I shut the door behind me as Leigh helped Mother down the dirt path. The docks were one town over, and it would be a long walk for her. I followed beside a still-limping Ryder. I knew better than to offer to help him.

"I can't believe you," I whispered.

"I know." He looked behind us. I peered back, too, my heart spinning in my chest, but nobody was there.

The sun was setting beautifully over the mountains, a pink and purple sky dotted with clouds. A single owl's hoot echoed through the rustling trees.

"I mean," I continued, "you went to war, left us for almost two years. I honestly thought you were dead. Then you come home, falling apart like a broken doll, with enough stolen riches to start a new life in a new kingdom. Who are you? A hero from a folk tale?"

"Arwen." He stopped and turned to face me. "I know you're scared." I attempted a weak protest, but he continued. "I am, too. But I saw an opportunity, and I took it. I don't want to spend the rest of my life fighting for the Kingdom of Amber any more than you want to spend the rest of your life living in it. This could change our lives. And for Mam, a chance at a cure. Or for Leigh, a chance for a better childhood. It's the right thing to do." He took my hand in his and squeezed. "I'm here to take care of us now. You don't have to worry."

I nodded, despite realizing how little my own brother knew about me. I would happily spend the rest of my life here. Maybe "happily" was the wrong word, but at least I'd be alive.

We continued walking, the sunset light fading behind the mountains and leaving us awash in dusty blues. Shadows stretched across the dirt road, and I flinched and spun at every sound, every skitter behind me, despite nobody ever being there.

I was peering deep into some bushes, looking for the source of what I swore were footsteps, when Leigh went rigid and turned to us with alarm.

"What is it?" I breathed, shielding her with my body.

"No, the pouch," she whispered, hands fishing through her little canvas sack in horror.

"What?" I asked, though my heart had stopped beating altogether.

She looked to our mother. "The vials in it are empty." Tears spilled onto her cheeks as she started back for our home. "Her medicine—we have to go back."

A vicious chill ran over me.

I hadn't poured the medicine into the vials in the pouch. I had let it steep, cooked dinner, Ryder came home—

In the commotion I had told Leigh to grab the pouch, but I never filled it.

Suddenly my heart was beating so fast I could hear it. "It's my fault," I breathed. "I need to run back for them. I'll be fast."

"No." My mother's voice was harsher than I'd ever heard it. "We are risking enough as it is. Who knows how long they were following your brother. I'll be fine."

"Mam, you need it. Arwen is fast." Ryder turned to me. "Run quickly, or you could miss the boat." But I knew what he was implying—that I could run into the soldiers that were on his tail. Leigh was crying in earnest now but trying gamely to cover up her sobs.

"I'll be right back, and I'll meet you at the docks. I promise." I sprinted off without waiting to hear their protests.

I couldn't believe how stupid I had been.

After all the pressure I had put on myself to provide for my family, to follow in Ryder's footsteps. To not be so afraid.

I raced up the dirt road, passing houses filled with families saying good night and putting out their hearths. The moon was now rising in the sky, the pale evening light replaced by midnight blue.

My mistake did have one silver lining. The sprint back to our house allowed me a much-needed moment of reprieve. A sense of calm washed over my anxious mind. My heartbeat became rhythmic. My footfalls, the same. *Thud, thud, thud.* By the time I got back to our home, I already felt better.

I hid for a moment behind a single apple tree, but there were no soldiers, no horses, no carts anywhere near our house. No noise or lights coming from inside.

Bells and Hooves were calm, both lazily grazing on hay.

I loosed an exhale, and sweat from the run cooled on my face.

Maybe Ryder had been wrong, and they had never followed him in the first place. Or, even more likely, they had given up hunting down one lone thief.

I could see now that everything would be all right.

As long as we were together, we could brave this journey. I could.

I opened our door with a soft creak, and came face-to-face with eleven Onyx soldiers, bathed in shadow, sitting around my kitchen table.

3

SOMEONE LEFT IN QUITE THE HURRY."

A rough voice scraped down my back like a dull knife.

It came from the menacing man lounging in front of me, his muddy boots propped up on the table Ryder had painstakingly carved so many summers ago.

Horror so crushing I could hardly think of anything else overtook me. My mouth was too dry to force a swallow. I didn't waste a moment assessing the rest of the scene in front of me—I turned on my heel and prepared to run for my life. But a young soldier with a pockmarked face yanked me backward by my hair with ease.

My scalp ached and I yelped in pain.

The door slammed behind me as the soldier dragged me inside and the metallic smell of blood met my nostrils. My eyes swept over my home—in the corner, bleeding out onto our wood floor, was a bald soldier in an ill-fitting Onyx uniform clearly too small for his large frame. He had a gaping wound practically bisecting his torso, and two stoic soldiers beside him were packing it with cloth to no success. The broad soldier moaned in agony, and the power in my fingers twitched with the urge to help him despite his creed and colors.

I tried not to think about what kind of convoy nearly loses a man and continues to break into homes, apprehending young girls by the hair like it's nothing, all in service of reclaiming lost coin.

Each Onyx soldier was clad in black leather armor, some with studded silver embellishments. A few wore dark helmets that resembled hollowed, threatening skulls and shimmered in the still-dwindling candlelight of my kitchen. Others had no helmet at all, which felt all the more frightening as I looked into their bloodied, cold faces.

None of the soldiers seemed at all bothered by the gruesome scene unfolding in the corner. Nothing like our Amber men, they made our soldiers look like little boys—which, in fairness, many were. These were menacing, brutal warriors who were never drafted to fight but rather trained their whole lives to kill and only to kill.

And what else was to be expected? The wicked king of Onyx was known for his cruelty, and his army was built in his likeness.

"What's your name, girl?" asked the same soldier who'd spoken first. He was one of the men whose leather armor was adorned with small silver studs. He wore no helmet, had a square face, small eyes, and no discernable smile lines to be found.

I recognized this type of man instantly.

Not in appearance, but rather his snarl, his cold confidence. The rage that simmered behind his eyes.

I had grown up with him.

A shaky breath rushed out of me. "Arwen Valondale. And yours?"

The men tittered, spite and cruel pity rolling off them in waves. I shrunk in on myself without meaning to.

"You can call me Lieutenant Bert," he said, lip curling. "How do you do?"

Some laughed harder now, encouraged by their leader. Others remained silent. Bored. I bit my tongue. There was something about them that I couldn't put into words. Power seemed to be rippling off them. I trembled, my knees knocking together in a discordant rhythm. It was no surprise that these monsters had killed Ryder's convoy easily. I silently thanked the Stones that he had somehow made it out alive.

"Let me make this quick for you, which is more than you'd be offered by some of my comrades. We followed a young man back to this house. He stole a great amount of coin from us, and we'd like it back. You tell us where he is, we kill you swiftly. Sound fair?"

I pulled my knees together and choked back a gasp.

"I don't know the man who lives here." I swallowed hard, racking my brain for any damning evidence in the home that could link me to Ryder. "I was just coming by to borrow milk. I saw they had a cow."

Bert's mouth pressed into a thin line. The seconds ticked by while he debated his next move. I knew he knew I was lying. I was a terrible liar. My heart spun inside my chest.

He gave me a smile with dead eyes, then nodded to the scarred man who still had my braid wrapped around his fist. "Kill her, then. She's no use to us."

The soldier behind me hesitated briefly, but dragged me back toward the front door.

"Wait!" I pleaded.

The soldier stopped short, looking down at me. Nothing but ice flashed in his dark brown eyes.

I had to think very, very fast.

"Your man there," I said directly to Bert, "is going to die within minutes if he doesn't get help."

Bert barked out a wet cackle. "Whatever gave you that idea? Perhaps his intestines hanging out?"

"I'm a healer," I said, mustering false courage. "They're packing his wound all wrong. He's going to go into sepsis." It was true. The man was convulsing, rivers of red dribbling from his abdomen and soaking into the wood of my home.

Bert shook his head. "I don't think he can be saved even by the likes of you."

But he was wrong. "Let me fix him in return for my life."

Bert chewed the inside of his cheek. I prayed to all the Stones that this broad, doughy, dying man was of some value.

Minutes passed.

Lifetimes.

"Everyone out," Bert finally barked at the rest of the men.

I let out a long slow breath, and the hold on my hair released. I rubbed at the back of my head, which felt bruised and tender. It was the least of my concerns.

The soldiers lumbered out one by one. Even the two who were tending to the injured man stood without question and filed through the door, faces expressionless, leaving me, Bert, and the patient on the floor all alone. The lieutenant hauled his feet off the table and stood with a sigh. He cracked his neck, seemingly exhausted by this turn of events, then nodded me over to the dying man.

My legs moved like lead in water until I knelt beside him. The smell of my mother's medicine mocked me, still steeping mere feet away. Bert hovered overhead.

"It would have been a real shame anyway," Bert said, kneeling closer to my face than I would have liked. "Such a sweet, soft girl. Dead so quickly. Before anyone had used her well." He smelled like ale, and I recoiled, which only delighted Bert all the more. "Fix him, and we'll see how generous I'm feeling."

I turned to the wounded man, his face a mask of dread.

I could relate. "It's all right, sir."

Two of his ribs had been shattered at an awkward angle and the flesh of his chest cavity was shredded and pulpy as if something had ripped right through him. This was neither a sword nor an arrow wound, and there were no burns to imply a cannon or explosion.

"What happened?" I breathed, without really thinking.

Broad Man tried to speak—a gruesome croak—but Bert cut him off. "There are grislier things out there than me, girl. Things you couldn't imagine."

I hated his voice, like the rattle of an empty gin bottle, and the way his eyes crawled over my body, eyeing my chest with no shame.

"I need alcohol and clean fabric. Can I walk around the house? See what I can find?"

Bert shook his head with a gleam in his eye. "Do you take me for a fool?" He pulled out a flask from his boot and handed it to me. "Here's your alcohol. You can use your tunic. Looks very clean to me."

With false coolness I took the flask from his hands, his knuckles caked in dirt, and looked over to the injured soldier.

I had gone my whole life keeping my power hidden. Never letting anyone see exactly what I was able to do. My mother had told me years ago that there would always be people who would try to take advantage of my gift, and that was before the war. Now everyone was suffering all the time, and my ability was even more valuable.

There was no way to heal this man without using my abilities. He would be dead within the hour, if not sooner. But I couldn't use my power without Bert seeing. Even if I faked an incantation, my power didn't look like witch magic. There was no earthy wind, no static. It just seeped out of my fingers.

Even if Bert *wasn't* leering behind me, if this broad soldier stood and walked out of the house after an injury like this, I wouldn't be able to credit my excellent surgical skills.

A furious shiver ran up my spine at the choice in front of me.

But it wasn't really a choice at all—I couldn't let this man die, nor could I let them kill me.

I steeled myself.

"This will hurt," I said to Broad Man.

He nodded stoically, and I poured the spirit on his bloody wound and my hands. He groaned in agony but held still.

Then I held my hands over his chest and breathed deeply.

Humming while my senses pulsed through the soldier, I felt his organs fuse back together, blood pumping slower, heart rate lowering. The fabric of his skin weaved into fresh, new flesh that bloomed under my palms.

My own heart rate slowed, too, adrenaline cooling in my veins and tension unfurling in my stomach. My eyes fluttered open and connected with Broad Man's. They were stunned, watching as his body put itself back together like a broken toy. The man's breathing returned to a less frightening pace, and the gash became an ugly, ragged pink scar across his abdomen.

I sighed as I closed my eyes, just long enough to gather some courage. All he needed now was a bandage, and I was not going to let the piggish lieutenant humiliate me. In one swift movement, I pulled my tunic over my head, leaving me in a thin, sleeveless camisole. I tried to ignore Bert's searing gaze on my breasts.

I wrapped the blouse around the Broad Man's injury and tied it tightly.

Bert stood up behind me and paced contemplatively through my kitchen. He was deciding my fate.

I could hardly breathe. I had never felt fear like this. Fear that shook my jaw, my hands, my very bones.

"Thank you, Lieutenant," Broad Man rasped, but Bert was still lost in thought. Broad Man turned one weak eye toward me.

"And thank you, girl."

I nodded my head imperceptibly.

"How did you do that? Are you a witch?"

I shook my head. "How are you feeling?" My words came out so soft I wasn't sure if I had really spoken.

"A lot less close to death."

"All right," Bert snapped. "Let's go find the kid. We'll take the girl with us."

No, no, no, no—

But I couldn't speak, couldn't breathe—too much terror was coursing through me; it was making my heart race so fast I was close to vomiting on the broad soldier beneath me.

I couldn't let them find my family. Bert couldn't be within a foot of Leigh. I shot a begging, pleading stare to Broad Man, who had the decency to look even more pained than he had when he was dying.

But two soldiers were already coming back in to help carry him.

I scanned the kitchen. Bert had walked out.

If I was going to run, this was likely my only shot.

Pulse thrumming in my ears, I sprang up and sprinted for the bedrooms. I had a better chance of making it through a window than the front door, with all the armored men waiting outside. The two soldiers shouted at me to stop, their voices deep bellows that rang through my bones, my teeth—but I kept moving, dodging one outstretched hand after another. Around the hearth, past the kitchen table, until I threw my mother's bedroom door open.

There was the window.

Right above her bed, sheets and blankets still rumpled. It smelled like her—sage and sweat and ginger.

I was so close.

So close—

But I was also so tired. Between healing Mr. Doyle, Ryder's shoulder, and the Broad Man's entire abdomen, I was dizzy and fatigued, my limbs weak, my breath uneven. I pushed my legs as hard as I could, vision blurring, and my fingers finally, *finally*, just barely grazed the checkered cloth curtains that framed the window—

Until a calloused hand wrapped around my shoulder and yanked me back with immeasurable force, slamming me into his chest.

No. *No.*

"She's a right quick one, isn't she?" he said to the panting soldier whom I had narrowly dodged around the hearth.

"Stones, yeah." He heaved, hands on his knees.

A scream flew from my throat—furious and wild and dripping with fear.

"Enough of that," the soldier snapped, throwing a dirt-caked hand over my mouth and nose.

I couldn't *breathe.*

My arms thrashed wildly, and he released his palm from my face to hold my arms with both hands.

"Don't make me knock you out, girl. I don't want to, but I will to shut you up."

I bit down on my tongue, hard enough to hurt.

I had to get ahold of myself. Had to—

The two soldiers guided me outside, where the rest of the Onyx men had now arrived with their horses. *Bleeding Stones*, even their horses were terrifying. Pure jet-black, with wild and unruly manes and eyes with no pupils.

I couldn't bring myself to look over at where we kept Bells and Hooves. I didn't want to know if these cruel men had left them alive. I thought of Leigh and my mother. What they might see if they came back for me. The blood on the floor . . .

I wrestled away from the soldier behind me—kicking and panting.

"Come on, girl. You've had your fun, that's enough." The soldier behind me pinned me to him until I fell still. He was so large, so much stronger—

And I was so depleted, so afraid, so cold—

I just couldn't let them go after Ryder, my mother, Leigh . . .

I whipped my face away from the soldier behind me and called out to Bert, who sat atop one of the midnight-black horses.

"Let my family be, and I'll go with you willingly."

Bert laughed and the gruesome noise rang through the night.

"Do I look scared of you putting up a fight? Just wait until the king sees you." His wretched smile gleamed in the pinpricks of moonlight that filtered through the trees, exposing all his yellowed teeth. "Besides, I thought you didn't know the kid."

My stomach threatened to empty itself all over the ground.

"He's my brother. But you have plenty of coin—how many healers? Willingly means I'll help you. Heal you and your men. Can your stolen coin do that?"

Bert didn't respond, and the soldiers turned to him expectantly. His silence bolstered my courage.

"If you go after them, I'll never work for you. You can torture me, kill me—I won't do anything if they are harmed."

I wasn't sure if it was a bluff or not.

"Fine."

It was all he said.

So abruptly that I almost forgot to feel relief.

Before I realized what he was doing, the soldier behind me tied my wrists together in front of me. The twine was sharp and scratchy on my skin, and my breaths began to come in strange, sharp bursts.

I did not like feeling trapped.

Heart and head whirling, I was in such shock I couldn't even cry. I was leaving Abbington. But not for Garnet, with my family.

No, to go to Onyx.

Alone.

The single most dangerous kingdom on our continent. With a herd of the deadliest men I had ever encountered.

I wondered absently if the king even knew about his errant lost coin. It seemed doubtful. This felt like a personal mission, orchestrated by a greedy lieutenant, who would return now with a new healer and boast of his findings.

Acid rose in my throat.

The soldier tugged me behind him as our lethal caravan filed into the night, some on horseback, some on foot. The only thing I could hold on to was the knowledge that my family was going to be safe. They had enough coin now to build a beautiful, safe, new life, and that was all I could possibly want. They deserved it.

I trembled again at the enormity of what I'd surrendered myself to. The horrors Bert alluded to. Most likely I was going to be raped, tortured, or killed, if not all three. What in the Stones had I done?

THE COOL EVENING AIR ASSAULTED MY FRAME, AND I REmembered how little I was wearing. My face flushed, but with my hands pulled in front of me, I couldn't cover myself.

We had been walking in silence for hours. At every hitch of someone's breath or errant comment among the men, my stomach dropped—sure they'd decided to kill me after all. Once in a while, one of the soldiers would actually say something to another and I'd I strain to hear, but for the most part, these men were noiseless and focused, like well-trained beasts.

I'd stopped recognizing anything, and all the trees and branches were beginning to look the same. I had also stopped wondering if these men ever planned to set up camp for the night. I'd seen a handful of maps in my life, especially when I was young and in classes, and from what I recalled Onyx was as far across the continent as was possible without crossing the Mineral Sea. I could only imagine we would be traveling for months, and my feet protested at the thought.

These men had no gear, no campsite, no carriages. How would they survive? How would I?

None of them even seemed tired. They were truly a different breed.

The soldier who bound me had taken to dragging me along behind him as my fatigue set in. Mentally I was exhausted, and physically I was getting there. When I stumbled over a few dead branches, he looked back at me with what was either pity or disgust. It was hard to tell through his helmet of bone and steel.

"Soon" was all he said.

It only made me feel worse.

Just as I was sure my body was mere minutes from giving out, we came to a glade. It must've been well past midnight. The stretch of dirt and straw was coated in a dim haze of night, and I had to squint to see where I was going. My feet and ankles and calves protested at each step, so sore that even standing still ached. The men came to a stop and looked around at one another in anticipation before I heard it.

Like the bang of a mighty drum or the crash of waves on an angry sea, a thunderous sound pierced the night. I startled and scanned the clearing for whatever monster must have made such a noise but saw nothing in the surrounding trees. The thuds grew louder, a deafening beat, reverberating in my skull.

Wind spun around us, blowing dust into my hair and face. With my hands tied, I could only screw my eyes shut and listen with unbridled fear as the noise grew louder. I was almost grateful to be surrounded by these men who felt more like weapons. Not that anyone's first intention would be to save me, but with them around I had a better shot at surviving whatever this thing was.

The ground shook as the creature landed on the grass ahead of us, lifting dirt up around me in clouds. I coughed, the rumble from the earth reverberating through my weakened knees and ankles. The woody blend of fir and crisp cedarwood stung my nose. When the dust settled, I opened my eyes.

Before me stood the most terrifying animal I had ever seen.

Not an animal, but a beast. A monster—

A full-grown, pitch-black dragon, covered in pointed, shimmering scales. More frightening, ancient, and powerful than anything I could have conjured from a book or children's story. It stretched its massive, bat-like wings, tipped by silver talons, exposing a glittering silver underbelly. A barbed, sable tail swung softly back and forth across the dirt.

The lieutenant approached the beast with no fear, and to my shock appeared to *speak* to the gargantuan creature.

I gawked.

Not a monster, then, but a . . . pet. The Onyx Kingdom had pet dragons?

I considered the other men, but none seemed frightened. They weren't even surprised. Rather, they made their way with ease onto the creature's back, which was long enough to have fit double the group if necessary.

When the soldier pulled me forward, I let out a small whine and dug my feet into the ground. I didn't even realize I was doing it—I wanted to be a brave, dragon-climbing girl, but alas, the night's events must have drained my reserves of courage. He yanked me closer despite my protests, until I was beside its sprawled right claw. The four sharpened nails were stained with a rusty red that I was going to pretend wasn't blood.

I willed my eyes to look anywhere else.

"It's all right. The beast won't hurt you," Broad Man said from his sprawled position on the back of the dragon, one hand pressed to his wound.

I nodded, but my mouth tasted like acid.

The soldier finally untied my wrists so I could hoist myself up. "Don't try anything smart, girl."

I was too exhausted to run anyway. "Not really anywhere for me to go."

The dragon's scales felt cool and smooth under my palms as I hauled myself up, getting a better look at its reptilian eye—blazing orange and ringed with gray. The dragon's gaze shifted to me and seemed to soften imperceptibly. It blinked once and cocked its head slightly. The simple act was so innocuous, so disarming, that I relaxed ever so slightly.

Once settled, I rubbed my aching wrists, which were torn and bleeding where the twine had been. My eyes landed on the back of the creature, toward the tail, where a huddled lump was wrapped in burlap, dotted with scarlet stains. A single Onyx boot stuck out from underneath.

Unease twisted low in my stomach.

There was a dead body on this beast with us.

I looked to Broad Man again. Something horrible must have happened tonight. Somewhere between Broad Man's wound, the blood on the dragon's claws, and the corpse aboard, was a story that I did not wish to piece together.

I tried to be grateful that at least nothing had punctured my torso. Yet.

Once all the soldiers had boarded, I barely had a moment to look back toward my town—my entire life—before the beast shot into the air. All of the breath ripped from my lungs as we soared upward. The air was thin and icy, and my eyes filled with water as cold night whipped at my face. I held on to the creature's ridged scales for dear life and hoped I wasn't hurting it with my vise grip.

The wind stung my eyes and I looked away from the skies and back to the soldiers. They seemed at ease now, some lying back against the dragon's outstretched wing, others with a casual arm wrapped around a talon. My gaze landed on Bert, only to catch him watching me with intent. Not just sexual, though his eyes were lascivious, too. But it felt more like he was boring into my soul. Like he was mesmerized. A furious shiver ran up my spine—he had seen my powers. That left me even more exposed than the camisole.

I shrank in on myself and trained my eyes away from his nasty face.

We sailed higher and higher, rising above the clouds. From up here, my world seemed even smaller than I had thought possible. This must be how the Onyx soldiers got around the continent so easily. I wondered how they didn't catch my brother sooner. The thought of him, and the rest of my family, made my heart seize up.

I was never going to see them again.

I clenched my jaw, teeth straining—I could not break down right now.

I had to hold it together until I had the right opportunity, and then I would allow myself to fully fall apart.

Now would be a great time for that optimism I'd been told I had in spades.

But I feared there was no positive spin for flying via massive, horned dragon as a prisoner into enemy territory. I looked down at the land below me, cloaked in darkness, and watched the only life I'd ever known disappear from sight.

4

A *BELT CRACKED ON MY BACK, QUICKLY REPLACED BY MY hands, deep inside a bloody, gaping chest wound. An orange, glowing eye peered at me—gazing into my soul. Power I couldn't describe tingled in my fingertips, in my bones, in the corners of my memory . . .*

I jolted awake.

The darkness around me was disorienting. I could almost make out the organic shapes of leaves and trunks and vines, but every thing was cloaked in shades of blue and black, barely lit by moonlight. Bodies shuffled around me one by one, and I suddenly remembered where I was and what had happened. Disorientation morphed into an onslaught of growing dread. Horror churned in my gut and tightened in my jaw. In my bones—

Broad Man, who was now moving at a steady, slow pace, much to the shock of his fellow men, nudged me forward, and I dismounted from the beast, my limbs moving before my mind instructed them to.

Without realizing it, I touched the long neck of the creature, steadying myself on shaking legs. Its peculiar eyes darted to me, and I mustered a weak smile. *Don't eat me* was all that came to mind. I had the vague, diluted thought that I was probably in shock.

Only then did I notice the unbearable chill. It was much colder here in the north, and my body was covered in gooseflesh, my lips and nose going numb.

The rest of the soldiers had walked ahead into the darkness, uninterested in the newly captured girl. A small mercy, maybe. Broad Man wrapped the twine around my wrists once more and I grimaced at the raw skin being abused again in the same spot.

A sound like lightning cracking startled me, and I turned just in time to see the creature take off into the skies, dirt flying into my eyes. By the time I pried them open again, I couldn't make the dragon out in the dark above any longer. Gone just as quickly as it had appeared, it was as if I had fabricated the creature out of my own imagination.

Except I never could have crafted something so disturbing.

I stared after the beast, into the textured darkness of night and forest and trees.

My only way back home, gone.

Broad Man jerked me forward and my wrists wailed in response. But I shuffled forward, one foot after the other, Bert and Broad Man before me, two of the soldiers carrying the burlap-wrapped body behind us.

All I could see in the slivers of moonlight were gnarled trees and lush greenery that came up to my shins as I stamped through.

We were clearly not in Willowridge, the capital of the Onyx Kingdom. There was no city, no life, no noise. Just a forest of some kind. The smell of damp moss, lilac, and night-blooming gardenia filled my nostrils. Different from any forest I had been in—no sweet spice or pumpkin or familiar decay of falling leaves. I had only ever been in forests that were endlessly brown and golden, or bare of leaves altogether. This wet, foggy enclave was already unlike anything I had seen or felt. All oaks and pines, cold and floral and crisp. For a single, nonsensical moment I could almost forget where I was, how I had ended up here.

My eyes were slowly adjusting to the night. We rounded a great, knotted willow tree, and in the distance loomed an imposing stone castle, with hundreds of lit-up tents in the field surrounding it. They were a cacophony of wartime colors, like a handful of mismatched jewels. Each a different size and shape, pitched alongside and on top of each other like picnic blankets on a summer day, haphazard and overlapping.

What . . . what was this?

We walked farther, and I finally heard something other than the crunch of our feet on the dirt—the sounds of people and music.

A wave of dread crashed over me.

It was more than just a castle or fortress, but rather an entire keep. Almost like a gated village of its own.

The hold was bordered on every side by the twisted woods we had traipsed through—no way in or out without making it across these haunted trees and vines and roots. No sign of life in any direction past the woods. Internally, I cursed myself for falling asleep on our ride here. A bird's-eye view would have been helpful. But the comedown from both the adrenaline of anxiety and then exertion of my powers on Ryder and the Broad Man had been a sedative I couldn't fight.

Vast iron gates appeared through the maze of trees, creaking open for us as we approached. I allowed Broad Man to pull me through, my eyes glued to the rolling land and castle before me.

"Welcome to Shadowhold, girl," Bert said, before striding ahead of the pack.

I shuddered.

As we walked along the road that bisected the sprawl of canvas tents within the castle gates, it dawned on me—this must be the Onyx army outpost, as evidenced by the blacksmith tables, cooking pots, and hung-up armor I spotted throughout the encampment. As we drew nearer, I noticed a few small cottages and huts to our left, and stables to our right.

Most must have been asleep, but a few soldiers were playing the lute and drinking by a crackling fire. Some looked up at the body being carried behind us, or at my half-clothed form, but all kept their eyes averted from their lieutenant.

I shivered against the freezing night, and tried to wrap my arms tightly around myself before remembering they were bound.

The longing to be back with my family was a greater pain than I had ever felt, far worse than any of Powell's beatings. It welled up inside of me, threatening to bring me to my knees at any moment.

What would they do then? Drag me along the dirt as I sobbed?

Yes. That's exactly what would happen.

I almost choked on the desperation—I wanted to be anywhere but here. Anywhere.

My feet towed along the gravel and dirt, dust forming a thin layer on my ankles, as Broad Man hauled me forward, and my eyes pulled up to the castle before me.

It was like nothing I had ever seen before.

This was the most chilling, twisted, somehow awe-inspiring fortress I could have imagined.

The all-stone stronghold was a feat of gothic architecture with towering turrets and strong, stone pillars. Stained glass windows glinted in the darkness, eerie in their glass depictions of war and brutality, a strange contrast to the warmth that radiated from within them. Inside, the light cast shadows in their frames that moved fluidly, like specters. The exterior, dotted by large black torches and a few heraldic flags showing the Onyx crest, only bolstered my assumption that the keep was the Onyx army base.

We reached the massive wooden doors, and my teeth clenched as I steeled myself. Broad Man tugged me once again, and my wrists lit with agony, pulling a strange whine from my lips.

Bert eyed me with a twisted, delighted gleam.

"Come, girl, you can stay with me tonight."

Horror blurred my vision.

I couldn't think of anything to say to save myself.

"Lieutenant, I think Commander Griffin wished to see us upon our return. I can throw the girl in the dungeons for now?" Broad Man offered.

Bert considered his soldier, then, annoyed, gave a gruff nod.

I heaved a small sigh of relief. I didn't know if the Broad Man was trying to help me or if it had just been dumb luck, but I was more grateful than I had been all day when Bert stalked off toward the castle. Broad Man pulled me away from the doors, and we filed past more guards and through a gate that led down a spiral of cobbled stone stairs.

Dread awoke inside my chest anew and my mouth went bone-dry.

"No, no . . ." I begged, pulling away from the shadowed cellar, but the Broad Man didn't seem to hear me.

Or to care.

Inside, the dungeon was dark and stale and reeked of brackish water and human filth. The incessant, slow drip of liquid echoed through the stairwell. Lanterns lit up a hallway filled with iron cells below us, and my heart jumped into my throat.

"No, wait," I pleaded again. "I can't go in there."

Broad Man gave me a curious look. "I'm not going to harm you. It's just a place to lay your head until the lieutenant decides what to do with you."

I tried to get my breathing under control.

"I just can't be locked in. Please. Where do the healers stay?"

Broad Man huffed and pushed me down through the dizzying stairwell. My lungs were collapsing in on themselves and by the time we reached the bottom, I could hardly breathe.

He pulled me behind him and along the maze of cells. The hoots and hollers of foul-mouthed prisoners paired with my heartbeat thundering in my ears became a vulgar symphony. I tried again in vain to cover myself.

Broad Man opened a cell door wide and shoved me in, tearing off my bindings. I stumbled, catching my palms on the rough, dirty stone beneath me. It was even smaller inside than it had looked. I spun, racing back toward the iron bars.

"Wait!" I yelled, but he was halfway down the hall and the cell was locked.

I heaved out a sob and backed into the corner, sinking down and bringing my knees to my chest. My head was swimming, my breath coming in irregular, uneven gasps. I tried to remember what

Mother had taught me all those years ago when I panicked, but my mind was in shambles.

Maybe now was the aforementioned time to fall apart.

How did this all happen? I tried to replay the evening's events in my head and it only hurt more. I finally gave in to the tears I had been holding back all night. They burst out of me and trickled in streams down my cheeks, splattering onto the floor. My wails were loud and choked, like a child's.

I wished I was more like Ryder. I hadn't seen him cry more than twice in our whole lives. Once, when he was fifteen, when he fell off our roof and broke his kneecap. Again when his father, Powell, died, seven years ago.

My stepfather died of a stroke, and when Mother told us, Ryder sobbed for days. His father was his best friend, and Powell worshipped his only son. Powell and I never had that kind of relationship, though. I wasn't sure if his hatred for me was born out of knowing I wasn't his or because I wasn't strong like Ryder, but either way, he carried a rampant disdain for me that I was shocked nobody else could see.

Unlike Ryder, I cried all the time. I cried when Leigh made me laugh too hard. I cried when I saw my mother in pain. I cried at the end of a great book, or when I heard a beautiful harmony. I cried when I lost a patient at the infirmary. I cried when I felt overwhelmed. It was the least brave quality—to be sensitive and fearful and full of tears.

But I let them flow freely now.

I sobbed for my family that I'd never be with again. For my stupid, rash decision to trade my life for theirs. I didn't regret it, but I hated that it had to happen. That I hadn't been able to come up with anything smarter. I cried for my future here, which I knew would be painful at best, short at worst. I tried to steel myself against a number of torments, which only made my mind run wild. What if they simply never let me leave this cell and I was trapped for eternity?

The unmistakable cry of a man in desperate pain clanged through the dungeon walls. I scanned the cells I had been dragged past. But almost all the other prisoners were sleeping.

The cry for help—for *anybody, please*—rang out again. There must have been another annex nearby for torture.

I pressed my palms to my ears tightly but couldn't drown out his sobs and pleas. It sounded as though he was being ripped in half.

I gulped and choked on air, panic back in full force.

I was suffocating.

Maybe I was dying. My mind was a clash of crawling dread and frantic energy, thoughts flitting from one to the next with no time to catch them. I was dizzy and panting, bracing myself against the stale floor beneath me.

Definitely dying.

I had to get out of here. *Right now.*

What had my mother told me to do? Why couldn't I remember? Was it—

Three Things.

That's what she had called it. Find and focus on three things you can name—I could do that.

One: Cobwebs. I spied cobwebs and mold atop the low ceiling of my cell. It smelled like mildew and damp, trapped air.

I sucked in a lungful of it.

Two: Lanterns. A few weak, flickering lanterns hung outside my cell. I couldn't feel the warmth of the flames, but the dim shafts of light cast shadows on the murky, wet floor.

Three . . . I looked around my small space and saw two buckets, one empty and one filled with water. *Three:* Buckets. I doubted either were clean, but I scrambled up and splashed my face. The freezing-cold water knocked the wind out of me, but the shock helped my system. I sat back on my heels and breathed a little easier.

"*Bleeding Stones.*" I put my head between my knees.

"Quite the mouth on you."

A voice, at once like thunder and a caress, purred through the iron bars beside me.

I whipped my head up. In my terror upon being thrown into the cell, I hadn't realized there was another prisoner in the one directly next to me; we were only separated by rusty metal bars.

I flushed. I'd had an audience for the most horrifically unpleasant moment of my life. And based on the continued cries of the person being tortured in some other wing of this dungeon, it was likely one of the last few.

"Sorry," I mumbled.

"It's just . . . a little dramatic, don't you think?" the dark voice said.

My skin bristled.

I squinted through the flickering shadows but couldn't see more than the outline of a figure slumped against a wall.

"I said I was sorry, what more do you want?" I was still trying to catch my rushed breaths.

Immediately I regretted my harsh tone. I couldn't make an enemy of the man I'd be trapped next to for who knew how long. He was probably a thief. Or a murderer.

Or something far, far worse.

But the prisoner only chuckled, the sound like the rumble of rocks down a mountain, reverberating in my chest.

"Some peace and quiet from your weeping would be nice."

As expected, but still—what a prick.

This time I didn't bother hiding my glare. I didn't know if he could even see me in the darkness.

"I'm done now," I admitted, drawing in a long breath. "It's not every day you get imprisoned. Or . . . maybe it is for you, but—not for me."

Please leave me alone, please leave me alone.

"I'm just saying, some of us are trying to get some sleep around here. Your theatrics and heaving bosom aren't going to change your situation." He paused. "Though the latter is nice to look at."

My stomach turned at his words.

Did I say "prick"? I meant "bastard." Vile bastard.

I had no reason to fight with him, and I shouldn't anger him—I had better survival instincts than that. But I had been through too much tonight.

I didn't have a single straw left in me.

"You're disgusting," I breathed.

"Someone's feeling brave with these bars between us."

"Not really," I admitted. "Just honest."

The conversation was a strange yet welcome distraction to my anxiety. Being alone with my thoughts sounded worse than almost anything.

The tortured man's wails had finally turned to whimpers. I hoped for his sake he might pass out soon. Now I heard only rustling as I watched the figure in the cell beside me stand up and stretch.

His shadow alone was imposing—at least a foot and some change taller than me, but the dim light hid the rest of his features. He stalked toward the bars that separated us. I fought the instinct to scramble backward and away from him, reminding myself that he couldn't reach me in here. I had to have some kind of backbone. Especially if this was to be my future.

"Are you trying to scare me?" I was aiming for bold, but it came out low and quiet.

"Something like that," he whispered through the bars. My heart leapt into my throat at his words, his voice soft and yet so deadly my toes curled in fear. I still couldn't make out his face among the shadows, but I could see his sharp, white teeth glinting above me in the lantern's buttery light.

"Well, you don't. Scare me, that is."

He laughed, but it felt cruel. "Such a brave bird. Good to hear. Perhaps now I can sleep."

What?

But . . . my thoughts were now flowing in a calm, even rhythm, compared to the frenetic mess they had been before.

My panic had subsided.

I took a soothing lungful of damp, dungeon air, and turned my eyes back up to the prisoner bathed in shadow beside me.

Had he known what he was doing when he was goading me? Definitely not, but the distraction had kept me from falling apart completely.

Still, I couldn't help glaring at him. "Your cruelty is a bit cliché."

He heaved a sigh that sounded suspiciously like a laugh and crouched down. Finally, the lantern outside his cell illuminated his face.

At first, all I could see were his eyes. Piercing, slate gray, and so bright they were nearly silver. They simmered under thick, prominent brows and obscenely long lashes. His dark hair had fallen casually across his forehead, and he coolly brushed it out of his face with a strong, broad hand. Perfect chiseled jaw. Full lips. It was indecent, frankly, how gorgeous he was.

Gorgeous, indecent, and deadly.

A chill ran through my entire body.

I felt more afraid now than I had all evening, and that included a literal ride through the skies on the back of a dragon. But despite the warning bells going off in every cell of my body, I couldn't look away.

He watched me examine him. There was a glint in his eye that I couldn't stop staring at. He smirked a bit and I came back to myself, heat reddening my cheeks.

"Why, because I'm imprisoned?"

"What?" I tried to shake off whatever was clouding my mind.

"The cliché, as you said."

"Yes." I lifted my chin. I had read enough books. "Cruel, dark prisoner. It's done to death."

He grasped at his heart in mock insult. "You wound me. Couldn't I say the same of you?"

I pursed my lips, and he grinned slightly.

He was right, of course. But I didn't want to share my sob story—how I wasn't actually a criminal like him—with this lethal, terrifying, profanely handsome stranger.

When he realized I wasn't going to offer any insight into my own situation, he sighed.

"You'll have to buck up a bit, bird. You're in Onyx now. It's not all mud-colored hair, ruddy cheeks, and squash farmers. Bastards like me are the least of your concern."

His voice carried an edge that stripped his words of any playfulness, and I couldn't help the shiver that slipped down my spine.

"How do you know I'm from Amber?"

He looked me over through the bars. Briefly, stupidly, I wondered how I must have appeared to him. Stuck in a grimy cell, shivering, feet and bare legs caked in dirt, hair a tangled mess, lips blue. *Ugh.* I crossed my arms over myself when I remembered how little I was wearing—the flimsy camisole—and what the cold had done to my chest.

His jaw ticked slightly. "What happened to the rest of your clothing?"

I squirmed under his unrelenting gaze, my face flushing. "It's a long story."

His expression was calm, but his eyes had gone black. "I've got time."

The last thing I needed was this dangerous prick knowing about my humiliation at the hands of Onyx's lieutenant. "I had to use my blouse to help someone. That's all."

He nodded with skepticism, but the intensity had cleared from his eyes. I shivered, an awkward convulsion against the chill in the air.

"Are you cold?"

"Yes," I admitted. "You aren't?"

"I must be used to it."

I wanted to ask how long he had been down here, and what he was in for. But I was leery of this strange, imposing man. His presence was almost too much to bear.

"Here," he offered, taking off his fur cloak and slipping it through the railing. "I can't listen to your teeth chattering a minute longer. It's grating on the nerves."

I hesitated, but survival instincts kicked in before pride. I took it from him, wrapping it around myself in one swift motion. The cloak was scented like cedarwood, whiskey, and velvety leather. And warm. *So* warm. I almost whimpered as the heat enveloped my freezing arms and legs.

"Thank you."

He watched me as my eyes fluttered closed, calmed by the warmth and heavy weight of his cloak. Even then I could feel his eyes on me, and my skin itched under his gaze.

For some bizarre reason, I couldn't stand the silence.

"Well, I'm not crying anymore. I'll try to keep it down."

But he didn't crawl back to his corner to sleep. Rather, he unfolded one leg out in front of him and brushed a large hand through his hair, sweeping it out of his face.

"Trying to get rid of me?"

"Yes," I admitted.

"She uses me for my fur and then kicks me to the curb. Women . . ."

I rolled my eyes, but I knew better than to be charmed. Obscene beauty or not, this man was locked up in an Onyx Kingdom stronghold dungeon. I just had to balance on the razor's edge between angering him and letting down my guard.

"Just practicing some self-preservation. You could be dangerous."

"True," he mused. "I could be. For what it's worth, I wouldn't care if you were dangerous."

I raised a skeptical brow and wrapped the fur around me tighter. "What's that supposed to mean?"

He gave a crooked grin and shrugged. "You're much too alluring. I'd just have to take my chances, and if you killed me"—he leaned in a bit—"well, it would be a good death."

I pressed my shoulder to my mouth to suppress a laugh. "I think you're a shameless flirt who has been down here alone for too long. Like a beast that likes to play with its prey."

He shook his head with self-deprecation, but the mirth had drained from his eyes. The realization that I may have struck a nerve sent a chill through my bones, and I scooted away from his shadowed form.

"If I'm a beast, so are you." He gestured with his broad hands to the cells that held us both.

For some reason, I felt tears spring to my eyes. The simple reminder was all it took.

Stones, I was so weak.

"The only thing we might have in common is a shared hatred for the wicked Onyx King that shackled us both in here."

"What's wrong with our king?"

His use of "our" answered one of my questions. So, he was from Onyx. Maybe that explained the aura of darkness that rippled off of him.

I tried to bite my tongue. I really did. But it was a sore subject.

"Besides decimating an innocent kingdom for their meager wealth and causing thousands upon thousands of innocent lives to be lost?" I asked. "Or training his soldiers to be more brutal, bloodthirsty, and violent than any other army in Evendell? Or what about his famed love of gleeful torture, senseless death, and ruthless gore?"

It seemed the cell I was in was not so great for my bedside manner.

His mouth lifted in a smile. "Sounds like you're afraid of him."

"I am. You should be, too." I shook my head. "Defending the very king who chained you up . . . King Ravenwood's soldiers slaughtered all of my brother's men. He was lucky to have made it out alive."

"Yes, bird. I've heard that does happen during wartime."

"Don't be glib."

"Don't be naive."

I stifled a groan—another sore subject. I snapped my mouth shut before insults flew out. Maybe it was time to put an end to this deadly tightrope walk of a conversation. I moved farther away and turned to face the empty cell on my other side.

But he sighed from behind me, resigned. "I shouldn't expect you to understand, bird."

Bleeding Stones.

I spun to face the bars again, ready to ask why he was so intent on talking to me all night when all he had wanted was sleep, but was caught off guard by the way his eyes bored into me.

Eyes like endless pools of liquid silver flickered with something far more intense than I had expected.

"Why do you keep calling me that?"

It wasn't what I had planned to say, but came out nonetheless.

For the first time, he faltered, and the intensity behind his eyes vanished as quickly as I had seen it. "I'm actually not sure," he said, laughing to himself. He looked down at his boots. "Just feels fitting." He met my eyes. "Perhaps given the cage."

I gave him a look that said, *Oh, right, that*, and closed my eyes again. "Well, this has been peachy, but unless you have some way out of here, I'm going to try to sleep now. I'm sure we can continue this tomorrow, and the next day, and the eternity after that."

I aimed for biting, but all fiery retorts and energy for banter had dissolved. The reality was worse than bleak. I was alone, exhausted, and more terrified than I could endure for long. I had nothing left in me tonight. Maybe tomorrow I'd figure out how in the world to get out of this keep, this kingdom, this whole mess I was in.

But tonight, I could only slump against the wall and let my eyes flutter closed. As I drifted off to sleep, I thought I heard the stranger whispering in hushed tones to someone else. I fought to stay awake and listen in, but my mind and body were too drained. Sleep came for me, swift and unyielding, against the muted sounds of men arguing.

5

I WOKE UP SORE AND STIFF, BUT OTHERWISE UNSCATHED. A few whispers of sunlight poured in through the window above me, but moments later the cloud cover was back, casting the cell in gloom. I tried to imagine the sun on my face.

Yesterday's events had felt like some kind of sickened fever dream—but awakening to the damp stone around me was as grounding as being slapped across the face. I was going to have to find some way out of here. No more blubbering. No more tears of any kind, actually. I steeled myself for the day ahead.

Unmistakable curiosity getting the best of me, I peered into the cell to my left. My eyes widened and my body went rigid to find it . . . empty. The man from last night was gone.

How had I not heard him be released? No bars clanking or soldiers escorting him out.

Could the argument last night have been between the stranger and a soldier? I hadn't heard any footsteps come toward us. I tried to peer farther through the bars into the cell on the far side of the stranger's. Was there anyone in there that he could have been fighting with? I couldn't tell.

Did he escape? Or—

My blood turned to ice at the new thought. An execution might have been silent. I felt a pang in my heart at the thought of his strong, tall frame hanging by a noose inside the castle gates. Or worse, his severed head on a spike.

The thought of my head next to his followed. If it happened to him, it could very well happen to me . . . I physically shook the dreadful images from my head.

I stared up at the gray, cracked stone ceiling, preparing for a day of being trapped in a damp cell, attempting to keep horrific thoughts and crippling panic at bay.

The sound of footsteps making their way down the dungeon hall drew my attention back. It was the Broad Man, and he was heading toward me. I ripped off the fur cloak and shoved it with shaking hands under the bench to my left. By the time I looked up he was working my cell door open. The lock was old and rusted and took an extra pull for him to wrench it free.

"Good morning," he offered. His face had gained some color back overnight. He looked much more . . . alive than he had when he brought me down here.

I scrambled back as far into the wall behind me as I could. "What's going on?"

"You're needed."

I prayed to the Stones that I was needed to heal someone, and not by the lieutenant. I tried to stay positive. At least I was leaving the cell.

He handed me a simple black dress and some aromatic dark

brown bread. My stomach grumbled at the smell. Surprisingly, Broad Man turned to give me privacy. I crammed a mouthful of bread in before shedding my Amber clothes with lightning speed and slipping on the black dress. It smelled of lilac soap.

"Thank you," I said when I was decent. The Broad Man turned, his eyes kind as they appraised me. I swallowed some fear and gestured toward his abdomen. "How are you feeling?"

"Better than I thought possible, thanks to you." He smiled awkwardly. "I'm Barney. Sorry about last night. For what it's worth, I didn't want to take you from your home."

Somehow, *It's fine, don't worry about it, Barney. These things happen*, didn't find its way out of my mouth.

"What happened to you anyway?" I asked instead.

He shook his head. "You first. What kind of magic was that?"

If only I knew.

There was something warm in Barney's eyes, though. A hint of a smile pressed at my lips. "I guess we'll both keep our secrets."

The walk out of the dungeon seemed shorter than the one inside last night. I followed Barney into the courtyard and immediately sucked in a wonderful lungful of fresh, morning air tinged with the smell of rain.

It was cloudy and frigid out, and once again I remembered how much chillier the north was. The fox fur cloak, courtesy of the dungeon stranger, was much warmer than my new black wool dress, with its leather corset and puffed antique sleeves. The dark realization that the stranger probably wouldn't need his fur anymore only made me shiver harder.

It was still early, and the castle grounds were quiet. I assumed everyone was sleeping, save for the sentries that manned the premises. I followed Barney through the large, wrought iron castle doors, and was greeted by the smells and sounds of a keep just waking up. Fresh bread baking somewhere in the kitchens, floors being scrubbed with various lavender and vanilla soaps. For an early morning, the keep's inhabitants were working overtime to make sure every surface shone and every window gleamed.

The castle was devastating in its haunting beauty. Having never been inside one before, I couldn't help my wonder. Shadowhold was still terrifying—eerie and gothic, like ghosts inhabited every shadowed corner and lurked behind every trapdoor—but there was no denying the majesty of it. Complex, sweeping stonework contrasted with the soft light that billowed through warped windows of colorful glass. Barney must have noticed my awe because he seemed to purposefully walk slower so I could take it all in.

Dusty blue and violet tapestries; rich, velvety green curtains; dark wood tables and chairs scarred with years of wear. Marble vases filled with the strangest flowers I had ever seen adorned the great hall as we walked through it. Spindly, sorrowful-looking things. Twisted vines and dark hues that set them apart from what grew in Amber. My mother would love them.

If I ever saw her again to tell her of them.

We trudged up a carved, stone staircase that wound around the keep, creating several little candlelit alcoves, and came to a stop in front of a door on the second floor, across from the gallery. A worn wooden sign read "Apothecary & Infirmary" and hung lopsided against the wood.

Fleeting relief crammed my heart back into my chest.

Not torture, nor instant death. Not the perverse lieutenant.

This I could do.

"This is where you will work. I'll stay outside to keep an eye on you, so don't do anything that would require the lieutenant." He said it like a warning, but I read a plea in his expression as well. "I'll take you back to the dungeon when the day is done."

I nodded, though the thought of the iron bars of the cell closing in on me sent dread skittering down my spine.

I'd have to save that panic for later.

Barney thought for a moment and added, "Our king is a man of justice. If he cannot persecute your brother for what he stole, he will take from you instead. Don't give him a reason to take more than your trade."

"Thank you, Barney."

Barney closed the door behind me, and I drew in a deep breath as I appraised the apothecary.

The wood-floored room had huge windows behind the counter that looked out onto the dizzying array of oaks and elms surrounding the keep. Strips of sunlight drifted in lazily, highlighting the specks of dust that floated through the musky air.

It smelled of arrowroot, lemongrass, and other salves—a mix of sweet, fragrant, and medicinal that I found strangely comforting. Rows and rows of shelves filled with various herbs and ointments took up most of the space, with a few nooks and crannies for more bizarre objects from around the continent, very few of which I had seen before.

Of course, I didn't plan to tell anyone that. I'd have to put my abysmal lying skills to the test if asked about anything in here, lest I be deemed useless to the castle. What would they do then? Kill me? Hunt my brother down again? I doubted the Onyx soldiers would be able to track down my family now, especially if they made it to the Garnet Kingdom. I winced at the irony. If King Ravenwood's men couldn't find my family, it was unlikely I would ever be able to, either.

"Hello? In here!" bellowed a man's voice.

My brows creased and tension coiled my hands into fists. I rolled up the sleeves of my dress before following the sound around the counter and to the right. Inside was a smaller room that must have been the infirmary. Sitting on a narrow daybed was a portly man with a red handlebar mustache. Despite his bulbous, purpled leg, he had a cheery smile on his face.

"Morning," he said, wincing. "Lovely day for an injury, don't you think?"

A small ripple of relief trickled over me. I had been anticipating a menacing general or soldier. Someone like Bert, whom I might have to heal quickly or risk death.

The sight of this man's mottled leg was a tonic to my racing heart and clenched jaw. Healing, in any capacity, calmed me. It was bizarrely exactly what I needed.

"What do you have going on there?" I leaned down to take a peek. The veins in his lower leg bulged angrily against his skin.

"I was out gathering firewood for the soldiers that have taken up residence within the castle gates. You can just tell by the morning's clouds that it's about to be a mighty cold evening. Walked through what must've been a bramble bush, and next thing I know my leg looks like an eggplant." He grimaced as I lifted his leg and placed it in my lap.

Good news was that this was a simple case of bramble poisoning. Completely treatable and fairly easy to do. Bad news was that draining the poison was agonizing, and I feared even this sturdy man might not be up for the experience.

I smiled at him evenly. "I can help you, sir, but I must warn you, it's fairly painful."

"Call me Owen. Are you the new healer? Our last one died on

the battlefield just a few miles from here. Heard she took an arrow through the eye socket." Owen gave me a bright look that said he thought this was a fun fact.

"Yes, well," I said, cringing at the mental image. "I'm Arwen."

"A beautiful name!"

I smiled despite myself.

I was tired. Exhausted, really. And no amount of sweet, mustached men would crumble the mountain of fear that had erupted in my soul at being here. But I couldn't go back in time. All I could do was try to take care of myself, and to do that, I needed to take care of Owen and his purple leg. Maybe if I did a decent enough job, someone might let me sleep in an actual bed.

"All right, Owen. Hold on tight."

"Do your worst," he said, cheeks rounding in merriment. Owen was an odd fellow, but it seemed I had met the one decent person in the keep.

Owen lay down and I got to work with my salves and tweezers. When he shut his eyes against the pain, I pulled the poison through my fingertips, watching as his veins became less and less swollen. His face turned a red that rivaled his mustache as he strained through the discomfort. I worked swiftly and finished before he could ask me to stop.

"I'd try to keep off it for a few hours and drink a lot of water today."

Owen looked at me with disbelief. "That was mighty fast, Arwen. We're lucky to have you."

I smiled and helped him hobble out, giving Barney a little wave through the open door.

Back inside, I looked through the books, scrolls, potions, and strange bottled creatures that adorned the apothecary walls. I devoured all the new information—so many ways to fix and mend and cure that I had never learned with Nora. Maybe something would spark an idea of how to escape from this place. I had more freedom than I would have expected as a prisoner, and with that came opportunity; I just needed a day or two to plan something that could actually work.

But after a few hours, the day started to crawl toward sundown. The minutes were like hours, the hours like lifetimes.

The reality of my situation had dawned on me around hour three, and I had been obsessing over it for the remainder of my sentence in the apothecary. I hadn't found anything of use to aid my escape, and every window, every door that I could see, was either locked or guarded. Not to mention my Barney-shaped shadow that I didn't think I was likely to shake anytime soon.

But even more difficult than breaking out of the castle would be surviving in the woods beyond. Even if, somehow, I beat those odds, I still had no idea how to navigate the enormity of Onyx. I was unskilled, weak, and uneducated on anything related to this kingdom. Completely unprepared for a life without the safety of my family. And where were they? Had they made it to Garnet? If so, what city? What village?

I slumped down behind the counter. Was it even worth fighting my fate?

But then I thought of Ryder. Of his strength.

He was everything I wasn't. Creative where I was practical, outgoing where I was shy. Brave, charismatic, popular, and adored by everyone. I was sure half the people I had grown up with wouldn't know my face from any other chocolate-haired Amber girl. He was the sun, and everyone circled around him, enchanted by his light. Which meant I was like some far-off planet, shrouded in a lonely expanse of space. Or maybe a lone meteor, trying with all its might to work its way into orbit.

But mostly, he was unbelievably brave.

And I was not. I had been crippled by fear my whole life.

Maybe I could pretend. Pretend I had his courage, heroism, and confidence, and see how far that got me. I was not as naturally daring as Ryder, but I was not ready to roll over and admit defeat just yet, either.

I stood up and hunted for anything that might be useful on my long and likely dangerous journey. Ointments and medical supplies from the drawers and cupboards around me, a sharp pair of shears, and some edible plants. I stuffed everything that I could into my skirt pockets. After, I looked for anything that would give me a sense of how or when to leave this place without being caught by the guards, but nothing jumped out.

As the sun set, I cleaned up for the day and thought of how to ask Barney to allow me to wander the castle so I could look for less frequented doorways, paths, or gates. Stopping to fix an off-kilter jar, I barely saw the mass of fiery-red hair that came barreling in and plowed right into me. My heart leapt from the shock as I grasped clumsily at the shelf behind me, and we both caught a few falling baubles that I had dislodged.

"Sorry! Sorry. *Ugh*, what a day," she said frantically. Her wavy mess of bright red hair framed a face with delicate features and a freckle-dotted nose. She smelled like cinnamon and cloves, and there was something about it that felt familiar and warm.

"It's fine, I—" Before I could finish, the spritely girl unceremoniously dumped her satchel on the floor and sank into one of the lambskin chairs in the center of the room. She tied her unruly hair up with a quill—a unique feat I hadn't seen done before—and kicked off her slippers, tucking her feet underneath her.

"My papa was in here earlier and left his sock behind. I told him we aren't so unfortunate to need a single sock back in our possession, but you know fathers," she said.

I stared blankly at her. I didn't, actually.

"Always *waste not, want not* and whatnot, so I told him I'd come fetch it on my way back from the library. But then I got stuck there until almost dusk. I guess every single person in the keep has decided today is the day they want to enrich their minds or just ruin my day or something, so here I am, hours later than planned, about to miss the first play of the spring, because of a damned sock."

I must have looked bewildered because her eyes widened at me before she let out a slight breath and laughed.

"Sorry. I'm Mari. My papa says my speed comes from my red hair. Makes me feisty, I guess. You must be Arwen. He said you were really spectacular. That you healed him quickly and without much pain. Thank you for that." She smiled at me kindly.

"Oh, yes. Of course. He was lovely." I leaned over the counter and produced the sock in question. "Here you go." I expected Mari to leave but she just took the sock and settled farther into the chair.

I shifted awkwardly on my feet. She didn't seem threatening, but I was still anxious. I peered around her and out at Barney, who looked like he had dozed off against a dark granite column in the gallery overlooking the courtyard.

Some bodyguard.

"So, new healer," Mari said. "How'd you end up here in Shadowhold?"

Like father, like daughter. Both Mari and Owen had a contagious ruddy cheer in their smiles, but Mari had a keen knowing to hers that Owen lacked. She seemed about my age, and was shockingly beautiful, in a slightly wild and breathless way. It was intimidating. She seemed like she might eat men for breakfast. Maybe there were men out there who would enjoy that.

I wasn't sure if I should tell her I was a prisoner. Would anyone trust me to heal them knowing I was from an enemy kingdom? I debated outright lying to her but remembered how that had worked for me last time. I fisted my hands in the thick skirts of my dress and settled for a half-truth.

"I just came here yesterday to fill the open position, and don't know much about the place."

I hoped that Mari's eagerness could help my predicament. Maybe she would tell me a bit too much, and I'd garner some information that might be useful in my escape. As long as she didn't ask where I was from. I knew better than to say Amber, but my lack of worldly experience made making something up impossible.

"Well, I can tell you everything you need to know. Most folk here are fairly dull and not too educated if I'm being honest. The keep houses soldiers and their families, the commander and generals of the army, some dignitaries and noblemen, and people like Papa and me who keep the place running.

"Anyway"—she shifted, pulling her knees up under her—"I've lived here all my life, only been into Willowridge once for a holiday and it was grand. So much history and loads of ancient books. But Shadowhold is lovely if you don't go outside much. I'm sure you already know, but the Shadow Woods aren't safe for anyone, even folk like me who know it inside and out. One too many creatures in those woods for my liking, and I'm pretty brave. Not to brag, but I'm not really humble, either."

She looked off for a moment, as if debating if she really *was* humble.

"What was I saying? Sorry. It has been such a day."

I gave her a warm smile. She was kind of charming. "That you've lived here all your life?"

"Right. The great hall serves a decent supper most nights. The rabbit stew is my favorite, but you can't go wrong with the brisket, either. People keep to themselves but are kind if you get to know the right folk, like me. I'd steer clear of the commanders and soldiers. They weren't too friendly before the war, and now they really have their trousers in a bunch. I'd especially keep clear of Lieutenant Bert. He's a foul brute. My papa thinks something horrible must have happened to him as a child because he's so twisted. That's just basic trauma, though. I have a lot of books on that if you're curious. He's been even worse lately. Ever since King Ravenwood arrived, they've all been more on edge."

My stomach suddenly felt like lead.

The wicked king was *here*? In the same castle as me?

"Do you know what he's doing here?" I tried to keep my question casual. I'm sure it was common for kings to leave their capitals and visit their army outposts, but I feared what it meant for our kingdom's position.

Mari frowned. "I'd imagine he's working with his army to plan their next attack on Amber. He's a brilliant war general, our king. Don't you think? Amber is an interesting kingdom to go after. No doubt it has its logistical perks. I just wish he had stronger diplomacy. No king can succeed with a reputation as a sadist and womanizer."

My eyes nearly popped out of my head—I would never speak so poorly of my own King Gareth, even if he was the half-wit son of our once great King Tyden, *Stones rest his soul*.

"What do you mean by that?" When Mari gave me a strange look, I quickly added, "I grew up in a very small town. Don't really know much about politics."

This was true, actually. A swift look of disappointment clouded Mari's dark caramel eyes, as if she had hoped her new acquaintance might have been brighter, but she seemed to think better of it when she realized she could educate me.

"Well, for starters, he's kind of a whore."

This time I snorted, and she broke into a bright laugh.

"It's true! I've heard he's slept with half the kingdom, but he never plans to take a queen. I think it's because he doesn't want to share any of his power. Which I guess is smart, politically speaking, but pretty cold if you ask me. But what should we expect? He's willing to do anything to get what he wants in battle. The history books already describe him as one of the fiercest rulers ever to grace the continent. He goes through lieutenants like pairs of undergarments. Nobody seems able to hold a position in his army for long, other than Commander Griffin. He's never even had much of a relationship with the noblemen or lords of the kingdom. Just cold and ruthless, like I said."

This fit with everything I had heard my whole life about King Ravenwood. I wasn't naive enough to think Amber's tales of Onyx's king and soldiers weren't a bit inflated, but to hear it from a member of the kingdom itself only proved the stories true.

Knowing he was now here, in the keep, only fueled my need for escape.

Mari stared at me, clearly wondering what I had drifted off thinking about.

"Sorry, it's just"—I hesitated—"horrible to hear bad things about our king. That's all news to me!" I cringed at the phony surprise in my voice. *Why was I so bad at this?* "I heard King Ravenwood keeps dragons, is that true?" I did not want to run into another one of those on my way out of here.

But she only laughed. "Only the one. I've seen it circling above the keep once or twice. Ghastly thing." Mari shuddered. "There are all kinds of beasts in the woods, though. Chimeras, ogres, goblins."

I twitched in quiet horror.

I hadn't ever considered such creatures might be real, hadn't given an ounce of credence to the rumors and gossip that swirled around my hometown. I had once seen a basilisk fang when a traveling merchant hawking oddities had passed through, and I had figured it was a hoax. "Those things are real?"

"You really are from a small town." Mari raised a skeptical eyebrow at me. "Next you'll be saying Garnet's salamanders or Pearl's snow wraiths are myths, too."

I tried to keep my jaw from falling through the floor.

"It's after dinnertime." Mari held her elbow out for me to take. "Shall we catch the tail end of this play together?"

But I shook my head. Given how much she feared King Ravenwood, I didn't think she'd want to befriend me further if she knew the truth: that I was a prisoner here and had to get back to my cell. Plus, I didn't want to venture farther into the castle—if those creatures prowled in the woods, what was inside the castle walls?

I looked over to Barney, who had awoken and was standing just outside the apothecary doors.

"Sorry, I'm exhausted from my first day and need some sleep."

"All right." Her face fell just a bit, but she rebounded quickly. "I'm sure I'll see you around. I have to come ask Dagan something tomorrow, anyway. Be well!" And with that, she was off.

"Wait, who is Dagan?" I called after her, but she had already made her way down the gallery hall toward the great stone staircase.

My raised voice did bring the needling eyes of both a broad-shouldered soldier with a skull helmet of bone and a noblewoman dressed in a dark lace corseted dress and violet and ebony jewelry.

Shit, shit, *shit*.

I winced before ducking back into the apothecary to catch my breath.

Everyone here scared me. They all brimmed with violent, shadowy power and cruel intent. Like I was meat, and they were starving.

Except maybe Owen. And his red-haired daughter. And maybe Barney—I wasn't sure about him yet. But regardless of the outliers, the Onyx people were to be avoided at all costs.

I waited until there was nobody in the gallery before leaving the apothecary. Barney was waiting outside as he had been all day and greeted me with a tired smile. I followed him down the stairs in silence. Gloomy portraits of Onyx royalty with pale, melancholy faces stared back at me alongside wrought iron candelabras and chandeliers.

I tried to avoid the threatening looks of the soldiers coming into the grand hall, and to keep myself from watching longingly as their families met them at the end of a long day to share a meal together. I missed Ryder, Leigh, and my mother desperately. I wondered where they were, and if they were as worried about me as I was about them.

The halls were growing dark as night cascaded on the castle, and I needed to find a way out that wasn't through the main castle doors, which were heavily guarded. Before we rounded the shadow-shrouded corner on our way back to the dungeons, hushed tones coming from a closed door down the hall caught my attention.

I could see a faint glow of candlelight emanating from below the wooden panels, and the slight gap in the frame allowed the sound to carry in my direction. The door had no guards—could this be another way out?

I peeked up at Barney.

"Can I look at this painting for a moment?" I asked, nodding to the one closest to the mysterious room. Upon actually looking at it, I winced. The painting was of a rather well-endowed nude man cradling his . . . endowment.

Barney turned pale with embarrassment. "Uh . . . sure."

I felt my face flush but counted my blessings. His discomfort at what he must have assumed was my sexual interest in the oil painting was probably all that stopped him from saying no.

I inched closer to the door while staring at the least fascinating painting of a naked man I'd ever seen, just in case Barney looked my way. I was about to try the handle when a harsh voice speaking in low tones filtered through.

"With all due respect, Your Majesty, that's what you said last time, and now we are losing men at an alarming rate. I can't train men as fast as they're disappearing."

Your Majesty? Was he talking to—

Another voice interjected.

"And with no respect whatsoever—you'll have to. Don't make me turn another one of your lieutenants into an example. You know how much I enjoy it."

I went stick straight, heart hammering in my chest.

The words were spoken with utter calm. Smooth as silk, even muffled through the stone wall.

King Ravenwood.

It had to be.

"You can brutalize whomever you'd like. It won't help us locate what we need in time. Just means I have to go find new lieutenants."

"Isn't that what I pay you so handsomely for?"

"What about taking a break from the search for a single week, just long enough to—"

"No—you know the seer's words as well as I do. Time is running out, Commander. We have less than a year."

A seer? What could—

Barney's rough hand encircled my arm, and I jumped nearly a foot in the air at the contact.

"That's enough. The painting will still be here tomorrow," he said, expression hard and cold. But his eyes flared with concern more than anything else. Had he, too, heard the furtive conversation? As he pulled me away, the other man—the one the king had called Commander—sighed, and I heard a chair scrape back.

"You used to be more fun."

Barney and I walked out into the chilly night air and away from the hushed argument. The last thing I heard was a dark chuckle that felt like a wave crashing inside my chest.

6

I WAS SURPRISED TO FIND SOMEONE ALREADY IN THE apothecary the next morning when Barney escorted me over. I studied the man reading behind the counter; he had gray hair with a few strands of black still woven throughout, a patchy beard, and a long, lean build. He looked up at me with stern eyes, and I noticed dark bags underneath them.

"You must be Arwen."

"Dagan?" I asked.

He gave a curt nod before going back to his book.

"Do you work here, too?"

He looked up at me as if I were bothering him. Which I probably was.

My cheeks went warm with the feeling of being a nuisance.

"Sometimes," he mumbled, before losing interest in me once again.

Lovely. I made myself busy sorting some of the dried herbs and reading a new healing text.

All I had been able to think of last night was the conversation I had overheard. I couldn't shake the feeling that if I were smarter, I could use some piece of information from the king's private argument to my advantage—to aid my escape plan. My very poorly constructed, not-really-existent-yet escape plan.

All I had gathered was that the king was clearly searching for something, and that time was running out . . .

I didn't know what to think about the mention of a seer. Yet another thing I had thought was only a fable. The power to see the future, to decree the Stones' will to us mere mortals. It was more than I could really comprehend.

My eyes flitted to Dagan. He looked like he had lived in Onyx all his life based on his menacing scowl and comfort behind the counter. Maybe I could ask him, very subtly . . .

"Do you . . ." I swallowed awkwardly. "Do you know—"

"I'll be back shortly," he said before heading for the door.

Oh. Great.

"All right." I sighed, confused. Remembering yesterday, I added, "I think Mari was hoping to come see you today. If she comes by while you're gone, shall I tell her you'll be back?"

Dagan looked like years had been taken off his already long life. I had a feeling he barely tolerated Mari's chaotic energy.

"No." And with that, he was off.

About an hour after that, my herbs had been sorted not only by color and place of origin, but also by how handsome I thought they would be as boys—cardamom clearly took the win there—and my boredom had become excruciating.

I stood up and clasped my hands together, bringing them over my head and leaning forward to stretch my back after hunching for so long over the dried leaves.

My hum of pleasure at the release was abruptly interrupted by the husky clearing of a throat.

"I hate to complain about the view, bird, but I fear I'm in need of some assistance."

My stomach felt like it had tripped over a cliff. I knew that voice.

I snapped up.

Before me stood my alarmingly handsome cellmate. Not dead after all, but not far from it. He was in nothing but a pair of trousers that had been shredded at one calf and were caked in dirt. His hair was stuck to his forehead with sweat and grime, and he held himself against a shelf with one arm.

It was a terrible time to notice, but his chest and abdomen were brilliantly sculpted, shiny with sweat, and dusted with a few fine dark curls. His cut arms flexed as he gritted his teeth and held himself upright. Despite his clear pain, he gave me a self-assured smile, which was both charming and infuriating at once. He had definitely caught me gawking.

I tried to avert my eyes—like a *lady*—when I saw it. His other hand pressed tightly to his right side. Sticky blood seeping in between his fingers and down his rib cage, pooling over his hip bone and into his waistband.

I rushed to his side but thought better of wrapping my arms around his hulking form—even injured, he looked like he could crush me with one hand if he wanted to—and instead guided him lightly onto the infirmary bed and slammed the door shut behind us. His body felt like chilled steel against my hands. The lack of heat radiating from him worried me. Too cold and clammy.

He'd lost a lot of blood.

The stranger closed his eyes with a pained grunt.

"What happened?" I asked as I filled a bowl with warm water and antiseptic. How in the world was he out of his cell and wandering the castle? With guards at every turn, in every nook and corridor?

"Just a tussle. I'm sure it's fine."

Anxiety crawled up my neck like spiders. "Can you show me?"

He released his hand from his side with caution, and I was instantly grateful for the wartime horrors I had witnessed these past few years back in Abbington—not so much for the medical experience, but so I knew not to gasp out loud at the gore and frighten my patient.

Keeping him calm was as important as stitching him up.

A massive chunk of flesh had been torn out right between his ribs. I could almost see the bone beneath the muscle.

"Is it the worst you've seen, bird?"

"Not by half. As you said, just a tussle. I'll have you stitched up in no time." I kept my voice relaxed as he opened his eyes and watched me gather my supplies.

He recoiled a little when my cloth first touched the wound. I could tell from the dozens of other scars on his arms and torso that this wasn't his first *tussle*. Still, when he flinched again, I felt the need to distract him, as he had done for me that first night in the dungeon.

"How did you get out?" I asked as I cleaned the gash. "I thought maybe something had happened . . ."

"Aw, bird. Were you worried about me? Scared you'd find my head on a stake?"

My mouth twitched, but I couldn't think of a witty barb fast enough. I actually had been worried about him, or at least what his fate meant for my own. His brows quirked up, and he quickly averted his eyes. But the flicker of disbelief I had seen in them surprised me.

Regardless, he had dodged my question, clearly uninterested in sharing his escape route.

Selfish prick.

"Do they know you made it out of the castle . . . or back into it? Why are you even still here?" I asked.

"Once I got this nasty thing, there weren't too many other places for me to go." He winced as I scraped dirt out of a particularly thrashed section of his side.

"So you doubled back to the keep you just escaped from? I figured someone like you would just keep running."

"So, someone very stupid?"

"You said it, not me."

He frowned. "In case you missed it, bird, there aren't any towns or villages for miles. What odds would you give me running for days with this kind of injury?"

But I was only half listening. I couldn't stop checking the infirmary door. Would Barney or Bert or another soldier barge in at any moment and kill him? Or me, for helping him? "Aren't you worried they'll catch you back here?"

He grimaced while I worked, lifting his left shoulder in a shrug. "I'm not the soldiers' top priority. We are at war, you know."

I swallowed thickly, hoping he was right.

He raised a curious brow in my direction. "You don't have to worry. They won't punish you for stitching me up."

"You don't know that," I hissed, my eyes darting to the door once more.

"So then why help me? If you think it could be your death sentence?"

My face flushed. He was right. This was a terrible idea.

"Because. You're hurt. And I'm a healer."

His gaze raked over my face. "You're very moral, bird. What's someone like you doing in an Onyx dungeon?"

Reluctance pulled my bottom lip into my mouth in thought. But he had successfully escaped his cell. I had been looking for a way out, and here it was. Maybe he would trade a secret for a secret. It seemed a worthy currency in a kingdom such as this one.

"My brother stole something from the king, and I made a deal to save his life," I said, eyes still on his wound.

After a too-long silence, I peered up to see the man's face had hardened. "Why?"

Defensiveness flooded me. "What do you mean, *why?* He's my brother. I couldn't let the Onyx bastards kill him."

His eyes bored into mine. A mix of coldness and curiosity.

"*Why* did you think your life was worth less than his?"

His words were not at all what I was expecting. "I—I didn't . . . It's not like that." For some reason, my face had flushed.

Growing up, I had always envied Ryder. Men wanted to be friends with him, women wanted to be with him. Powell and my mother adored him. In their eyes, he could do no wrong. With that came an incredible sense of self-assurance that in turn only made him more successful at everything he attempted.

Maybe I had felt like if someone had to make the sacrifice, better it was me than him. Shame coated my tongue, rang through my ears. My cheeks felt hot. I looked down at the wound I was cleaning. The sooner I could get him out of here the better. The prisoner watched me carefully, and I hid from his prying eyes and finished my work.

Once the wound was clean and dressed with ointments, I began to stitch him up. He lay still, barely flinching as I sewed through his skin.

It was now or never. I was almost done—

I thought of the lieutenant, the fact that King Ravenwood was somewhere in this castle, and weighed my next words carefully. I only had one chance at this.

"I could use your help."

His eyebrows shot up, but he waited for me to continue. I turned around the truth in my mind. I couldn't trust this man, of course, but time was running out. As soon as he was healed, he'd be gone, and with him, my only chance at freedom.

As if he saw me debating whether to open up, he said, "You've helped me quite a bit—let me return the favor."

I swallowed against the bile burning in my throat.

"Help me escape. You've clearly had success in doing exactly that. Take me with you, please."

His brows pulled together, but he didn't say anything. I finished my last stitch and began wrapping the wound in bandages.

"Can't. Sorry. I still have some business to attend to here."

Business!

"You're a fugitive," I said, a laugh that was more shock than anything else slipping out. "What *business* do you have other than getting out of this Stones-forsaken place alive?"

Maybe it was his ego—maybe he needed me to beg him for help. I wasn't above that. I'd do whatever I had to do. He grinned and sat up, taking the last few bandages from my hands and finishing the job himself.

"A fair point from a wise woman, but sadly I can't tell you much more, except that the woods around Shadowhold are fierce and filled with creatures I wouldn't advise you to face alone."

"So I've heard. Is that how you got this injury? Something took a bite out of you on your way out?"

A laugh breezed out of him, and he winced. "You're not so far off."

He swung his legs around and stood up gingerly.

"Wait." I motioned back to the bed. "I wasn't done. One last ointment."

His brow furrowed but he gestured toward himself as if to say, *Fine, hurry up, then.*

I grabbed a healing salve and crossed the room to stand beside him. Stones, he was tall. He towered over me. Even misted in sweat and pale from blood loss, his beauty was painful. Heartbreaking.

And he really needed to put a shirt on. I took a tentative breath and slipped my hands under the bandages with the guise of applying the ointment. His breath hitched at my touch, and I let droplets of my power spill out into his skin and pull his ripped flesh together, reinforcing the stitches and calming the swelling.

"Why won't you help me? I won't be a burden to you. I promise."

I peered up at him.

His eyes were soft but wounded. Maybe he was just in a great deal of pain from his injury.

"I'm sorry, bird. I fear you're needed here."

I pulled my hands away and his gaze dragged over me, slow and savoring and shockingly intimate. The space between us crackled.

Using my powers always drained me a little, and I could feel a slight fatigue beginning to set in. His eyes narrowed and he stepped even closer, his bewitching woody scent filling my senses.

"Are you all right?"

"Just tired."

He nodded. "Happens to me, too."

My brows knit inward. "You . . . get tired?"

It almost looked like his cheeks were flushing, but before he could respond the loud slam of the apothecary door swinging open in the next room pulled his gaze from mine. Without missing a beat, the man shot me an apologetic smile and hoisted himself out the window.

"Shit!" I whisper-shrieked, running around the table to the windowsill, but he was out with a grunt before I could stop him. I looked down at the dusty ground below and drew in a true gasp.

He was gone.

How?

I spun around right as a handsome man with honey hair and clear green eyes like sea glass came barreling into the room.

My chest expanded as I tried to remember to breathe. Adrenaline still simmered in my veins.

"Where is he?" The broad-shouldered man was almost as tall as the prisoner, and possibly stronger. He wore an Onyx uniform with glistening studs along the black leather harness. Turning in circles, he inspected the small room. Then his threatening, vicious gaze dragged over me.

I swallowed hard, shifting under his unflinching eyes. "I'm Arwen, the new healer. Who are you looking for?"

He shot me a devastating glare and I cowered. Without saying anything further, he turned on his heel and slammed the door behind him.

7

J UST ONE DAY AFTER THE RIDICULOUS WINDOW ESCAPE, A
miracle happened—I found my way out.

And his name was Jaem.

Jaem was the butcher's son. Today, he had come in with two
mangled fingers. While trying to flatten a cut of pork, he had
caught the eye of a lovely young woman named Lucinda. With her
long, fair hair and narrow nose, she took Jaem's breath away, and
he had hammered right down onto his own hand. Poor kid. While
I fit the digits that looked more like ground meat into a splint, he
told me he was hoping to bring something back from town tomorrow for Lucinda. He went into the capital once a week to sell the
keep's leftover meats and hides and didn't tell his father so that he
could keep the extra coin. He left each week at midnight.

Tonight, I was going to sneak onto his cart.

I had realized my cell lock was rusted on my first morning here,
but I'd yet to find a way to use that to my advantage—until now.
Once inside the Onyx capital, I could get to a port city and find
safe passage on a ship. I had a little coin still on me from the night

we had tried to leave Abbington hidden in my skirt pockets, and I hoped that would be enough to pay for travel from the Onyx coast to Garnet. As long as I could navigate the capital, and whatever creatures or villains lived within its walls . . . But my unease about being in Willowridge was nothing compared to my fear of the Shadow Woods. If I could get through them safely in Jaem's cart, I could manage whatever was in the city.

The fear that Barney or Bert—or, Stones forbid, the king himself—might realize I helped the prisoner escape the other day was a constant rattle in my mind. Each day there was a new, more pressing reason why the sooner I got out of this keep, the better.

Still, I found I had replayed my conversation with the stranger more than a hundred times in my head. What could possibly have kept him in Shadowhold after finding a way out of his cell? Why had he disappeared before hitting the ground? Surely my eyes had played some kind of trick on me.

That, and the conversation between the king and his commander I had overheard, spun in my mind on a constant loop each night when I was locked in my cell—they were all that distracted me from the clawing, dripping fear.

"Does the myrtle leaf go here?" I asked Dagan, pulling myself back to the herbs in front of me.

A slow nod.

I should have known. It was all I ever got from the older man. He seemed to despise me for some reason, and I tried to keep my mouth closed around him as much as I could. We worked in silence as the final hours of the day crept by.

Now that I knew midnight meant I might be able to leave, the day was kicking and screaming its way toward dusk.

"Hi, you two! What a party it is in here."

Mari's chipper sarcasm as she bounded through the apothecary door was a welcome reprieve from the monotony.

"What's that?" I asked by way of greeting, pointing to the leathery book in her hands.

"A witch's grimoire. I think it's over a hundred years old. I've translated as much as I can, but, Dagan, I thought you might be able to help with the rest?"

Dagan huffed but I could tell he was pleased with the request. Maybe he was just as bored as I was. The thought made me laugh. He took the book from Mari and went into the closet, presumably for something to help him translate.

I whispered to Mari while he was out of earshot. "I think he's said about six words to me today. Not a chatty fellow. Who is he, exactly?"

Mari giggled. "He used to be an advisor or something to the king before Kane Ravenwood, and before that, I think he served in the Onyx army, but now he just works in the apothecary. Some of the younger kids think he's a warlock and that's why King Ravenwood keeps him here, but I've never seen him use any magic." She tapped her fingers on the wood counter in thought. "He pretends I annoy him, but I can see right through it. I know he loves to help me with old texts and my research on Fae and witches. He's just a lonely old man. I'm not sure he ever had a family or anything."

A twinge twisted in my heart for Dagan.

"I have to get back to the library, but maybe we can have supper together tonight? It's the brisket I told you about."

I wasn't sure why I felt guilty turning Mari down again. I didn't even know her that well. But it had been a long time since I'd had an invitation of friendship from anyone. Plus, I had avoided the great hall for the week I had been here. I had avoided everything except this room, the infirmary attached to it, and my cell.

Even if I was daring and decided to brave the rest of the shadow-filled castle, I didn't see Barney approving of a dinner date with a new friend.

"Tomorrow?" I wouldn't be here then, Stones-willing.

If I was successful tonight, I'd likely never see her again. The somber thought surprised me. I hoped she wouldn't think it had anything to do with her.

Her expression told me she knew I was holding something back. "What's wrong?"

"Just a little homesick. That's all."

Another half truth.

"All right. We'll see how you feel tomorrow." Mari gave my arm a squeeze before turning to leave.

Dagan and I continued to work, with only a few other patients— all soldiers—coming in throughout the day. He let me do all of the healing, checking on me once in a while to make sure I hadn't made any obvious mistakes. I tried not to take it personally.

I was just cleaning up in the infirmary after an unusually gory javelin wound when I heard a gruff voice that made my stomach swirl with unease.

"Dagan, welcome back," Bert said. "Commander tells me the Jade Islands were a bust. Pity." The sound of boots scraping toward me was slow and persistent, like the dread unfurling in my chest. "Where's the girl?"

Shit. I couldn't be this close to freedom and fall into Bert's hands now.

Silently, carefully, with such gentleness my hands shook, I closed the infirmary door, then pushed the daybed up against the lock.

I had to get out of here before Dagan brought Bert in here to take me. But my heart pounded so loudly in my ears, I couldn't think.

The window.

If the stranger could do it with the wound he had, I could, too.

My fingers reached the glass before I had full awareness of it, and I pushed and pushed and pushed.

The latch wouldn't budge. *The latch wouldn't budge* and I was stuck in here, like a mouse in a trap.

Had it been sealed since the day the prisoner had fled? I slammed myself into the frame over and over, pain searing through the muscles and bones in my shoulder and forearm.

Sweat beaded at my brow, at my hairline.

I licked my lips and strained with the effort, teeth clenched, ears ringing.

Come on, come on, *come on*.

Finally, it gave with a *pop*.

Thank the Stones.

I lifted it up, and a cool breeze kissed over my face. My vision narrowed on the view beneath me. The soldiers milling about. The blacksmith slamming his hammer like an executioner. My palms itched at the sight—I would never make it to the stables. I would probably never make it at all. It was a steeper drop than I was expecting, even from the second floor. I still had no idea how the prisoner had done it.

The doorknob to the infirmary jiggled and I hoisted myself up.

"Arwen? Why is this locked?" I pulled in a sharp inhale.

It was Dagan.

I listened for Bert's voice, one foot dangling out the window, wind snapping at my ankle—but didn't hear anything.

"Arwen?"

I hadn't heard Bert's voice again. The banging continued, and I said a silent prayer to the Stones that this was the right decision before pulling myself back inside.

By the time I moved the bed away and opened the door, Dagan was red in the face.

"What were you doing in there?"

I cradled my bruised arm. "I . . . got stuck."

Dagan shook his head and retreated into the apothecary.

I followed him, asking, "Did I hear the lieutenant?" I tried to sound casual, but it came out two octaves too high.

Dagan made a disgruntled sound. "Unfortunately."

"Not a fan of his?"

"Is anyone?"

A smile twitched at my lips. "How'd you get him to leave?"

Dagan gave me a pointed look. "I did not have what he was looking for."

A huge exhale found its way out of my lungs. I hadn't even been aware I was holding my breath.

Relief had my eyes on the clock—it had to be midnight by now, right? I needed to leave Shadowhold more than I needed my heart to beat or my lungs to breathe.

But it was only dusk.

"Dagan . . . I'm not feeling too well. I think my porridge was a bit off this morning. Do you mind if I head out a little early?" I grasped at my stomach a beat too late to sell the story.

He looked at me, suspicion in his eyes. "If you must."

"Thank you." I almost said that I'd see him tomorrow, but I felt like I'd done enough lying for a lifetime.

Barney walked me back to the cells in uncomfortable silence. Clearly something was on his mind, but I didn't care to know what. I had a single mission this evening. I had plotted all day as I stitched and mended, and now it was time to see if I had learned anything from a lifetime growing up with Ryder. It was all I could do not to fall apart at the enormity of the danger that stood before me if I succeeded.

We arrived at my cell and Barney closed the door behind me, pushing the iron key into the lock.

"Barney," I asked, grasping his hand through the bars. He flinched slightly but met my gaze as he waited for me to continue.

"I just wanted to say. I am so grateful to you. For your kindness and your bravery."

As I spoke, my heart spun inside my chest. Using my foot, I slowly pulled the cell door inward, toward me, inch by inch. So careful to make sure he didn't notice the rusted lock would only close properly if it was pulled tight. So subtly that I could hardly tell if I had actually moved it at all. So slight that he would never have noticed the misalignment of the dead bolt to the strike.

"You're so thoughtful and have made me feel so at home here. To be honest"—I looked down demurely and thought I saw Barney blush—"you're . . . the only thing getting me through this difficult time. I just wanted to say thank you."

Barney regarded me with painfully uncomfortable silence and pink cheeks. ". . . All right."

He shook his head in confusion and finished turning the key before heading back up toward the spiral stone steps, faster than I'd seen him move before.

Once he was gone, I released an exhale I felt like I had been holding for a hundred years. I had been hoping to charm him, but making him aggressively uncomfortable had worked just fine, too. My hands wrapped around the iron bars with care, and ever so slowly I inched the cell door open with a creak.

Open.

It was open. Not locked.

Barney had turned the key into the rusted lock, and the dead bolt had slid right past the strike.

I was free.

But I couldn't celebrate yet.

I pulled the food and supplies that I had pilfered from my few days in the apothecary out of my skirt pocket and found the paper with a rough map I had drawn of the outer courtyard inside one of the empty buckets. I had everything I needed, including a small pack I had swiped from a snobbish nobleman's wife who came into the infirmary with a scratchy throat. Who knew I was such a good little thief? Must run in the family.

Now came the hardest part. Sitting in my open cell, knowing I could leave at any moment, but waiting for midnight, for Jacm, for the chime of the bell.

⁂

I WAS JOSTLED OUT OF A HALF SLEEP BY GROANING.

A prisoner so bruised his face looked like a plum was dragged along the wet cobblestones before me and brought back to his cell from the sealed-off annex at the end of the dungeon's passageway. Night after night of tucking my head under the fox fur to hide from weeping, gurgling, and wailing had told me exactly what went on in there.

Three fingers were missing from his hand, and he had a festering wound where his ear had once been. A terrible gasp slipped out of me.

He was bloodied and retching, almost skeletal, and barely able to take three steps forward. Finally, the soldiers reached his cell and threw him in with the sickening slap of skin against stone. It was the cell two over from mine, directly next to where the handsome stranger had been kept. I was certain now that the pulp of a man had been who the stranger had argued with on my first night.

Dusk had slipped into night, and my mind never stopped racing. After one uniquely unpleasant imagined scenario in which I only made it steps out of my cell before a soldier found me and sliced me in half for my treason, I turned on my side and released a pent-up groan into my cloak.

"Tough day?"

His voice did something to my heart that I didn't want to look at too closely—an uncanny blend of relief and excitement and genuine fear. When I turned around, the stranger I was thinking about was standing across from my cell, leaning back against the cool, lantern-lit stone of the dungeon, face awash in blue light. One foot up against the wall behind him, and arms crossed—the picture of leisure.

I gripped my hands around my knees to keep them from shaking.

"What are you doing down here?" I asked, my voice a mere rasp. There were no prisoners in the cells directly next to me, but there were a few who could likely hear us farther out.

"What a lovely cell you have. Much nicer than mine was. A bench, a bucket. How'd you sway the bald oaf to set you up so nicely?" He gave me a lazy smile and leaned closer. "Did you bribe him with your gorgeous, pouty lips?"

I didn't attempt to hide my disgust. "Get your mind out of the gutter. He's a kind soldier. One of the rare few here, it seems."

His eyes sparkled as he walked up to my cell and peered down at me.

My instincts had clearly been right about him—to be slipping in and out of the castle so easily, and with such cool, unnerving calm. He must have been more cunning, more dangerous than I had even realized.

I just didn't trust him.

And clearly, the feeling was mutual. He hadn't been interested in telling me anything about his escape. Irritation pricked at my skin. This stranger couldn't help me, but he had ample time to stroll through the dungeons and be irritating?

"Your healing skills are top-notch, bird," he purred. "I feel like I'm in one piece again." He lifted his shirt, showing me a slice of dazzling, near-carved, golden-brown torso with a single stitched line across it.

I scowled. "You must have a death wish. Why are you back?"

Remembering my cell was open, I crawled toward the door until my feet were pressed up against it, holding it closed. A sinking feeling snaked through me at the thought of him being this close without a real partition between us. He was much more menacing tonight than he had been in the infirmary. I wondered if it was the clammy pallor that had come with his chest wound. The look in his eyes when he feared for his life.

"I told you, I have a few things to attend to. Some of which are down here in this dungeon." He pulled his gaze from me and peered down the dark corridor. "Don't worry," he continued, looking back at me. "I won't get you in any trouble."

The clock tower outside struck, sounding that it was only two hours until Jaem would ride for Willowridge, and I'd need to slip out of my cell.

"Right," I said, but I wasn't really listening anymore. Fear and self-doubt were creeping in like they always did. I couldn't do this. I wouldn't make it out alive. I—

"What's wrong?" His voice had lost its playful purr.

"What? Nothing."

I trembled, anticipation and anxiety physically shaking my body. My bones. The sun was setting, and I had no real plan for getting past the dungeon guards at the top of the stairs. What was I thinking, attempting this? Maybe I had a death wish, too.

"Hey," he said more sharply, crouching down and slipping a large hand through the bars to grasp my arm. "Talk to me."

I winced at the pressure on my forearm. I hadn't healed myself in hopes of retaining all my power, all my energy, for tonight. He released me instantly, his face contorting in horror. "You're hurt. Why didn't you say something?"

"It's nothing, just a bruise."

Anger simmered in his eyes. "Who did this to you?"

"I stupidly did it to myself, I was trying to—" What? What was I trying to do? I wasn't going to tell him I was trying to throw myself out the same window that he did.

He waited for me to continue.

"Doesn't matter. Why are you even talking to me? Are you going to tell me anything about yourself, how you escaped? Or just keep bothering me at inopportune times?"

"Is there a more opportune time you would prefer?" he asked, arching a playful brow. "Maybe in the middle of the night? When you are all alone down here, thinking of me?"

I shook my head in exasperation.

He huffed a quiet laugh. "In truth, bird, your cell is the last place I should be, but"—he sighed—"I can't seem to keep away from you."

A shiver kissed up my spine.

"Well." I searched for the right words. "It is nice to not feel completely alone."

His brows lifted slightly. "I can't imagine a woman like you feels alone often."

I shot him a look. "Excuse me!"

"That came out wrong," he said, dragging a hand over his face to hide a smile. I had to force myself to look down. The dimples. They were killing me.

"I only meant that you are warm and funny and very pleasant to be around. I would assume you are rarely left alone by men or women."

His words were like a loaf of bread rising in my chest. Warm and gooey and soft.

But they soured quickly. "You would assume incorrectly. I haven't had too many friends in my life. Certainly no *men*. My town was small, very few children my age. Everyone was close to my brother, and I sort of just . . . tagged along."

"Then they're all half-wits. Sounds like a blessing, leaving that collection of huts."

"Maybe. Sometimes . . . I don't know."

"Tell me. Sometimes what?"

Why did I feel the words bubbling out of me? Words I had folded so deeply inside myself for so long I had almost successfully forgotten they existed. I forced a slow breath into my lungs.

"Sometimes, I wished for more."

His eyes flickered, waiting for me to continue.

"Growing up . . . I didn't learn much, or meet many people, or try many things. It's shameful, frankly, how little I know about the world." I thought about Mari. How much she had seen and learned and lived in her twenty years. I'd bet she was even well versed in the mysterious, far corners of the continent. Kingdoms I knew nothing of, like Jade and Citrine. I shook my head. "In just a few days, I've met people here who have seen and done so much more than me. It makes me feel like I've barely lived."

"Why didn't you leave?"

Fear. Constant and cloying fear that dripped down my neck like thick syrup each and every day.

"I had a lot of responsibilities. I couldn't," I said instead.

"That sounds like a load of shit to me."

I stiffened. "You're foul."

"I'm honest."

My fingers pinched the bridge of my nose. Forget foul—this man was maddening.

"Never mind. I'm going to sleep."

I made to crawl back to my corner, but he grasped between the bars and wrapped a strong hand around my bare ankle. His touch was firm enough to hold me in place, but gentle around the sensitive skin. A chill ran up my calf and settled between my legs. I shivered.

"Come on, bird. You've got no reason to lie to me. Why did you stay?"

"Let go of me."

He did so at once and without hesitation.

"I told you. My mother was ill. My sister was young. Even before my brother had been sent off to fight in your king's war, someone had to help take care of them."

He shook his head and an uncomfortable silence stretched between us like a long and unending sea.

"And I had a person there that I cared about."

The stranger's full brows quirked up in interest. "I thought you said no men."

Halden wasn't a *man*. He was . . . Halden. It was—

I didn't need to explain myself to this stranger. I opened my mouth to say exactly that.

But he just shook his head. "Nah."

I crossed my arms. "What do you mean, 'nah'?"

He shrugged. "He wasn't much to you."

"What?"

"You don't light up when you speak of him. You clearly never think of him. Try again."

"You're so dismissive. How could you possibly know that?"

"Trust me, I know these things." His eyes bored into mine. "Why did you *stay*?"

Ugh. Enough already. What did it matter, anyway? "I was scared."

"Of what?"

"Of everything!" I gestured wildly at the bars surrounding me where I was held against my will in the most treacherous kingdom in Evendell. "Look what happens when you take one step out of your tiny, suffocatingly safe life!"

Why did I feel so guilty saying it out loud?

"Fair point, bird. Prison's not the ideal result of adventure, I'll give you that."

I laughed hard—drained and frustrated and so, so tired. I heard a grunt from a cell farther back and quieted myself.

"All right, so maybe I traded one prison for another. I will say, at least I'm constantly learning here. There are herbs and medicines in that apothecary I've never even heard of, let alone seen in person."

"Your positivity baffles me."

I lifted a brow in question.

"The way you look at things. It's just . . ." His hand disappeared in his dark locks. "Refreshing."

I considered him. Perfect, dark hair curling over his forehead and down at the base of his neck. The tiniest bit of scruff along a jawline that rivaled jutting cliffs. Those clear, slate eyes. My heart was thrumming.

"What?" he said with a roguish grin. No. Not the teeth. The full smile was arresting. It was uncanny, seeing someone so stunning, so clearly powerful, so dangerous, share something as intimate as a smile. Knowing any attempt at a lie would be abysmal, I tried to cover with something honest.

"Just trying to understand you."

His smile faded and he lifted his eyes to the ceiling in thought. Then he stood abruptly.

"Time for me to go." He tried for lighthearted. "I promised you no trouble, right?"

I nodded but struggled to find words.

He turned back to me before leaving. "Keep your chin up, bird. You're not alone here."

"Well, I will be, when you finally finish whatever it is that keeps you hanging around Shadowhold."

I sounded so pathetic my toes curled inside my shoes.

But he just regarded me with those shining eyes and an elegant smile. "I don't see that happening anytime soon."

And with that, he slipped down the passageway like a shadow

and up the stairs into the night. I almost felt bad—I hadn't told him that even if he was planning on staying here, I wasn't.

I curled up in the corner. The journey ahead of me would be more dangerous and unpleasant than anything I had ever experienced. And that was *if* I even made it out tonight alive. I rolled to my side and wound myself into a ball, wishing I didn't feel so afraid.

8

I AWOKE WITH A START AT THE BELLS THAT CHIMED MID-
night.

It was now or never.

My mind was still bathed in the fog of restless sleep, but adrenaline pumped steadily through my veins, forcing me up to my feet.
Wrapping myself in the stranger's fox fur cloak, I tied my long hair
back in a loose braid and made sure the pack was secured tightly to
my hip. I didn't need anything getting in my way if I had to run
from something or someone.

I opened my cell door with a creak and swept my attention over
the hallway dotted by crumbs of light from flickering lanterns—
eerily silent and empty, as always. I tiptoed down the corridor and
toward the spiral stairs. When I reached the bottom, I braced myself with a deep breath. It was a terrible plan. The worst plan anyone had ever tried in the history of the continent. I had no faith in
it whatsoever, but it was all I had.

One more deep breath, then—

"Help!" I yelped upward.

My stomach threatened to crawl into my throat. I fisted and released my hands.

Silence stretched through the night.

"Hello? Help!" I yelled again.

A few grumbles from fellow prisoners, irked by the jarring disruption to their sleep.

But nothing else.

I called out one last time and then sprinted up the stairs until I reached the slatted wooden door of the dungeon. I held myself to the wall behind it and tried not to breathe.

I waited and waited, so long it felt like years were passing by.

My lungs were burning.

My heart—racing like the wings of a hummingbird.

I waited until the door pushed open, pinning me to the stone wall, and a guard still bleary with sleep sauntered right past me and down the stairs.

No air in or out of my lungs. None—

"Oi, shut up, whoever you are," he called down.

Once he cleared a full spiral, I slipped out and hurried into the night, never stopping to catch my breath.

The castle was frozen in a deep and silent slumber. I sped along the same path I had taken that first night I arrived, through the field, alongside the soldiers' painted camps.

I wished I had known about Jaem earlier—once out of my cell, this wasn't as hard as I thought it might be. If Jaem successfully got me through the Shadow Woods to Willowridge, I might just—

Voices rang into the night, and I froze.

But it was just a few soldiers telling stories into the late hours beside dying, dancing firelight. My chest caved in with relief, and I kept moving, blanketed by darkness and staying close to the tents to keep out of sight. I carefully edged through mazes of sleeping soldiers, my back flush against canvas, peering around each corner before I turned. My slippers squashed in the cold, wet mud. I winced as icy water soaked between my toes.

Finally—I spied Jaem's cart pulling up at the end of the dirt road ahead of me. His horse nickered softly, and I could just make out a wagon filled with dried meats and pelts. If I sprinted now, I would make it to the cart right before Jaem reached the main gates of the keep.

I took a step forward and a tin cup clanged beneath my foot. I silently cursed men and their inability to pick up after themselves and looked around for any sign that someone had heard. When nobody came for me, I puffed out a breath and turned to make my sprint for the wagon, and ran face-first into a large, sweaty body.

Bert.

Just as surprised to see me in his camp as I was to see him.

My heart thumped loudly in my eardrums as his disbelief warped into sinister delight.

"Look what I found. Little magic girl out here all on her own," he hissed. "All the coin in Evendell says you aren't supposed to be out of your cell in the middle of the night."

My throat constricted with a silent scream. I wouldn't be able to reach the shears in my pack in time. Even if I could, I wasn't sure I had the strength—mentally or physically—to plunge them into his heart, his neck. But I could outrun him. He was inebriated and wearing a heavy suit of armor, and I was fast.

Even faster with fear on my side.

But if I ran, would he call after me and alert all the other sleeping soldiers? I didn't like my odds of outrunning hundreds of Onyx men.

"You're wrong," I said, mustering false courage. "The king knows I'm here."

Bert let loose a low rumble of a laugh, but his smile didn't reach his eyes. Something in my gut shifted, souring my stomach. I suddenly knew with absolute certainty that I should run. I turned on my heel just as I felt his rough hand grip around my elbow.

"Then I'll take you right to him," he said more to himself, hauling me backward.

My entire body shook so hard I thought I'd vomit.

I had to get away from him. Before he brought me into his tent. I had to—

"Let go of me!" I hated how shrill my voice sounded, how scared. I tried to pry his fingers off my arm, but he only grasped tighter, his nails digging into my skin and drawing blood. "I am a prisoner of the king!"

A sinister laugh slithered out of him. "Exactly. *Prisoner.* What is it you think that means?"

"Let me go right now," I demanded, but my words were a strangled wheeze, and tears pricked at my eyes. "Let me go or I'll scream."

"Be my guest," he whispered up against my ear, his breath hot and stale. "You think you'd be the first?"

I didn't let my shock keep me silent for long. I would have rather been caught and spend the rest of my life in that dungeon than experience whatever it was Bert had planned for me. I sucked in a deep breath to call for help but Bert clamped his meaty hand over my mouth and held it tight. I tried to shove him away, off of me, gagging with fear and disgust and nausea—but he was so much stronger than me. I thrashed and bit, straining for breath, but he dragged me farther toward his tent.

"If your mouth feels this good on my palm, I can't wait until you're on your knees. Magic girl with the magic mouth."

Tears had begun to pour down my cheeks in earnest.

I choked on a single, mangled sob.

He took us to the opening of his tent, and I could see the pallet and pelts inside. My stomach roiled.

No, no, *no*.

I struggled, pushed, and writhed, anything to get away—

I couldn't go in there.

He couldn't make me do this. I wouldn't let him. I—

"What the fuck is going on here?" growled a low voice behind us. Cold as death and just as violent.

Bert spun us to face the man, but I already knew who would be standing there.

I knew his voice like my own by now.

"No." The word fell from my mouth. Bert would surely kill him.

The prisoner's familiar, towering frame, blazing silver eyes, and a more mercenary expression than I had ever seen stared back at us. Fury simmered in his gaze—fury and the promise of death.

But he didn't move to draw a sword or rush the lieutenant.

Instead, for no reason at all, Bert released me, and I fell unceremoniously to the ground.

Confusion rang through my chest alongside my relief, my heartbeat still pounding with residual adrenaline.

Bert stumbled and arched a bow before the stranger.

My hammering heart stopped cold.

Why would—

"My king," Bert sputtered, face aimed at the dirt beneath him.

My vision tunneled until all I could see was the prisoner standing before me. The weight of realization like a boulder on my chest, crushing, horrifying—

No air.

I had no air. I wasn't breathing. I—

His gray eyes didn't meet my gaping stare. They were too busy, too focused, flickering with white-hot rage, like burning liquid silver, directed at the hunched lieutenant.

I could feel Bert wobble beside me, trying in vain to hold his bow.

A cold rush of humiliation flooded my veins as I took one small inhale.

"You?" The word came out far too hoarse. I cleared my throat. "You're the . . . you're King Kane Ravenwood? How?"

"Questions later," the king bit out, but his seething tone wasn't directed at me.

I watched from the mud as he stalked forward, like shadowed death incarnate, and put both his hands on Bert's still bowed shoulders, kneeing him in the face with so much force it reverberated through the ground beneath me.

With a wet crunch, Bert flew backward and landed with a sickening thud. He moaned in agony, his nose clearly shattered at a hideous angle, lip busted, and one eye already swelling shut. I thought I might have even seen the moonlight glint off a few teeth in the wet grass.

For once, I felt no inclination to heal.

The king crouched over him and spoke so quietly, it was almost a whisper—a sinister sigh alongside the night's fog. "You disgusting piece of filth—a festering blemish in my army and among men. You will regret every single step that led you to this moment. You will *pray* for death."

Bert just groaned, and then fell back into the grass, unconscious. The king stood up, brushed some mud from his knees, and turned to face me. His expression was a careful mask of calm, as if he knew that if he either softened toward me or revealed the depths of his rage I might fall into hysterics.

And he would be right. I was mortified and sick with fear. I couldn't form a single coherent thought around the resounding roar of betrayal whirring through my ears.

A handful of soldiers had heard the commotion. They rushed out of their tents, some with glinting metal swords at the ready, others sleep addled and still pulling on pants—but each one bowed when they saw their king.

"Take this sack of shit to the dungeons," he said to them. "And tell Commander Griffin"—King Ravenwood nodded toward Bert's mangled face—"I want him to *suffer*."

The soldiers didn't hesitate, picking Bert up from the muddy ground and carrying him off toward the castle as he moaned.

The rest of them stood by, ready for further orders from their king.

Their *king*.

"As you were." His words sent the men scattering back into their tents and left us alone beneath the shining night sky. Horror swirled in my gut like blood in water as I regarded King Ravenwood.

He took a tentative step forward and offered me his hand. His eyes still burned like ice.

I stared at his palm before pushing myself up off the grass without his help.

My breathing had gone so shallow, and I was shaking in awkward, jarring spasms. I didn't want to be touched by anyone at this moment, least of all him.

The King flexed his outstretched hand and pocketed it as if he didn't know what else to do with the appendage. "Are you all right?"

Was I *all right*?

"No." I wiped the cool, drying tears from my face.

King Ravenwood looked physically pained as his eyes followed my hands on my cheeks. "I swear he will not live to touch another woman."

Emotions warred inside my heart. Shame at how I had so easily been played for a fool, fury at his betrayal and toward his twisted lieutenant—how close he had come to hurting me . . . and terror. Such terror of the wicked king of legend who stood before me, I thought I might faint.

Fury—the easiest to grasp and harness in my mind—won out, and I glared at him.

He rubbed a hand down his face like a long-suffering children's teacher.

"Arwen—"

I made a noise that was somewhere between a scoff and a gasp. I had to get out of here.

Right now.

But Jaem was long gone, so my feet began to carry me back toward the castle. The gorgeous deceiver followed me closely.

He looped in front of me, and I stopped short.

Our chests were a single breath apart, and I cowered back from his broad form. From the wicked, predatory power that seeped from him.

"I was going to tell you." He surveyed me from head to toe, seemingly checking for injury.

What would he do to me now? Now that I had tried to escape?

He must have seen the horror on my face because a bitter smile replaced his frown. "I'm not going to torture you for your failed attempt to run, though that would be fitting of the merciless king you think I am."

"Thank you," I whispered dumbly.

King Ravenwood pressed his lips into a thin line.

"I need to know if you're all right," he said firmly. "Did he hurt you?"

It was like the words were blades in his mouth.

"Why were you chained up in your own dungeon?" I asked. It was all I could force out.

His jaw clenched. "I had to talk to someone down there. And not as . . . myself."

I remembered the hushed argument that first night. The husk of a man that had been brought back to his cell this evening.

"Are. You. Hurt?" His words punched through clenched teeth.

"No," I said, lower than a whisper.

He nodded, eyes softening with relief.

"Why . . . continue to lie to me in the infirmary?"

His brows furrowed. "Maybe you wouldn't have healed me if you knew who I was. All I had taken from you."

I would have, but I wondered if he knew that. If that was another one of his many lies.

I didn't know why I even bothered to ask—it wasn't like I could trust a word he said. Alongside my fear, searing humiliation funneled through me. I had allowed a monster to lie to me, deceive me, and coax some of my deepest truths from my lips. It had all been a nasty, dirty trick. The red haze of anger that veiled my vision intensified.

I was weak and stupid—first with Bert, and now with King Ravenwood.

"Are you really going to kill him?" I asked.

The king's jaw tightened. "Yes. I am going to kill him."

"Of course." I looked down, but my tone had conveyed my disgust.

"You are impossible. I just saved you from a fucking rapist. Now you judge me for how I wish to punish him for hurting you?"

"He was your own corrupt lieutenant!" I bit my tongue. I was too angry to be near him. I would say something that would get me killed, too.

"Yes, and that will haunt me for a long time, Arwen. I had no idea . . . who he was." He sighed. "They should have told me. My men. About him. I don't know why they didn't."

"Maybe the other kingdoms aren't the only ones who fear the Onyx king."

His eyebrows creased together as he looked down at me, and I wondered if it was shame that played across his face. Whatever it was, it hardened into something cruel and cold and glinting with intrigue.

"And what about you, bird?"

I stayed silent. He was too smug . . . I knew where this was going. He leaned against the wall beside us. The corner of his mouth perked up just slightly.

"Do you fear me?

His teeth gleamed like a wolf's in the moonlight.

"Yes." I wouldn't be able to lie convincingly. I knew my fear was written plainly on my face.

"Good. Maybe then you'll listen when I ask you to do something for me."

My stomach heaved at the thought of what he might ask. He must have seen the revulsion on my face because a muscle in his jaw ticked.

"No, nothing like that, bird. I wouldn't say you're exactly my type." My face flushed with the sting of his words. "I had warned you that escape would be dangerous. Yet you tried anyway. I know you wish to return to your family, but I ask that you stay here in Shadowhold and continue your work as a healer. Consider it payment for your brother's debt."

I hadn't been expecting that.

It had dawned on me a day or two ago that there were far fewer people in need of healing here than I expected. If the king was so desperate for my healing abilities, wouldn't I have been more useful on the front lines? I had more patients back in Abbington.

"Why do you want me to stay here? You don't even have many patients."

"Perhaps I am . . . intrigued by your particular skills."

My face flushed. I didn't want to be his trophy—to be kept here like one of the jarred creatures in the apothecary.

"And in return for your commitment to Onyx, I will find your family and make sure they are safe," he added, like the only thing that mattered to me in this world was simply an afterthought.

I knew I couldn't trust him, but the relief at the thought of their safety was like a cold gulp of water filling my chest. The king would have the resources to find them. Spies and messengers, a dragon to cross the seas faster than a thousand ships. He could probably track them down in mere weeks, while it might take me years. A lifetime, even.

Maybe he knew I'd always keep trying to run unless he bribed me otherwise.

"How do I know you'll keep your word?" My voice had gained a semblance of strength.

Humor danced in his eyes as he ran a hand through his tousled dark hair. "I realize how this sounds, but you may just have to trust me."

The very thought turned my insides cold. Stupid—that's what I had been to even consider it. I couldn't form words, so I continued my hasty walk toward the dungeon. The king easily fell into step beside me. Damn those long legs.

"Is that a yes, then?"

I shuddered. "No."

"Well then you're headed in the wrong direction, I fear."

I went still as death. "What do you mean?"

He grinned a feral smile that made my blood freeze in my veins.

"You think I'm going to allow you the luxury of the cell you just slipped out of when you have no intention of heeding my warnings about escape or accepting my deal? No, I think I'll place you somewhere a little less . . . comfortable."

I went stiff as a corpse.

The annex. Where all the screams and wails were born.

Blood was rushing in my ears as delight at my torment danced in his eyes.

"You said you wouldn't." I sounded like a petulant child, and the words turned to ash on my tongue.

He shrugged. "Did I? Must've changed my mind. The stretcher can be very effective, you know."

He was taking too much pleasure from my horrified expression. I hoped he saw how much I hated him. More than I had ever hated anyone. Even Powell. "You are everything I thought you were, and so much worse."

His slate eyes twinkled. "Perhaps so. Still, your pick."

The idea of spending the rest of my life here was enough to make me physically sick. But what were my options, really? Endure whatever he had planned to force me into submission? Images of racks and ripped-out fingernails danced in my mind. And then what? I'd be weaker and more traumatized and even less likely to successfully escape. Wasn't agreeing to stay and letting him at least find my family the better of two evils? And the one that I could more likely work to my advantage?

"Fine," I said, biting down on the nausea turning over inside me. "But I have—" I swallowed hard. "I have a request."

The king took a step closer and looked down at me with curiosity. Curiosity and . . . something else. Something . . . hungry. I froze. When I didn't continue, he murmured, "Let's hear it, bird."

"You find my family now. Not eventually. And deliver a letter to them, with proof that they received it," I forced out.

His face softened. "Done."

"And you must swear not to harm my brother," I breathed. "I am serving his sentence."

"Of course," he said, though his mouth soured.

"And . . . I want out of the dungeons. If I am going to live here, I cannot sleep in a cell forever. I need to be allowed to roam the castle freely. No more Barney hovering over me."

He looked at me, lethal and unforgiving. "Fine. You can have all of your requests, but hear me, bird. You will not run again. If you do, your family, once I find them, will suffer for it."

Blood leeched from my face, but I nodded in silence as still as death.

"It's dangerous out there," he added. "If you can believe it, I don't wish to see you harmed."

Despite everything that had happened, I exhaled a long slow breath. If he kept his word, I would be able to get a message to my family. Maybe I'd even see them again one day, if I behaved. And if he was lying, I'd know soon enough, when he had no proof of my family's safety, and I could try to escape again then, once I had made him believe I had no intention of doing so.

Still, bitterness coated my tongue. I couldn't help the words that flew from my mouth at him as our eyes met under the twinkling light of the moon.

"I wish whatever attacked you in the woods had succeeded."

Eyes laced with deadly power gazed back at me.

"No, you do not."

9

⁓⟐⁓

"Y OU'RE POUTIER THAN USUAL TODAY."

Dagan eyed me, and I shifted to stare sullenly out the window at the woods, thinking of all I had lost in so little time.

The chambers I was taken to last night in the servants' quarters were nothing special, but larger than the room Leigh and I had shared back in Abbington. The thought depressed me for more than a few reasons. But the white linens had been cool on my skin, and a small fireplace emanated a low, temperate heat. Despite my worry that anxiety-driven nightmares would keep me up all night, sleep had come for me swiftly. Thoughts of darkened dragon scales, bloody fingernails, and careless gray eyes had followed me into a dreamless slumber.

Yesterday, I had thought it would be my last afternoon in this apothecary. Now, it was a lifetime. Dagan's tense mood paired well with mine, and the two of us only highlighted the coldness of the castle. While I could appreciate the keep's impressive towers, delicate chandeliers, and expensive textured furniture, all I could think of as I had walked to the apothecary this morning was an entire existence spent here against my will.

"I had a long night," I said.

Dagan waited for me to continue. I very much did not want to talk about this, but he also had never cared before to get to know me—if we were to continue working together, I felt like I should take advantage of his interest.

"I found out someone had been lying to me. And I was roughed up a bit. By the lieutenant. I'm fine, though."

Maybe I expected the same protective, furious anger that I had felt from the king, but Dagan just continued to watch me, expressionless.

"He tried to assault me," I said, finding myself looking for an outraged reaction. I wanted to know what Dagan thought of Bert. Of King Ravenwood. Was he not upset by this? Did nobody in this Stones-forsaken castle have a conscience? "But the king stepped in . . . and sentenced him to death."

Still nothing.

"By *torture*." I glared at the older man.

Dagan huffed and closed his book, reaching under the cabinet.

"Thanks for your concern," I said, under my breath.

He pulled out a parcel wrapped in burlap and rounded the counter for the door. I must have really been boring him today.

"You coming?"

I stared at him, stunned.

Coming? With *him*?

"Where are you going?"

"Only one way to find out," he said, more bored than anything.

I looked around the apothecary. I was never going to find out more about this castle—this kingdom—stuck in here each day. And if I had learned anything last night, it was that knowledge was power, and I was powerless unless I pushed my fear aside and braved the rest of this keep.

I followed him out into the gallery without another question.

We strolled silently through the castle, passing corners shrouded in shadow and soldiers speaking in hushed tones. When I felt their inquisitive eyes on me, I sped up to keep closer to the old man.

My freedom from Barney's watchful eye felt eerie—almost too good to be true. But I allowed a single splinter of hope to pierce my heart. Maybe the king intended to keep his promises, and my independence in the castle was the first.

Instead of taking the route I had grown so accustomed to—down the sprawling stairs, through the hall of oil paintings, and out the front doors to the dungeon—we made an unexpected left and filed down a hallway dotted with statues. A pale marble woman in the throes of ecstasy wrapped in sheer fabric made me blush, while a wolf frozen in obsidian with teeth bared felt almost too lifelike to be art. The passage ended with a wooden door that a single guard opened for us.

Misty morning air filled my lungs.

We trudged silently down a damp, stone staircase until I couldn't hold my unease in any longer.

"Where are we going?"

Of course he didn't answer me. I should have expected as much.

This staircase led down to a grand lawn behind the castle—vast and emerald green. As I stood at the precipice of the expanse, I took in the wide, open space and inhaled dewy pine and freshly cut grass. It reminded me of my morning runs in Abbington, though far greener and more damp. My feet squished in the cold lawn as I followed Dagan down through the clearing and noted the way the trees and wildflowers ringed the field walled in stone.

It was like an arena.

Lost in my appreciation for the textures and colors of the glade, I almost didn't notice Dagan stopping short in the middle of it as he dropped the wrapped parcel in front of me. It landed with a metallic clang. He gestured toward it, my pulse skittering at the invitation.

I knelt down slowly to inspect the parcel's contents, and my mouth fell open like a book.

Inside were two massive, glittering silver swords. The blades glistened with the early sun, which filtered through the burlap. The grip and pommel of one were covered in intricate metalwork that resembled the vines of a dense forest.

I bristled with horror.

"What are you going to do to me?"

Dagan's brows furrowed. "When I was growing up, what nearly happened to you last night happened to more girls than not, and there weren't any kings around to save them."

My blood ran cold as I thought of the girls who had not been as lucky as I had. Was he going to finish where Bert had left off?

"I taught the few I could with that same blade."

In an instant, fear melted into relief, which gave way to confusion.

He walked toward me and lifted both swords, handing the smaller, less elaborate one to me.

"We'll start with a basic strike from above. Evenly distribute your body weight between your feet, leading foot in front, and face your opponent."

I nodded but still made no move to lift my sword.

"Any day now."

He was going to teach me? To wield a sword?

I wasn't even very good with a butcher knife.

But his eyes were shifting from stern to irritated, and with the metal weapon in his hand, I didn't wish to make the old man angry. I tried the stance, and he lifted my elbow slightly.

"Hold your sword at shoulder level. Good. First, close the line between your opponent and yourself by bringing your sword forward, like this." He demonstrated for me, his movement fluid like running water. "Then, step toward your opponent and a little to your right, to avoid a counterattack. Then you can bring down your blade in a straight line to strike."

I was mirroring his movements, watching my feet placement, and running through about a hundred ways to take the sword and race for the wall behind me that separated us from the woods, when he snapped, "Now, look alive."

Before I could exhale, he charged me. The man had to be in his seventies, but he moved like a jungle cat. I must have screeched as I dropped my sword like a hotcake and sprinted in the opposite direction. I heard Dagan bark out a genuine laugh before I turned around and stared at him, stupefied.

"What in the Stones was that?" I gasped.

"Let's try again."

Dagan backed up and waited for me to pick up my sword. This time when he charged at me, I dodged to the left, still holding my sword but dragging it behind me like a dead weight. He really was . . . teaching me. And maybe messing with me, a little.

"Good. Hold your sword upright. It's a weapon, not a broomstick."

"You wouldn't say that if I was a man," I huffed, lifting the sword into the air. Its weight pulled at my wrists and forearms. I would be sore tomorrow.

Dagan repeated the move, but this time when I ducked, he swung the sword back in my direction. I bobbed and then backed up, but he stayed on me. I continued to skirt his blows, swinging the way he had instructed, but eventually his sword made contact with my shoulder. I braced for pain but found just a tap in its place. I assumed it took some skill to swing with such precision and vigor but make sure the blow was slowed just in time.

"Good," he breathed. "Again."

We continued for the next forty minutes or so, moving into how to block and the basics of a parry. He corrected my stance, my elbows, the direction my feet pointed. By the end I was dripping sweat, my face hot and salty.

The familiar ache in my muscles, in my joints, was more welcome than I could have anticipated. I hadn't gone this long without running in years, and expelling some of my pent-up energy was almost as calming as healing.

"Well done," Dagan conceded as he wrapped up the swords in their parcel. "Again tomorrow, same place and time. We'll do this each morning before the apothecary opens."

"All right." I wasn't going to fight him when he was quite literally teaching me to defend myself from the very men that kept me in this castle. And the practice had brought me . . . joy. I was terrible at it, but there was something about holding the weapon and moving with it that was invigorating. I pictured ramming my sword into King Ravenwood's arrogant face and a thrill thrummed in my veins.

I fought to catch my breath as we walked back to the castle in oddly comfortable silence. The dark sky above us promised a day of welcome rain, and my overheated body craved it.

"Dagan?" I asked eventually. "You're a skilled swordsman. What are you doing running an apothecary?"

He squinted up at the heavy clouds above us. "I was in the Onyx army. Some years back."

I shook my head. "No, I've seen soldiers. That was something much more. You're a master."

"I had a worthy teacher in my father," he said, looking down.

"Well, thank you for trying to teach me. I'll give it the best I've got."

He hiked up the stairs, a grin twitching on his lips.

Later, back in the apothecary, I realized that had been the only time I'd ever seen him smile.

—⚓—

IF I WASN'T TOO SORE TO WALK AFTER A MORNING SPENT AT-tempting to outmaneuver a master swordsman, the hike up the stairs to the library was sure to do the trick. Keeping the oath I had made to myself this morning to discover more of the castle and build up a defense of knowledge, I had decided to start somewhere that scared me the least—visiting Mari where she worked. I hoped she might have more information on the king, the seer, and the castle itself. But also, I just liked the girl.

When I reached the top of the near-endless stairs, I was met by books upon books sprawled across spirals and rows of shelves. I'd never seen so many of anything in my life. The library was all warm shades of tea and tan, with worn reading desks and antique velvet chairs strewn throughout. By the time I found Mari in the

"Gnomes and Sprites" section, I still had just barely caught my breath.

"Hello," I squeaked, irrationally afraid of disturbing the books' peace. The room felt like a temple—reverent in its silence.

"Arwen." She beamed, flitting over to me. "I can't believe you actually came up here. It's quite the climb, isn't it? Papa said no job is worth the trudge up those stairs each day, but I don't mind."

"The view must be unbelievable way up here."

Mari gave a knowing smile and walked us over to one of the stained glass windows that looked down onto the forest below. The pines and oaks looked even more foreboding from above, filtered through the colored glass. Acres upon acres of deep, crisp greens and gloomy black. A crack of thunder made me jump, and Mari turned, getting a better look at me.

"What's with you? You look terrible!"

I slumped against the window. "Thanks."

She leaned even closer, inspecting my face. "Ugh, and you're sweaty!"

"This is going to sound bizarre—" I started, but realized I wasn't sure how to finish the sentence. If I was going to live here, at least for the time being, I needed one person I could open up to. Last night had been—

I couldn't sit alone with all the feelings much longer.

". . . Yes?" she prompted, going back to putting books away.

Pushing off the glass, I followed her and scanned the library. An older, bespectacled woman was reading in a corner to our left, and two men who looked like generals were perusing the maps section.

Keeping my voice low, I started small, to test her out. "I spent the morning learning to sword fight with Dagan."

Mari whirled to face me. "What? Why?"

And here was the hard part . . . Could I trust Mari? My instincts were never this strong, and they were pushing me to open up to her. She had only ever been kind to me, sought out my friendship, tried to make the transition—though she didn't know the whole truth of it—easier for me.

I blew out a breath.

"I came here because my brother was going to be sentenced to death for theft, and I offered to work as a healer to pay off his debt. I spent my first night in the castle dungeon and the king was in the adjoining cell, pretending to be a prisoner in his own keep." When her face contorted, I cut in. "I would tell you why, if I knew."

"You met King Kane Ravenwood? And spoke to him? What was he like?"

"Horrible," I snapped. "And miserably handsome. An awful combination."

Mari laughed. "That does seem to be the consensus throughout the kingdom. How does that lead to a sword fight with Dagan?"

I told Mari everything. King Ravenwood's lies, the awful lieutenant, my attempt to run, our wretched agreement, and my exchange with Dagan this morning. I told her of my mother, my siblings, my childhood in Abbington. Everything except for Powell's abuse.

Mari sagged against a tall bookcase beside me. She actually seemed at a loss for words for the first time since I had met her.

"I'm so sorry you're stuck here," she finally said. "Shadowhold isn't that bad, though. It'll grow on you, I'm sure of it. I'm even more sorry about your mother's ailment. I can't imagine what it would be like to see Papa suffer like that."

My heart hurt when I thought of my mother, attempting a journey to safer lands in her condition, and without her medicine, as I never made it back with it that night. "The healers in my town weren't ever able to figure out what it was. We tried every single potion, ointment, and therapy we knew. Eventually they told me to stop trying to heal her and just keep her comfortable while we waited for the inevitable." I thought back to the day Nora gave me the stern talking-to. I had never felt so defeated.

"I am so sorry, Arwen. At least your small town had a healer. There are many who have to travel for medical help. In Serpent Spring, on the border of Peridot, there aren't any healers for miles. Once a man had his arm lopped off by a windmill and had to be flown via wyvern to Willowridge. Why he was up there, I don't care to know."

"Mari, how do you even know that?"

"I read it in a medical text." She shrugged.

This woman was a wealth of knowledge. She—

My breath caught in my throat.

A medical text.

Could that be it?

I searched the shelves around me until I saw it, and made a beeline for the section marked "Medicine." Our small town had none of the resources of this castle, such as a library like this that must have been imported from the bustling capital, and surely other cities over the decades, too.

"How could I have been so stupid to only think of this now?" I said to Mari, who trailed behind. It should have been my first thought in a castle such as this one.

"Think of what?" Mari called after me before being met with a loud hush from the woman in spectacles.

But I had already found what I was looking for. Row after row on various illnesses, ailments, and their cures. If there was anything that could help my mother, it was within these pages.

It wasn't even as terrible a plan as some of my others this week had been—do a decent job here, heal the soldiers, learn to fight. And all the while hunt for a cure for my mother. Once I found it, I could insist King Ravenwood get it to her, or I'd threaten to stop working for him.

"Mari." I spun to her, true hope alight in my chest for the first time since I left Abbington. "Will you help me? I know it's a lot but—"

"There are three things I love in this world. Reading, a challenge, and proving others wrong."

I laughed, bright and loud. "And helping people?"

"Sure." She shrugged. "That, too."

⚬

THE AFTERNOON HAD CREPT INTO NIGHT AS WE FLIPPED through over half the books in the section. When my eyes had become so tired of medical jargon that I could barely hold them in a squint, and we hadn't found anything of use, I stood on wobbly knees and promised Mari I'd come back tomorrow morning before my work in the apothecary. Then I made the treacherous walk down the stone stairs.

When I reached the hallway of oil paintings, I spontaneously turned right, inspired by my dedication to leave no stone in the castle unturned. Actively exploring the castle in pursuit of any knowledge that could help me had felt much better than cowering in the apothecary.

The new, darkened hallway was aglow with iron candlesticks and chandeliers, and I willed myself to be brave. Shadows couldn't hurt me. Neither could ornate stonework or hushed whispers from hidden alcoves.

One foot in front of the other—that was all I had to do.

At the end of the winding passage stood lofty, night-dark doors that were flanked by four sentries.

A curse bellowed through them and into the hall, stunning me and stealing the air from my lungs. That low voice was all too familiar, and I couldn't help the undiluted terror that pinched in my gut at the sound. Even the guards in their leather-harnessed armor and skull-like helmets flinched.

Every cell in my body urged me to run in the other direction. Away from that lethal roar. But maybe I could hear another snippet of the king's struggles with the seer if I stood by and listened . . .

I'd just take a few steps closer . . .

The massive black stone doors swung open and a sobbing, blubbering mess stormed out and barreled directly into me. I stumbled backward, my ankle rolling in on itself.

"Vengeful bloody monster is going to get every last one of us fucking killed."

The force of the whimpering man nearly sent me to the ground—he was huge. At least six feet tall, built like a stack of bricks, and sniveling like an overtired toddler. I was not going to stick around to find out what King Ravenwood had done to reduce this mountain of a human into a puddle of tears.

I turned on my heel before hearing the king's voice boom out into the corridor. "Well, look who it is."

Shit.

Despite the acid burning in my veins, I knew better than to run away from him. The looming threat of the dungeon was only a fraction of what he was capable of.

I turned and lifted my chin.

Walking into King Ravenwood's throne room was like stepping inside a thundercloud. Black and gray stonework made the room feel cavernous, and the twisted throne he sat upon was a monolith of carved black vines. Torches lit the room in columns of flickering light, but there was no hiding the harshness of the space, which was only amplified by the king's dark expression.

I forced a simple curtsy at King Ravenwood's feet, despite the way it soured my stomach.

He arched a single brow, his usually sparkling eyes weary this evening.

"What were you doing out there? Miss me already?"

"So, not such an insightful king," I mumbled.

I really had to get a lid on my anger, but I couldn't help the fire that raged inside of me every time he spoke. And today was especially painful. He was in such a position of power—legs spread, jaw relaxed, a hand adorned in silver rings slung casually over one arm of his throne.

The self-satisfied prick was practically begging for my barbs.

But the guards behind him fell deadly quiet, and I recognized the blond soldier who'd snapped at me in the infirmary as he stepped forward with lethal intent, his green eyes promising murder.

I swallowed, considering the stoic young soldier. He had chased his own king down that day, though Ravenwood hadn't actually been an escaped prisoner . . . Why had he run after him?

"You may want to watch your tongue," King Ravenwood drawled. "Commander Griffin can be a little sensitive about name-calling."

Commander?

The man looked awfully young to be the commander of the Onyx Army. I understood a young king like Ravenwood, likely twenty-five or twenty-six. Royalty had no control over when their parents passed, leaving the crown to them.

But Commander Griffin looked to be about the king's age. I wondered how he had risen within the ranks so quickly.

The man in question rolled his eyes but kept his stance next to the king, watching me as if I were a threat. The thought made me smirk.

"Something funny to you, bird?"

"Not in the slightest," I said, schooling my face. "If anything, the mood seems quite . . . somber."

The king rolled up the ornate sleeves of his black shirt and crossed an ankle over his knee. His forearms were golden from sun and corded with lean muscle as they rested on either side of him.

"If you must know, it's been a horrible fucking day."

"Tragic," I mused. Not rude, but not . . . polite, either.

His answering smile was feral, and the wooden arms of his throne groaned beneath his grip. When had I become so bold?

"So easy for you to mock, isn't it? When you know absolutely nothing about what is going on around you. When you have so little awareness of the sacrifices kings and queens have to make for their subjects, the lives lost, the choices that can't be reversed."

I tried not to scoff as anger built inside me. He was waging a war on one of the feeblest kingdoms in all of Evendell. He was a bully, not a martyr.

"I struggle to find sympathy," I admitted through clenched teeth. I needed to leave this room before I said something I regretted.

But the king's expression only intensified. Simmered under thick, furrowed brows.

"You have no idea how dangerous things are becoming. How precarious is the fate of every single person that you know. That you've ever met. That you love."

I scowled at his attempts to scare me but couldn't stop the shiver that slipped down my spine.

"So tell me," I said. "What's really at stake for you, King Ravenwood? Or are you scared that I might know the truth? That the only thing that matters to you is your own greed?"

His face hardened into a mask of cruel calm, and he stood, stalking closer.

I fought the urge to flinch as his face drew near my own and he murmured in my ear. "Firstly, you may call me Kane. King Ravenwood is a little formal from someone I've made blush as many times as you."

Punishing embarrassment burned my cheeks. The guards behind the king shifted. I opened my mouth to protest his outrageous claim, but he continued. "Secondly, Arwen, having only lived a 'tiny, suffocatingly safe life' for twenty years, never having seen anything, been anywhere, felt any man . . . what could you possibly *know* at all?"

Without a second thought, I reared back and the flat of my palm connected with his smug, male face.

I waited in still silence for his anger. His fury.

But King Ravenwood had the audacity to look oddly pleased, a strange smile spreading across his face.

As soon as the stark noise had resonated through the room, Commander Griffin was behind me and had my arms in a vise grip.

A wave of panic crashed inside my chest and my heart slammed against my throat.

I yanked away in earnest, but the commander was absurdly strong and pulled me backward. His rough hands dug into my skin.

"Unhand her," the king snapped, rubbing his jaw and turning back to his throne. "She's nothing more than a nuisance."

His words stung. I hoped the slap had, too. How dare he throw my own words back at me? Words I had shared with him in confidence when I had thought he was someone else. It was a low blow, aimed to elicit a response from me.

The commander did as he was told and let me go without another word.

"Can I leave?" I asked the king, trying not to sound like Leigh when she wanted to be excused from supper.

"By all means," the king said, and gestured toward the door.

I raced back to my bedroom in the servants' quarters, shame and rage warring inside me. I couldn't believe I had stooped to his level. I crawled under a woven blanket, the firm mattress dipping slightly under my sore limbs. The day had started so promisingly, with Dagan and Mari and my new outlook. The first ray of light in a never-ending chasm of darkness that had enveloped my life.

And now I just wanted it all to be over. Again.

Try as I might to fight it, the king's words had struck a chord of shame in me so sensitive, so personal, it had felt almost invasive. Like he could see right through me and had reached inside my hollow rib cage to fish around for the thoughts I had hidden in the deepest corners of my heart.

I *had* started to resent my home in Abbington. All the ways my life there had underserved me. And I still hated Shadowhold, even more now that I knew I'd likely be here forever. It didn't leave many options for anywhere I truly belonged. Somehow, despite the many long, empty days of my childhood, or the recent nights spent in a leaky, stone cell, I had never felt more alone.

10

⚜

Dear Mother, Leigh, and Ryder,

If you are receiving this letter, it means you are finally somewhere safe, and maybe warm? Surrounded by exotic foods and fruits? Or is that just my grumbling stomach talking? I wish we could be together, but just know I'm taken care of in Onyx. It's a long story that I hope to tell you all in person one day. In the meantime, please use this coin to help build your new lives. Knowing Ryder, half the sack he stole is likely gone already. Leigh, don't let all this change frighten you. I know that leaving Abbington was hard, but as long as you are with Ryder and Mother, you are still home. Mother, I am searching this new kingdom for any information on your illness that I can find. Don't lose hope! And, Ryder, please take care of them. They need you.

All of my love,
Arwen

I had been carrying the letter around with me for days like a child with a safety blanket. I just couldn't bring myself to ask the bastard to make good on his promise, especially after the last time I had seen him, when I'd behaved like a maniac. I debated giving the letter to Barney, whom I passed in the great hall or gallery every so often, but I'd get a better sense of whether or not King Ravenwood was planning to keep his promises if I could talk to him one-on-one and somehow make up for my outburst.

I had never been so outspoken with anyone in my life. I hated him, I didn't respect him, I didn't trust him, and I could not for the life of me keep my thoughts off him and his smug, cruel words. But I needed to harness that fury and put on a pleasant face if I was to ask him to send the letter.

I arrived at the dimly lit library after another morning training with Dagan. Mari was slumped over three books in various stages of completion, snoring like a bear in hibernation.

"Mari?"

"Ah!" She gasped, shooting up like a firecracker, red hair spilling over her face.

"Did you fall asleep up here?"

"Ugh, yes," she croaked. "The last time I did that was before I took the barrister's exam."

"You took the barrister's exam? Are you going to become a barrister?"

"Oh, Stones, no." She shook her head, patting down her hair.

"Then . . . why?"

"Just to see if I could ace it." She gave me a knowing smile that said she very clearly had.

I shook my head. "You're a nut." Her smile broadened, pulling a grin from my own lips. "And I'm really glad your father left his sock in my infirmary."

"Me, too. I haven't had a new friend in some time," she said as she stood up and stretched. "I think I annoy people sometimes."

Before I could disagree, she continued.

"Anyway, look what I found." Mari pointed to the book in front of us, and I followed her fingers across the worn, sand-colored page. "Fatigue, muscle decay, headaches, weight loss . . ."

The page detailed my mother's condition to a tee, down to the aching joints, headaches, and drowsy spells.

A spark lit inside me—guarded hope and a sliver of sheer joy.

"What is it?"

"The book is from the Pearl Mountains, so you know it's accurate," she started. The kingdom was known for its vast wealth of knowledge and towering libraries built into and floating among the city's peaks.

"It says the illness is called Plait's Disorder and has a surprisingly simple cure. 'One concoction, taken each day, abated most patient symptoms and improved both quality of life and life expectancy.'"

The sliver of joy widened to an entire slice. It was too good to be true.

"Mari! You're a genius."

She beamed at me, still looking like she needed a good comb. "I'm just a power reader. It was your idea to search the library."

The concoction's ingredients weren't too common, but luckily the castle's apothecary had all but one. I had never heard of burrow-root, and after organizing the apothecary inventory about three times a day, each day, I knew we didn't have any.

"Damn," I muttered as I read. "Do you know anything about burrowroot?"

Mari nodded. "It's native to the Onyx Kingdom, so it probably grows in the woods around here. But it only blossoms during the lunar eclipse, which is in two months, and only about eight minutes long from start to finish."

I grimaced as disappointment washed over me. So close, and yet—

"How can I find it on the eclipse?"

"It leaves this iridescent residue year-round wherever it grows, so if you had some way of braving the forest, you could look for it now. Then you'd have to find your way back to the spot on the evening of the eclipse . . ." As if she saw my mind turning, she added, "Please don't do anything completely stupid."

"I won't," I lied.

I was getting good at that.

⬥

IF STEP ONE OF BEING BRAVE WAS ACKNOWLEDGING THAT I had to see the king again, both to get him my letter and now to find the burrowroot residue in the Shadow Woods, then step two was actually doing something about it.

It was my day off from the apothecary—I guessed Dagan needed a break from the constant chatting and giggling that occurred now that Mari liked to visit me each day—and I was making my way toward the throne room. To ask the wicked king for his help. Like an idiot.

The castle was quiet and sleepy as I wandered the halls, observing the families and soldiers as they enjoyed breakfast in the great hall. My stomach grumbled. In just two weeks, I had become shamefully accustomed to the Onyx Kingdom's cloverbread. The dark brown loaves were made from obsidian wheat native to the land, blended with molasses and caraway. I slathered my dense and slightly sweet slices in melting butter each morning. Watching a mother and son tear into a piping hot loaf as they looked over a picture book made my heart ache.

I had to admit, if this castle was anything to go by, maybe the Onyx Kingdom was not the land of horrors that everyone I had grown up with claimed it was. None of these people had gnarled horns or grotesque claws, and definitely no wings. Besides Bert, nobody had even been too unkind to me. Despite all the times my mother had said to never judge a book by its cover, I had done just that. I wondered if these people also despised the war just as much as we had back in Amber. I was sure they, too, had lost homes and family members.

The thought made me furious with King Ravenwood all over again. What kind of man, let alone a king, did this to so many innocents? And for what? More land? More riches?

Along with my disgust for King Ravenwood, I felt disgust for myself. How could I ever have harbored any kind of positive feelings for such a selfish, vile, arrogant, violent—

"Arwen?"

I spun around, bumping face-first into a strong, warm chest. "Ouch," I muttered, rubbing my sore nose like a child.

The king peered down at me, humor in his eyes, but his mouth held a firm line. He was flanked by four soldiers, all adorned with hunting gear.

"Good morning, Kane," I said. Commander Griffin cleared his throat. "Or do you prefer Your Majesty?"

He grimaced. "Kane is fine. Don't worry about Commander Griffin."

Griffin arched a skeptical brow.

The king's dark hair was swept back, out of his face. He wore a leather jacket and tunic, hunting boots, and a sword at his hip, clearly headed out for some kind of expedition. But fear was written starkly across each of the lantern-lit faces of the men standing behind him in the hallway. Today was not a jovial outing, it seemed.

Now that he was in front of me, I wasn't sure how to proceed. Maybe he'd deliver the letter, but I wasn't sure about the burrow-root. I could try to coerce him, say I would refuse to heal anyone until he procured it for me, but there was no way around sharing that it was for my mother. There was a reason the apothecary didn't have it—it wasn't usually used for healing. He was bound to ask me why I wanted it, and I wasn't about to share my deepest desires and weaknesses with the prick. Again.

An idea dawned on me.

I put on my most appealing smile and fluttered my biggest doe eyes. "Actually, I was just looking for you, my king." I cringed internally. Probably laying it on a bit too thick. But Kane's eyes gleamed and his lips quirked in amusement.

"Is that so?"

"Oh, yes. I had to apologize for my behavior the other day. It was outrageous. I was very sleep-deprived and think I must have been coming down with something. Can you forgive me?"

He only raised a brow in interest. "Your fury didn't seem fever addled to me. But I'm glad you're feeling better."

"I was just so very grateful for your kindness toward me the other night, allowing me to stay here in your keep. I thought I could give you the letter I wished to send my family, for you to share once you find them." I produced the letter from my dress pocket and handed it to him.

He held the envelope and turned it around in his hands in confusion. "Why is it so heavy?"

I reddened. "I thought I'd send them some coin. In case they are in need."

The king weighed the letter in one large palm. "Quite a bit you've put in here. Is this all you have?"

"Nearly, yes."

"Doesn't your brother have enough of our coin to last a few lifetimes?"

I hated when he spoke of my brother like that. He wouldn't have needed it had our village not been ravaged the past five years. But I held my tongue.

"I just want to help them. This is the only way I can."

His brows drew together, the flickering lights dotting the hall shining on his stern face. He didn't say more.

"Will you deliver it to them?" I pressed. "When you find them? When we separated, they were headed for Garnet."

The king eyed me thoughtfully, something like pity in his quicksilver eyes.

I bristled.

"I gave you my word, did I not?"

Yes, but I value your word about as much as a sack of potatoes.

I swallowed hard. If anything I had heard about this king was true, flattery and imagined power over his subjects were the only ways to get what I needed from him.

"Yes, of course, my king."

His eyes went heavy-lidded, and a seductive smile played at his lips. "You're going to have to stop with that term of endearment, bird."

My breath caught and my cheeks grew hot. The commander

cleared his throat a second time, and I swallowed again. Why was my mouth so dry? Kane drew a hand down his face to hide his smile.

"That day . . . it was not my intention to offend you."

"Yes, it was," I said, before cursing myself internally. The men behind the king shifted just a little. *Be agreeable, Arwen.*

King Ravenwood scratched his jaw in thought.

"Perhaps you know my intentions even better than I do. More ardently, then, I am sorry," he said, his voice low. And in his eyes, a new expression—one I hadn't seen in them before.

I stood there, dumbfounded. Was this a real apology? From him?

The king and his men moved to walk past me, down the hall and surely toward the castle gates. But I couldn't give up on the second part of my plan. I needed to find the spot where the burrow-root grew.

"Actually, I know how you could make it up to me." He turned, allowing me to continue. Confusing admission of guilt aside, I knew the bastard was fighting the urge to raise a suggestive brow.

"Could I join you today?"

"No," Griffin bit out.

"But—"

"Sure." Kane smiled. Griffin muttered something under his breath and headed down the hallway.

I beamed at the king, giving him my best *this means a lot to me* face.

"I promise not to be a bother at all," I assured him. "I'm very easygoing."

11

❧

"No WAY IN THE STONES." I PUT MY FOOT DOWN HARD FOR emphasis.

Kane rolled his eyes. "Suit yourself," he said, and strolled toward the stables.

His men were mounting their horses around us. It was a rare sunny day that hinted at the coming of summer. A welcome warm breeze wafted through the pine trees of the woods, filling the horse stables with a now familiar sweet and refreshing scent. Though I trained with Dagan each morning, the nature of the lessons left little room to appreciate my surroundings. I hadn't had any real time to enjoy the outdoors in weeks, and I longed for the feel of grass between my toes and sun on my face.

Not to mention I had somehow succeeded in charming Kane into taking me into the woods with him, which was the only way I was going to find the burrowroot residue. This was my chance—I couldn't squander it over a single, unpleasant horseback ride.

I made a face at the Stones above to grant me strength, and followed behind Kane.

"Fine!" I called after him. "Fine. But I'll have you know I have ridden many a horse in my day. I don't know why you're treating me like a child."

He said nothing but stood patiently, waiting for me to mount the creature. I did so with ease, nearly kicking the king in the face on my way up. I thought I heard him chuckle before he hopped on, but all thoughts fell out of my brain as soon as he was seated behind me.

His warm, impressive form now enclosed me from behind, like a broad hand around a tiny pebble. A heady mix of fir, leather, and mint filled my nose as his strong muscled arms wrapped around me to grasp the reins. I leaned back into his unintentional embrace. Really, there was nowhere else for me to go.

"Comfortable, bird?" he murmured beside my ear. I closed my eyes without thinking.

"No." But the drowsy huskiness of my own voice had my eyes flashing open in alarm. Kane laughed, a sensual sound that conjured bedsheets and soft hums, and brought our horse alongside the other men.

Stones, he was always so self-assured.

I hated it.

Griffin appraised us with a frown. "You two look cozy."

"I told him I could ride alone." I don't know why I felt the need to justify my position to these men—they all knew my hatred for the king. Had seen my outburst in the throne room. But I didn't want them to think of me as weak.

It was a thought I hadn't ever had before and was now having all the time.

"And I told her if she could protect herself, she'd be welcome to have at it. Let's go."

I wondered if he knew about my morning lessons with Dagan. But before I could ask, Kane and I took off at a fast clip and the men followed behind us in formation through the Shadowhold gates.

I braced myself for the horrific creatures and deadly twists and turns of the Shadow Woods—but the gnarled trees weren't as frightening in the bright light of day. I wondered why the forest had appeared so terrifying to me before, and hoped it had nothing to do with the legends surrounding the staggeringly lethal man flush against my back. Every time my anger bubbled up at him, I reminded myself of the plan—be agreeable, find the burrowroot, make it through today, then ignore Kane for the rest of eternity. I kept an eye out for the burrowroot's shimmery residue while trying to memorize everything around me.

I'd still have to make it out here again the night of the eclipse, which meant eventually, I'd have to tell someone my plan—even if the woods weren't as terrifying as I expected, I couldn't risk my family's safety by breaking my deal with Kane and sneaking out. But that was a problem for two months from now. Maybe someone would have killed him by then. A girl could dream . . .

Lofty pines and willows, knotted elm trees forming hidden nooks and crannies, and baby blue wildflowers were all rooted in the verdant grass and tufts of moss scattered along the forest floor. Little creatures scurried about as we rode through the woodland, and pockets of sunshine dappled through the dense tree leaves.

It was nothing like the forest of my home in Amber, which was golden and rusty scarlet all year round. Our leaves fell like rain each morning and crunched under my feet each night. I had never seen this much green before—it nearly hurt my eyes.

Kane had been quiet on our ride despite the intimate position. I had been awaiting lecherous jokes and revolting touches, but he had been almost . . . uncomfortably reserved. I wanted to break the tense silence but couldn't think of a single pleasant thing to say. It was odd being pressed so close to someone I felt such loathing for.

Especially because his arms wrapped tightly around my middle were like iron bands of heat, and I desperately needed to take my mind off of them.

"Do you often take leisurely afternoon jaunts into the forest?" I finally asked.

"I'm a little busy for such distractions."

I rolled my eyes. "Busy with what exactly? Bedding women and killing people for sport?"

His voice was like a deep, satisfied purr. "Don't tempt me, bird."

I swallowed against my heart, which had lodged itself in my throat. I didn't want to know which of the two was tempting to him.

Agreeable, right.

"So, what is the purpose of today's excursion?" I tried.

"Why did you ask to come if you didn't know?"

A fair question. I tried for half honesty. "I needed to get out of the castle. I was feeling a bit cooped up."

"You get that way a lot, don't you?"

So, the self-involved king was observant. "I have an . . . unpleasant response to being trapped."

"I remember—your first night in the cells."

I tried not to spasm from the weight compressing my chest that accompanied the memory. Or of Kane when he was pretending to be someone else. It was infuriating, still not understanding why he had lied to me for so long.

Agreeable, agreeable, agreeable.

Ryder had been charming for nineteen years. I could do it for a single afternoon.

"I never thanked you. For moving me into the servants' quarters and letting Barney off his post."

"Seemed a smart punishment for trying to run away." I could hear the wry smile in his voice.

"In all fairness, I did warn you I was thinking about it."

"No," he chided. "You were looking for help. You told me as a friend."

The reminder of my foolishness was like being doused in ice water. And something else . . . a small, strange hurt pinched in my heart. For the closeness I had felt to him that final night before I fled and learned the truth.

"Yes," I admitted. "We were almost friends, weren't we?"

"Mhm," he murmured. "Friends."

"Why did you come back to my cell that night, hiding your identity?"

His voice took on a razor's edge. "Maybe I wanted to see if you were still planning to run."

"If you had wanted me not to, you could have kept me better guarded," I snipped.

"Right. How easy it is to keep someone who is deathly afraid of being confined from escaping."

Traitorous surprise bloomed in my chest at the thought of him struggling to keep my anxiety at bay. I looked out at the forest ahead of us, the sunbeams filtering through emerald leaves. If there was an ounce of kindness in this man that I had missed, I'd have to find a way to use it to my advantage.

"Didn't matter anyway," he continued. "You never even made it to my sentries."

"Sentries?"

"I had guards waiting at the perimeter of the woods each night after your confession in the infirmary. If you had made it there, they would have stopped you. But, of course, you didn't." His knuckles went white with tension on the reins, while his body stiffened behind me.

"Right."

Minutes of piercing silence stretched while we rode through the towering trees, branches entwined as if woven together.

"Dare I ask where Bert is now?"

"I wouldn't," he said, his low voice like a dagger's caress against my cheek. But he shifted even closer, his hand splaying taut across my stomach, holding me to him.

The ride was long, and I was growing tired of our proximity. But I couldn't hold myself ramrod straight any longer—my back was beginning to ache, my knees and thighs sore from gripping the horse to hold me upright. I gingerly leaned back into Kane, just a little, and let my head rest on his chest.

He flinched and I wanted to say, *I don't like it any more than you do,* but feared his undoubtedly cocky response.

Finally, Griffin's horse overtook ours. He shot a pointed glare my way as he passed and I sat up self-consciously, my back aching in protest.

When Kane spoke, his voice was a little hoarse. "Don't mind him."

"I think he hates me," I joked, but it came out without humor.

"It's not you he's upset with, bird."

I wanted to ask what he meant, but we had arrived at a clearing.

The open glade was brighter than our journey to it—bathed in rays of sunlight that highlighted insects and fluttery things lazily drifting through the breeze.

But Kane had gone stiff behind me, and in the distance, I saw why.

It looked to be the aftermath of some kind of attack. Dirt and rocks were flung about as if someone had been dragged back and forth. We drew nearer, and I noticed blood coating the grass. I prayed the muddied, fleshy masses amid the leaves weren't viscera, but I had worked with war injuries long enough to know it was a waste of a prayer.

Kane reined our horse in while Griffin dismounted. The other men came to a stop behind us.

"What happened here?" I breathed.

"That's what we're trying to figure out," said Griffin, stalking closer to the scene amid the tall, muddied grass.

Kane and the rest of the men climbed off their horses to get a closer look. I followed suit, listening as the men assessed the scene in hushed tones.

My stomach fell further the more closely I looked at the gore below us.

Mari hadn't been kidding about creatures lurking in these woods. I had no idea what could have mauled a person so thoroughly to leave a sight like this behind.

I shoved the thought from my mind.

While the men were distracted, I needed to survey the woods for the burrowroot. I hadn't seen any residue on the ride here, but I could probably locate it much better now that I was on the ground. How hard could it be? Find the residue, remember the spot, find a way back here safely for the eclipse.

Easy.

I slipped behind a handful of trees and inspected the forest floor. The grass was high and unkempt, and it was hard to see among all the clovers and dead leaves and tiny crawling bugs that looked like little seeds.

But around the corner of one thick oak, something reflected a ray of sunlight. I flicked my eyes back to Kane, but he and Griffin and the others were still looking around the area of the attack, discussing what they thought had happened.

I ducked behind the oak and knelt to the ground. Sure enough, slimy, shimmering goop was slathered over the roots of the tree. Unless this was the scene of some kind of unicorn intimacy that I did not want to be privy to, burrowroot would grow here the night of the eclipse. Adrenaline zipped through my system. After all these years, I had finally found something that could actually help to heal my mother.

I stood up and tried to memorize the area. About twenty paces off the clearing, below the largest oak tree, and the clearing was thirty minutes on horseback into the forest, to the east of the keep.

I could find this spot again.

"I think we're done here," I heard Kane say. "Arwen, what are you doing?"

I stiffened and rounded the oak. "Just looking at the flowers."

The soldiers heeded orders and hopped back atop their steeds. I let out a sigh at the realization that I was headed back to Shadowhold. It was a gorgeous day, the woods no longer felt so terrifying, and I would have given almost anything to skip another spring afternoon spent in my room.

Kane's gaze held mine. "What is it?"

My face flushed. What a silly thing to concern myself with. "Nothing." I made my way back to our horse. But Kane stayed put.

"Try me."

I observed him cautiously. He had been uncharacteristically kind to me today. I was sure it was a ploy of some sort, but maybe, just maybe, my attempt at charm had worked better than I'd hoped.

Here went nothing. "I wanted to . . . stay. For a bit."

"Stay," he repeated. "In the woods?"

I nodded brightly. "It's beautiful out. And nice and warm, finally. Do you think there's a pond somewhere around here?" I spun around and listened for the telltale gurgling of a babbling brook.

Kane's mouth twitched up at the corners. He was weighing, debating. Then he said simply, "Fine, let's go find you a pond. Griff, we'll meet you back at the keep."

Griffin made no move to leave.

"Don't worry, I'll bring him back in one piece," I said with a grin. I couldn't help the spark of joy from my gamble paying off.

"I should bloody hope so. We only have one king," he said. There wasn't a trace of humor. There never was with the commander.

He held firm, staring at the two of us until Kane said pointedly, "You heard the woman. I'll be in safe hands."

Griffin's face was a mask of reluctance, but still, he turned his horse and trotted off, leaving Kane and me alone in the woods.

Melodic, chirping birds swooped overhead, and a warm breeze brushed my hair into my face. I combed it back self-consciously.

Kane's eyes lingered on me.

The clearing was suddenly far too small for the both of us.

I fidgeted under his gaze. I had no idea what to do with my hands. I wondered if he could tell.

This had been a truly terrible idea. What was I thinking?

"Come on." He broke the strange energy with a laugh and headed off through a worn path in between the trees. I followed close behind him, my heart still thundering in my chest.

I turned back to spy his horse grazing in the glade where we left him.

"Will your horse stay put there?"

"Yes."

"What if one of the creatures that live out here finds him?"

Kane stepped over a protruding tree root and motioned for me to do the same. "He'll be fine. He's very fast."

"What if one of them finds us?"

He stopped short before spinning to face me. "You have a lot of questions all of a sudden. Are you nervous?"

Yes. "No, why would I be nervous?"

"I thought you were terrified of me," he said, his eyes gleaming.

I am. But . . . "If you were going to hurt me, I think you would have already." The truth of the words surprised me.

He flashed a knowing smile before trudging ahead.

He was too pretty. What a disaster.

Time to change the subject. "What was that back there in the clearing?"

I felt his energy shift like a dense cloud passing over a summer sun. His pace slowed but he didn't look back at me as he spoke.

"Two of our men never made it back from where I sent them. A guard found their remains this morning."

Fear coiled in my gut, slick and slippery.

"You think they were killed by something that lives out here? An animal?" *A monster?*

"It's complicated."

Another nonanswer. I don't know what I expected. I wished I could see his face as I followed him down the narrow path. Aside from the rustling of leaves and chirping of birds the forest was blanketed in a quiet calm. The tension that had been twisting along my nerves since Griffin and his men left intensified.

I breathed deeply through my nose. I couldn't ask to go back now; it would show too much weakness.

"I'm sorry," I said. "About your men."

But he didn't answer me.

We hiked in silence until the steep, leaf-shrouded pathway finally gave way to an opening. A long, rolling field dotted with soft pink thistle and lavender stretched before us. In the distance, tucked up against a rocky, mountainous wall, was a glittering, turquoise pool.

My heart leaped, anxiety momentarily forgotten. It was more beautiful than anything I had seen in Abbington. In my life, really.

I peered up at Kane, sweaty from our hike. I wanted to cut through that smug exterior more than I could explain. "Race you there?"

Kane's eyes widened and he laughed—a real, booming peal that seemed to surprise even him. "Should we make it interesting?"

Though my heart spun at his words, I tapped my finger to my lips in playful thought. His eyes followed my finger to my mouth intently. "If I win, you have to answer any one question I ask with complete honesty."

He pulled his shirt over his head and then removed his boots. His broad chest was even more magnificent than it had been that day in the infirmary. When our eyes met, my stomach flipped on itself.

Bad, bad, bad.

I dipped my eyes down to my heavy, dark clothing, and unlaced my corset.

"I must say I admire your determination," he said, squinting up at the blue sky. "Fine. But if I win"—he flicked his gaze to me—"you tell me why you really wanted to come out here."

I halted mid–pulling off my boot and gaped at him.

"I am not quite as gullible as you think I am," he added with a smirk.

Shit.

"A truth for a truth," I said. "Sounds fair."

Kane looked positively delighted, and I let confidence color my gaze back at him. Matching his arrogance sent a surge of exhilaration through me. We stood there grinning at each other like idiots.

He broke first. "We go on the count of three. First one to hit the water wins?"

I nodded.

"One. Two. Th—"

"Wait!" I stopped him. I couldn't run well in this thick, wool dress, and our wager had left me feeling bold. I wanted to see him cave, or falter in some way. I slipped the heavy dress over my head, leaving me in a sleeveless chemise and thin undergarments.

A soft breeze kissed over my body, and I stretched like a cat in the sun.

I felt Kane's gaze on me and peered over at him. His shadowed eyes traveled over my bare toes, up my exposed calves and thighs, roamed my silk-covered stomach and breasts, and landed on my face.

He looked pained.

"You all right over there?"

He shook his head. "Wicked little bird."

I tried to conceal my smile.

I wasn't sure what was going on—he had always been attractive. As a prisoner, as an infirmary patient, and even as a wicked king.

But some of my searing hate had begun to slip through my fingers . . .

He cleared his throat. "All right, before you kill me. One. Two. Three."

We both took off with blistering speed. I pumped my arms at my sides as the balls of my feet landed lightly on the mossy grass. I felt like I was running on air. The wind pulled my hair back and cooled my sunshine-warmed limbs. It had been too long—the sprint felt like coming home. I breathed in fresh, pine-laced air.

A wave of euphoria crashed over me and spurred me on faster.

To my right, Kane kept pace. His muscles flexed with each pump of his powerful arms, and he looked about as happy as I felt.

But he was picking up speed.

I dug deeper, upping my pace and leaning forward. This was the only thing I knew I was great at. Whenever I felt trapped, alone, pathetic . . . running reminded me that I could be strong. That all I needed were my own two feet and I could go anywhere. I gained on Kane with ease and saw a look of shock register on his face.

It was delicious.

We were only yards away from the water now and still almost neck and neck. I pushed harder until my lungs were burning, my shins were aching, and my heart raced in my ears. I thought of Kane's face when he saw me undress and felt even stronger. I leaped into the air just a second before him and landed in the cold water with a splash.

"Aha!" I yelped, surfacing and wiping water from my face. "I won."

Kane shook his hair out like a dog and attempted to knock some water from his ear. "Yeah, yeah, I saw," he said, catching his breath.

I grinned and fell back into the pond, letting the chilly fresh water tickle over my scalp.

He studied me with amusement. "You are fast. Like a gazelle or something."

"Thank you."

"It must be because you're so small. Less for your legs to carry." He gestured at his broad torso.

I rolled my eyes. "Are you bragging, King Ravenwood? About your muscled form?" I tutted in mock disappointment.

"I'm touched you noticed."

I knew we were flirting. It was despicable. But I was having a good time. It had been a very long while since I'd done anything of the sort.

He studied me, sparkling water raining into his eyes. "What are you thinking?"

I was sick of the half-truths. "That I am having fun. Somehow."

The expression on Kane's face said it was a better answer than he could have hoped for.

I waded through the pond, stretching my limbs and avoiding rocks and skinny orange fish.

"You have plenty of fun, I'm sure, but it's been a little while for me. Not so lovely back home in a town reduced to the used handkerchief of war. Or trapped in a cell in a foreign kingdom without your loved ones . . ."

I hadn't meant to sound so bitter, but once the truth gates were opened it was hard to pull them shut.

Kane studied me with wary interest, and something like pity settled on his face.

"I can only imagine what you think of the choices that I've made." He swam closer to me, intensity brewing in his silver eyes.

"Actually, I don't need to imagine—you've told me, haven't you?" I swallowed hard and waded away from him. "Just know . . . they are not made without understanding the sacrifice. The loss, as I told you in the throne room. I don't have as much *fun* as you think."

It must have been the cool water breaking gooseflesh out across my limbs. I forced my gaze away from his, the sincerity there too raw. Too intimate.

"What did you do for fun when you were younger, then?" I missed how I felt mere minutes ago. How light and airy our conversation had been.

"I liked to play the lute. My mother taught me. It was something we did together." It seemed like a happy memory, but when I lifted my eyes to him, he had gone still, and his expression was almost distraught.

So much for light and airy.

"Was that your hard-won question?" he asked, brow quirked. "Seems a bit of a waste for the insatiable curiosity I've come to expect from you."

Kane waded closer to me, his broad chest rippling with each movement, hair dripping gleaming beads of water onto his face. He pushed it back as he looked down at me.

"No, I—"

I couldn't be so close to him. He was too beautiful and magnetic and threatening. But he stalked toward me, the pond undulating around the defined vee at the base of his hips. I scrambled backward, feet slipping over the mossy bottom of the pond until my back pressed against the stone behind me. The waterfall from the rocks above trickled down my back like rain. Kane placed his hands on either side of my head and leaned forward so that the water sprinkled along his hands and forearms, sparkling droplets like falling stars twinkling around us.

His eyes were all pupil as they flared at me. That earlier sincerity and sorrow were replaced by a singular, burning attention that landed on my mouth. I was sure he could see my thrumming heartbeat pulse along my neck. I was near trembling. From fear, but also—

Finding my footing, I stood up, to gain some ground, to steady myself—

But the pond was shallower by the rocks. I felt my chemise go flush against my breasts, soaked and clinging to my body. I covered my pointed nipples with crossed arms, peering up at Kane. His jaw was tight, but he had already averted his slate-gray eyes and was gazing at the falls above us.

"Don't worry, bird. I'm not looking."

Once again, where I expected insult, teasing, cruelty, instead I found consideration. Even kindness—

The words spilled out of my mouth before I could catch them.

"Set me free," I breathed.

"What?" His eyes pinned mine.

I felt my face flush red. But I had already said it.

"Please," I begged. "I don't belong here. You barely need me. Let me go back to my family."

Kane's jaw had gone rigid, his slate eyes simmering. He pushed himself off the rocks and moved away from me.

"I can't do that," he bit out.

"Why not?" I waded after him. I had never felt so small. So vulnerable. Not since I was a little girl.

But I was not above begging for my life. He had shown me

kindness today. Maybe there was a part of him that had empathy—that might be swayed.

"Please," I asked again.

He opened his mouth to speak, but thought better of it, and shut it once again.

Tears began to prickle at my eyes.

Now that the adrenaline from the run, my plea, and . . . other things was subsiding, I noticed the sun skulking behind the trees, and felt my limbs ripple with goose bumps in the cold water.

"Let's get back," he finally said, eyes on my shivering shoulders. "You can ask me your question on our way home."

12

⁕

THE RIDE BACK WAS A THOUSAND TIMES WORSE THAN THE ride into the woods. After he lent me his shirt to wring out my wet hair, Kane and I dressed quickly and made our way through the woods, less clothed than we had been before.

He was such a miserable prick. Playful and charming and surprisingly caring when he chose to be, but as selfish as they came. I kicked myself internally for wasting a plea for my freedom on him.

To make matters infinitely worse, I couldn't take my mind off the bastard's slick chest as it stuck to my back, my dress pooled around my middle so my chemise could dry. His hands held the reins in front of me innocently enough, but watching him grasp the leather straps was so sensual it made my toes curl. I was acutely aware of his controlled breathing on the back of my neck and swore I could feel his heart hammering against my shoulder blade. The way our legs were spread in tandem over the sides of the saddle felt disturbingly erotic and I kept having to pull my wandering mind back from downright filthy places.

I was furious with the man. So, so furious. But I also wanted to lick his neck. It was complicated.

Our horse sidestepped quickly to avoid a fallen log, and Kane's hand splayed tightly against my stomach to hold me in place against him. His pinky just barely grazed my lower stomach, but I felt the sensation in my core and a deep need grew within me. Kane's chest expanded, and he let out a shaky breath before removing his hand, as if my thin, wet chemise was soaked in fire.

Thankfully, we reached the castle soon after, and Kane dismounted faster than I'd ever seen the man do anything, and we had quite literally just been sprinting. I thought he might have adjusted himself while I got down from the horse, but I averted my eyes.

"Well, thanks," I said, and turned on my heel to head into the keep.

"Arwen," he called after me. "Wait!"

I tried to will the red from my cheeks before peeking behind me, only to see that he was bringing me my boots. My eyes fell to my bare toes.

"I don't think you meant to go in there barefoot, but I know better than to tell you what to do."

"Thank you." A thought struck me, my head now clear from whatever had clouded it on our ride. "I didn't get to ask you my question."

Amusement flashed in his silver eyes. "I thought you might have forgotten. Go ahead."

There were so many things I could ask. *Why did you declare war in the first place? Why was Griffin upset with you today? Who were you talking to in the dungeon that first night? For someone who has an entire kingdom to take care of, you are supremely selfish.* I guess that last one wasn't a question.

But what I really wanted to know toppled out of my mouth like a rock rolling down a mountainside.

"Why do you allow everyone—your own subjects, those across all of Evendell—to think you are such a monster?"

Kane's brows shot up in surprise. "You don't think that anymore?"

I answered honestly. "I'm not sure, but you definitely play into the persona."

His jaw ticked, but his eyes were thoughtful, not angry. He sighed, looking toward the now cloudy sky above us. Then his eyes dropped down to me.

"Most of the rumors I'd imagine you've heard about me are true. I don't allow vulnerability to get in the way of my duties."

For some reason, his words were like a slap. "So, you see compromise, mercy, love . . . as vulnerability? Weakness?"

He seemed to be trying very hard not to roll his eyes. His jaw tensed. "Yes, actually. Kings who are ruled by emotion make decisions that hurt their people. My only job is to keep my kingdom safe."

"King Gareth is a kind and just king," I said, lifting my chin. "He keeps his people safe and is always merciful. He allows them a choice."

Kane's jaw hardened. "I've never forced my people to join my army."

My protest went stale in my mouth. But he continued, stepping close enough that a single breath separated us.

"And does he keep his people safe?" His eyes seared into mine. "You're here, aren't you? A captive of his greatest enemy. Gareth is a sniveling *worm*."

I fisted my hands at my sides. "You are needlessly cruel."

He stepped back, an unkind laugh escaping him. "There's just so much you don't know."

"Then tell me."

He sighed, but when his eyes found mine again, they looked almost wounded. "How many times do I have to tell you—I *can't*."

I clenched my jaw. "I guess trust is another one of those pesky weaknesses you don't like to indulge in."

My heart raged in my chest. What was I doing? Standing out here, arguing with him once again? Taking his secrecy personally? He didn't owe me anything.

I needed serious help.

I stormed off toward the keep and tried not to feel anything when he didn't call after me.

⚜

MY STOMACH MADE A GURGLING SOUND AS I TOOK THE STAIRS two at a time to meet Mari in the great hall. The castle was eerily beautiful at night, faint music and the hum of suppertime chatter floating through the halls. I hadn't eaten anything since returning from the Shadow Woods last night, opting instead to crawl into bed and drown out my thoughts in a restless sleep. And a fidgety morning. And an anxious afternoon—

It was evening now, and I was starving.

"I finally found a book on Faeries, but it was all children's stories," Mari huffed, blowing one red curl out of her face once I had caught up to her in line for dinner. She was fascinated with Fae lore, but there was very little reading material on the beings. Some books claimed the creatures were a myth altogether. Mari wasn't sure yet.

"Why not go back to your research on witches? I thought you were enjoying that. Dagan should have that grimoire translated soon, right?" Maybe he could help me get the burrowroot on the night of the eclipse. He seemed willing to help Mari, and he was kind enough to teach me sword fighting.

I stepped aside, allowing a group of handsome young soldiers to bypass us. Mari looked lovely in her blue dress and black Onyx bow. Each of the young men eyed her thoroughly, but Mari didn't seem to notice.

She only rolled her eyes at me. "Witches are far less interesting. Everything we think we know about the Fae—the wings, the pointed ears, the claws—might not even be accurate. The fact that I can't find a single definitive text is making me bonkers. Witches are just women who can master a few spells. It's boring, honestly." She chewed her lip.

I narrowed my eyes at her.

"What are you not telling me?"

"Nothing!" But the deafening pitch of her voice said otherwise. We stood there in rare silence until finally we were served our brisket. Tender, caramelized, and smelling of spice and sweetness—I couldn't wait to stuff my face. We sat down in a corner lit by both lantern flames and fireflies that sometimes drifted into the hall from the courtyard. Their flickering glow danced across Mari's preoccupied eyes.

"If you aren't going to tell me what's really going on with you, how am I supposed to tell you about the disaster that was the day I spent with the king yesterday?" I feigned genuine puzzlement and took a huge bite.

"What? When?"

I shook my head as I chewed.

"Fine," she relented. "I'm trying out some spells and have not had . . . much luck."

My mouth hung open. Mari was a witch?

She had said it like it was the most obvious thing in the world, but only those with a witch or warlock in their ancestry could practice witchcraft. Magic wasn't uncommon, but I had only met a handful of witches in my life, their spells used for crafting or cooking, sometimes to make sleeping potions or tonics for luck that only worked half the time. Though I imagined, knowing what I did of Mari, she didn't intend to perform such common witchcraft, but rather, something far more impressive. Far more powerful.

"I finally figured out how to fix the issue, but it's a little tricky." I got the feeling admitting defeat physically pained her.

But I was still hung up on the magic part. "Spells? You have witch lineage?"

She nodded. "My mother was a witch."

Mari hadn't spoken much of her mother, and for someone who talked as much as she did, there must have been a reason it was a sore subject. I wanted to know why and what she was keeping from me but swallowed my curiosity. I wasn't ready to tell her about Powell yet, so it didn't feel fair to pry.

"How can I help?" I asked instead.

Mari shook her head. "There's nothing you can do."

"Come on, I'm happy to be a test subject. Want to try a wakefulness spell on me? I'm exhausted."

She laughed, then chewed on her lip, and I knew if I waited there was a good chance she would open up. I had a suspicion that secrets didn't last very long in Mari's internal vault.

Finally, she caved as I had hoped. "All right. What I need is Briar's amulet. It's a relic that belonged to one of the greatest witches in history, Briar Creighton. She lived hundreds of years ago, but she's still alive today, as fair and youthful as she ever was. At least, that's what I've heard. She put quite a bit of her sorcery into this locket before she was rumored to gift it to . . . well, you can guess."

I already feared the answer. "King Kane Ravenwood?"

"Yes! Apparently, they were lovers when he was young."

"Of course, they were." I pinched the bridge of my nose. I wasn't judging Kane for sleeping with a hundred-year-old witch who probably didn't look a day over my age, but still. I suddenly had a terrible headache. "So you want me to ask him for it?"

Mari's eyes nearly jumped from her head. "No! Holy Stones, Arwen, of course not. He'd never give that to you, or to me."

I heaved a sigh of relief. Thank the Stones, because I was done with anything related to—

"I want to steal it from his study."

Now it was my eyes that bulged. "Tell me you aren't serious."

"You asked me to be honest with you," she said with a shrug.

I massaged my temples. My headache was becoming a full-blown migraine.

"It's too dangerous," I said. "King Ravenwood would have your head for far less."

"He'll never know. He's out in the woods today—the blacksmith told me this morning. It's the perfect time." She bit at her lip before turning her pleading eyes on me. "The only time."

Guilt squeezed my stomach. I had pushed Mari to be honest with me. We had been friends for only a few weeks, but I knew with absolute certainty that she was going to enact this idiotic plan with or without me. And truthfully, I felt braver now than I ever had before. I had survived a lot worse than sneaking into a study.

"I'm going to do it either way," Mari said, as if she could read my thoughts.

"All right, fine," I conceded. "What's your plan?"

Mari's answering smile was so pure, so joyous, it pulled a reluctant grin to my cheeks as well, despite my exhaustion, and fear that this would be a complete disaster.

"It'll be easy." She beamed. "And then you'll tell me all about your day with the king. Follow me."

"Now?" I said, but she was already up and bounding down out of the great hall. I cursed under my breath and shoved one last forkful into my mouth before following after her.

We leaped up the sprawling stone staircase, through the gallery above the courtyard, and past the apothecary, locked for the evening.

I wrestled to slow my shallow breathing as we walked with urgency.

We'd be in and out in no time.

"How do you know the amulet is even real, let alone in his study?"

"I've lived here all my life, Arwen. I know every secret the castle has, and even a few the king himself doesn't yet know about."

Shoving away panic and nerves, we rounded yet another corner and found ourselves in a passage I hadn't been down before. It had the same sophisticated stonework and shadowed nooks and crannies as the rest of the keep but was narrower and filled with fewer lanterns. As if to tell guests, *This hallway isn't for you.*

At the end were two ornate doors covered in inky, iron filigree, guarded by stoic sentries. But Mari led us past them quickly, and around a final corner to a lone display case. Inside were treasures I could never have imagined, like wartime armor belonging to the original king of Onyx, encrusted with diamonds and amethysts like a mouth crowded with teeth. Below that, a gangly amphibian creature with delicate lace wings was suspended in some kind of preservative. And farther below, a massive harpy's talon, taller and wider than me altogether.

Every day in this kingdom my understanding of this continent— this world—expanded.

"Come on," Mari whispered, pulling me from the enchanting artifacts.

I spun, looking around. "There's nothing here."

Mari murmured a phrase and, with a rumble I felt in my toes, the case that housed the unique items shifted and groaned, revealing a small alcove.

"What was that?"

"Secret password," Mari said under her breath. "The door is spelled to only open when it's uttered."

How very surreptitious of Kane, having a hidden entry to his private study. Fitting for a man who prized his secrets above all else.

Mari slipped inside and I followed, heart a furious beat inside my chest.

It was like stepping into a jewelry box. An ornate rug—clearly from Garnet or Rose due to its elaborate detail—spread below my feet, sprawling over the floor and underneath bookcases, statues, and a leather love seat with intricately stitched plush pillows. A stone-wrapped fireplace holding logs still adorned with cooling embers like jewels. Vases overflowing with the chilling Onyx lilies and violets I had come to love. Moonlight filtered in through a domed glass ceiling that seemed to reach up and up without end. It must have been the inside of the spiral tip of the castle, a tall and pointed spire that pierced through the clouds.

And in the center of the dazzling nook, a large reading desk—wood the color of copper and with nearly as much shine, and a delicious black leather chair with four clawed feet that begged to be sunk into. The desk was laden with shiny books, worn scrolls, and quills, even a leftover goblet cast aside still marked with the stain of wine.

"Wow."

"Yeah, I said that when I first saw it, too."

"You've been in here before?" Mari was more of a rebel than I would have guessed.

"Only once or twice," she said, peeking through drawers and shelves. "Maybe a few more . . . After one of the kitchen maids spilled the passphrase to enter back when I was young, I'd sneak in every once in a while. I would just snoop around to see what treasures the king had collected. Or to hide from bullies."

She said the last part so offhandedly I almost didn't catch it. I wanted to press further, but she hurried over to a shelf filled with weathered texts and began to rifle through them.

"So, if you can get in so easily, why did you need my help?"

"I had heard rumors that as of recently, he was keeping his pet in here. I thought I might need a spare pair of hands. But it looks like we're alone, so this should be a breeze."

Pet? The thought of Kane running around with a wide-eyed and scruffy pup melted my heart. I shook the images out of my head, and my eyes landed on a small, unimpressive wooden door nestled in the corner.

"Where do you think that leads?"

"The king's quarters. But I don't have a way in there."

I hummed my understanding, but my thoughts were elsewhere. There was something startlingly erotic about thinking of Kane's bedroom. What he did in there when he was completely alone. How he slept, who he thought of. I tried not to shiver.

It probably looked like the dungeons or his throne room—all stone and steel. A dark, cold room for a dark, cold person.

I could hear Mari's eye roll in her voice. "You are king crazy."

I flushed at the realization that I had been gazing longingly at a wooden door.

"All right." She approached the desk. "Briar's amulet, where are you?"

Before I could join her, a haunting cry, like a widow's wail, cut through the room.

A scream lodged in my throat at the sound, and Mari and I both whirled around, caught.

A feathered creature prowled out from behind the love seat, stretching like it might have been asleep. It was a strange, gangly thing that stared back at us. At first glance, it seemed like a large owl. But upon closer inspection, I recoiled from beady, humanlike eyes and bony shoulders that folded underneath its raven-feathered wings. It crept toward us with impish delight, lanky legs, and a twitching cock of its head. As if said owl had mated with an underfed, demonic child.

It halted, regarding us peculiarly, then squawked again, revealing rows and rows of pointed white teeth.

"Mari. Is that Kane's 'pet'?" My voice didn't sound like my own.

"Yes, can you distract it? I'm almost done." She was pushing through every drawer of the desk, rummaging for the locket. The owl-thing hooted again and stretched its clawed feet. Unblinking eyes bored into me, following my every move.

"Distract it? Mari!" I hissed.

"It's just a strix. If it was going to eat us, it would have already."

I released some of the tension in my locked-up knees and clenched jaw. "Oh. So they don't eat humans?"

Her voice was an echo, the result of her head being deep underneath the cavity of the wood. "No, no. They absolutely do. But he hasn't yet, so . . ."

I sucked in a shaking breath.

This woman was out of her mind.

"Good owl creature. What lovely fangs you have." Was this distracting? I tried to speak affectionately, as I would have with Bells and Hooves back home. It came out harried and unhinged.

The creature only inched closer. Its eyes had gone predatory, the three spindly fingers of its ghoulish claws reaching outward. My breath was coming in uneven bursts.

"Mari, come on. *Now.*"

"Almost . . . done . . ." she grunted, her voice muffled.

The strix, still staring daggers into my soul, spread its wings wide, the feathers inky black and sleek as if they had been dipped in oil. I jumped backward at the sight.

"Ah! Found it."

At Mari's exclamation, the owl-like being flashed its teeth once more and charged at me.

Heart thumping in my ears, I ran for the secret entrance, burying myself against the wall and faintly making out Mari's low hum behind me. The rush of wind at my back had me spinning around, and I watched as the strix shot up into the air with a strangled hoot, suspended there and thrashing.

Bleeding Stones.

I slumped with relief, supporting my body's weight against the hidden door and sucking in the musty air of the study.

"Are you doing that?" I motioned toward the strix, fighting to get back down from its hovering spot in midair.

"Yes!" Mari cried, running over to me. A thin leather rope held a purple gem around her neck. "Holy Stones! I can feel her power. I can't believe it."

"That is so great. I'm thrilled for you. But." I looked up at the hovering beast, angling down to swipe at us but unable to move. "What do we do about that? We can't leave him up there."

"Sure we can."

I shot her a glare. "*No*, we can't."

I couldn't do that to Kane or the creature, no matter how much it had wanted to eat my eyeballs and feast on my flesh. At least, that was what I felt like it had been trying to communicate to me. "Bring him down, and we'll run out before he can get us."

Mari frowned but held the amulet tightly against her chest with determination. She focused on the swatting, squawking owl and began a haunting chant under her breath.

Seeing magic done was always awe-inspiring, even when I was shaking so hard my jaw hurt. The static wind, the slight hum in the air—our town dressmaker's little spell to get a bottle of dye from a high shelf; a brief enchantment by a barkeep on a drunken patron to help him leave without trouble.

It had never looked as raw or visceral as what Mari was doing.

She continued her chant, but the creature didn't budge.

Mari and I exchanged a look of concern. The strix looked concerned as well, cocking his feathered head.

The thump of footsteps echoed through the wooden door—the one that led to Kane's bedroom. All three of us whirled at the sound and the filtered noises of men next door seeping inside.

"And Eryx seems pleased with our offer." Kane's deep, unmistakable voice. *"We may have an ally yet. And just in the nick of time."*

"That's a stretch." Griffin's voice.

"Oh, for Stone's sake, Mari! Try again!" I hissed. I didn't know what it said about me, but I was significantly more terrified of running into Kane than I was of death by strix.

"Always so upbeat, Commander. Can't we have one meager success?"

Griffin scoffed through the wall. *"Fine. But what about Amelia?"*

Kane's casual laugh carried through the door into my bones.

My face heated.

I did not want to hear more of their conversation. Mari's face scrunched up as she continued to chant the spell, grasping at the amulet around her neck.

"Griff, do you honestly think, with all that is at stake right now, that—"

The strix hooted loudly, flapping its staggering plumes against the magical strain.

Oh, Stones. My heart was in my throat. I was choking on it—

We had to leave right now.

"What is that?" The thumps of guards' boots were a steady rhythm from the king's room heading toward us.

"Mari!" I hissed.

Suddenly Mari's hold on the strix released and the creature fell halfway from the lofted ceiling to the ground, catching itself mere inches from the floor with outspread wings and murder in its eyes. Mari and I slipped through the alcove right before the guards pushed in or the owl-like creature could have us for dinner.

We heaved twin sighs of relief in the hallway and walked as fast as looked natural in the other direction. When we rounded the corner, I was practically vibrating with anger.

"Mari. That was—"

"I am so sorry, Arwen," she said before turning her chestnut eyes on me. "It was so dangerous and completely stupid. I can't believe you agreed to it, honestly."

I could feel my all-too-familiar headache returning.

"You almost got us killed," I snipped. "How could you think—"

I snapped my mouth shut as we passed by two strolling sentries in the torchlit hall. Mari and I smiled—warm and broad and phony as charlatans.

They passed us and I readied myself to lay into her further, but she slowed at the gallery, looking down at the people milling about the courtyard below us.

She looked stricken.

Had the strix scared her that much?

"I had to get the amulet," she said. "I couldn't fail." She turned to face me, eyes grave. "Being good at things, knowledgeable about everything. I don't know. It's all I'm worth, I think."

Irritation still prickled at my skin, but her words made my heart hurt, too.

"Mari, that's not true and you know it. How can you say that?"

"I didn't have any friends here growing up. It's an army stronghold, for Stone's sake. There were very few kids, and of them, the girls were sent to take classes in Willowridge, and the boys were taught to fight. I think Papa never sent me away because he didn't want to be alone."

The image of a small, lonely Mari, red curls taking up half her face, bullied by young boy soldiers and hiding in Kane's ornate study, made me want to hug her.

"My mother died giving birth to me. I never knew her, but I knew from what Papa told me about her that she was a brilliant witch, and good at everything else she did. He was so enamored with her, and every day growing up he told me how alike we were.

"I loved reading, just like she did. It felt so good to have something that I could take pride in. Feeling like she and I were the same. Then it didn't matter what anyone thought of me. I had my mind, just like my mother, and that was all I needed. I was so afraid of failing at these spells, Arwen—at failing at something she was great at that I had set my mind to—that I almost got us both killed. I am so profoundly sorry. I just didn't know who I would be if I tried witchcraft and didn't succeed."

All the fury swept out of me like a snuffed candle.

I knew what she meant.

Maybe not about the incredible pressure she put on herself, but my childhood loneliness also led to some poor adult choices. Truthfully, had I found something when I was young that I was as great at as Mari was at academia, I might have grown up with some of the sense of self and confidence that she possessed.

I turned her to face me.

"Mari, if you never pulled a random fact out of thin air again, or quoted a text I'd never heard of, or mastered a new spell or translation, I wouldn't think of you any differently. Your brilliance and fierce determination are only two of the many, many qualities that make you my friend."

Her eyes brightened. "Thanks for saying that."

"It's true. I'm a terrible liar."

We resumed our stroll, and this time the silence was pleasant— a nightcap to accompany the balmy evening that had somehow not ended in our death.

"So," she said after a few minutes, "are we going to talk about what we heard?"

My cheeks reddened. *Amelia.*

"My ego is still recovering from the fact that Kane seems to have slept with half the kingdom, including century-old witches, and shows no interest in me," I said. It was a joke, but it didn't come out like one.

Mari grabbed my arm tightly and swung me into her eyeline.

"Let's not follow that train of thought," she said, grimacing. "You don't want to be wanted by a man like that anyway. You hate him, and with good reason." Her voice was warm, yet firm. "You are a bright light, Arwen. And he is not worthy of you."

I nodded but my heart had seized up in my chest.

Maybe, as much as I thought Mari couldn't see herself accurately, it was possible neither could I.

13

I THWACKED AT THE TREE WITH ALL MY MIGHT BUT BARELY
made a dent in the bark. Even when I imagined it was Kane's
arrogant face, or someone named *Amelia*, my slashes were mere
scratches against the wood. After all the mornings I had spent with
steel in my hands, I still felt like my strength had not improved
at all.

I wiped the sweat from my eyes and peered up at Dagan.

"This isn't training. This is free labor. If you need more firewood, I bet Owen would be happy to oblige."

Dagan loosed a chuckle, the novelty of which still hadn't faded.
Nothing seemed to bring the curmudgeon as much joy as these
morning lessons. I couldn't tell if he was secretly endeared by my
learning, or just a sadist. Probably both.

"Give me four more blows and we'll call it a day."

I rolled my shoulders back and took the axe to the tree four
more times, leaving a shallow gash in the wood.

"There you go," he praised. "That's something. We'll get it
down one day."

"I still don't understand what this has to do with sword fighting."

Dagan offered me his sword in return for the axe I was holding. I made the trade and instantly felt my arm pull toward the ground.

"Dagan!" I gasped. "What is your sword made of? Bricks?" I couldn't hold it even with two hands, let alone wield it expertly with one.

"The sword you've been training with is for a child. Five or six years old at best." My jaw practically unhinged. "You need to grow stronger so that you can use a proper one soon."

I respected his dedication to my self-defense, but the urgency was unsettling. Did he think I'd be in peril again in the near future?

Despite the shudder that ran through me, I was grateful for the reminder not to get too comfortable here—that Onyx was still dangerous.

"I'm sorry, I don't mean to complain. I'm just a little tired."

Late last night, I had healed two injured soldiers who had returned from a mission with significant stab wounds, and it had taken nearly everything out of me.

I dropped his sword and leaned back against the marred tree. Dagan stared at me, sympathy and curiosity twisting in his expression.

"Do you get tired when you work in the apothecary?"

I knew confusion was written plainly across my face. "Sometimes the hours are long . . . Why?"

"That's not what I mean." Dagan took his sword back, swiping the blade across his palm.

"Dagan! What—" I reached for the sword, but he swatted me away.

"Here, heal this."

I narrowed my eyes at him but followed his request. Taking his calloused hand in mine, I closed my eyes and felt the familiar tingle in my fingers.

"Now, I want you to try something new. Don't pull power from within but try to harness what's around you instead."

"What's around me?" My eyes popped open and I scanned the area. "Like you? My sword?"

"Not exactly. Sometimes it's water. Sometimes it's earth. My guess for you is atmosphere. So try to pull the very air around you into my palm, if you can."

"Dagan." Cautious hope bubbled in my chest. "Do you know what these powers are? I've wanted to understand my entire life. If you know something, you have to tell me."

Abbington hadn't had libraries or scholars, so after exhausting all forms of research, I had given up on trying to understand this part of myself. I had even searched the Shadowhold library a few weeks ago to no avail. I had told myself it was better this way—that I preferred not to know.

But Dagan's eyes only scanned the field around us. "This technique has helped others with their witchcraft. That's all. I thought it might be worth trying."

I knew he was keeping something from me. He wasn't as bad of a liar as I was, but it was close. I knew witches never pulled their power from air or water or earth. Mari had made it very clear as she walked me through all of her research on her new skills that a witch's power came from her lineage.

However, when he didn't say more, I caved and gave it a shot. I imagined pulling the very air around me into his palm, sealing up the small river of blood that had spilled out. My fingers twitched and I watched in awe as his hand found its way back together again, without leaving me exhausted or dizzy.

"How . . . ?"

Dagan's lips pursed in a knowing smile. "Good. That may help. Let me know."

And then he headed back to the castle.

———✧———

I WAS SO SORE I COULD HARDLY WALK BACK TO MY ROOM. I was going to draw myself a piping hot bath and fill it with salts from the apothecary to ease my aching muscles. Another facet of my strange powers was the ability to heal quickly. I was never sick for long, and my cuts became scars sometimes overnight. One long bath and I'd be good as new by tomorrow.

It was an oddly cloudy day despite the crawl toward summer, and my private washroom was dim and quiet. I lit two lanterns and a handful of candles to brighten the space and began boiling the water. The white porcelain of the clawfoot tub was cracked, and it had some rust here and there, but I had fallen a little in love with it. Back in Abbington, we had a communal bathhouse, which was almost solely used by teenagers who wanted to screw away from the intrusive eyes of their parents.

I tried to remember the fleeting, foreboding feeling I had when training with Dagan today—a reminder not to let my guard down completely. But my life here in Shadowhold was far more decent than I had ever imagined it could be. I had even caught myself forgetting about plotting or scheming a way to escape, enjoying Mari and Dagan's company, even Barney when I saw him in the great hall.

I pushed back against the guilt that scratched at my heart.

I was surviving.

That was all I could do. Guilt had also been swimming in my mind ever since we stole Briar's amulet. I had hoped Kane wouldn't notice, that he wouldn't come after Mari for it.

A small part of me hoped he wouldn't feel betrayed.

The irony was so ridiculous I nearly gave myself a headache.

Once the water was close to scalding, I poured it into the tub and peeled off my sweat-stained, dirt-ridden leathers. I dipped one blistered toe into the steaming water. There wasn't a single part of me that wasn't raw and achy from the morning's exercises.

Dagan was definitely a sadist.

I added the salts and the clear water bloomed milky white, smelling of eucalyptus and lilies. As I lowered myself into the tub inch by inch, at least half the tension left my body like steam off a cup of tea in winter air. I submerged and lifted my feet out, resting them on the lip of the tub in a position fit for a queen.

I had been this sore after my footrace with Kane, too. It had been a while since I had exerted my muscles that much, but my aching legs had been far more welcome than whatever this full-body bruise from training was. Thinking of my day with Kane brought all kinds of conflicting feelings to mind. His infuriating arrogance. Our argument. His stance on love and trust. But also his willingness to bring me along into the woods just because I needed to get out. Our playful wager. Our swim.

That ride back to the castle . . .

The thought of him behind me, glistening as the sun went down, maybe even hardening at the sensation of my body in his arms . . . I didn't want to feel anything for him, but I couldn't help it. The memory brought back an intense ache in my core and my nipples pebbled even in the warm water.

Alone, in the privacy of the washroom, surrounded by the candles' dim light, I allowed myself to slip a hand down my stomach and between my legs. It was an entirely different feeling thinking of Kane rather than Halden—a want so pure and demanding, I couldn't bear to leave it unanswered. I thought of Kane's wicked grin, his deep and husky laugh, and the way he nearly pressed me up against the rocks in the pond.

I wondered what might have happened had I not been so focused on escape. What if I had taken the sheer camisole off altogether? Would he have been able to hold himself back? Or would he have ravaged me, consuming me completely until we were one?

I imagined his hands grasping at me, coaxing a moan from my lips, whispering in my ear what my most intimate sounds were doing to him. I rubbed circles between my legs, feeling the pressure build throughout my body, want pooling low in my belly.

I ached for him.

I wanted him to touch me so desperately it was all-consuming. I brought my other hand up to my breast and massaged it gently, thinking of his hands, their strength, and how his rough touch would feel. He was so dangerous, so lethal. It was shameful— mortifying—how much it had begun to turn me on.

As I pictured Kane, his name slipped out of my lips in a soft gasp. Even in the water, I felt wetness pooling at my center, and I pushed one finger in slowly. I moaned, eyes screwed shut in pleasure, as my release built. Withdrawing nearly to the tip before plunging back in, I imagined it was Kane's hand, using me, playing with me, wringing cries from my throat and tears of ecstasy from my eyes. Would he be rough? Jaw tight, hands punishing, demanding moan after moan, sob after sob . . . or would the wicked king be surprisingly gentle? Restraining himself, afraid to thrust too hard, shaking with the need to keep himself in control . . . My fantasies were unhinged. I was so close, I could almost feel his tongue on my neck, his grunts against me, the way—

I was shaken from my filthy imagination by the sound of heavy footsteps coming from my bedroom.

Fear cut through me.

I stood up, dousing the floor in water, prepared for whatever might come through the washroom doors. I looked around for some kind of weapon and grabbed the nearest candlestick.

"Arwen? Are you al—" Kane barged in, hand on his sheathed sword, but stopped short upon seeing my soaked, naked form. He made a guttural noise that sounded almost like a whimper and turned around quickly.

"Fuck." His voice cracked, and he cleared his throat. "Sorry."

I dropped down into the tub with an ungraceful splash to hide my body. "What are you doing in here? Don't you knock?" I asked, but it came out like a shriek.

"I was coming to ask you a question and then I heard— I thought you were hurt," he said to the wall, still facing away from me. "I— Never mind."

I squirmed. Still hot all over—from the steaming bath, from embarrassment, from . . . I shook the images of Kane's lust-soaked eyes and parted, breathless lips from my mind.

"Well, I'm fine. And you can turn back around now."

Kane slowly faced me. I had wrapped my arms around my chest, and the tub covered the rest of my body. The salts had made the water opaque, like a blanket of liquid white. Somehow, he looked almost as embarrassed as I felt.

A horrible thought entered my mind, and all others eddied out.

"What made you think I was hurt?" I tried not to sound hysterical.

"I thought I heard . . ." Now his cheeks were truly flushed. I couldn't tell if it was from arousal or shame. Maybe both.

I recovered quickly. "Don't be crude, Kane. I'm just sore. Dagan is teaching me to sword fight. Haven't you ever had a sore muscle? Or were you born looking Stones-carved?"

Ugh. I was overdoing it.

He relaxed a bit and his wolfish grin returned. He leaned against the wall. "Someone's spirited this morning."

I shook my head and closed my eyes, lying back in the tub. I let the warm water rise up around my neck and calm me down before I looked at him again.

"Smells nice." He wandered closer but kept a respectful distance. I wasn't sure if I appreciated that or hated it more than anything.

"The salts are scented with white lilies. They're my favorite flower."

He smiled a new smile, a relaxed and pleasant look I rarely saw on him. It took my breath away.

"We don't get many of those here in Onyx."

"I know," I said. "My mother told me they only bloom in Amber. That's why it's my middle name; she said I was born surrounded by them."

"Arwen Lily Valondale," he mused. My name on his lips was like a prayer, if a prayer could be sensual. It was nearly enough to make me whimper.

I cleared my throat.

"How do you know my surname?"

He clucked his tongue, shaking his head in playful reprimand, and my breasts tightened in response. *Damn him.* He shouldn't do anything that made me look at his mouth.

"You think I let prisoners roam free in my keep without doing my research?"

He sauntered closer and my lower stomach clenched. I was still *so* naked.

He had to go.

"Last time I checked, the tub was a private space, not a common room. Why were you in my quarters in the first place?"

Kane inched toward me farther and knelt so as to not see inside the tub. When we were at eye level he said, "I wanted to ask . . ." He scratched at his jaw.

A terrible thought occurred to me too late. Did he know it had been Mari and me in his study? Was that why he was here? Had he realized Briar's amulet was missing? I tried to make my face appear indifferent.

He sighed. "If you might join me for something tomorrow night. I think it may help you understand this kingdom a bit more."

"Surprised" was an understatement. I dipped a little lower in the tub to buy some time.

"Why should I?"

"Because I am telling you to?"

I scowled.

He laughed a warm and genuine laugh like I was hilarious. "Yeah, I didn't think that would mean much. How about because it will ease your insatiable curiosity about me and this kingdom, and the war that you have so many opinions on."

"Fine." I nearly smiled. He had me there.

"Good." He grinned. "I'll have Barney bring you."

I turned, reaching for my robes behind me, when I heard his sharp inhale. I spun back to him and waited for whatever was on the tip of his tongue, but I already knew what was coming.

He looked stricken.

"You have scars." He said it like he could break iron with his fists.

Despite the hot water, a shiver ran across my back.

"Yes" was all I could manage. That was not a part of my life I wanted to share with anyone, especially him.

"Who did that to you?" he said in a low tone I could barely hear.

Images of Powell and his belt assaulted my mind's eye.

I flushed. "It was a long time ago."

As if he could see what the memories did to me, he didn't push further, for which I was grateful. Instead, he swallowed and held my eyes.

When I didn't look away, he leaned slightly closer, his expression one I couldn't read. His jaw was still as hard as granite.

The space between us pulsed with slow, agonizing energy.

My core still ached.

Our faces were far too close for how naked I was. And how near to coming I had been mere moments ago. I could smell his leathery, woodsy scent, and it was mind-altering.

I drew my tongue across my bottom lip and watched him follow the movement with something like a wince—as if the movement pained him. His eyes had gone fully black, all pupil. Not an ounce of the slate gray that usually stared back at me. They followed a line down the column of my neck, to my collarbone, to where my breasts were pushed together underneath my folded arms. His lips parted slightly.

But he didn't look lower, and I felt both relief and disappointment.

I angled my face up toward him. I wanted him to kiss me. I could admit it to myself—I wanted his lips on mine more than I wanted my next breath.

But his brows creased and he shook his head, cleared his throat, and stood up.

"I'm sorry," he said, before walking out of the washroom without another word, and leaving me breathless.

14

I FOLLOWED BARNEY OUT INTO THE SEA OF TENTS. A WIDE and shining harvest moon hung in the crisp night sky, and it glowed on his soft, familiar face. I was stunned to realize I had missed the sweet, doughy man.

I had borrowed a dress from Mari and a few of the black ribbons so often found in Onyx women's hair. I had no idea what Kane wanted me to see, and neither did she. She had mused that maybe he was going to bring me to the front lines and show me the realities of war so I could see why he ruled so cruelly. I couldn't imagine anything more terrible.

Dagan had been even less helpful this morning. I only revealed that the king had asked me to join him for something that evening, and of course left out all of the needy wanting and aggressive eye contact that seemed to overcome the two of us the past few days. I had a feeling Dagan knew something else was going on, though. Every time I spoke of Kane my cheeks grew hot. When I had asked if he knew why the king might wish for me to join him tonight, he only rolled his eyes and left me alone in the apothecary for the rest of the day. *Reminder: do not ask Dagan for relationship advice.*

The sound of fire crackling in my ears, Barney and I passed by men cooking pots of stew, dealing cards, and drinking ale. The soldiers who had been so fearsome to me just a few weeks ago now seemed like Ryder and his friends—playful, boyish, and all too young.

We rounded a boisterous corner and came across a tall, pitch-black tent. It was more like a pavilion—adorned with silver filigree around the entrance and banners on each side with the Onyx emblem.

I recognized the area, and nausea flitted through me.

Behind us was the exact spot where Bert had tried to assault me. Kane must have been in this very tent the night he heard my struggle. I shuddered, thinking of what might have happened had he not been there. Begrudging gratitude had blossomed inside me toward my training. Had I had a sword with me that night, and known how to wield it, I could have at least been able to fight back.

The tent was not at all what I expected upon entering. In the middle of the room sat a sizable textured map of Evendell, with various pieces representing each kingdom's many battalions spread about. Leather chairs and furs in an array of sand and chocolate shades filled the rest of the space, as well as gothic lanterns and black taper candles that bathed the room in streaks of butterscotch light.

Men and women held copper chalices and ate cloverbread, chicken, and steak. Ginger, citrus, rum, and cloves wafted through the air, mingling with gardenia and lilac—the most common Onyx flowers, I'd discovered. The glowing lights made for a warm, pleasant ambience.

I realized, belatedly, that I was pressing my hands to my heart in awe, and . . . excitement.

Barney guided me over to Kane, sitting on a velvet throne. To his side was a man with dark skin and a strong jaw, whom I didn't recognize.

"Lady Arwen, Your Majesty."

Kane stood to greet me. Tonight, he was dressed as a true king—black robes, a few silver rings, hair slicked back, and a delicate crown of onyx branches encircling his head. He was breathtaking.

I swallowed any residual embarrassment at our almost-kiss in my washroom yesterday and greeted him with a simple curtsy. Kane examined me with a slow sweep from my boots to my black ribbon, a spark dancing in his eyes. I wondered if he noticed that I was dressed like one of them.

But his usual playfulness and charm were absent tonight. No flirtatious comments, no witty banter.

"I'm glad you could join us," he said. "I'll just be a minute. Please, sit." He motioned to the plum velvet chair beside him before resuming a heated conversation with the man to his right.

I fought against the urge to look out at the small sea of nobles that filled the tent. Their eyes, curious but also territorial, bored into my back like the pointed ends of a hundred swords. Instead, I looked to my other side, where my biggest fan, Griffin, sat. I wanted to ask him or Kane exactly what this was, but he, too, was entangled in a conversation I feared interrupting. I found myself wishing Barney were still here.

Staring at my hands, I turned my ears to the conversations around me. Kane was discussing the Opal Territories' peace treaty, but I could only pick up on a word here or there. The room was growing noisy and restless.

To my left, Griffin was engaged in a surprisingly jovial discussion with a beautiful blonde woman. It was fascinating to see Griffin laugh when he had always been so stoic around me. He actually had a warm and friendly smile when he chose to show it.

"Wild, right?"

I turned to Kane. "I think it's the first time I've seen his teeth. Other than when he's baring them at me, at least."

Kane smirked, but it didn't reach his eyes. Something was clearly on his mind tonight. "As I said, it's not you, it's me."

I hummed my understanding but didn't say more. Griffin and Kane might not have been brothers, but clearly, there was some deep-rooted, almost familial tension between them that I had no intention of getting involved in.

The commander in question stood, and the crowd of chattering dignitaries quieted, turning their attention to him. "Tonight's forum is regarding the Opal Territories," he said. "Amber has been running soldiers through Opal's Midnight Pass illegally. They're getting to our men quicker because of it."

My heart dropped into my stomach with a thud.

Oh, no.

My eyes flashed to Kane, but his were trained on his commander.

I racked my brain for what I knew about the Midnight Pass, the treaty. This was information I had learned as a kid in childhood classes. Opal's land was free and clear of any one ruler. It was a wild and rocky place with many different groups and divisions. If I recalled correctly, decades ago the territories had collectively signed a peace treaty with the other eight kingdoms that declared them neutral in any wartime event.

Unfortunately, both Opal and Peridot were right in the middle of Amber and Onyx's conflict. Soldiers from both sides had to go around via the Mineral Sea and the Quartz of Rose, both of which took much longer than just cutting a straight line through Opal.

My excitement at joining this forum had rapidly soured in my stomach, warping into grave concern. What would they do to the Amber soldiers? How ruthless would they be?

Or did they not care? Maybe it was Opal's problem to deal with.

"Thank you all for joining us," Griffin finished. "The forum is now open."

Almost immediately, a portly man with an impressive beard stood. "My king, I've said this before, but I'll say it again gladly. If Amber can break the territories' rules with no consequences, so can we. Let's get our men in there tonight. Even the playing field. There's no time to discuss alternatives."

The blonde woman sitting next to Griffin scoffed, standing up and facing Kane. Her eyes were pleading. "Your Majesty, with all due respect to Sir Phylip, Amber's actions are not without consequence. My spies have heard that the territories are launching an attack on King Gareth any day now in retribution for using their land as a shortcut and going against the treaty. That will help our cause. Let us not end up on the receiving end of their fury, too."

Sir Phylip dragged a hand down his face. It seemed these two may have had this argument before.

"If we go in there," she continued, "we will only bring danger to this kingdom and cause more blood to be shed in Opal."

Kane spoke for the first time. "Lady Kleio is right: we don't go through Opal out of respect, not fear. Amber may be bastards, but we aren't."

Opal had created the treaty to keep their lands and people safe—I didn't believe Gareth would disregard that for his own gain. That sounded more like Kane, if anyone.

The man next to Kane stood, his baritone voice rumbling through the forum and commanding attention. "I have advised our king to meet with the various tribe and division leaders to enact a new treaty allowing only Onyx safe passage. If we want to send a wave of troops to meet Amber, we will need their help."

Both Sir Phylip and Lady Kleio rolled their eyes at this almost in unison. Kleio spoke first. "Lieutenant Eardley, tracking each leader down, even with our best intelligence officers, will take months. It's time we don't have."

Unease churned in my gut. I didn't want to hurt my kingdom, but I did want to help avoid more bloodshed altogether. The lack of dignitaries standing up against Phylip's plan for carnage worried me. If they utilized his plan, thousands of Onyx, Opal, and Amber lives would be lost within the next few days.

But the predicament did remind me of something—

It was a stretch but, when I didn't want a medication to hit the nervous system too quickly, I'd put certain herbs or elements into my concoctions to act as blockers, allowing the medication to find other routes through the body and the effects to last longer for the patient.

That was what Onyx needed. Something to block the Amber soldiers, forcing them to abandon the pass. If going through Opal took the same amount of time as the other routes, they'd stop seeing it as a shortcut and leave the territory altogether.

My eyes cut to Kane. Leaning back, ankle crossed over his

knee, fingers steepled in his lap, he was the epitome of calm. I had to admit I was wrong about the way I assumed he ran his kingdom. He was giving every noble, lieutenant, and dignitary in his court a chance to voice their thoughts and come up with a decision together. It was surprisingly fair.

As if he could sense my staring, Kane turned and caught my eye. He waggled his fingers at me in a coy wave. I smiled but shook my head—I wasn't saying hello. I motioned to the group and then pointed at myself. He raised an eyebrow but nodded once in suspicious approval.

My stomach made a little heave of anxiety, and I fisted my hands in my dress to suppress their shaking.

When a curly-haired older woman had finished making her point about stationing Onyx men at the border of Opal and Amber, and Griffin had shot that down as a waste of their troops, I took in one more deep breath and stood.

"Good evening," I started. The room was silent. Everyone seemed to look to Kane for his endorsement. I turned to him as well. He watched me with the same detached expression that he had held throughout the entire forum but didn't make a move to stop me.

"I have no military training," I said, turning back to the small crowd. "I'm not nobility, and I've only seen two maps of our continent in my life." Beside me, Griffin placed his head in his hands. Kane stifled a laugh at his commander.

"What are you doing here, then?" asked a gruff voice from the other side of the tent. Voices tittered with humor, and I strained but couldn't see who had said it. My cheeks heated, sweat prickling at my hairline.

Kane shot the man a look of pure venom. "I don't believe the lady was finished speaking. You'd be wise to watch your tongue in her presence."

Deadly silence followed.

But his words bolstered me and I continued, voice a little less wobbly this time. "It could be fruitful to render the Midnight Pass ineffective."

Despite there being no moisture in my mouth or throat whatsoever, I tried in vain to swallow. I waited for the rumble of disagreements I knew was coming, but all I could feel were their eyes lingering on me, waiting for me to continue. There was no way to look at Kane for some kind of approval without showing weakness.

And I didn't need to.

This was a good idea. I knew it was.

"Not only would this stop Amber soldiers from getting to our borders faster than we can get to theirs, but it would be doing the Opal Territories a favor. We'd be keeping war out of their land for free, and later down the line, they might be happy to do us a favor in return."

"We can use the dragon and our hydras," a nobleman added from my right. "It'll be faster and more covert than having a battalion transport the blockade."

"Our ore deposits will work to block the pass. They'll never have enough manpower to move them out of the way," Griffin added, deep in thought.

Pride warmed my bones as I sat. I couldn't help looking at Kane now. He continued to watch the discussion play out but shot me a small nod, a smile twinkling in his eyes.

Kleio stood next. "Thank you . . . ?"

"Arwen," I supplied.

"Thank you, Arwen." She smiled. "It's not a bad idea. I have some spies in Opal as we speak. They could track down—"

Kleio was interrupted by heavy boots marching toward the tent.

Murmurs of concern danced through the forum, and I felt dread pull low and deep in my stomach.

Seven fully armored Onyx soldiers pushed through the tent's flaps and marched straight through the forum on a track toward Kane.

The king shot out of his chair with something I had never seen in his eyes before—pure fear.

My throat had constricted, and I fought to swallow nothing at all.

The soldier whose armor was studded with silver spoke to Kane in hushed tones. I recognized the armor but not the man, and realized he must have taken Lieutenant Bert's position.

I waited and waited and waited.

The atmosphere crackled with horrific anticipation.

But as soon as they exchanged a few words Kane's shoulders relaxed. And mine followed suit. Whatever was happening, it wasn't what he dreaded. The fleeting relief came and went before Kane faced the forum.

"Enough for tonight. Lady Kleio, see to it that your spies make sure the pass is cleared. Utilize Eryx if need be. My men will begin to harvest and transport the ore." With that, the entire tent cleared out in a matter of minutes, leaving only Kane, Griffin, Lieutenant Eardley, and the soldiers.

And me.

Griffin ordered men to cover up the war table. I waited for

someone to tell me what to do or where to go, but no instruction came. Kane nodded to the lieutenant, who left the tent and returned with three more Onyx soldiers.

The sight before me filled my stomach with a twisted queasiness, and I dug my fingernails into the wooden arms of my chair. Each soldier held a man whose arms and legs were bound by chains and with a sack hanging over his head.

I drew in a quick breath—prisoners.

They were prisoners of war.

Kane turned his attention to the men forced to their knees in front of him.

The lieutenant cleared his throat. "These three Amber soldiers were found in our keep, trying to access the vault. They killed six of our men and three bystanders. I believe them to be a specialized team of King Gareth's. How do you wish to proceed, my king?"

Kane's face was pure steel. Cool, calm fury. Not a single ounce of the man I had come to know was left. He looked like death and violence personified, and fear rippled through me. Not for myself, but for the men who knelt before him.

"Off," he commanded, and the soldiers removed the men's hoods.

I nearly fainted.

Before me, dirtied, nose bloodied, and wincing in agony, was Halden.

15

WITHOUT THINKING I MOVED TOWARD HIM, HANDS outstretched.

No, no, no, *no*—

Griffin grabbed me by the arm, yanking me backward.

"What do you think you're doing?" he whispered.

I felt frantic. The tent was far too hot, the candles suffocating.

"I know him!" I whispered back. "He's a friend. There has to be some kind of mistake."

I couldn't believe he was alive. And here in Onyx. And imprisoned. And—

Griffin's hold on my arm tightened. "You have to get out of here, now." He stepped in front of me, shielding me behind him, but it was too late.

"Arwen?" croaked Halden. His hair was a dirty mop on his head, painted red with blood. His nose was swollen, his cheek bruised—but his brown eyes looked just as they had the day he left for battle. Round, sincere, and pained.

"Shut up." The soldier behind him smacked Halden across the back of his head.

"Stop that!" I couldn't stand to see him like this. I lunged forward again.

Kane whirled to me. "You know this boy?"

Before I could speak, Halden answered. "She was going to be my wife."

I went still.

The entire tent did.

Halden, you *Stones-damned* idiot.

Kane looked positively livid, and even Griffin had gone pale.

"No, that's not . . . It's not exactly—" Words were not coming to my brain in time.

Kane didn't even wait for me to finish. He stalked over to Halden, eerily calm. "You love this woman?"

Halden looked right at me with fervor. "More than anything."

Bleeding. Stones.

Kane nodded curtly. "Good." Then he looked to the soldiers behind Halden. "Kill him."

"No!" I shouted.

Did anyone else hear that ringing in their ears? What was happening right now?

"Are you out of your mind?" I pleaded.

But Kane had stopped looking at me. He sauntered over to his leather chair and picked up a glass of dark liquid, sipping slowly. Leisurely, as I struggled for air.

The soldiers began to drag Halden and the other two young men away.

"Stop!" I raged. "Right now!"

But Griffin's hold on my arm was like a metal cuff. He wasn't even straining to keep me in place.

Kane studied my face, cold and unfeeling as tears brimmed in my eyes. The boy to Halden's right began to plead and the one on his left loosed urine down his leg as he shook. Kane said nothing as I wailed in earnest.

No, no, no. Please, no—

Finally, Griffin interjected. "My king. May I suggest we discuss the benefits of keeping even one of these rodents alive? They may have some information of value. Shall we let them rot in the dungeon while we confer?"

Kane rolled his eyes and tensed his jaw, taking another sip of his drink, but eventually he nodded to the lieutenant. "As the commander wishes. Take them to the dungeons for now."

All three prisoners let out tandem exhales. Halden's eyes never left mine. He mouthed something to me before being pulled out of the tent, but I couldn't see through the blur of salt water in my eyes. Kane seemed to catch whatever it was, though, and sneered in disgust.

"Everyone out," Kane said with a snarl. The room quickly emptied, leaving just him, Griffin, and myself.

I was going to pummel Kane's cruel, bored face.

Griffin let go of my arm, and I launched myself at him.

"You are a monster. What is wrong with you?" I seethed. "You were going to kill those boys? They're barely men! And you knew I knew him? Cared for him? I can't even look at you." I just *barely* managed to stop myself from throwing my fist into his jaw. I would not stoop to his level again.

Kane studied me with indifference. The only signs of his rage were his hands balled into fists, the skin of his knuckles white with pressure.

"They killed my men. They killed innocents. That doesn't bother you?" he asked with quiet venom.

I shook my head. "You don't know anything for sure. You sentenced them to die without a second thought. How can anyone who rules a kingdom be so impulsive?"

"The healer's right, actually," Griffin interrupted. "That was supremely stupid, my friend."

I couldn't believe my ears. "Thank you!" I turned back to the king, emphatic. "We can't just kill people whenever we feel like it, Kane."

Griffin shook his head. "No, now we absolutely have to kill them."

"Exactly. Wait—what?" I spun back to Griffin. "Why?"

Griffin sighed and poured himself a glass of whiskey. "Kane just showed his hand. Your lover tested him, and he failed. Now all three men know that the king of the Onyx Kingdom cares for his healer, and that gives Kane a weakness. They can't live knowing that information. I'm sorry."

My head was swimming. There was far too much going on. Was Griffin right? Was Kane's violence due to Halden's implication that he and I had been in love back in Abbington? And did Halden do that on purpose? In hopes of saving his own skin? Did he know, somehow, in just the few minutes he was in here, that Kane valued me?

I was an idiot. Of course he did. Why else would I be in this tent with the king's army, seated directly next to Kane, draped in an Onyx dress, black ribbons in my hair, sipping lavender whiskey with the rest of them . . . unless Kane had valued me?

I was a dirty traitor.

I slumped down into a leather chair and stared at the floor.

Kane turned to Griffin. "They were dead men walking, regardless. If they made it to the vault, they already know too much to be allowed to go back to Gareth."

I began to weep.

I couldn't help it. I hadn't thought of Halden at all in quite some time, but that didn't mean I wanted to see him dead.

It was too horrible to fathom, the ending of his life. And it somehow being my fault.

Kane considered me with a quiet rage. "I'm sorry, Arwen. About the man you love."

I peered up at him through tears, furious. "I never said I was *in love* with him. He is one of my oldest friends from childhood. One of my brother's best friends."

"No wonder he's a thief, too," Griffin mumbled into his drink. I ignored him.

"He's like *family*," I continued. "I haven't seen him since the day he was sent off to battle *your* soldiers in *your* bleeding, pointless war!"

I was getting hysterical, my pulse ratcheting up in my ears.

"But he's in love with you and planned to wed you?" Kane pressed.

"That's not the point!"

"I'm curious."

Too bad, I thought. But I took a deep breath. If there was ever a time to coax out the best part of Kane, the version of him from our day in the pond, it was this very moment.

"Yes, fine. We were—romantic. But then he left, and I didn't think I'd ever see him again. I thought it was just for fun, not that he ever thought *that* way about me."

Kane softened slightly. "How could he not?"

"Please," I begged. "Don't kill him."

Griffin looked nauseated. "I think it's time the healer returned to her quarters, don't you?"

~✦~

AFTER A FITFUL NIGHT OF SLEEP, I WOKE BEFORE DAYBREAK and made my way down the stairs. My cloak fought against the morning chill, and I blew hot air into my hands. I had smuggled a few slices of bread, some dried meats, a needle, and some bandages with me and wrapped them in the fur draped around my body.

I had to find a way to see Halden, and I figured sticking as close to the truth as possible was likely my best way in.

"Morning," I chirped to the young guard on duty. "Just visiting the prisoner."

"Which prisoner?"

I feigned confusion. "Mathis. The one with the festering wound." Enough time spent in a kingdom run by a liar, and the lies were coming to me easily now.

"Who are you again?"

"I'm Arwen. The healer. Commander Griffin sent me here to stitch Mathis up." I waved my medical supplies at the guard.

His brows knit together, lips pursed in doubt.

"All right, suit yourself," I said with a sigh. "I don't want to be working this early anyway." I turned to leave, then spun around. "If Mathis dies of blood loss before they can get information out of him, just tell Commander Griffin you didn't recognize the prison healer. I'm sure he'll understand. He's such a warm, forgiving man."

I started walking and held my breath. After a slew of grumbling, the guard finally shouted after me. "Fine, fine, just make it quick."

I was delighted, but plastered a mask of boredom on my face before turning around. "Thanks, shouldn't be too long."

Inside, the cells were as soggy and miserable as I remembered. My heart ached for Halden—it had been the most hopeless I had ever felt, inside these walls.

I found his cell faster than I could have hoped. His white-blond hair stood out among all the gray. He was sleeping in a heap, shivering and caked in dried blood. I hissed his name until he woke with a start.

"Arwen, what are you doing here?" He looked dreadful. His eye was now swollen shut and a bruise the size of a squash blossomed on his chin.

"I brought you some things."

I pulled out the contraband and slipped it through the bars, not unlike what Kane had done for me so long ago. I pushed the memory from my mind.

Halden reached for the bundle and his bruised knuckles brushed over my fingers. My hands itched to hold him, to comfort him.

"Thank you." He looked over the items and tucked them behind a bucket. "But I didn't mean what are you doing down here in the cells. How did you end up at the Onyx Kingdom's outpost?"

"It's a long story. But I'm safe. I'll tell you all about it when we have more time."

"I doubt I have much time left at all."

"Don't think like that. We'll figure something out."

He studied me curiously. "You seem different."

I felt my cheeks go hot. "How so?"

He looked uncomfortable. "I'm not sure. What have they done to you?"

Something like defensiveness bubbled up. Halden had a way of reminding me of Powell on occasion. Making me feel small. "Nothing. They've been surprisingly kind, actually." It was the truth.

"Yeah, I saw that." Halden's eyes narrowed. "Maybe you can reason with the king. He cares for you, you know. You should have seen his face when I called you my wife. He looked like I'd killed his pet."

For whatever reason, I thought of the strix. My lips twitched thinking of Kane's relationship with the foul beast—teaching it to come when called and how to do tricks. *Bleeding Stones,* how did I still feel anything warm and gooey for the man?

Halden. I had to focus on Halden.

"Why did you say I was to be your wife? We never spoke of things like that."

Halden bit his nail in thought. "I did hope when I returned, we might be married." I waited for him to continue. "But when I saw you in there, unchained, not as a servant, seated directly next to the king . . . I knew you were in some kind of position of power here. I thought if I tied myself to you, I might be spared."

Something like unease spread through me, oily and cloying. So Griffin had been right. Halden was more manipulative than I thought. I never knew that side of him. I guessed he was doing what he needed to survive.

"Maybe." I let the thought linger, unsure how to finish. I wasn't sure if I wanted Halden to be right. If I wanted Kane to feel that way about me anymore.

"Trust me. If he didn't care for you, I'd be dead right now."

Something about his assertion drained the color from my face. "Why? What did you do?"

Halden jerked back as if I had slapped him. "What did *I* do? I'm fighting for our home."

But still, my gut told me his words had meant more than he intended to share. "Last night. They said you killed three innocent bystanders. Is that true?"

"Arwen." His eyes were so wounded. "Of course not. How can you believe anything they say? And about me?"

Shame heated my face. "I don't know. Why would they lie?"

Halden bit at his nail again. "Why? Because they're demons, Arwen. They've clearly gotten to you already. I don't know why you're here, but I promise, I'll get you out. I told you last night I'd save you." He looked at me earnestly and I tried to feel something positive: hope, love, relief. But all I felt was nausea.

"We have a plan," he continued, nodding toward the cells to his right, in which the other two Amber men slept. "We just need some kind of commotion. Can you think of anything that might spread the guards out?"

I racked my brain, but nothing came to mind. "It's pretty isolated here. What's your plan?"

He shook his head as if to calm his own frantic thoughts. "Once something comes up that might work, you'll find a way to tell me, yeah? I can explain then. And get us both out of here."

Footsteps echoed down into the cells from the top of the stairs.

"Yes. I'll keep my eyes and ears open. In the meantime, stay alive." I turned to run.

"Arwen!" he rasped. I turned and looked back at his hands curled around the cell bars. "I've really missed you."

I waited for my heart to leap at his words, but it never did.

Instead, I gave him an almost-smile and hurried out, winding my way up the musty stairs and past the young guard.

"Handled?" he asked.

"What?" My mind was still reeling from my encounter with Halden. It had not been at all what I was expecting . . . "Oh. Oh! Yes, Martin is all healed. Thanks."

"Martin?"

Shit. "Mathis! Oops. Too early for me, back to bed I go!" I scurried away before the suspicious look on his face could become anything else.

Halfway back to my quarters, I slowed down to catch my breath.

Halden didn't seem the same. But hadn't he said the same about me, too? How could I judge him? Who knew what horrors he had seen on the battlefield? My heart hurt for him. For all he had been through.

Crossing the stone courtyard, I noticed the sun peek over the castle spires. A soft, lilac-scented wind blew my hair from my face. Despite the horribleness of the past few hours, the quiet dawn brought me some strange peace.

"This is my favorite time of day," a deep voice crooned behind me. "The sun rising over the castle feels like a fresh start. A re-birth."

I closed my eyes. I did not have the mental energy for this man right now.

"Please," I whispered. "Leave me alone."

"I behaved abominably last night. I let my rage consume me. It wasn't befitting of a king. Or a man, frankly."

I hesitated, then turned to face Kane.

My heart almost couldn't take the sight of him.

He looked as if he hadn't slept all night, his hair disheveled, his eyes red.

And still he was nearly too handsome to behold.

Exhaustion lined his expression as he regarded me. "I am so sorry," he said, his voice weary. "And for whatever it's worth, you were incredible in the forum. As brilliant as you are beautiful."

My traitorous heart tried to soar, but I caught it and crammed it back down. No warm feelings for the sweet-talking king today. Absolutely none. "Did you follow me this morning?"

"No." He paused. "But I know you went to see the boy. Arwen, he's not who you think he is."

I was so tired of there being so much I didn't know. "Really? Enlighten me."

Kane's brows creased, troubled. He weighed his words carefully before answering. "I'm not sure I can trust you, bird."

If I rolled my eyes any harder, they would have lodged in my skull. "*You* can't trust *me*?"

He laughed bitterly. "I'm aware of our history. But I have never lied to you."

"What? What about the entire *I'm a prisoner, too* façade?"

"I didn't mention my royal lineage, but I never lied."

"And I haven't lied to you, Kane."

He stepped closer and I flinched back reflexively. His face fell.

"Last night, you arrived at the forum in Onyx colors, referred to my people as *ours* and this kingdom as *we*."

My stomach twisted. He was right. Before Halden's capture, I had been starting to feel like a part of this land. I had made an unexpected home here. Kane noticed the shift in my attitude and continued, outrage twisting his face.

"Then, your lover shows up at my home, kills my people, and

tries to take what is mine. You fight for him, steal for him, and plot to help him escape, and tell me that isn't lying?"

My stomach jumped into my throat. "I thought you weren't following me."

"I have eyes all over this castle. How could you have expected any less?"

Kane stalked past me, fury rippling off of him.

Heat lit my face. I should have known he'd never actually leave me unguarded. I clenched my teeth against the rage.

"I'm not 'yours,' by the way." I wasn't even sure why I said it. I wanted him to hurt, too.

He faced me, but his expression gave nothing away. "Of course not."

"You just said, 'take what is mine.'"

Kane pinned a cruel grin on me. "Well, aren't we cocky? I wasn't actually referring to you. Would you like me to have been?"

The words stung more than I anticipated they would.

"No, of course not," I said, shaking my head emphatically to further prove my point. "I don't even know you."

The corner of his mouth quirked in a sly grin. "Well, when you've forgiven me for my outburst, we'll have to remedy that."

I was never going to forgive him for sentencing Halden to die. "So you aren't going to kill them, even after what Griffin said?"

"Not yet."

DINNER HOUR IN THE GREAT HALL WAS BOISTEROUS AND full of life, but I could barely look up from my stew of eggplant and bell peppers. Mari watched me carefully, as she had all day, until she couldn't take it anymore.

"All right, Arwen. Enough. What is going on with you?"

I laid my head down on the cool wood and made a guttural noise into the table.

"Sorry, I don't speak *miserable*. Talk to me."

I looked up at Mari. Her freckle-dusted face was stern, but underneath that I felt only empathy and warmth. I heaved a sigh. "It's kind of a lot."

Mari looked relieved. "I'm all ears."

I told Mari the entire saga. How maybe, despite my realizing it, I had developed a slight crush on the king. How much I had appreciated his wartime forum, and the respect I felt for his egalitarian process. How I was just starting to find my footing here, and with him, when Halden was captured. How much I despised him now, more than I ever had before. How Kane had agreed to spare his life for the time being. How I knew I had to help Halden escape before he changed his mind.

"There's no other way. He'll die here if I don't help him get out somehow."

Mari chewed her food slowly, processing. "The king hasn't been seen with any women in weeks. It's all over the castle. I wonder if that's because of you."

"Yeah, right," I chided. "I haven't heard any such thing."

"Yeah, because you don't talk to anyone but me. I'm telling you: there is no shortage of beautiful women around here who would love to be the queen of Onyx. Or just to sleep with him. They have been throwing themselves at him ever since he arrived at the keep. His reputation was well-known, and they are very disappointed."

I tried with every cell in my body to feel nothing at all.

"Well, that's not the point, Mar. Forget Kane. What about Halden?"

Mari rolled her eyes. "Didn't I say the king's wartime tactics weren't foolproof? Now his own subject"—she pointed at herself with theatrical flair—"is going to help commit treason to save a boy's life. We'll get him out. Don't worry about it."

I raised a brow. "Please, do share."

She gave me a classic Mari look, equal parts coolly self-assured and itching with excitement. "I was actually dying to tell you this all day, but you were in a funk. I was waiting until I could get the full range of Arwen excitement. The night before the eclipse, King Eryx of Peridot is coming here with his daughter. King Ravenwood is throwing a banquet for their arrival. There will be food, wine, liquor—everyone will be caught up in the revelry, if not completely smashed!"

I must have been missing something. Mari watched me eagerly, waiting for my "full range of excitement" to kick in. When it didn't, she continued impatiently. "Everyone, including most of the dungeon guards! We never have festivals or celebrations out here in the middle of the woods. They will be preoccupied and Halden can make his escape."

I shot her a stern glance and looked around to make sure nobody in the great hall had heard us, but the rowdy dinner crowd kept the long tables nearby at a high decibel.

"Whoops," she said sheepishly.

"Now I just have to figure out how to tell Halden."

"I think I can help with that, too."

"Mari, you're a lifesaver."

"Quite literally, huh?" She laughed, but I didn't have high enough hopes yet to join her.

16

THE ENTIRE CASTLE HAD FELT ON EDGE LATELY—SERVANTS rushing and whispering, soldiers even more brutish and poised for a fight than before. I had hoped it was only due to the pressure to prepare for the upcoming festivities. I tried not to worry that something more foreboding was afoot.

It wasn't like I could ask Kane what was going on—I had decided, with Mari's encouragement, to let go of all my complicated feelings for the king. He was a charming, powerful man, with a good sense of humor and a killer crooked grin, but was also a hothead, a manipulator, and a liar, with no sense of morality or compassion. Not a fair trade in my book.

But my heart hadn't quite agreed to the new arrangement yet, so I was avoiding him—to the point of ducking behind columns whenever he stalked through the halls. Not the most mature way to carry myself, but I had bigger issues to deal with.

All that mattered was helping Halden.

I didn't think I could fake my way into the dungeons a second time, especially with Kane's eyes all over the castle, as he had said, so weeks went by with no clue as to how Halden was doing. Still, I was determined to help him escape; I couldn't sit around and wait for Kane to use him as a bargaining chip with King Gareth or kill him in another bout of jealous rage. Hopefully neither of which had happened already.

Mari had promised me she had a plan, but that she just needed a bit longer for it to work.

To take my mind off it all, I trained with my sword in the mornings, healed soldiers in the afternoons, and spent most evenings with Mari in the library. Summer had fully arrived, and with it I experienced my first real seasonal shift. Onyx's spring hadn't been too dissimilar from Amber's year-round chill, but summer here was like a bath of light and heat. With the soft, blustery winds and days that never seemed to grow dark came an abundance of bluebells and violets, which I had taken to stealing and keeping in glass vases in my bedroom. When they wilted, I was so unable to part with the spectacular blooms, I'd press them in my books until they were delicate, thin memories of the blossoms they once were. It wasn't too far off from how I was feeling about myself recently, as I wandered from apothecary to bed each day in a daze.

I was in desperate need of positive Arwen. Where had she gone?

As I folded bandages in the apothecary, the dim light of afternoon slipping behind the pine trees outside, I tried to play rose and thorn, as if my mother was here with me.

Rose: I was finally using an adult's sword, but still nothing like the one Dagan wielded.

Thorn—

The sound of grunts and boots scuffing against the apothecary floor had my eyes lifting up from the bandages and landing on a couple of armor-clad soldiers supporting a sweating, shivering man, paler than any person should be.

"Here." I motioned to the infirmary. "You can place him on the daybed."

"Thank you." The voice came from behind the men, like midnight. Quiet, soft, and pitch-black.

Bleeding Stones.

Kane stepped into the apothecary behind them. He was wearing a simple unbuttoned white shirt, his few silver rings, and black pants, and seductiveness dripped from him like rain down a window. Even after everything, I was so affected by his presence.

"What do you want? I have a patient to tend to." I hoped my breathy voice might be accredited to shock.

"You've been avoiding me."

I swore steam was curling out of my ears. "Could you be any more self-obsessed? This man is *dying*."

"Yes, and I'm here to help," he said. "Lance is one of my best soldiers."

Such an obnoxious liar. "Pretty despicable to use your own soldier's illness as justification to come bother me," I said as I followed the men into the infirmary.

The two soldiers looked anywhere but at us. Kane bristled, turning to them. "Leave us. *Now*."

They scurried out without hesitation, one even bumping into my herbs in his rush and knocking sage and poppy seeds all over the floor.

A wet, hacking, cough drew my attention away from the spilled jars.

Lance was not doing well.

He was shivering despite the blanket I had pulled atop him and sweating profusely. I would have thought it the flu or a fever, had I not noticed the two puncture wounds near his wrist, rusty with dried blood.

"What happened?"

"He was bitten. I believe the creature's venom is what's slowly killing him. Well, not that slowly, it seems."

"Always so compassionate." I scowled at him. "What bit him?"

Lance moaned incoherently, and Kane didn't take his eyes off the shuddering man. "Can't say for sure. Do you need to know in order to heal him?"

"It would help." I moved into the apothecary to look through the shelves of antivenom. "Funnel-web spider, stone goblin, horned ember snake . . . any of those?"

Kane followed me out, away from Lance's bedside. "It's not anything your ointments will work on. He needs you," he demanded, with uncharacteristic sincerity. "Your abilities."

"Fine." I scooted past him and back into the infirmary, before placing my palms on Lance's clammy face. He had started convulsing and twitching. Cranking the window open, I let the lilac-scented evening air waft into the room. I needed to work fast.

Ever since Dagan had shown me how to harness the atmosphere around me, I had been using it in small doses for particularly dire patients or overcrowded days. A soft wind breezed in like steam from a bubbling pot, and I redirected it into my palms, which in turn seeped power into Lance's head. It funneled through him, a potent tonic to his pain. He gasped as the air itself poured through him, purging the venom from his bones, lungs, and skin. Lance shuddered out a heaving exhale and weak color began to return to his wet cheeks.

I exhaled, breath coming out of me like a burst ball. It was getting easier and easier to use the elements around me, and I was never left craving quite the nap as before. I tucked the knit blanket around Lance's body as he drifted off.

"He should be all right now, but I'll stay here with him for a few hours to make sure."

"Nicely done, bird," Kane murmured.

"I didn't ask for your approval."

He chuckled as I placed a cold compress on Lance's head and poured a glass of water for when he awoke.

"I've been working on it," I admitted, as he left the infirmary to pace around the apothecary. "If you must know." I followed him out, twisting my fingers in my skirts, then restraining my restless hands behind my back.

He needed to leave.

"Well, I'm impressed," Kane said, eyes glinting. "And proud to have such a skilled healer in my own keep." He continued his slow perusal of the space, which was now awash in buttery candlelight spilling in from the hallway. It gleamed off his rings and in his slate eyes. He was always glowing.

"Don't you have something better to do?" I asked.

He lifted a brow. "You're going to be here all night watching poor Lance sleep. I'm just offering some company."

I scoffed. "I'm all right. Thanks, though."

He turned toward me, his eyes searing into mine. "Perhaps I just like to watch you squirm in my presence."

My brows knit together. I had no more bite left in me. "Why are you like this?" I asked, exasperation seeping into my voice.

Kane threw me a sideways grin. "You don't even want to scratch the surface of that question, bird."

He was probably right about that.

"Have you found my family?" I asked.

"Not yet," he said, strolling through the apothecary, opening and closing jars and drawers. "But I will."

"I don't believe you," I snapped.

He spun to me. "It's like searching for a needle in a haystack. Three needles actually . . . Give me some time."

I gritted my teeth, about to lay into him, when an awkward grumble erupted from my stomach. I pressed my hand into my dress to quiet it, but I had been in the apothecary all day and hadn't eaten since I'd had a peach that morning on my way in. My abdomen protested again, and I grimaced.

Kane raised a single curious brow in my direction and a slight tickle of embarrassment climbed up my neck.

"What?" I asked, feigning ignorance.

But he just walked toward the apothecary door and pulled it open, sending the wooden sign swinging.

"Barney," he called into the gallery, "can you send for Lady Arwen's supper to be brought to the apothecary?"

Oh, Stones.

The tickle of embarrassment had become an all out assault.

"Of course, Your Majesty." Barney's familiar, sweet voice echoed in from the hall.

Kane made to close the door, but stopped right before it shut, swinging it open once more. "And extra cloverbread," he said. "Two loaves. Thank you."

When he shut the door and spun back to me, he looked very pleased with himself.

"That was not necessary," I said, picking up the fallen herbs and throwing them in the waste bin.

"Sure it was. Someone has to take care of you if you won't."

I stared daggers at him. "Is that what you think you're doing? Taking care of me? By keeping me here against my will and threatening to murder my friends?"

His playful expression faded, replaced by something far colder. Far more frightening. I swallowed hard.

"That boy is not your friend."

I shook my head. I didn't want to have this conversation with him.

Not tonight.

Preferably, not ever.

He loosed a sigh and ran a beleaguered hand through his hair before turning and strolling casually around the apothecary. The sun had finally disappeared, and the room was beginning to become cloaked in a sleepy, evening darkness.

I fished through the drawer nearest to me for a match to light the room's lanterns.

Kane tapped the glass case in front of him and my eyes flashed to him.

"What's that?" he asked.

I flared my nostrils. "None of your business."

"Come on, it's so spindly. I'm fascinated."

I sighed. "It's a preserved jellyfish. They have healing enzymes embedded in their tissue, and the dried membrane can be used like a second skin over cuts and scrapes."

"I love to listen to you explain medicinal practices," he purred.

"And I'd love to listen to you fall off a cliff."

He visibly shook, suppressing a laugh.

The man was infuriating. Coming in here, irritating me, trying to bribe me with food.

Speaking ill of Halden after everything.

Halden and his men wouldn't have been in his vault in the first place had he not attacked the Kingdom of Amber. I rubbed my temples. All I wanted were some damn answers.

"Why did you attack Amber?" I said, stepping around the counter and closer to him. "Give me *something*."

"I've told you," he said, eyes still on the jellyfish. "Gareth is a weasel and doesn't deserve to rule his own kingdom."

"That's not a reason to murder thousands in a war, and you know it."

His gaze hardened but still never left the glass case. "It's all I can tell you."

The roaring in my ears was so loud I could barely hear myself say, "Then get out of my apothecary."

"Arwen," he said, eyes finally meeting mine. "As charmed as I am by your fire, you're going to have to forgive me eventually."

I gritted my teeth. "No, I really, *really* won't."

He prowled closer to me, and I could almost feel him. Touch him. Smell him. His brows knitted together. "I can't stomach you hating me forever." His gaze was unflinching.

I couldn't help my response. "Well, you should have thought of that before you sentenced Halden to die."

Something predatory flickered in his eyes before he clenched his jaw and placed his hands in his pockets.

"Fine. Have it your way."

"Is that a threat?" I couldn't help the fear that crept into my voice.

He glared at me until finally, he sighed, resigned. "If it was, you'd know it. Have a nice evening."

17

DESPITE MY LOVE FOR THE WARM, FRAGRANT EVENING breeze I had come to know as summer wind, it wasn't doing much to calm my nerves. I had finally gotten Mari to share her "plan," which turned out to be a complex spell she needed to get just right.

Today she was ready to give it a try.

"All right. One more time, please," I said, voice low, twisting my sweaty hands in my skirts. We were hidden behind a hedge by the dungeon stairs, where we had agreed to meet.

"Calm down. I've practiced over and over. It's second nature now." Mari sounded confident, and I wanted to believe her. She had been working on the spell for weeks and was delighted when she was able to use it successfully on a squirrel. He hadn't been able to see a walnut right in front of him for hours.

She clutched at the violet amulet. "It's a simple cloaking spell. I'll perform it on the guard and, to him, you'll be invisible for a little while."

"How long is 'a little while'?"

Mari stared straight ahead, raising her head high. "I don't know."

"What!"

"Shh!" she hissed. "It's fine! How long could it take for you to get in and out? And I'll be here waiting for you."

"Mar," I tried. "You know it's all right if you aren't perfect at this the very first time. We can always try something else."

She gave me a look that said, *Don't you dare*, so I nodded, but couldn't stop shifting beside her.

"Stand still or I'll be too distracted to get this right." Mari closed her eyes and brought her hands out in front of her as if she could touch the guard in the distance. She hummed a low tune and whispered words in a primeval language I couldn't understand. The tall grass at her feet began to rustle in the sudden wind, a wind that smelled of rain and earth, despite the sunny day. A few of her long hairs gradually rose around her, encircling her in red strands that mimicked flames. Her knuckles cracked as she clenched her outstretched fingers.

And then she stopped.

She blinked her eyes open, looking a bit disoriented. She reached a hand out to hold on to me and I grasped her tightly. "Are you all right?"

She stared at me, dazed. "Who are you?"

My heart dropped into my stomach.

A wide smile grew on her face. "Kidding!"

I let out a breath that was almost a laugh. *Almost.* "You're the worst."

"Go on," she said.

I hurried toward the bearded guard, never succumbing to a run, which might have appeared suspicious to anyone else who could actually see me.

The guard was about my age. Ruddy pink cheeks, scruffy blond beard and brows. When I stood before him, an eerie sensation licked down my neck. He looked into my eyes and yet saw right through me. I waved a tentative hand in his face, but he just rubbed his nose in boredom and continued to stand watch. I wasn't going to stick around to count on my luck.

Sneaking past him, I ran through the dark spiral once more. I had the fleeting thought that if I was truly lucky, this would be the last time I ever had to come down here.

I rapped the bars on Halden's cell. "Pst! Halden!" He was asleep under the fur that I had brought him, curled up in a dark corner like a wounded animal, his white-blond hair now almost gray with dirt and soot.

"You made it back," he said, voice coated in sleep. He sounded almost reverent.

"Yes, but I have to be quick." I passed him some more food I had smuggled. "In one week, the night before the eclipse, there will be a banquet at sundown. That will be the best time for you to attempt your escape."

Halden nodded. "Who's the banquet for?"

"King Eryx of Peridot. I'd assume they're trying to make an alliance."

He bit at his nail and spat the clipping to the left. It was a nasty habit I somehow used to find attractive.

"Have you met any halflings here at Shadowhold?"

My brow creased. Halden believed in Fae now? And their descendants?

"What? Not that I know of." Though now that I thought of it, some of the soldiers I had healed or passed by had seemed so powerful and so menacing . . . But it wasn't worth sharing that with Halden. "I don't even know how to tell a halfling from a mortal."

Halden sighed, sitting back on his heels. "You can't really. It's hard to know without researching a person's ancestry. They say Onyx is filled with them."

"Why do you ask?"

He gave me a half grin. "Morbid curiosity, I guess. Has the king said anything to you about something he is looking for? A relic of some kind?"

Unease dipped in my belly. "Halden, why are you grilling me? You know I would tell you anything that could help you escape."

"Of course. Just another tall tale I was told by some soldiers in my battalion. Too much empty time to think down here is all."

My mind flashed to the night I had heard Kane talking with Griffin about the seer, about whatever he had been searching for. It felt like a lifetime ago. Could that be the same thing Halden was talking about?

"Since when do you care about Onyx and their secrets? You were more reluctant to serve than anyone else in Abbington."

I recalled my displeasure, well over two years ago, when he had cared so little about fighting the wicked kingdom in the north. How his apathy had made me feel irritated and alone.

How much things had changed, in so little time.

He shook his head. "I was a child then, Arwen. I've learned more about King Gareth since, of what he fights for. There's just a lot you wouldn't understand."

I was so, so sick of men that I was romantically interested in saying that to me. I made a face.

"And what about you? You don't care about our kingdom anymore?"

"No, of course I do," I said, my face growing hot. "I care about the people who are dying because of senseless greed for land and coin."

"I don't want to argue. The night of the banquet—where will I find you?" Halden asked.

It was the question I was dreading. It would be the night before the eclipse. When I needed to make it back into the woods for the burrowroot. And, truthfully, I wasn't sure if I was any more likely to reach my family if I fled with Halden.

"The king is trying to track down my family. If he finds them, and I'm gone . . ." I wasn't sure how to finish that thought. Would Kane harm them out of anger?

"I can protect you, Arwen. King Gareth's spies are just as good if not better than Onyx's. We can find your family together."

Some part of me still softened at his comforting words. His self-assured smile, even behind bars. "How are you going to get out of your cell? Even if most of the guards are caught up in the revelry, how will you get through the woods?"

Halden snorted. "The woods aren't as dangerous as I'm sure they've led you to believe. Just trust me. The night of the feast, when you hear an explosion, you'll have a few minutes to get to the North Gate. Can you do that?"

But shock had my heart rattling in my chest, making it hard to respond.

"An *explosion*? What in the Stones are you planning?"

"The less you know, the better," he said with sincerity.

"I need more than that. You cannot hurt the people of this castle. They are innocents."

He shook his head. "Of course not. Is that really what you think of me?"

I didn't know how to answer that. Guilt seeped in like red wine on a white dress—sticky and spreading and impossible to ignore.

Halden exhaled, and bit at his thumbnail again. "One of my men is a warlock. He can blow these cell doors open anytime. The explosion will free a path for us out of here and barely rattle the great hall above us." He gestured upward. "But even then, we'd never make it past the soldiers that guard the North Gate. The night of the banquet they'll be underprepared and overwhelmed with people. It's our best shot. I promise, nobody will get hurt."

It seemed like a fine plan. Not foolproof, but the best they could do on such short notice.

"I have to go. I don't have much time." I stood to leave but Halden grabbed my hand through the bars.

"Wait." He pulled me so I was pressed into the railing, and his rough hands enclosed my own through the bars. "Do you remember when we watched those shooting stars on the roof of the Tipsy Boar?"

I pictured the chilly night, bundled up in his arms atop the local tavern. He had seen the stars falling and wanted a better view. Somehow, he had convinced me to climb up there with him. I was sure at any moment the whole structure would crumble under our weight and we would land in a heap of ale and glass.

"Of course," I said.

His russet eyes had gone heavy-lidded and seeped in lust. "And do you remember what we did when the last star had faded from the sky?" His voice took on a huskier tone, and my cheeks warmed.

"Of course," I repeated.

"I think of that night constantly . . . Just in case something goes wrong, I'd never forgive myself for not kissing you one last time."

Before I could register his intent, Halden pulled me toward him until the cool iron pressed against the sides of my face, and his warm lips brushed mine. It was a tentative kiss. Safe and familiar. I had missed him so terribly after he left, and fantasized of a moment like this—well, without the dungeon element. But now . . . I couldn't place the feeling exactly. It was soothing to be so close to him again. My toes still curled at his touch. But something was missing.

He pulled away, his gaze holding mine, and squeezed my hands tightly. "You'll meet me there, at the North Gate?"

Would I?

Halden could help me find the burrowroot in the woods, more likely than I could ever find it alone. He cared about me, and always would. And I couldn't stay here another minute with Kane after who he had revealed himself to be, time and time again. I doubted he ever really planned to find my family for me. He was a liar, and always had been, so what kind of future did I have here in Shadowhold? It was safer to stick with the man I knew than the king I didn't.

"Yes," I finally answered. "Good luck."

I made my way up the stairs two at a time and exhaled a breath I wasn't even aware I was holding when the guard from earlier was still standing watch. I breezed past him and didn't slow until Mari and I had made it all the way back into the apothecary.

~⚬~

THE SLICE OF THE SWORD SAILING THROUGH THE AIR NEXT to my head was a little too close for comfort.

"Watch it!" I said, dodging just in time.

Dagan continued his attack, coming at me with a ferocity I hadn't seen from him before. But I wasn't afraid. I parried each blow and used my size and agility to my benefit. Dagan was older, taller, and slower than me. Which meant I could be scrappy and move around him with ease. With a second to spare, I caught my breath and swung at him, nipping his leather armor.

He paused to study the nick, wiping sweat from his brow. A smile played on his lips, but he said nothing. I wanted terribly to gloat or jump in the air at my slight victory, but overexertion forced me to brace my hands on my knees and catch my breath instead.

"Last lesson for the day," he said.

Thank the Stones. It was only morning, but the week had flown by, and I had too much to do before the banquet tonight. Dagan unstrapped his outer armor, dropping it on the grass unceremoniously. He sat down and motioned for me to sit across from him. The grass was cool on my palms, and I inhaled the scent of blossoming gardenia. There was so much I took for granted about these mornings out here. Now that this was my last one, I realized I would miss it quite terribly.

"What are we doing?" I asked.

"Using a different kind of weapon. Close your eyes."

I did as I was told. I had learned not to question Dagan. When it came to self-defense, the man knew what he was talking about.

"Think of your greatest strength. Tell me what you feel."

My brows knitted together. My greatest strength? Nothing really came to mind. I was proud of my ability to heal people, but it wasn't as much a strength as an ability. A gift, maybe. I felt strong when I ran, but did that qualify as a strength? I had never thought of it as such. My family came to mind—how taking care of them made me feel strong. But I had never been as good at it as Ryder had.

"I can't think of anything," I admitted. It was more shameful than I cared to admit.

"That's not what I asked. What do you *feel*?"

I sat stubbornly still. Something about having my eyes closed brought emotions I wasn't aware of to the surface. "Sad. And alone. Which makes me feel afraid."

"Stay with that feeling. What does the fear make you feel?"

I sighed. "Trapped. Sometimes it's just hard. To wake up each day knowing how much of my life will be ruled by it, by being afraid."

"That feeling you have when your heart is racing, chest is tight, mouth is dry. Do you know what that is?"

I nodded. "Terror."

"No, Arwen. It is power."

I was trying to follow his guidance, but it didn't really make any sense.

"Dagan, I don't think this is working. Whatever this is. Can we stop for today?" I peeked one eye open.

His words were instantaneous. "Eyes closed."

"How—?"

"Eyes. Closed."

The wind was howling through the trees in our training field. With my eyes shut, the noises of the keep preparing for tonight were heightened—carts being loaded and furniture being moved in the distance.

"When you are afraid," Dagan continued, "your body fuels you to run or to fight. Filling you with the power to protect yourself, one way or another. You are an excellent runner. Now you are becoming an excellent fighter as well. I cannot say those feelings of fear will ever dissipate. But you can harness them. Make them work for you. Turn that fear into courage. After all, they are one and the same."

There was some truth to his words. The panic attacks I suffered, medically speaking, were just a torrential influx of adrenaline. But when I was ensnared by them, it was nearly debilitating. Very hard to see that as some kind of untapped power.

I sat in silence as instructed until my back ached and my tailbone went numb. When whatever Dagan hoped for hadn't happened, he stopped us.

"We'll try again tomorrow."

I pushed myself up with a groan. "Somehow I think I'll miss the sword fighting." It didn't come out playful like I'd hoped.

Dagan considered me.

"Who do you think is more courageous when charging into battle? The knight who has nothing to fear, surrounded by hundreds of his fellow men, armed with all the weapons on the continent, or the lone knight, with no one beside him, nothing but his fists, and everything to lose?"

For reasons that I couldn't comprehend, the question made me feel like crying. "The latter."

"Why?" he asked.

"Because he knows he can't win, and he chooses to fight anyway."

"There is only true courage in facing what frightens you. What you call fear is indeed power, and you can wield it for good."

I looked down, deflecting his searching gaze.

I felt doomed to fail him. Whatever he hoped was within me, I was sure it was not.

"You remind me of . . . I would have been very proud to see my daughter grow up like you, Arwen."

For a moment I was speechless. It was the kindest thing I'd ever heard him say. It was maybe the kindest thing anyone besides my own mother had ever said to me.

"What happened to her?" I asked tentatively. I wasn't sure I wanted to know.

Dagan bent down to pick up the swords and wrap them in their coverings. "My wife and infant daughter were killed by the very man that Kane wages war against." I staggered back at the horror of his words. "That grief, that anger. I find a way to harness it each morning to face the day, and each night to go to sleep. We all have demons. What defines us is how we choose to face them."

My heart twisted and cracked inside of me.

"I am so sorry." It was all I could find.

"Thank you." He nodded to me, and we headed back to the keep in our usual silence.

I felt sick to my stomach. For Dagan, and for the fact that I was planning to leave tonight, and possibly to return to the kingdom responsible for his loss? All of it suddenly felt very wrong.

18

THE REFLECTION STARING BACK AT ME IN THE GILDED mirror barely resembled my face. I had never seen so much charcoal in my life—Mari had painted my eyes with the smoky mixture and my lips a dark scarlet.

"That's enough. Honestly, Mar. I look like a pirate. Or a lady of the night."

"Or both! A beautiful pirate whore," Mari said, dusting more dark powder onto my eyelids.

The look wasn't helped by the off-the-shoulder night-black gown she had squeezed me into.

"This is so unfair. Why can't I wear something like you?"

"Because," Mari said, twirling in her high-necked pine dress, "I'm not seeing an ex-lover tonight."

"He's not an ex-lover by any stretch of the imagination. He's the king, and I doubt we'll even see each other."

Mari ignored me and brushed my hair, letting chocolatey locks fall down my back, one section at a time.

"Tonight . . ." I started but didn't quite know how to finish the thought.

"I know." I couldn't see her face in the mirror, so I swiveled to look at her.

But I couldn't bring myself to say the words. I felt strangled by emotion I hadn't seen coming.

"I understand, Arwen," she said, taking my hand in hers. "If Halden can get out, you're going to go with him. I'm sure I'd do the same."

"Yes. But it's a big *if*."

"No, it's not. He doesn't want to die. He'll find a way out."

I felt tears sting my eyes.

"Oh, Arwen. Don't cry. He's going to be all right."

Guilt coursed through me—it wasn't Halden I was crying for. "I'm going to miss you."

Mari's eyes were like wet glass as she pulled me into a hug.

"Me, too."

She released me and wiped at my cheeks, clearing the blackened streaks that ran down my face. "But you'll find a way to write to me. I know we'll see each other again. Now let me fix this. *Sad* pirate whore is definitely not the look we are going for."

⊰✦⊱

THE GREAT HALL WAS ELEGANT AND CELEBRATORY TONIGHT, lit with candles of every shape and size and adorned with wreaths of Onyx flowers. Heat from the shadowy lanterns, the piping hot food, and the crowding of bodies all warmed my skin. A haunting tune from the harmony of four different string instruments reverberated through the hall, calling me to dance. Outside, the white, elegant horses of Peridot were stark next to Onyx's brutal, demonic-looking ones, as tanned, blond Peridot dignitaries and nobles dressed in sultry warm colors filtered in.

I had lost Mari a while ago. She and a librarian from Peridot had hidden in a corner, drunk on birchwine and analyzing some old Fae text. But I didn't mind walking through the festivities alone. Despite my earlier complaints, I felt rather pretty in my silk-draped gown and the way it hugged my curves, melting against my body like candle wax.

I grabbed a cup of wine and took a sip. The bitter taste was foreign to me—Amber wine was notoriously sweet and caramel colored. This drink was the color of currants and I instantly felt it in my bones after only two sips. I maneuvered my way past sweaty, joyful strangers and toward the dancing. I wasn't normally a reveler, but the level of anonymity at tonight's festivities gave me a sense of freedom I hadn't ever felt. Before I could throw myself into the merriment, something caught my eye. No—someone.

A woman so stunning it was arresting, lithe with milky white hair and a delicate crown of leaves, was laughing uproariously at a certain dark king.

Kane propped himself against the wall behind her with one outstretched arm, and grinned into his ale. Her laugh was like a peal of bells, light and melodic. As he continued whatever story he was telling, the mystery woman listened intently, her eyes following every word off his lips. After one particularly hilarious aside, she reached a delicate hand out to encircle his bicep, and I found my feet moving before my mind had a chance to follow.

"Good evening," I said, stumbling into them with a little too much gusto.

Kane appraised me, his eyes traveling down my body deliciously slowly. But it was the expression he held when he settled on my face that took my breath away.

"Arwen. You look . . . so beautiful."

We held each other's eyes a beat too long, a smile that was almost awe growing on his face.

But then Kane seemed to remember where he was, cleared his throat, and gestured to the woman next to him. "Arwen, this is Princess Amelia. Princess, this is Lady Arwen. She is our keep's healer."

Amelia. She was the princess of the Peridot Provinces, the luscious jungled peninsula that bordered Onyx, and the daughter of the banquet's guest of honor, King Eryx.

Shame colored my face.

"Your Highness." I curtsied.

The princess said nothing, but her narrowed eyes told me she didn't appreciate my interruption.

The three of us stood around limply until I couldn't stand the tension any longer. Clearly, I had interrupted a moment between them. Why had I rushed over here, anyway? To ruin Kane's night? Wasn't I the one who wished he would leave me be? Who planned to flee this very evening? The birchwine was making my head swim.

"Well. Enjoy the banquet! The mutton is excellent," I said, overly chipper. I winced as I turned to leave.

Kane's warm hand wrapped around my arm with ease as he pulled me back toward him. "Your Highness," he said to the princess, still grasping me tightly, "I must have a brief word with Lady Arwen. Can I come find you in a short while?"

"You'd better," she said, without much humor. She was as severe as she was stunning.

I gave her my best *don't look at me* shrug as Kane drew me away.

We crossed the great hall swiftly. When I realized he was pulling me away from the banquet, I struggled against him. "Where are you taking me? Let go. I won't bother you again, I want to stay and enjoy the dancing."

Kane was either ignoring me or couldn't hear my protests over the music and revelry. We exited the grand room through a hidden corridor, flew down tight stone steps, and slipped inside the nearby wine cellar.

Kane closed the heavy stone door behind him, shutting out the noise of the banquet and drowning us in silence. My ears felt like they were full of cotton.

The small space was musty and dry, filled to the brim with barrels of wine. There was little room for both him and me. Kane's impressive height didn't help. I felt small, both in stature and behavior.

"*Bleeding Stones*, Kane. This is ridiculous."

"You really do have a mouth like a sailor." He laughed, leaning against the door.

"Don't think about my mouth."

His eyes turned from playful to deadly in a heartbeat. "How I wish I could stop, bird."

I snorted. "You're incorrigible."

"And you're jealous." His smile was like a wolf's.

"That's ridiculous. You disgust me. I'm—" I paused, trying to gather myself. What was I? "I'm sorry I interrupted you and the princess. That was rude." I crossed my arms, and then quickly un-crossed them so as not to appear defensive.

His eyes gave nothing away. "We are at war. I am trying to so-lidify an ally. You think I'm just playing around? Do I strike you as a huge fan of banquets?"

I pressed my lips into a line. "Who knew political warfare could look so intimate?"

The corner of Kane's mouth turned up. "Aw, bird. Did you burn with rage at the thought of me with another woman?"

"Don't be silly. By all means, have at it. She's just a little young for you, don't you think?"

Kane actually looked offended. "How old do you think I am?"

"Never mind. It doesn't matter." I tried to push past him, but he blocked my path.

"Well, I should hope not. You have a man behind bars a few feet beneath us who believes you to be his wife."

"Of course. Halden. Thank you for sparing him."

"Of course," he mimicked, a gleam in his eyes. "I'm not such a cruel king after all."

"I really should get back. Mari will be—"

A shock wave radiated through my body, throwing me into Kane with brutal force. My chin snapped against his sternum and searing pain bloomed in my jaw. Kane wrapped his arms around me, cradling my body to his as the force knocked us to the floor.

Wine sloshed as barrels fell on each other, breaking apart. The faint roar of screaming echoed from the great hall above us, and I squeezed my eyes shut. The ground continued to shake.

"I've got you," Kane grunted, as wine barrels tipped off the shelves and landed on his back. Every muscle in my body was tight as a coil as I prayed for the shuddering to end.

Stop, stop, *stop*.

When the aftershocks subsided, Kane's face was inches from mine, the length of his body pressing down on me. It was overwhelming to feel him everywhere—muscular torso pressed to my breasts, our thighs intertwined, his corded arms protecting my head. And a strong hand still cradling my neck gently—ever so gently. Much, much too gently. At the first hitch of my breath, he disentangled from me with lightning speed.

My heart still pounding from the shock, I assessed the damage.

The wine cellar was decimated.

Dust and debris cluttered the shelves and floor, and we were both soaked in dark red. Kane's eyes lit with horror as he searched my body.

"Are you hurt?"

"No, it's just wine," I said. But I brought my hand to my mouth and felt where I had bitten through my lip in our collision.

He cradled my jaw with a gentleness that nearly made me pant. Using his thumb, he carefully pulled my lower lip down to inspect the wound. I felt my whole body flush from the intimacy of the touch.

"Ouch. Sorry, bird. Have some of this, it'll keep it clean." His thumb released my lip, and he reached for an unbroken bottle, dusted off the dirt, and handed it to me. I took a slow sip, holding his gaze.

He exhaled a shaky breath as he watched me drink deeply from the bottle and set it down beside me.

"What was that?" I asked, massaging my jaw.

But it hit me a moment too late. Halden's explosion. It had been much bigger than he had let on, whatever it was he did.

If anyone had been hurt because of this, I—

"Perhaps an earthquake." Kane stood up and pushed through the debris to reach the door. "Stay here. I'll send Barney for you."

Before I could argue he pushed at the door. But it didn't budge. My stomach sank in an instant.

"Kane."

My chest began to shudder. He pushed again, hard, using his whole frame. The muscles on his back rippled under his shirt; the cords in his neck bulged.

"Kane."

My palms were sweating. Heart racing. Kane let go, pushed the hair out of his face, and cracked his knuckles. Once more he heaved forward, but nothing happened.

"Kane!"

"What?" He swiveled. I was on my hands and knees, heaving for air. He rushed to me and placed a calming hand on my back. "Fuck. You're all right, little bird. Trust me. You can't die from fear alone. There's plenty of air in here."

He was saying the right things. All the things I had told myself a thousand times. That Nora had tried to walk me through, or my mother when I was young. But it made no difference now. My chest felt like it was caving in on itself. My whole body shook with adrenaline and my thoughts swam. I had to get out of here.

Now, now, *now.*

"I can't stay in here." I took in another huge gulp of air.

"Try to sit back," he said. I scrambled up and pushed myself against the wall, eyes squeezed shut.

"Good. Slow breaths now. In through your nose, out through your mouth."

This room had plenty of air. I was not going to be stuck forever.

I squeezed Kane's hand and fought the urge to breathe in by the mouthful.

"What a grip. Your training with Dagan must be going well."

I nodded, my eyes still screwed closed. "I'm so strong, I could strangle you."

Kane chuckled and the sound relaxed me more.

"You are strong. You're doing great." The words of encouragement brought tears to my eyes. "Tell me how you'd strangle me."

"What?" I said, my eyes snapping to his.

"You heard me. I want to know—help prepare me for the attack."

I knew what he was doing. But I needed the diversion.

"I'd make Griffin smile. Shock alone would be enough to distract you. Then I'd squeeze the life out of your thick neck."

Kane laughed hard—his addicting, hearty laugh.

I wanted to chew on it. Stuff it into my mouth so nobody else could have it.

"Keep going. This is my new favorite pastime. Death by bird."

I screwed my eyes shut and leaned back once more.

Breathe in, breathe out.

"Well, you'd be dead then. So I'd take over the Onyx Kingdom and rule with Barney at my side."

At his wheeze, I peered one eye open. Tears had gathered in the corners of his eyes. My lips perked up, too. His laugh was contagious.

One more slow inhale, and finally, the adrenaline abated. I was still on edge, but my heart rate had slowed and I could swallow again. I blew out a breath.

"Thank you."

He smiled that crooked smile at me, wiping tears from his eyes.

"No, thank *you*." Slowly he rubbed circles along my palm with his thumb. The sensation was meant to calm me, but I only felt liquid heat course through my veins from the slight contact. I pulled my hand from his.

"Don't worry, bird. We won't be in here long. They'll be looking for us. Someone has to notice the king is missing eventually."

Resting my forehead on up-tucked knees, I shuddered out an exhale. I heard him stand and peered up to see Kane chugging from a birchwine bottle. The long column of his throat glistened with sweat in the dim cellar lighting as he drank. He took a final swig and pointed the bottle in my direction.

"Can I offer you a drink?"

"You really can't get that door open?"

He took a seat next to me, passing the wine. A flicker of worry passed over his expression, there and gone in an instant. "I'm afraid not."

The liquid was bitter and heavy on my tongue. I drank and drank, hoping the spirit would relieve even a little of the tension coiled in my body. The guilt that had crept in once again for having fun with him. Even if I was trying to suppress sheer, unrelenting panic.

"All right, that's enough." Kane motioned for the wine. I continued to sip until it was empty. I was going to need all the help I could get, stuck in here with him.

"Let's try another form of distraction," Kane said, prying the bottle from my hands.

My body quickly felt the effects of the spirit, loosening and thrumming with a subtle buzz. I looked over at Kane, for what felt like the first time since we were trapped in here. His dark hair was pushed out of his face, damp from sweat and possibly spilled wine.

His crown was slightly askew. Before I knew what I was doing, I reached up and carefully set it straight on his head. His remarkable quicksilver eyes studied my face. I drew my hand back and let it fall lifelessly into my lap.

"Want to lecture me on all I don't understand about the continent and how pathetic I am?"

"Don't sell yourself so short, bird. I'm never trying to insult you. You have no idea how exceptional I think you are."

I snorted. "What a line. Trust me, there's nothing special about me."

He cleared his throat and looked up at the ceiling as if he were asking some unknown entity to grant him strength. He, too, must have been miserable about our predicament.

"What did you actually have in mind? For a distraction?" I asked.

"I'm not sure. What do you and your pretty redhead friend do for fun?"

A genuine laugh burst out of me, and I wasn't even sure why. I reached for a second bottle above my head and yanked it open.

"What is so funny?" Kane asked. "Besides you guzzling through the castle's most expensive wine as if it were water."

I laughed harder and took another mouthful. "I don't know." I giggled. "I think it's funny that you don't know how to have fun."

Kane looked at me in pretend outrage. It was painfully adorable. "Using my pond confession against me, it seems. I used to have loads of fun. I was sort of known for it, actually."

I snorted. "Yeah, that's not the kind of 'fun' Mari and I have."

"That is devastating news."

For some reason, I could not keep it together. I doubled over laughing. "Keep it in your trousers, Kane. You're not her type."

"I'm everyone's type."

I faked a dry heave, and this time Kane was the one to laugh. The noise was a deep rumble from his chest, and a smile glowed in his eyes.

"I know. It's the worst," I said.

"Ah. My poor jealous bird. I told you, I'm not interested in the princess anymore."

I shook my head. He had it all wrong—I wasn't talking about her. I was talking about m—

Then my brain stopped working.

"Anymore?" I asked, barely keeping the horror at bay.

He grimaced. "We have spent some time together. Intimately. Many years ago."

I gasped like I was in a bad theater production, and Kane laughed harder. I tried to laugh with him, but the image of them together made me want to set myself on fire. Her long, white hair threaded through his strong hands. His grunts of pleasure as he buried himself between her—

"Arwen—" Mercifully, he interrupted my revolting train of thought. "It was nothing. I had no feelings for her."

"Oh, so you used her?"

He threw his head backward, smacking into the wine barrels behind us and wincing.

"Always so difficult. It was mutual. An agreement between old friends. It was . . . before."

"Before what?" I asked, guarded hope lilting my words.

His eyes narrowed on my lips, but he didn't answer.

For a moment all I heard was the steady drip of spilled wine falling on the stone floor.

"You don't have much of a right to be jealous anyway," he

finally said, finishing off the next bottle. "Seeing as you're still so hung up on that human filth in the cells beneath us."

The thought of Halden killed my happy buzz almost immediately.

I looked down at my hands. "I don't think he's below us anymore."

"Not an earthquake, then?"

I shook my head.

"And you knew?"

I couldn't bear to look up and see his rage at my betrayal. I didn't say anything.

"Well, I hope for your sake he escaped. If my men caught him, he won't live to see daybreak."

I turned my face farther away from Kane, so he couldn't see my expression. It would give away the pain that I felt at the thought of Halden's death.

"What did they want? In the vault?" I asked.

"Something that hasn't been there for a long while."

Kane stood and began to pace in the small space. He reminded me of a caged beast, hackles raised and power rippling off him. The musty cellar with its low ceiling was too small to hold all of him in.

He cursed under his breath and turned to me. "I have to leave tomorrow. I'll be back as quickly as I can. But, Arwen, don't go chasing after him while I'm gone." He knelt down. "There is evil lurking beyond these walls, waiting for you to make a single misstep."

I turned his plea over in my mind. I had heard these warnings before, but Halden's voice echoed in my ears. *The woods aren't as dangerous as I'm sure they've led you to believe.*

He could tell I didn't believe him. I could see it in his eyes. He looked like he was on the precipice of an enormously difficult decision.

"I have to explain something to you."

I wanted to urge him to continue—I'd kill for answers—but felt at any moment he might change his mind.

"Arwen." He paused, running his hands through his hair in exasperation. "He's a murderer."

19

A SICKENING SHIVER KISSED DOWN MY SPINE.
What was he talking about? I shook my head. "No, you're a murderer."

Kane looked around in exasperation. "Perhaps so, but I do not make a habit of killing innocents in cold blood."

My body went rigid. "Neither does Halden."

"He was an assassin for the Amber king. He—"

"I'm sure you have assassins." I could hear my voice rising in pitch.

Kane's face hardened.

I remembered what sheer power he possessed and felt myself shrink backward.

"What is your obsession with comparing us? I'm not claiming to be anything I am not." When I didn't respond, he softened, but his tone was still bitter. "Your precious King Gareth sent Halden's unit into Onyx to kill Fae."

My entire body seized. I couldn't move—couldn't breathe. I pressed my hands against the cool stone floor to ground myself.

"I didn't tell you because it is a burden to understand what is truly at stake. I didn't wish to hurt you. But watching you pine over the spineless twit is making me . . . aggravated."

The room wouldn't stay still. My heart spun in my chest.

"So they're . . ." I swallowed a lump in my throat. "They're real?"

"How much do you know of them . . . the Fae?"

"Not much," I admitted, still reeling. "Ancient, violent creatures. Very scary, very old, very dead."

"Centuries ago, there was an entire realm of them. Mortals, too. But the Fae were a dying breed and eventually their king was the last true Fae that lived."

I had gone completely rigid. My eyes felt as wide as the sea, and I tried to get a handle on my breathing and my swimming thoughts. The wine was really not helping.

"What does that mean? 'True Fae'?"

"He was full-blooded. No mortal heritage. But he was the last one. Even his children weren't full-blooded, since his queen's grandmother had been a witch. The land they inhabited, the Fae Realm, was growing bare of resources. Fae children were rare, but mortals were fertile, and the more mortal children born into the realm, the more mouths to feed, homes to build, and wars to fight.

"The realm functioned on a unique Fae power, called lighte, which every Fae was born with. It could be bottled and sold, used to fuel anything. It could heal, build, destroy. But it came to them from deep within the Fae land, and it wasn't infinite. That's why Faeries aren't born here in Evendell.

"With fewer Fae, lighte grew rarer and even more valuable. Soon, the realm couldn't support the influx of people, turning the once magical world into a barren wasteland. Ash rained from the sky; lush green meadows turned to cracked, dry earth. Earthquakes, fire rain, and the birth of demons that thrived in such conditions plagued the realm. The people starved and suffered. They begged the Fae king, Lazarus, to be kinder to the realm, to ration the lighte, to find other resources, but he refused."

"How do I not know any of this?" The story was like an old cautionary tale. I thought better of my question. "Or, how do scholars and bookworms like Mari not know any of this?"

"Only high-ranking nobles and royalty from Onyx know the truth. And you." Warmth flashed across his face. My heart fluttered.

"Why only Onyx?" I asked.

"When refugees from the realm began to make their way over to Evendell, Onyx was the closest kingdom. Some traveled instantly with lighte or witch magic. Others braced themselves for the long and treacherous journey across forbidden lands and seas. Few survived. When Lazarus realized his subjects were leaving, he built a wall to keep his people in. He convinced them it kept them safe from all those who wished to steal their lighte.

"A seer, a type of Fae whose power draws visions from the future, was pulled from slumber one night to deliver a prophecy."

The seer was *Fae* . . . and the prophecy Kane had referenced all those months ago had been about the Fae king. But what did that have to do with him? Or Halden?

"A small but powerful group used her foresight to lead a rebellion to save the realm, but it failed." He clenched his jaw. "Thousands died. In their retreat, a mere hundred Fae got out and came here to Onyx, to start fresh. Which is why there are still Fae and halflings in the kingdom to this day."

Horror at his words made my heart rattle in my chest.

"How did they get out?" I asked.

His eyes had turned sorrowful. "At enormous personal cost."

My mind was reeling. All along, the Fae had been real. And some even lived here, today, in Onyx.

I shook my head, unable to find adequate words for my shock.

"I have about a hundred questions," I said, staring at the barrels of wine in front of me. Kane's answering smirk said, *What a surprise.*

"But what does this history lesson have to do with Halden?"

His pupils flared. "About three years ago, my spies informed me that King Gareth had struck a deal with King Lazarus."

Icy dread slunk down my spine.

"He's still alive?"

"Any Fae that are more than half-blooded can live for a very long time. Lazarus is probably encroaching on a millennium. He promised Gareth and his highest dignitaries untold power, riches, and lighte in return for fresh land devoid of people."

"How . . . ?" I didn't know how to finish the sentence. Unimaginable horror washed over me. I reached for another bottle of birchwine.

"Lazarus will have no problem turning an entire mortal kingdom to ash if it means a fresh start for the Fae left in his kingdom," said Kane, watching a stream of spilled wine slowly crawl across the dusty cellar floor.

"So, he destroyed his world with greed and now that it can no longer serve him, he wants to take ours?"

Kane's jaw clenched. "Exactly. I tried to convince Gareth that he couldn't trust Lazarus, that I could give him any riches he desired. But the imbecile wouldn't be swayed. Now, Lazarus and Gareth are gathering more allies to wage war on Evendell."

"I still don't understand why Gareth and Lazarus would want the Fae murdered. Aren't those Lazarus's people? His subjects?"

Kane heaved a heavy sigh. "They're his *defectors*. Any Fae here in Onyx or otherwise are living proof of those that escaped his realm." Kane rubbed his jaw in thought. "He's a very vengeful king. Likely makes everything you once thought about me look like child's play."

Guilt bubbled up inside me.

"Is that why Onyx attacked Amber? Those with Fae blood live in your kingdom, and Gareth was murdering them?" Hadn't Halden said something like that? My mind was like tangled bedsheets. I couldn't believe Halden had lied to me. I wanted to punch him in the face.

"In part. It's more complicated than that."

It always was. "Why are you here, then? And not in Willowridge, protecting your people?"

Kane ran a hand down his face, clearly regretting his decision to share anything with me. "The Fae king wants me. Even more than the defectors. I'm keeping my city safe by staying here, in the stronghold. Away from them."

Fear that I never expected crept into my soul. Fear of my own King Gareth, of what might happen if his army took the castle. "Are we safe here?"

"For now. Unless the half-wit tells Gareth I'm here."

It wasn't the most comforting answer.

"Great," I said, my voice dripping with sarcasm. "I helped set free a murderer who has been killing innocents, and I get the pleasure of being a prisoner in a castle that is doomed to fall any day now to a vicious Fae king because of it. I'm on quite the roll."

Kane scoffed. "We both know you haven't been a prisoner here in a long time. Yet you stay."

The too-familiar stab of guilt bloomed in my chest once more. I shouldn't tell him.

I didn't *have* to tell him anything.

But still—the words pressed on my tongue, as he beheld me with soft curiosity.

No. He had kept so much from me, I didn't owe him anything. Why did I feel the need to—

"I was going to leave," I blurted. "Tonight." *Damned wine.*

Kane's expression was unreadable.

"But I ended up stuck in here, so Halden's likely gone without me." I wouldn't have known Kane's fury had I not glanced at his hands. His knuckles were rigid and white along his fists as he clenched and unclenched his palms. "I don't understand why it matters to you. I'm not your property."

"I know that." He sounded exasperated.

"And I'm grateful that you are trying to find my family, and I'm not as miserable here as a healer as I thought I would be, but you have to understand. Halden was like family. I had to leave with him if I had a chance."

"I know."

"And had I just—"

"Arwen." He turned to face me, his expression one of frustration more than rage. "I am not angry that you planned to leave. I am angry that the imbecile left you behind."

Now I was completely confused. And it was not the wine's fault.

"What? You wanted me to leave with a Faerie murderer?"

Kane's mouth quirked slightly. "No," he said, trying for patience. "Never mind."

I shook my head.

He was upset about . . . my honor.

I almost laughed.

After everything, he hadn't really been a monster. Not at all.

"So all the things I thought of you—that the entire continent thought, the war you waged—it was all to fight this Fae king?"

"Well," he said ruefully, a slight grin working its way onto his face, "don't chalk it all up to virtue. I am still a bit of a prick."

I couldn't even muster a smile at his words. I was still trying to put all the pieces together in my mind.

The Fae, the upcoming war, the even *more* wicked king. The prophecy . . .

I recalled the words that had kept me up so many nights here in Shadowhold.

"You know the seer's words as well as I do. Time is running out. We have less than a year."

"What did the prophecy foretell?"

"That is a conversation for another day." His tired gaze raked down the column of my throat. "A more sober day."

I nodded. It was enough information—I wasn't sure I could take any more.

He finished the next bottle of birchwine and lay back against the wall beside me, closing his eyes. After long minutes passed like water droplets sliding off a sweating glass, my mind spinning with knowledge of all that I had misunderstood, I couldn't stand the silence anymore.

"Have we been in here for a hundred years?" I asked, watching him rest. His face was magnificent. As if it had been carved by the Stones themselves.

I wondered if he felt any relief in sharing so much with me, or if that intimacy had scared him. Made him feel weak, as he had once feared.

"Yes," he said, eyes still closed. "Why are you staring at me?"

I looked away instantly. "I'm not."

"It's only fair. I've stared at you. Most of the time, I can't seem to look at anything else."

I turned to face him again and found him looking right at me, just as he said. Like this, our faces were far too close together. I needed to pull away but felt inexplicably tied to his gaze. His restless eyes studied mine, slate gray on olive green, and my heart hammered in my chest.

His hand made its way to my face, carefully, as if not to spook me. He brushed a thumb against my cheek, and I let out an involuntary hum.

Kane's expression shifted. I knew it was need in his eyes, and that they reflected the need in my own. I couldn't deny it a minute longer. The attraction I felt for him was like a dull ache that never left me. I licked my bottom lip, in hopes of conveying exactly what I wanted. Had I been a little braver—or had one more swig of wine—I might have just taken it for myself. But there was something about him that was still frightening, only maybe now for different reasons.

He watched as my tongue caressed my bottom lip, and his hand laced through my hair, cupping the side of my face. Tightening just enough to make my toes curl. I must have whimpered, because he pulled himself closer to me until I could feel the heat of his breath on my mouth. He smelled like wine, leather, and mint. I closed my eyes and leaned into his touch.

"Oh, for fuck's sake." An exasperated male voice came from the doorway, which had been wrenched open.

I jumped about a foot in the air and scrambled away from Kane, who stayed perfectly still on the floor. Griffin and a handful of soldiers and guards crowded the doorway.

"Commander." Kane greeted him casually. "It's about time."

─────── ✦ ───────

AFTER WE HAD LEFT THE WINE CELLAR, KANE SENT ME TO the infirmary while he and Griffin surveyed the damage. Thankfully, very few had been harmed in the explosion. I tended to a few concussed Peridot and Onyx revelers, and two prison guards who had taken the brunt of the burns from Halden's explosion. It may not have been my finest work, as I was still fairly sloshed, but thankfully my healing abilities were second nature. I hadn't gotten back to my room until the wee hours of the morning.

My feet ached as I opened the door to my quarters.

I felt his presence in the dimly lit bedroom instantly. Kane was lying on my bed, one hand behind his head—the picture of comfort.

"If I had a sack of coin for every time I found you somewhere you shouldn't be, I would be a very rich healer."

A laugh breezed out of him. "How was the infirmary?"

I slipped my shoes off, feet aching, and climbed into bed beside him in all my clothes.

"Exhausting. And I may have operated on some soldiers a little smashed. But they're tough. Who needs all five fingers anyway?"

He stared at me in shock until a laugh burst out of me. "Kidding. Everyone seems to be fine, if a little shaken up."

Sighing, I studied the knots in the wooden ceiling above us. He followed suit.

"I'm glad to hear it."

I turned to face him. "So, what happens now?"

"My best spies are tracking the Amber men as we speak. Tomorrow, Griffin and I will go after any leads they find. We need to catch them before they give Gareth and Lazarus any intel on me, or Shadowhold. The entire keep and visiting Peridot nobles believe the disruption to be a kitchen mishap. Not much else we can do tonight."

"And how much trouble am I in?" I prepared myself for the worst.

"Truth be told, bird, I only blame myself. I should have known to never threaten someone you care about. You love too fiercely."

I wanted to remind him I wasn't in love with Halden before I realized he didn't mean romantic love. His tolerance toward my betrayal was shocking.

"Well. I am sorry for my part in it. Had I known who he was . . ." I had no idea how to finish that sentence.

Kane just nodded and stared once more at the wooden slats of the ceiling above us.

"I have so many questions from earlier. About the history of the Fae. Mari would probably vibrate with curiosity."

Kane's mouth quirked up, but he didn't say more, and I didn't ask. Maybe I felt like, after what I had done to help Halden escape, I didn't deserve to grill him.

We lay in comfortable silence for a moment. I wasn't sure if it was the wine still coursing through my veins, the relief of finally understanding the man beside me, or the late, strange hour of the night, but I couldn't find it in me to make myself hate Kane a minute longer.

Truth was, I probably hadn't really hated him since our day in the forest.

"Tell me about Abbington."

His words caught me off guard and I stiffened imperceptibly. "I've already told you. What did you call it? A 'collection of huts'?"

But he only shook his head and fixed his gaze on me. "No, the good—tell me what you liked about growing up there."

It was easier than I expected to step back into the glade outside my house, the cobblestone streets, the small cottages and farmhouses. I could smell the crisp air, the year-round corn harvest, the steam billowing off my cranberry and apple tea, warm inside my chilly kitchen.

"It wasn't glamorous. We didn't have the finery that you have even here in the middle of the woods. But everyone was kind, tried to help each other. The taverns were warm and full, the sunsets were spectacular each night over the mountains. I don't know . . . It was home."

"And your family? What are they like?"

"Leigh, my little sister, is a menace. She's way too smart for her age, and always speaks whatever is on her mind. But she's so sharp, so witty. She really makes me laugh. You would love her. Ryder is the charmer. He has the kind of confidence even charlatans would follow blindly. I've never met anyone who wasn't completely enamored with him. Even our parents. And my mother . . ." I turned to face Kane, whose expression had grown wistful. The twist in my heart forced me to trail off.

"Your mother?"

I cleared my throat. "She used to sing while she cooked, when she was healthier. She always made up these songs that never sounded quite right. Trying to rhyme 'celery' and 'friendly' and things like that." I smiled even though my throat was squeezing. "She made everything better. Every bad day in school, every splinter, every time I felt so scared I couldn't breathe. She was ill my whole life and never complained. Not once."

"I'm sorry," Kane said, eyes almost wounded. "About what this war has done to your home and to your family. I swear, I will find them for you." I nodded because I believed him. "And one day, when Lazarus is defeated, I will rebuild all the cities and villages like yours that fell. Restore homes, heal the injured."

"I can help you with that last one," I said, before realizing how pathetic it sounded. Practically begging him to keep me around. Take me with him.

His eyes lit with a new expression. Something I couldn't quite place, there and gone like a flash of lightning. "Is healing your favorite thing to do, bird? Or do you do it simply because of your gift?"

"I do love it. Healing people. And I like that I'm good at it. Is that conceited?"

His mouth lifted in a smile. "Of course not."

"But my favorite thing to do . . . I love running. If I could, I would run each morning and night. I'd sleep like a baby. I really love flowers, too. I think I could have enjoyed being an herbalist. And Mari's gotten me quite into reading. I like the love stories and the epic, fantastical tales of pirates and conquerors."

He huffed in amusement.

"You don't like to read?" I asked.

"I do." He tucked a rogue brown strand that had cluttered my face behind my ear, and my whole body lit up like a matchstick. I willed myself to be calm, but my toes twitched, and I was sure that he saw. "But as you said tonight, I am old and dull. I like political tomes."

I feigned dying slowly from boredom, which earned me a gorgeous grin.

"Fine. What else do you love?" I needed more. I loved learning about the non-wicked-king side of Kane. I pictured him in another life, buttering cloverbread and reading a large, boring book in a little cottage by the sea, while babies slept in the next room. Whether or not I was somewhere else in that cottage, taking a soapy bath, I tried not to dwell on.

"Well, you know I loved playing the lute growing up. I like to play chess with Griffin. He's the only one who can beat me."

"Such a humble king," I teased.

"Truth is, I don't do too much that I enjoy anymore."

The thought made me unbearably sad. "Well, we'll have to change that. When this war is over, and you can spare a moment from your kingly duties, I will take you to my favorite grassy hill above my home in Amber. There is nothing a mug of cider and a sunset over the town square in Abbington can't cure."

"You're very good at that."

"Good at what?"

"Relentless positivity."

Humor twitched at my lips. "That doesn't sound like a good thing."

"There is nothing more valuable in a world as dark as ours."

We were both on our sides now, staring at one another. There was far too little space between us and also, somehow, too much. It was torturous. I searched my brain for another question to break the tension.

"The last time you surprised me like this, I still thought you were a prisoner. Why did you come visit me that night?"

"What do you mean?"

"The first time we met, you were in the dungeons to manipulate someone else for information. The second, you needed medical assistance. I'm the only healer, you thought I might not help you if you admitted you were the king—fine, makes sense. But the third time you were just outside my cell, waiting for me. You told me you were seeing if I was still planning to run. But I didn't believe you then and I sure don't now. So, why?"

He ran a hand over his jaw in thought. "What I told you that night was true. I had been dealing with something unpleasant. Afterward, I think I just wanted to . . . be near you."

My pulse quickened and I waited for more. More, more, *more*.

"Not as the king I knew you hated. But as a man you had come to like." He shook his head and sighed. "And a man I had come to like."

So I had been right, after the day we raced to the pond.

The monster act was a purposeful one, to be to others what he felt inside. I chose my next words carefully. "You said a while ago that maybe I didn't think so highly of myself." Heat burned my cheeks at the admission, but I pressed on. "That I had thought my life was worth less than my brother's. I realized not too long after how little I had stood up for myself or thought of myself for so many years. Is it possible you suffer from a similar affliction?"

Kane wove my hand in his. His palm was rough and warm and dwarfed mine twice over.

"Such a perceptive bird. I fear my condition is far worse. You have been surrounded by people who have told you such things. Dim-witted fools, all of them."

He was warring with whatever he wanted to say next, I could tell. I waited patiently.

"I have harmed many people, Arwen. I bring pain wherever I go. I hurt people. Often those I care about most."

I knew it was true, but it was worse hearing him admit it.

"There is always another day, Kane. A chance to make things right with them."

"No, there isn't."

His grave eyes glinted in the candlelight, and I released a slow breath.

"Isn't that a little . . . definitive? Everyone is capable of redemption."

"They're dead, Arwen. Because of me." I started at the harshness of his words. The self-loathing and pain entwined in them—no wonder he thought he was a monster. "There is no redemption," he continued, pulling his hand from mine. "Only revenge."

"Sounds like a very lonely way to live."

"Yes." He said it like he deserved such an existence.

"Is that why . . ." It was a delicate question to phrase, but it had been burning in my mind for too long. "You've never taken a queen?"

"I'm not sure that's a fitting punishment for anyone," he said, a bitter laugh falling from his lips. "Even by my standards, and 'love of torture,' as you like to say. Nobody deserves to suffer the eternal fate of being my wife."

Self-deprecating Kane—that was new.

Or maybe not. I hadn't known him all that well until tonight, I realized.

He sat up a little bit. "For what it's worth, Griffin is a much bigger fan of those tactics you claim I love than I've ever been. Very tough military parents. He even once suggested we get you to talk in such a way." Kane's eyes went viciously black at some memory, and my heart raced.

"Get me to talk? To say what?"

"There was a blade taken from my vault years ago. Griffin thought maybe you might know something, since our last lead at the time was in Amber. It's what your pigeon-brained *lover* was looking for." He said the word with a grimace.

I was sick of Kane assuming Halden and I had been together in that way when we hadn't. Especially now that I knew what Halden was capable of.

"He was never my lover. We didn't . . ." I drew in an awkward breath.

"Ah."

"I haven't. With anyone." He had been right, that day in the throne room. And something about the strange hour of the night, like a private pocket of our own, coupled with our closeness on a bed, was pulling intimate admissions from me. Maybe I was still drunk.

His expression was unreadable, but he had the decency to move past my unnecessary confession.

"But you felt something for him."

"I'm not sure. I think he was what was expected of me, and I wanted very badly to be what my family wanted. I didn't feel anything when we kissed in the dungeons, though." *Shit*. Definitely still drunk.

Kane's eyes were like razors skating over me. His jaw had gone rigid.

I cringed. "What?"

"Fuck." He sighed, running a hand down his tense face. "I want to eradicate him for getting to touch you, let alone kiss you. It's making me physically sick." He rested his face in his hand. "Since when am I such a jealous schoolboy?"

My heart walloped and I fought a smile. I was becoming addicted to his confessions.

"But if I recall, I'm 'not exactly your type'?"

His face twisted, dark brows pulling in. "I'm not sure what ever compelled me to say that."

"I think I had insulted you."

"Ah, one of the many attractive things you do so well."

The word "attractive" falling from his mouth imprinted on my brain like a wax seal, and I blushed, suddenly wishing my room was even darker. There was nowhere to hide my face this close to his. His golden skin glowed in the soft candlelight. His beauty was almost alarming this close up.

He looked at me in earnest. "It was a very rude thing of me to say, and likely said in . . . self-preservation. Forgive me, Arwen. Nothing has ever been further from the truth."

Maybe I should have told him how I felt. But it was too much for me to even begin to share. Bigger than me. Bigger than him.

Truthfully, it frightened me.

All I knew for certain was that I trusted him more now than I had ever expected to, and that I should tell him about my plans to get the burrowroot tomorrow night, during the eclipse. Maybe he could help me make it safely in and out of the woods unscathed.

But I didn't have the energy left to argue with him if he deemed it unsafe. After everything he had told me about the Fae king and the woods beyond the castle, I doubted he'd want to risk any of his guards' lives, or even less his own, to get a single blossom for my mother—who I might never see again—for a potion that might not even work.

My eyelids had started to feel like lead pulling my lashes down. My entire head was heavy from the wine, and the onslaught of information I had learned tonight.

Kane ran a few lazy fingers through my hair, lulling my eyes shut and slowing my spinning mind.

I'd ask him about the burrowroot first thing tomorrow.

20

The pounding in my skull was an outrageous cacophony of pain. It was as if my head was a cellar below a ballroom of giants. Clumsy, drunken giants.

I groaned as I stumbled from bed and splashed my face with lukewarm water in the washroom. Summer was here in earnest, and I was dripping with sweat despite the hour. I had slept until late afternoon and then lain in bed until sundown, unable to move, contemplating everything Kane had said last night, both in the wine cellar and afterward.

Halden's questions in the dungeon felt so obvious now. I wondered how much Gareth had told him about his plans to sell all of Evendell out to Lazarus. A small corner of my mind told me Halden likely knew it all, and still fought for him.

The guilt of helping him escape was crushing, and yet Kane had not mocked me for my choices, nor had he threatened me with any punishment. I had quite literally committed treason, and all he felt was rage on my behalf. Fury that someone had left me behind.

Truth was, he was more furious than I had been. Even before

Kane revealed the truth about Halden or the Fae, I knew I had never felt as much for Halden as I had for Kane in just the past few months. Granted, some of what I felt had been pure, seething hatred, but still. It was wild how just a little time away from Amber had completely changed my almost lifelong feelings for the fair-haired boy. What once felt all-consuming and charged was a blurry memory to me now, the same way one might look back on their first novel or taste of chocolate and think it was the best the continent had to offer. I didn't know how many other facets of my previous life would suffer from a similar realization.

Kane was gone when I rose with the setting sun, as I knew he would be, and I was grateful. I needed to talk to Mari. She didn't know I was still here. For all she knew, I had left with Halden and the others. I needed to tell her everything Kane had revealed, and also that we had almost kissed. Knowing Mari, that would interest her even more.

Leigh would have been the most thrilled. Her crush back in Abbington may have been right all along. Minus the wings, there were likely Fae all over this kingdom. At the thought of Leigh, my blood ran cold.

My mother, the eclipse. Shit, I had slept too late.

Shit, shit, shit.

The eclipse was tonight. I grabbed my pack and threw my training leathers on frantically. How could I have been so stupid? So sick from wine and caught up in my own ridiculous almost-romance with some dark king that I had nearly missed the chance to save my own mother.

I had to focus.

If I failed tonight, there would be plenty of time to beat myself up over the next year while I waited for the moon to hide itself again.

I needed to find Kane, and quickly. He had been honest with me last night, and now I was going to be honest with him. I would beg him to take me back to the site of the burrowroot. I wasn't daring enough to face the forest at night alone, and he was the only person I trusted to get me there safely.

When I made it to the throne room, the sentries regarded me with ice in their eyes. I didn't blame them; three prisoners had escaped last night. I would be on edge, too.

"Good evening. I'd like an audience with the king. Can you tell him it's Arwen Valondale?"

"He's not here, Lady Arwen."

"Where can I find him? Or Commander Griffin?"

The taller guard looked at the one with the mustache. Mustache shook his head.

"They're not in Shadowhold, miss," said Tall.

My stomach sank to the floor.

"Well, where are they? When will they be back?"

Then I remembered. Kane had said he'd be tracking down Halden.

Shit.

Too much wine was my enemy yet again.

Mustache widened his stance and put his hands on his waist as if trying to intimidate an animal.

"I think you'd best run along."

I could have fought with them, begged for more information, but time was running out. I turned on my heel and ran toward the apothecary.

The lanterns were all out in the small room.

"Dagan!" I shouted, but the hollow bounce of my own voice against the wooden walls told me I was alone. He would have been a tough sell anyway.

I looked through the marbled windows at the warped moon in the sky. I had an hour at most. Silver moonlight glistened on something out of the corner of my eye, and I spun to see Dagan's sword and scabbard tossed in the closet. He must have left it there when I missed my lesson this morning. I made a mental note to apologize for that and for what I was about to do. I grabbed the heavy weapon, slung it over my back, and hurtled toward the stables.

Once there, I guided a horse from her stall and hoped the sound of her hooves on the dirt path wasn't as loud to everyone else as it was to me. I squinted in the clear night air but could only discern a couple of guards. The North Gate was much smaller than the castle entrance, as it was backed up against a denser expanse of forest. Past the woods was a smattering of mountains, meaning it was much harder for enemies to gain access this way.

I had to think quickly. The moon was high in the sky, and I had exactly zero idea how to get myself and a horse past the six or so guards at the gate. I could probably find a way alone, but the horse was going to be a no-go.

Maybe that was it—the horse was impossible to hide. She could serve as my decoy. I'd have to run to get to the clearing in time, but I had a shot. Without another thought, I whispered an apology to the horse and smacked her hindquarters.

She took off like a creature possessed. The guards followed her, trying to grasp at her reins, but the poor thing was spooked and beyond catching. I hoped they would be kind to her once she was returned to the stables.

When there was only one guard still standing by the gate—the others trying to corner the rogue mare—I bolted. If I could make it through the metal entrance before he caught me, I knew I could outrun the guard. In the time it would take for the Onyx soldiers to get their steeds and catch me, I would have the burrowroot. I could face the consequences after.

I moved swiftly, sticking to the dark corners of the castle's outer edge. I was almost at the gates when I lost my footing and flew forward. I landed hard on my wrist and felt instant, searing pain.

But that was going to have to be a problem for later.

Looking behind me I saw the spiked metal trap embedded in the grass. It was peppered throughout the entire courtyard that surrounded the North Gate. So less manned, but not less protected. I should have known.

I shot up.

And my heart dropped into my stomach with a thud.

I was staring directly at the guard. It was the same rosy-cheeked, yellow-bearded young man from the day Mari helped me visit Halden in his cell.

I braced myself to be manhandled back into the castle. Possibly the dungeons.

My mouth opened, an argument prepared on my tongue. But I hesitated.

His expression. It was—blank.

He said nothing as he stared at me. Not even *at* me, though. Almost . . . right *through* me.

As if I wasn't standing right in front of him, covered in dirt and clutching my wrist, the guard furrowed his brow at something just past my head and tracked past me toward where I had fallen. He kicked at the metal trap with his shoe in confusion. I had no idea how I had gotten so lucky, but I wasn't going to wait around to find out. I took off through the gate for the clearing.

As I ran, it hit me—Mari's spell had never worn off. I had to remember to tell her that her "simple cloaking spell" might have worked a bit too well. Was it Briar's amulet? Maybe it was time to return the enchanted item to Kane's study.

The Shadow Woods were far more ominous at night. Gnarled branches made monstrous shapes in the shadows, and thorny bushes tore at my leathers. It was also far colder. Despite being at the peak of a sweltering summer, the enchanted, ancient Shadow Woods were chilling at nighttime, and a cool fog swam around my ankles. I wished I had brought the fox fur—for warmth and comfort. Like a little girl, afraid of things I couldn't see in the dark. I tried to remind myself that I had been here during the daytime and felt safe, but it was less than helpful. I had been safe because I was surrounded by guards and horses. Men who could protect me. And Kane.

I ran hard, breath punching out of my lungs. Nothing better for my fear than sprinting.

Still, my thoughts landed back on the king. I had done exactly what he'd asked me not to do. Snuck into the woods, at night, while he was gone. Even though I was no longer planning my escape, he would still be furious.

The feeling of weakness was back once again as I rounded a fallen log and recalled how close I was to the clearing. It felt like more of my life than not was spent feeling weak and guilty. A small corner of my mind wondered if ending up in Shadowhold might have been my only chance at changing that. The heavy thump from Dagan's sword hitting my back with each step told me maybe that instinct was right.

I still hoped I wouldn't have to use it, though. It would be my first time fighting something other than Dagan, who, despite not being the warmest fellow, did not actually wish to see me dead. Plus, I had Dagan's sword, not my own. It was heavier than mine by at least double and required both hands to wield, while mine only needed one. I didn't want to think of how difficult it would be to swing the piece around with my now sprained wrist.

My lungs weren't as accustomed to runs such as these anymore, and by the time I arrived at the clearing, I was gasping. In the watery moonlight, the wet grass shone silver and the trees looked like one tangled, black spiderweb. I had been fortunate to find my way through the dark maze, despite coming from the North Gate this time. Now, I needed to find the oak tree—but it all looked the same, and the eclipse would be any minute. I was running out of time.

"Bleeding Stones," I breathed. I couldn't have made it all this way in time for nothing.

Deep in the spiky bushes behind me, a wet, sloshing sound cut through the deafening quiet of night. I went stiff as a corpse and whirled my head to listen closer—my whole body recoiling at the undeniable sound of a creature feasting on something—or someone—that had not survived the night.

I dropped to the ground and crawled toward the bushes on my knees and elbows. Through the scraping twigs and spongy moss, I slinked until I could see through the thorns of the bushes and just barely make out the carcass of a deer.

A scream lodged in my throat at the sight before me.

Devouring the deer's supple body were two lionlike creatures. I recognized them as chimeras, and particularly nasty ones at that. I had never seen the nocturnal creatures before but had read about them in one of Mari's favorite books: *Onyx's Most Foul.*

Beady eyes with no pupils. Gruesome, snarling snouts. Long, fanged teeth protruding from their mouths, coated in drool and meat. Their faces were so sleek and threatening, their gnarled claws so caked with dirt and blood, that my stomach turned from pure fear and I thought I might vomit.

Before I could scramble backward and heave out last night's wine, I noticed where they were feasting. The poor doe was laid across the roots of the familiar oak tree.

Shit.

I racked my brain. What did that *Stones-damned* book say about chimeras?

Mari had been talking nonstop that day in the library, so I had only made it a few sentences through the chapter on chimeras. Instead of knowledge of the creatures, I knew every detail of Mari's favorite swimming hole in the Shadow Woods, which her father would take her to when the summers became too hot to bear. I knew nothing about the beasts in front of me, but I *did* know how Owen always made sure to bring an altruistic soldier or two with them, because the woods were so unsafe. How her favorite guard had been an older man who always called her "brainy braids," because she would wear these braids that—

Oh, Stones.

That was it.

The water. It was safe—chimeras couldn't swim.

My eyes found the tree-covered path that Kane had taken me through all those months ago. This was a uniquely stupid plan— even for me—but I had no other options. I needed the creatures away from the oak tree so I could access the root when it bloomed. I was not going to turn around and spend the rest of my life knowing that if I ever saw my mother again I'd had the chance to help her and didn't take it out of fear.

I dumped the sword and slid it under the bush in front of me. I couldn't run fast enough with it strapped to my back, and it would be a good marker for the burrowroot when I made my way back. *If* I made my way back. And to be honest, I couldn't use it with my wrist in this shape anyway. I would leave it in the woods altogether if it weren't Dagan's. It would be a shame to defeat not one but two horrific creatures only for Dagan to kill me.

I made my way to the hollowed-out path in the trees that Kane had shown me, took a breath to quiet my nerves, and whistled at the chimeras. The piercing tune sliced through the silent woods and sent smaller animals scurrying. The two vicious creatures turned to face me, confusion and hunger in their eyes.

The smaller of the two, with small, pointed ears, a wild mane, and rigid goat horns, ambled toward me, seemingly more curious than anything else. But that was all I needed. I picked up a couple of pebbles and nailed her in the head once, then twice. She pawed at her jutting brow and picked up speed, snarling.

And then I ran.

21

I RACED THROUGH THE LEAFY CORRIDOR THAT KANE AND I had once traipsed through. Through dew-covered spiderwebs and spindly twigs, I threw myself forward at a pace that had my pulse screaming in my head, hearing the lumbering thumps of the chimera's footfalls behind me all the while.

I just had to get her in the water, and then I could double back for the burrowroot.

Finally, I made it to the pond.

I turned on a heel and waited for the creature to lunge for me.

It didn't take long—the chimera snarled, moonlight glinting off its bone-white fangs. All the breath puffed out of my lungs, and when it charged, I grabbed its fur and threw us both into the pond.

The freezing water paralyzed me, and for a moment I couldn't move any of my limbs. All I knew was ice so cold it felt like fire, and my mind and body froze into utter stillness, too shocked to breathe or move or think. But I had to—

I forced my head out of the suffocating blanket of cold and gasped for breath. A wave sent me back under, filling my mouth and lungs and nose, as the chimera thrashed and displaced half the pond's water. The frigid rush sent me flying toward the rocky outcrop. I slammed into it, the breath knocked from me, and surfaced again, like a moth in rain, fighting against the dark waves and searching for anything to grab on to.

Why was the water so cold? I had been here mere months ago, in the spring, too, and it had been lovely. I knew the forest was enchanted, but it was clear Mari and Kane had been right—the Shadow Wood was no place to be at night.

I reached for a branch and swung myself up and out of the water, sending my wrist into torturous spasms. Freezing water gurgled out of my mouth. I panted for air.

A horrific wail of agony shook me from my reprieve.

I looked to the pond, but the chimera was unconscious, possibly dead already. One down, one to go—and quickly, if I was to avoid whatever was making those noises. Or inflicting them.

Water and algae sluiced from my leathers. I ran for the clearing and prayed the action would pump heat into my chattering bones. In the moonlight, I could scarcely make out the large, sleek form hurtling toward me.

The noise pierced through the night again, ripping from its jaws in a strangled roar. The other chimera. Crying in agony for its mate.

I ran in the other direction, doubling back to the pond.

But he was too close. I wasn't going to make it to the water before he reached me. I braced myself for impact.

Which never came.

The second creature tore directly past me and landed in the water with a splash. He whined in distress and tried to nudge his unconscious mate awake, but the frigid water overwhelmed him and sent him thrashing.

I could go right now. Back to the oak. Against every single odd, my plan had worked, and I could get to the burrowroot before the eclipse. I looked up at the moon. I still had time. Maybe a few minutes.

One last haunting wail ripped from the surfaced creature, still trying miserably to stay afloat and save his mate. He let out a strangled cry that reverberated through the trees, then gurgled as the water pulled him under.

Bleeding Stones.

I could not believe I was going to do this.

I dove back into the water.

Agony clawed at my skin once more. This dive was a thousand times worse, now that I knew how cold it would be. I swam toward the first chimera, who was still unconscious. Thankfully, the water buoyed the creature, allowing me to move her to shore. I pushed her massive body toward the edge of the pond and rolled her onto the grass.

The second was going to be harder. I swam toward the sputtering chimera, and tried to get under his huge front paws, but took a flailing claw to the face instead, a flash of burning pain ripping across my cheekbone. I braced myself and dove underneath the icy depths.

Silence enveloped me.

Pushing him forward, I tried to maneuver the beast to shallower water. I pushed and grunted, feet scraping along the pond's algae-covered bottom, until the creature finally clawed himself out of the pond and choked out water and half-digested deer. The stench was nauseating, but there was no time to retch.

The first chimera wasn't breathing.

I reached her quickly and began chest compressions. As soon as my hands touched her fur, though, I knew.

No, no, *no*.

It was too late.

Swallowing a sob, I placed my hands over the fur of the creature's chest and hummed. Dagan's words had been clear: focus on how I felt, not what I thought. Or what I feared.

I felt remorse. Deep, painful, and specific, like a needle piercing my gut. Remorse that I had almost killed two innocent creatures out of terror.

Through my palms, golden light blazed, and I pushed the cold water through the chimera's lungs like a maze. Encouraged, I moved my hands up along its esophagus. The light that emanated from my hands grew brighter over the chimera's throat as I worked. Pushing and plying, I drove the water out with careful focus.

The second creature had stalked over. He menaced toward me with a roar that shook the trees above us.

But I didn't have time to feel afraid.

"She's going to live," I said, my teeth chattering around the words. I knew he couldn't understand me. "I can save her, if you don't maul me." I pushed power from my fingertips into her torso as the water lodged in her lungs worked its way out.

The other chimera considered me, then looked down. Slowly he lay next to his mate, tucking his snout between her back and the forest floor, whining softly.

After one final push, a spray of putrid wet flew out the chimera's mouth and I ducked. She rolled over and choked on air, and I exhaled my own in turn. The relief was like a solid weight in my palms. Tangible and grounding.

Thank the Bleeding Stones.

The chimera I had saved sluggishly climbed onto all fours and shook out her wet fur. Her mate nuzzled and licked at her before turning back toward the woods. I took that as my cue to leave and gave one last glance at the two creatures, but they were already retreating in the other direction. The larger chimera looked back to me once, and his melancholy, white eyes held mine for a single moment.

But I was most definitely out of time. The eclipse was high in the sky, painting the entire forest an unnerving blue. My limbs were heavy with the exertion of my power, but I raced for the clearing and turned right at the glistening silver of Dagan's sword. I pushed aside the deer carcass and saw each burrowroot leaf below me had blossomed into a stunning lotus underneath my fingertips. I plucked as many as I could, jamming them into my pack. Within an instant, the eclipse was over, and the blossoms were gone. The twisted wood was cloaked once again in pale, shadowy moonlight.

I could have cried with relief.

I had done it.

I was freezing and was likely going to need six or seven warm tubs to thaw out. I was soaking wet, covered in dirt, dripping blood from my face, and had sprained the shit out of my wrist. I was still nauseous and achy from last night's terrible wine-related choices, but I was alive.

And I had the burrowroot.

The thought of giving my mother some kind of hope for the first time in years overwhelmed me. A sob racked through me, and I bent over, bracing my hands on my knees. It was time to head back.

I reached for Dagan's sword, stood up, and saw it.

A more horrific creature than I thought possible.

Yellow, slitted eyes. A rabid, snarling mouth lined with pointed teeth. A wet, slick snout. And worse yet—the broad stature and build of a violent, possessed man. I went rigid, my skin prickling and my insides turning cold. Despite my trembling hands and heart, I turned and ran back toward the castle as fast as my legs could carry me.

The wolfbeast chased after me on all fours, all knees and elbows and odd angles. An uncanny sight I'd likely never erase from my mind. I knew it was faster than me. I choked on a sob as tears sprang to my eyes. I ran and ran and ran—terror pulsing in my joints, my legs, my lungs. This could not be how I died.

I took a hard right in hopes of losing the wolfbeast, but his snarls followed me around the bend, and on through the maze of oaks and pines. I cut another right, but he gained on me with ease. Stumbling and slipping on the twisted branches below, I whipped back and swore I saw primal pleasure in his eyes. A predator that enjoyed the hunt.

I was never going to outrun him.

There was only one way I was making it out of these woods with my life.

I stopped in my tracks, slung out Dagan's blade, and leveled it at the beast.

My lungs burned.

The creature skidded to a halt, and I swung, missing his neck by a mile and slashing his bicep instead. The creature whined at the incision, then roared at me. I didn't have the breath to weep or sob or beg.

"You insipid child!" His voice was like a razor against metal—inhuman and repulsive. A scream ripped out of me at the shock that he could speak, and I paced backward, still holding my sword out.

Every time I thought I understood the depths of the dangers of this world, something new and even more horrific than the last came for me.

The beast lunged, and this time he slammed me to the ground, knocking the breath out of me and grinding my spine into the rocks below. A sob split from my throat—furious and wild and dripping with agony.

But I shoved him away with every single ounce of strength I had, and scrambled back up before he could sink his claws into my body. I lifted the sword once more—Dagan would not have been pleased with my form. Between my exhaustion and my sprained wrist, I was holding it less like a sword and more like a bat.

The wolfbeast's face twisted and I understood then the term "wolfish grin" with complete clarity. He was amused. "Didn't expect the wolf to speak?"

I tried to respond but couldn't find my voice as he closed in on me. I wanted to scream, but only a whimper slipped out. My trembling palms were sweating against the leather pommel of the sword.

"You're tougher than they said you'd be, but nothing I can't handle. I can already taste you from here." The wolf licked at the air with his long, canine tongue.

I shivered at the thought of its rough texture sliding over my bones.

The wolfbeast lunged at me again and this time made contact, his claws ripping out a chunk of my hair. I yelped in pain, which only seemed to excite the monster. He dove for me again, knocking my body into the mossy ground below. Pain bloomed in my shoulder and elbow, my wrist already pulsing in agony. The wolf's breath washed over me and smelled of something more powerful than magic—metallic and astringent.

I realized with utter clarity I was not going to survive this.

As if the beast had heard my thoughts, he reared back with a violent howl and lunged forward to dig his razor teeth into my abdomen. I screwed my eyes shut.

I just hoped it would be swift.

Please, please, please, *please*—

But the pain never came.

Instead, I heard the deafening wail of a creature howling in agony.

I could hardly understand the sight before me. Gray and golden fur rolled in a heap on the forest floor, a tumbling mess of snarling, blood, and whimpers—the chimera. He had lunged at the wolf-beast, effectively saving my life. And now, he was ensnared in the monster's claws. Like a dogfight, they were moving so quickly I couldn't intercept. I waited for the right moment and lunged forward, driving my blade into gray fur, and knocking the wolf into a tree.

The chimera fell to the ground, one goatlike horn severed, and a piercing wound spurting blood from his neck.

No! A cry caught in my throat.

The wolfbeast cackled, exposing rows of pointed teeth, and stood before me. I looked down at the wheezing animal at my feet who had given his life for mine.

For the chimera, I was going to pretend to be someone brave until I was one. I angled my hips toward the beast, swung the sword to shoulder level, and brought it down on the wolf. He dodged, then charged me, but my body took over. Weeks of training—of sweat and blisters and aching arms and sheer determination—all came together in an instant like a key sliding into a lock. I swung repeatedly, nipping him on the shoulder, the neck, the arm. His howls became my fuel, and each time my blade found its mark, I was emboldened. Stronger. The sword felt lighter in my hands. More than that—it was an extension of me.

Of my rage.

I moved like Dagan, step after careful step, circling the creature. When he charged me, I brought my sword down on him and sliced one of his claws clean off. He howled and I felt it in my bones.

I was not capable of stopping.

The clearing glowed. I could see him better in the soft, yellow light that surrounded us. Sweat poured down my brow but a breeze I couldn't place warmed and cooled me at once.

I felt taller. Fiercer. More whole.

I could have sworn I saw fear enter the wolfbeast's eyes. He lunged at me once more, and with everything I had left I stabbed forward, burying my sword to the hilt in his chest.

He gurgled out a screech that felt ancient in its power, and with a dying breath reached his remaining clawed hand out toward me. If he made contact, I didn't know. I turned and ran for the chimera, bloodied sword still dangling from my hands. The golden creature was whimpering, bleeding out onto the damp leaves of the forest.

"No, no, no," I pleaded. "You're all right."

It was the larger chimera. He had come back to help me. A kindness shown for saving his mate's life, when I had been the one to cause her near death in the first place. I could not let him die for me. Tears rolled down my cheeks and landed in his fur.

His eyes were dimming—there wasn't enough time.

I pushed my hand into the chimera's neck wound and closed my eyes, focusing on his pain. But I was so tired, so weak—I had used my powers up on his mate, and then some. Nothing came out, or even pricked at my fingers.

"Please, please, please." I wasn't sure who or what I was praying to.

I thought of that day with Dagan. The way I had pulled warmth and light from the atmosphere. I pictured taking what little moonlight still shone, sucking it into my fingertips, and redirecting it through me and into the softly crying creature.

Something beneath me shone bright like a sunrise. Emboldened, I strained against the weakness and focused further on the ether—the sky itself. I could harness it. Make it work for me. The glowing intensified. I could almost hear the chimera's lungs filling up with air once again.

But the forest was starting to feel very hot.

Which made no sense.

It was summertime, but the Shadow Woods had been icy all night. My hands were shaking, and the ground felt uneven. Was the earth moving? No, the trees were moving. The chimera was now up and looking at me curiously. His neck . . .

It was better. Healed. How?

Physical relief surged through my bones. I tried to get a better look, but the creature's coarse, honeyed fur was blurring into the moonlit night.

A wave of nausea rolled through me. Something sticky was dripping down my body. The chimera tried to nudge me with his furry snout, but I tipped backward and landed on the dirt with a thud.

Something was very wrong.

A voice thundered my name a million miles away.

The chimera took off into the woods at the sound echoing off the trees. I tried to tell him goodbye.

A man's blurry figure, with a familiar cedar-and-leather scent, rushed to me, hands pressing into my chest like a heavy weight.

"No, not goodbye," the figure assured me, but the voice was panicked. "You are going to be fine."

Slowly, pained quicksilver eyes and a clenched jaw came into focus.

It was Kane.

He loosened the sword from my rigid fingers, uncurling each one carefully until the metal hit the dirt with a resonant clang. I looked up at him, bewildered. Where had he come from?

Behind the king were at least seven men on horseback, all with swords drawn. Kane's eyes were wide, his jaw locked tight. He wrapped his arms around my chest tightly, holding me from behind.

"Stay with me, Arwen. Can you hear me?"

When I laughed, something wet and phlegmy rattled in my chest, which made me hack up a cough. I wiped at my mouth. "So dramatic, my k—" The bright smear of red on my hand turned my words into a single choke.

I peered downward. My chest was sputtering blood between Kane's fingers. I lifted his hand ever so slightly and could see my own collarbone beneath my ripped and frayed flesh.

Everything blurred and I felt darkness overtake me, sudden and unyielding.

22

RELENTLESS, EXCRUCIATING PAIN COURSED THROUGH MY body, shocking me into consciousness. I sucked in a lungful of air and swallowed hard. Salt dripped into my eyelashes. My mouth tasted like coins.

I could barely make out the shapes moving like a dust storm around me. Women with damp cloths and a man wrapping my wrist in gauze. Someone was stitching up my face. The needle tugging at my skin was a dull ache compared to the searing in my chest and roaring behind my eyes.

Some cobwebbed, rational corner of my mind wondered who was healing me if I was the castle healer. I laughed out loud, and the focused men and women exchanged furtive looks and only seemed spurred to work more quickly.

I tried to press my palm into my chest, but the woman next to me kept pushing my hand out of the way. It didn't matter. I had no power left. I had used all my healing abilities on the chimera. When had that been?

I could barely keep my eyes from fluttering closed and fought to peer through the sheer drapery that surrounded me.

It was a room I had never been in, shrouded in navy curtains and filled with leather furniture. A handful of black candles with curled wicks burned in the dim light. Something smelled familiar, like home, but I couldn't place it.

Lilies in stone vases peppered the space. Where had those come from? The delicate white flowers played against the soft candlelight.

Beautiful.

Also, sweltering.

About a million degrees and suffocating me. I tried to sit up. I needed fresh air, right now.

Warm, broad hands held me down.

"Try to stay still," Kane murmured, his voice hard as steel. "It's almost over."

I whimpered and turned my face away from him, my head foggy and nausea coating my stomach. I was dizzy and hot and freezing. *I need water.*

"I'll get it for you." His familiar scent disappeared, and my throat closed up at the loss. He was back moments later and gently pressed the glass to my dry, cracked lips.

A sharp burst of pain echoed through my chest, and I choked on the agony.

"You're torturing her!" Kane roared at someone, but I could not see anything through the blinding anguish. I heard the glass of water shatter on the floor.

"The venom has to be purged, my king. This is all that we can do."

"Please," he begged. Actually *begged*. "Then please, just work faster."

"We are trying, but—" A woman's voice. The fear in her words was contagious and soaked into my already shivering bones.

"No," he breathed. It was almost a sob.

"There might not be—"

The truest, most piercing agony I had ever felt seared through my chest, into my heart, down to my toes, through my very soul—

I screamed a bloody, gargled wail into the overheated room. Sweat dripped from my brows and stung my eyes.

I couldn't endure it. I couldn't I couldn't I couldn't—

"No!" he roared, and this time, wisps of twisted black shadow filled the tented gossamer of the bed, snuffing out all the light and bathing the room in stark black midnight.

The specters drowned out my suffering in an instant. What was anguish—pure anguish—was now . . . nothing. Numb, cold nothing. I reached for Kane, in relief, confusion—but found only the swift and heavy comfort of sleep as my eyes fell closed instead.

<hr />

A SHARP STAB OF PAIN EXPLODED THROUGH MY BACK. I snapped my eyes open and was somewhere unfamiliar.

Or worse, somewhere all too familiar—a place I hadn't been in years.

I was staring at the dark wood floor of Powell's work shed. It wasn't even worth looking to the door or windows. I knew they were locked, that I was trapped inside. I braced myself for another lash of pain, but it didn't come. I peered up and instantly regretted it. Powell stood over me, face bright red and snarling, belt raised.

"Weak girl," he said, spitting. Tears spilled over my cheeks and snot bubbled at my nose.

"I have asked you three times this week not to play in the kitchen," he said, voice booming off the walls of the cold, empty shed. I didn't want to cower, but I couldn't help it. I shrank into myself, hoping my back might soon stop pulsing in pain. I knew better than to speak.

"You're infuriating. Making me teach you this way." He was right. He only ever hurt me because I was the worst. Why couldn't I be stronger? Smarter? I hated that everything he said about me was true.

"You are a poison in this family, Arwen. You're killing your mother."

As he lifted his hand to strike me again, I called out, begging him to stop, but nobody heard me.

~❦~

"SHH, ARWEN. NOBODY IS HURTING YOU. YOU'RE GOING TO BE all right."

I sobbed and sobbed, cries racking through me at the pain.

Please stop, I thought. *I can't take any more.*

"Stop what? Arwen?" He sounded frantic. Scared.

But so was I.

~❦~

THE BED WAS LIKE A BATH OF SILK, SOAKING ME IN SHEETS and leaving me weightless. Layers of gossamer lined the four posts and twinkling lights peeked through in pockets. I hadn't noticed a fireplace before, but the fickle, dancing flames through the canopy were a comfort. A slow lullaby sounded from an instrument somewhere. Haunted and bewitching, the notes weaved through the room like wisps of moonlight. It made me want to sing. Or maybe cry.

"You're awake," Kane said from a corner of the room I couldn't see.

My eyes ached with tears at the soft sound of his voice.

The melancholy song ceased, and I heard him place something on the floor.

What had I seen before falling unconscious? The images of black, mistlike smoke coiling around me, lulling me into sleep, were hazy, but I knew I had seen them. The feeling—it hadn't been like anything I had felt before. Not like magic, not like a potion. It was as if something had seeped inside my soul and eased my anguish. It was a dark and twisted mercy of some kind.

Kane approached me slowly and held his cool palm on my forehead. It felt delicious. I leaned into it like an animal, rubbing my hot face on his hand.

"I have something even better for you."

I whimpered at the loss of contact. The bed shifted and Kane was beside me, pulling my body against his and laying a cold compress on my forehead. It felt like heaven, and I turned my face away so he could run it along my neck and shoulders and arms—

My eyes shot open. "What am I wearing?" I could hear the slurring of my words.

Kane blushed. *He is so cute.*

"Thank you, bird. You're in one of my shirts. It was all I had."

I nodded my face into his body, cradling my aching wrist against his chest.

"You're warm," I said.

"Not as warm as you. Your fever hasn't subsided."

I hummed.

"Arwen," he continued. "Why were you in the woods tonight?" He paused. His poor eyes were anguished. "I could have lost you."

He held my wrist to him like it was very delicate. My heart thumped.

"I tried to find you." I peered up and was met with a pained expression. I reached my good hand toward his rumpled brows and touched his temple. "It's all right, I got what I needed."

"And what was that?"

"For my mother. To heal her."

Kane nodded, but I could tell he had no idea what I was saying. "Sleep, little bird. I'll be right here."

So I did.

I WOKE TO SHUDDERING AND GASPING. I LOOKED AROUND for the source only to realize the grotesque noises were coming from me. It was midday, and I felt like a hog roasting over a spit. I lashed at the sheets and rolled around, searching for some relief from the mountains of covers that swallowed me whole. I rolled onto a hard body and knew from the familiar scent it was Kane. He smelled like a sweaty cedar tree. *If it had been doused in whiskey and set on fire.*

"Clearly, I need to bathe," he said, his voice laced with sleep.

I had to stop doing that—my fever was making it impossible to tell my thoughts from my words. I was a delirious mess, everything was blurring together, and I thought I might have been babbling. *Damn this fever.*

Kane's answering laugh shook the mattress beneath us. *Ugh.* Had I said that out loud, too?

"Why are you in my bed?" I asked. I was aiming for snarky, but it came out like a lost child.

"Actually, you are in my bed."

I held my ground. "Why am I in your bed?"

Kane laughed again, a bright and hearty boom that brought a lopsided grin to my groggy face.

"It's so good to have you back, even just a little."

I wasn't sure where I had gone but I smiled anyway. "You're welcome."

"Can you eat?" He made to leave the bed in search of food, but I wrapped my arms and legs around him like a vine.

"Don't leave." I was pathetic. It was all right. *I had made peace with it in death.*

"You aren't dead, Arwen."

Of course I was. *He was reading my mind, and I was pantsless.*

"I'm not reading your mind; you're talking to me. And you're pants-less because you keep taking off your pants." He motioned toward the floor, and I peered over to see my leathers in a heap. I whispered an internal prayer of thanks to the Stones that there were no undergarments down there as well. I curled toward him again.

"I can't keep holding you like this," he said. His body had tensed. I couldn't tell if I had dreamt it. "But I can't seem to let you go, either."

"What was that?" I asked. "The . . ." I didn't know how to explain it. The twisted darkness that had filled his room like living shadows.

But he knew.

"I want to share everything, Arwen . . . but it would only bring you more suffering."

I pried one eye open to look at him, but he was staring out the window at the sun as it slipped behind the woods below us.

"I'm stronger than you think."

"No, bird. You're stronger than any of us. It is only you who doesn't think so."

⚛

THE CLUMSY GIANTS WERE BACK, BUT THIS TIME THEY HAD brought friends who also lacked rhythm. I rubbed at my temples and tried to swallow, my mouth feeling like cotton. But my vision and thoughts were clear—the fever had finally passed.

I sat up and stretched. Every joint in my body, from my fingers to my neck, popped and cracked with relief.

And I was starving.

I slipped out of the bed, my bare feet on the cool wood floor, and assessed the room that smelled so brightly of lilies. So these were Kane's private quarters. They were more colorful than I had expected. Whimsical blue throws and sultry violet curtains popped against the dark wood floors, stone walls, and cluttered shelves. Stacks of the historical books he had told me about framed his bedside. It was so lived-in, so masculine. Not at all cold or sterile as I had once imagined.

The balcony doors were open and I stepped outside, soaking in the fresh air and summer sunshine like a wilted flower after a storm. I stretched my arms high above my head, and the breeze grazed over my thighs and bottom.

Oh, right. No pants.

I went back inside for them, but my leathers were so stiff and caked in dirt, blood, and pond water I couldn't bear to slide them on.

Behind the four-poster bed was a closet filled with mostly black, kingly attire. In the far corner was a full-length mirror. I prepared myself for the worst and approached.

In some ways, it wasn't as bad as I expected. My legs were mostly fine, minus a few scrapes and bruises. I was grateful to be in undergarments that covered my ass and most of my stomach. Kane's large black tunic fit me more like a dress, and I heaved a sigh of relief. One point scored for modesty.

In other ways, it was really, very bad.

My face looked horrific. Like a deranged swamp witch. My eyes lacked their usual olive color, I was too pale, and my lips were cracked. The stitches on my cheek cut across me like tracks, and my lower lip was still bruised from the night of the explosion. Even my wrist, despite the wrappings, was purple and swollen.

I held my palm to my cheek and breathed deeply, feeling the welcome sting of my skin lacing itself together again and pushing the stitches out of my face. I was still so weak—but I had enough left to make a slight dent in the healing process. Within a couple of days, it would barely be noticeable. But that wasn't the worst of it.

It was time to see the real damage.

The buttons of Kane's tunic were easy to undo, but I was terrified to look at my reflection. I wasn't necessarily a vain person, but I knew whatever injury I had sustained from the wolfbeast would be with me for life.

Peeling back the bandages revealed a large gash that ripped me from my collarbone to the top of my breast. The healers had stitched it up beautifully. I would have to thank them somehow.

For the first time, I'd had someone actually tend to me after I had been injured. It was a strange comfort, to not have been alone healing my wounds.

But in looking at the stitches, an image of the white of my own collarbone flashed in my mind, and I gripped the ornate armoire to steady myself. I wasn't squeamish; my professional assessment was that the dizzy spell was more likely due to dehydration. I made my way back into the bedroom and found Kane setting a breakfast tray on the bed for me.

"You're up," he said, eyes following my bare legs. A grin tugged at my lips. His shameless ogling felt like a sign that I was no longer his patient. I self-consciously patted my wild hair.

"I am," I said. "What's this?"

I climbed into bed and tucked a rebellious lock behind my ear. Fine, I wanted to look nice for him. Maybe hours of fevered, sweaty, bloodied Arwen could be erased by a decent comb.

"This is breakfast. How's the wound?"

"It's uncomfortable," I admitted. "But better than I expected given the fever. I don't want to know what kind of venom was in the beast's claws. Thank you, Kane. For everything."

He only nodded.

The food before me was mouthwatering. Three boiled eggs, two loaves of cloverbread with a dollop of honeyed butter, a sliced apple, and some grilled pork. I practically drooled.

And, candidly, it wasn't the only mouthwatering part of breakfast. Kane looked downright delectable. His shirt was unbuttoned, exposing a slight dusting of dark, curled chest hair. His black locks were swept away from his face, and slight stubble sprinkled his chin. I hadn't ever seen him with facial hair before. I resisted the all-consuming urge to cup his jaw in my hand.

"You have a beard," I said around a mouthful of apple.

He cocked his head and joined me on the bed, resting his hand on my forehead.

I laughed and covered my mouth. "Not the fever talking. Just a lack of filter." A horrific thought dawned on me as I wondered what humiliating things I must have said while sick. As if he could read my mind, Kane's lips curved in a mischievous smile. I raised an eyebrow in question.

"Oh, you don't even want to know," he purred.

"Stop that. You're lying." I was going for outrage, but his charm had turned my admonishment into flirting. *Damn him*.

"You'll never know."

"Add it to the list," I mumbled, and took a huge bite of the sweet bread.

When he didn't respond I turned to face him, but he was lost in thought.

"I don't mean to keep things from you, Arwen." I didn't like when he used my name. Not that I fully understood the feathered nickname, but I had come to learn that "Arwen" meant only bad news. "There is some knowledge that would only bring you more pain."

His words brought back a singular memory of the strange power that had seeped out from him when I was dying, and brought me into a sleeplike state. Stronger than any medicine, but not quite unconsciousness.

My breathing went shallow.

I scrambled back on the bed away from him. "You . . ."

"So you remember that," he said, his face solemn, resigned.

"What was that? Are you . . . some kind of warlock?" But I knew—that had not been magic.

He frowned. "Perhaps if I had told you weeks ago, you wouldn't have nearly died."

I wanted to ask how the two things were at all related.

"Finish eating," he said after a moment. "Then let's take a walk."

23

$$\sim\!\!\diamond\!\!\sim$$

SHADOWHOLD'S GARDENS WERE A WELCOME SIGHT FOR MY weakened eyes. Trellises of the expected gardenia and lilac surrounded pitch-black fountains with floating blossoms. Velvety purple roses bloomed alongside twisted black voodoo lilies, and ethereal violet and wisteria hung overhead. Flowers I now knew were called bat flower, dragon arum, and spider orchid flourished in abundance. It was a gothic display of beauty, but one I had come to love. I wondered if part of me always knew there was more to this place than horror.

Kane strolled alongside me, but I kept my distance. I knew he wouldn't hurt me—he had just saved my life.

But I was uneasy, to say the least. Confused, afraid—I felt like I was on the precipice of something that I wasn't sure I wanted to know. But it was too late for that now. The Arwen who would rather stay in the dark, naively waiting for everyone to take care of her, make decisions for her . . .

The thought of that version of myself brought me to the brink of nausea.

We moved slowly, taking in the stillness and chirping birds. After bathing quickly and putting on a clean dress, I had met him out in the early evening air.

And he had yet to say a word.

"I need answers, Kane," I said, not unkindly. But it was true. Enough was enough.

"I know," he said, resolve fading from his eyes. "I just need to . . . think."

Fine. I could be patient.

We strolled through the garden in silence until we passed the same gloomy flowers, which reminded me of something. "The white lilies. In your room."

It wasn't really a question, but he answered me anyway.

"I thought they might remind you of home."

My heart swelled. "They did. Thank you."

He hesitated. "Happy memories, I hope?"

I turned his question around in my head. "Mostly."

When he didn't respond I looked up. He was watching me with a strange intensity.

"What is it?"

"While you slept, you were calling out for someone to stop. I thought you might have been dreaming of the beast that attacked you, but then you kept saying this man's name." I could tell he was trying with all of his internal strength to be gentle, but his eyes were all pupil. "I never stopped thinking of those scars I saw on your back in your washroom. Arwen, did someone hurt you?"

Something about the kindness in his voice made me feel sick. I didn't want to be saved anymore. Pitied.

"No. I mean, yes. A long time ago, when I was young. I'm fine now." I watched him watching me. "Obviously," I added dumbly.

Kane looked like he could topple mountains.

"Who?" He gritted the word out.

I hadn't told anyone this in a long time. Only Ryder, actually. Once I was old enough that the memories felt like someone else's life. I had made him promise to never tell Leigh or our mother.

A truth for a truth, maybe.

I steeled myself.

"My stepfather, Powell, would beat me. I don't really know why. I think he hated me because I wasn't his. It's not a very good reason. But sometimes people are just looking to give their pain to someone else and will use any excuse they can find. My family never knew."

"How?" he asked.

"My mother was always sick; I knew she couldn't live without him. I couldn't put that on her. Leigh was too young to burden. Ryder and Powell were so close. I could heal my broken bones and welts pretty quickly."

"And where is that pathetic creature now? With your family?"

I shook my head. "He died years ago. A stroke."

"Shame." Kane's eyes simmered.

I gave him a questioning look.

"Bastard got off far too easily," he said, looking down, jaw tight. When I didn't respond he added, "I'm sorry you had to suffer alone. I'm sorry you had to suffer at all." Again, with that pained gentleness.

"Thank you," I said. And I meant it. "But now it's your turn. No more stalling." I steeled myself. "What did I see?"

He crossed his arms over his chest, a gesture I'd never seen him do, and then uncrossed them just as quickly. He ran a hand through his raven hair.

I reined in the urge to physically choke the answers out of him.

"In my defense," he finally said, "you had been drinking."

I waited for that to make any sense.

"It didn't feel like the right time to tell you, in the wine cellar. And . . ." Kane sighed. "I didn't want to scare you."

His words had the opposite effect as fear coiled in my gut, but I kept my gaze neutral.

"You remember the rebellion, led against the Fae king," he said, and I nodded. "It was orchestrated by a small group that wished to save the realm. To bring down the impenetrable walls and free those within them. The attempt . . . It was led by Lazarus' son."

"The Fae king's son tried to overthrow his own father?"

"Both of his sons did, actually. But yes, the rebellion was led by his youngest."

A tiny, spindly talon of dread scraped gently down my spine. "And how does that relate to what I saw?"

Kane clenched his jaw, a flicker of shame in his eyes. "It was me. I'm Lazarus's son, Arwen."

But I couldn't hear him over the roaring in my ears.

"Arwen?" Kane said, studying me.

Kane was *Fae*?

The beings I had feared as a child. The stories intended to scare and shock, told over a bonfire. The thing I had been sure—so sure—did not exist at all until two nights ago was now standing right in front of me?

The words fell out of my mouth. "You fought against your own father?"

Kane's eyes watched mine fiercely, searching for something. "I tried to. But failed."

His expression was unreadable. I twined my shaking hands in my loose skirt.

"It was the worst mistake of my life. It cost me, and those closest to me, everything they cared about. It cost most of them their lives."

His bitterness, his rage, seeped out like ink in water.

He had said he hurt those he loved, but this . . . This was—

"I hate Lazarus more than you can fathom. I will avenge those we lost and save this mortal continent, Arwen. I have to. It is not a question of *if*—only *when*."

I dipped my head in a nod. I believed him—how could I not? I had never seen anyone more steadfast about anything.

But I was also still absolutely reeling.

"Do your men know what you are? Does your kingdom?"

He took a shuddering breath as if to calm himself before shaking his head.

"So what I saw when I was . . ." I swallowed the word "dying." "That was lighte?"

"Yes. Each Fae has a different variation of it, so it won't always look like that. There is something . . . dark laced within mine. Something I inherited from my mother's witch ancestry. I try to use the power as little as I can manage." Kane's face barely concealed his disgust.

"But you used it last night. On me," I said.

"To silence your pain, your suffering. Yes." He looked at me, eyes clear. "And I'd do it again. A hundred times over."

"Thank you," I whispered.

He only nodded.

I rubbed at my temples and stared ahead at the sprawling hedges before us. A slight summer wind blew my skirts around my ankles.

It was just dawning on me that Kane was probably over a hundred years old. The onslaught of information of the last few days mixed with my fragile physical state was teetering me toward a mental breakdown.

"You're taking all of this surprisingly well," he offered.

I turned to him, inspecting his youthful face, smooth skin, strong jaw. "How old are you?"

He covered a smile with his hand, rubbing his stubble. "About two hundred and fifteen." My mouth fell open. "To be honest, I've lost track over the years."

I shook my head, trying to rattle my thoughts around. "When was the rebellion? How long have you been ruling the Onyx Kingdom?"

"I left the Fae Realm with the few I could get out fifty years ago. I took over Onyx from the king at the time, an older monarch with no living heir. Part of the 'persona' as you had called it—the mystery, the foreboding—I've crafted with my closest advisors for that very reason."

"So nobody will know how you look, or notice when you don't age."

"Correct," he said.

"What about your allies? King Eryx and Princess Amelia?"

"They know. Both of my lineage and Lazarus's intent. They plan to fight against him. For Evendell."

The reminder of the impending doom of the entire continent was like ice water running through my veins. There was truly nowhere to run. No way to save everyone.

No matter what happened, who won, so, so many were fated to die.

He grimaced, as if following my train of thought. "There's not much time left. The mercenaries from the Fae Realm are coming for me while Lazarus prepares for war." Kane swallowed once. "That's who attacked you in the forest."

I froze mid-step. "The wolf was a . . . Fae mercenary?" The thought that I had killed a Fae felt like a sick joke. "That's not possible."

"Very powerful Faeries have the ability to shape-shift into a creature form. It's incredibly rare and uses a huge amount of lighte. I'd imagine Lazarus is devastated to have lost one of such power. He can't have more than a hundred left in his army." I wondered if it was pride that glowed in Kane's eyes.

"That's what killed your man in the Shadow Woods. When you brought me with you?"

"Yes. Also what 'took a bite' out of me, as you said that day in the infirmary." He smiled at the memory. "My father's mercenaries have been coming for me for months now." All the mysterious injuries that nobody would explain to me . . . Lance's bite, Barney's wound that first night . . . "We've killed as many as we can to keep them from reporting my whereabouts, but we can only hold them at bay for so long."

The thought of them coming after Kane forced the color from my face.

"It gets worse, I'm afraid."

I braced myself. "How did I know that was coming?"

"The Kingdom of Amber has taken Garnet."

The entire garden stilled along with my heart. My family—they were there.

"My family sailed for Garnet. At least, that's where they planned to go. You have to take me there. To find them."

Kane's expression softened. "My spies are close. As soon as I find your family, I'll get you to them. But I fear Lazarus may be confident enough to attack now. He has two mortal armies." Kane took hold of my upper arms. I didn't flinch at his touch, and his eyes seemed to notice, growing warm. His broad hands radiated that heat throughout my body. "You can't stay here a day longer, Arwen. The keep is no longer safe for you, or anyone. He is coming for me. Any day now, I'm sure of it."

I swallowed hard. Lazarus couldn't have Kane—all other thoughts had slipped from my mind but that. He *could not* have him.

"But as you know, Peridot and Onyx have struck an alliance. You need to leave tonight for the Peridot capital of Siren's Cove, where you'll be safe. Griffin will take you."

"Griffin?" My stomach sank. "What about you?"

"I will join you when I can."

Then he let go of me, and I missed his touch like warmth in the dead of winter. "Where are you going?"

"That's enough honesty for today, I think." He tried for a smile, but it didn't reach his eyes.

"But you've told me everything now? No more secrets? I can't live like this anymore, Kane. Especially now. I need to know this is everything."

He pressed a soft kiss to my forehead. Cedarwood and crisp mint flooded my senses.

"Yes."

A weight I hadn't anticipated rose off my chest. He had told me weeks ago that he didn't indulge in trusting others, and that he couldn't trust me. Yet slowly, torturously slowly, he'd let me in. Knowing he had changed his mind, for me alone—allowed me to share these burdens with him—cracked me open completely.

I sighed so deeply my lungs hurt.

As we rounded the same hedge as before, I noticed a handful

of soldiers had lined up to meet us. Griffin stood chief among them, his face stoic.

"Now?" The familiar rise of panic turned my stomach. I was terrified to leave him. The enormity of my feelings for Kane drenched me like a torrent. I nearly fell to the ground—all this time I had thought I wasn't capable of such feelings at all. I thought Powell had so thoroughly ruined me, that I would never feel anything close to this. And yet—

Kane's brows knit together in pain at my pleading. "Yes, now."

"Wait." I had to get my racing heart under control. "Please, can Mari come with me?" I couldn't leave her here if the castle was likely to fall.

"I'll have Griffin send for her."

He watched me closely, brows pulling together, something warring in his expression.

I didn't care anymore how pathetic I sounded, how weak, how afraid. How ridiculous it was to have fallen for a lethal, breath-taking Fae king. "Will I see you again?" I said.

I felt like I might cry.

Kane looked like he could hear my heart splitting open. "I hope so, bird."

I reached up to touch the dark scruff that had grown across his jaw and neck. The slight bags under his eyes. I realized, belatedly, that he was a wreck.

Carefully, as if I were a wild animal, he brushed a hand against my cheek. I was vaguely aware of the handful of soldiers who suddenly found their shoes exceedingly interesting.

"I must tell you one last thing."

His eyes didn't leave my face.

"I was wrong that day, to say you thought you were worth less than your brother. You made a heroic choice the night you came here. It took tremendous courage. I have been king a long time, and rarely, if ever, do I see that even from my greatest warriors."

My eyes found his through a cloud of tears.

"You showed extraordinary bravery when you had no hope it would save you. Whether you know it or not, Arwen, there is a wild strength inside of you. You don't need Ryder, or Dagan, or me, or anyone else to take care of you. Remember that. You are enough."

His words were a prayer, devastating and empowering at once. We were mere inches apart, and I could feel the tickle of his breath across my lips, his fingers weaving through my still-damp hair. Kane studied me closely, brows pulling together, and tentatively wrapped his other hand around my waist. His eyes searched mine once more as if to make sure, without a shadow of a doubt, that I wanted this, too. I hoped he could see that I had never wanted anything more in my life.

He let out a shaky breath and, with unexpected tenderness, brought his mouth to mine.

As my lips brushed his, he released a guttural sigh into my mouth, as if he had been holding his breath for days. Years, maybe. Waiting for this very moment. I could relate—feeling his mouth envelop mine, being held inside his arms, knowing he somehow felt the same—it was better than anything I could have dreamed.

His lips were soft and wet and searching. He took his time with me, savoring and gently caressing my lips with his, sending shivers into every nerve ending in my body. When his grip tightened in my hair just enough to pull me closer, I lit up and moaned into him. My fingers slid delicately, softly, achingly against his neck, and a groan fell out of his mouth into mine. I caught his bottom lip between my teeth and sucked—I wanted another one of those low, rumbling, male noises. I wanted it more than air in my lungs.

As if he could feel my need, he deepened the kiss, his restraint slipping from gentle into something hungrier, something far more desperate. He brought his hand from my waist to the side of my face, angling my jaw closer and sweeping my mouth with his tongue until I couldn't help a gasp, and I swore I felt a wicked chuckle rumble through his chest against mine.

And then, it was over.

He pulled back, lips bruised and parted, chest heaving, and looked at me only once with enough longing to weaken my already shaking knees. I felt the absence of him like a chair being pulled out from under me. I swayed with the loss of contact and watched as he walked away all too quickly.

24

I WAS BEING COOKED ALIVE. THE ONYX SUMMER WAS RE-lentless, and the warmth was intensified inside our stuffy carriage. Mari and I had been assured by Griffin and the four other soldiers with us that Peridot was only a week's ride away, but by day two it already felt longer.

When I asked Griffin why we weren't traveling by dragon again, he had said the dragon was "more of a symbol for Onyx power than a mode of transport" in that signature dry way of his.

Still, the dragon would have been less hot.

I watched Onyx's landscape pass by through the carriage window while Mari slept. I was shocked to find myself missing Shadowhold. Maybe it was the constant smell of lilac in the air, or the gothic library and its wrought iron chandeliers. Gardenia against stone. Velvet chairs and Kane's grin.

I missed my work in the apothecary and all the faces I'd likely never see again. Dagan's furrowed brow. I couldn't stop thinking about how I had fought a Fae creature and won with everything he had taught me. I wondered if I'd ever get to tell him of my battle. He would be so proud. I hadn't even gotten to say goodbye.

The moments after Kane left had been a blur. Griffin sent soldiers with me as I threw the few belongings I had in a sack, whirling around my room like a tornado. The burrowroot was still safely lodged in my satchel, and I gathered the remaining ingredients for the concoction from the apothecary before we were rushed out of the keep for good.

On our first night in the carriage, I confessed everything to Mari, who played a masterful game of catch-up. We covered the impending doom of the continent, Fae history lesson, horrific wolf-induced wound, Kane's immortality and overall not-humanness, and the deeply inappropriate corners of my mind that despite all of the above wanted to strip him bare and lick him from head to toe.

Mari wasn't her usual sunshine self, of course. Upon hearing the news of the war's advancement—Fae-related details were kept under wraps—her father rode for a small town outside of the capital to gather his sister and her six children. Mari didn't know if he'd meet her in Peridot, and she was trying to keep the thought from her mind entirely.

Mostly, though, I missed Kane. It had been only two days, and I knew I wasn't missing him as much as preparing to miss him. It seemed very unlikely he would come hide out in Peridot with me anytime soon with this war against his father on the horizon. A chasm had opened in my heart, and I felt like I was drowning inside of it.

The carriage slowed to a halt, shaking me from my longing and

Mari from her sleep. The sun had gone down and we pulled off in front of a strange, lopsided inn with a thatched roof.

"Where are we?" I called out of the window.

"Serpent Spring, and keep your voices down," Griffin said before tying up his horse and heading inside.

"He is so bossy," Mari said, shaking out her red curls. Sleep had set them askew, and she looked like a frayed edge. "Hand me my books? And that cloak? Come on, hurry up," she added, as she climbed outside into the dull evening heat.

I rolled my eyes.

⬧

THE INN WAS SWELTERING AND DISCONCERTINGLY EMPTY. Griffin, Mari, and I ate a late supper at a rickety wooden table. We were alone, save for a snoring older man with a handlebar mustache and two rowdy local boys well into their fifth drinks of the night.

"In this one, I found a few mentions of Fae society, but nothing about a power source," Mari continued, poring over the leather-bound tome on the table beside her stew. She was over the moon about the new insight into the history of the Fae and had spent all subsequent waking hours on the journey thus far researching.

"Quieter, please." Griffin's jaw tightened as he rubbed at his temples. He was not a fan of Mari's, it seemed. Even less so when, after needing his expertise on a few Fae-related questions, we had admitted to him that she knew about Lazarus and the Fae Realm. I wondered if he resented babysitting the object of his king's affection and her friend when a battle such as this one was brewing.

"I know, I know, the whole concept of a book is so hard for

you," Mari said. "These are *words*," she enunciated slowly before turning back to me. I covered my laugh with a bite of potato.

"All I'm asking for is discretion. You weren't supposed to know any of this." Griffin shot a pointed look in my direction. "And you never know who could be listening."

Mari nodded in a fake display of sincerity, her brown eyes big and innocent. "You're right. I think Sleepy behind us is working for the enemy. Good eye, Commander."

Griffin stared down at his stew, possibly contemplating all of his life choices. I shot him my best *Thank you for bringing her along* smile. He got up from the table, leaving his dinner behind.

"Mar, why do you antagonize him?"

Mari looked back at her book while she shoveled a spoonful into her mouth.

"I don't mean to."

I glared at her.

"Anyways," she continued, lowering her voice, "I'm not sure why lighte is what interests you the most out of what Kane told you. There's nothing in here about it."

Damn. "That's the whole issue. Even if by some unlikely odds we defeat this king—"

"Which I don't see happening."

I shot her another glare.

"Sorry," she added.

"Even if we *did*, there are tens of thousands of mortals and Fae living in a hellscape realm. It isn't right. And we can't save their lands or bring them here without learning more about lighte."

I pushed my plate away from me. My stomach had soured and suddenly nothing sounded worse than the starchy, grainy mush.

Mari eyed me suspiciously. "Since when do you care so much? About a realm you only learned of five days ago?"

I couldn't really answer her. I wasn't sure. The feeling of help-lessness was an all-too-familiar one. One I had experienced every day of my life until I came to Onyx. But I had learned to live with-out my family. To sword fight, to be bold. I had survived an attack from a Fae mercenary. And now Kane was leaning on me, counting on me—he had called it relentless positivity, but despite all the helplessness, there was another feeling blossoming inside me.

And maybe it was hope.

~✦~

THE PATCHWORK BLANKET WAS ROUGH AGAINST MY SKIN and the bed smelled of mothballs and sour laundry. I turned to my other side to see if somehow that configuration would be more comfortable.

It wasn't.

The pillow was hot against my cheek no matter which way I flipped it, and the stagnant air of the inn was suffocating me. I threw on my boots and made my way down the stairs before I knew where I was going.

Outside, the cool air was like a caress against my face. I took a deep inhale of obsidian wheat and cut grass. I had fallen a bit in love with the rough Onyx land. Lemongrass, lilac, lavender. The sticky, sweet fragrances of my childhood town now felt cloying in comparison.

I poured water from the inn's well into my cupped palms and splashed my face. The sound of metal on metal surprised me, and I turned to see two men fighting in the distance. When one called out for mercy, my legs began moving of their own accord.

It wasn't yet morning, so I rubbed my eyes and squinted into the dim light, looking for some kind of weapon to stop them. All I saw was a long piece of wood.

That would have to do.

I ran toward the men, prepared to break up the fight with a branch, when I heard a deep peal of male laughter.

The exhale that puffed out of me was almost comical.

Griffin was shirtless and dripping sweat. His blond hair was matted to his forehead. Across from him, a mop-headed young soldier we had been traveling with lunged. Griffin parried the overhead blow with ease, then clocked him in the head with his pommel.

"Ouch!"

"Less talking, more focus on your distance. You're getting too close," said Griffin. His eyebrows perked up when he saw me.

"Morning, healer." Griffin ducked under the next attack and hit the boy in the stomach with his other hand. "If I had my dagger, Rolph, you'd be dead."

Rolph dropped his sword and flopped down on a nearby bale of hay. "All right. I'm dead."

"What kind of attitude is that?" Griffin asked, but Rolph had already stalked back toward the well, surely for water and to tend to his bruised ego.

"You could go a little easier on him," I said, picking up his discarded weapon.

"And then what would he learn?"

I turned the sword over in my hands. "You could be a little easier on Mari, too."

Griffin's playful energy shifted. "Did she say that? That I was hard on her?"

I shook my head. "No, I'm saying that."

Griffin hummed a nonanswer.

I had missed the feeling of steel in my hands. The power I felt when I wielded a sword.

"Care for a wager?"

Griffin raised a sweating brow at me. "You've been spending too much time with our king," he said. Then, after a moment, "Try me."

"If I can land a single blow on you, even one, you have to say something kind to Mari. A genuine compliment."

Griffin rolled his eyes. "What are we, schoolchildren?"

I grinned.

"Fine. If you can't, though, what do I get?"

I thought for a beat. "Griffin, I don't think I know anything about you. What would you want?"

"A silent dinner tonight. If I have to play sitter for you two until we reach Siren's Cove, at least make it tolerable."

"You're terrible. And boring."

Now it was Griffin's turn to grin. "It's the little things."

Before I could respond, he came at me, sword flying. I parried as many blows as I could, but a few hits landed on my arms, abdomen, and back. Griffin had experience teaching, it seemed, as each blow was harnessed with such skill, it would hurtle toward me with speed but land with nothing more than a sting. Griffin's style was much faster and scrappier than Dagan's; he tossed his sword from right hand to left and jumped over my attempted low blows.

Ten minutes later, my legs could barely keep me standing up. "All right, all right," I panted. "Enough."

Griffin shot me an infuriating grin. I blew the hair out of my face like an aggravated horse. Griffin laughed. "Don't be too glum. You're much better than I expected. The old man taught you well."

"Did Kane tell you?"

Griffin nodded, but behind his eyes was something I couldn't place.

"Get cleaned up. We head out in an hour."

I huffed. So much for strong, powerful, Fae-slaying Arwen.

"You could be decent with a bit more practice. Let me know if you want to keep working on it."

I paused. "I thought you hated me."

Griffin's expression barely changed, but his eyes had grown solemn.

"No, healer. I don't hate you." He heaved a sigh and sat down on the bale of hay beside me. The sun was just beginning to rise, and the flickers of light picked up golden strands in his hair.

A thought dawned on me, something I had been wondering for months now.

"Why did you chase after Kane that day in the infirmary? He wasn't really an escaped prisoner."

A rueful smile tugged at the commander's cheeks. It was still strange to see him grin.

"He needed to be healed but didn't want to tell you who he was just yet. We argued about it." Griffin's jaw tightened at the memory. "He gave me the slip."

A laugh popped out of me. "You *chased* him down?"

Griffin's grin was gone, though. "My job is to protect my king. You are—" He scratched at his chin, trying to find the words. "Dangerous for him."

I scoffed. "Right. The great Kane Ravenwood taken down by Arwen from Abbington. Terrifying."

Griffin stood. "It is no laughing matter. He cannot have a single weakness when he goes up against Lazarus, and yet, you are his. Nothing could be more perilous for Evendell."

⟶✦⟵

THAT NIGHT, AFTER YET ANOTHER SUFFOCATING CARRIAGE ride, we sat down at a different little inn. This one was owned by a sweet, plump family, and smelled strongly of pork.

Dinner was an awkward event. While the rest of the guards we traveled with sat around the inn's dormant hearth—it was far too warm for even a single flame—drinking ale and telling stories, the three of us sat in aggressive silence, picking at our food. Mari was displeased, to say the least, about my silent dinner bargain. I had to sway her with the promise of three new books when we arrived in Peridot.

The silence was deafening, but the looks between my two dinner guests were even worse. Mari glared at Griffin with the fury of a soaked cat. Griffin was the embodiment of smug calm, which only made Mari angrier.

The minutes ticked by torturously. I ate as quickly as I could. Mari stared at Griffin until her anger seemed to slip into something else altogether. Her eyes shifted and his peace turned into suspicion.

I didn't dare ask what was going on.

Suddenly Mari turned bright red and looked down at her food. It seemed the poorly cooked pork had become very fascinating in the last minute. I looked from my pork to hers but didn't see anything of note.

I peered back up at Griffin. He was watching Mari's averted chocolate eyes with something like remorse.

He cleared his throat.

"Your hair is radiant. Like sunshine after a storm."

Mari's mouth fell open, and Griffin stood up abruptly, his too-long legs banging the table and making the cutlery jump. He left the table early for the second night in a row.

"What . . . was that?" I asked her. She looked even more shocked than I did.

"I have no idea," Mari said, for the first time since I'd known her. Maybe in her life. She ran an idle finger through her curls and went back to her dinner.

25

I KNEW WE HAD REACHED THE COAST BEFORE I EVEN opened my eyes. A salty breeze wafted in through our carriage window and the temperature dropped about twenty degrees.

"Oh, thank the Stones," I mumbled, my mouth still thick with sleep.

"Arwen, get up!" Mari's voice sounded far away. I cracked one eye open to see her pressed up against the carriage side, head out the window, eyes squinting against the bright sun.

"It's so beautiful," she said.

I couldn't help a smile before I squeezed in beside her.

My heart shone in my chest at the sight, matching the bright sun outside.

Peridot was lusher and more breathtaking than anything I could have imagined. Once again, the weight of how little of Evendell I had experienced hit me like a gut punch.

The castle that sprawled before us atop the highest hill was like a ranch. Bamboo beams, a large, thatched gate, and miles of exotic, textured land spread in every direction. The smell of salt-water and plumeria filtered in as I spied cows, horses, and goats. Bright green hills rolled beyond the castle gates like waves in a sea, all dotted with tropical flowers. I'd have to look into their names now, too.

The city itself stretched beyond the fortress, weaving into the trees and hills and growing denser until I had to squint to make it out. As if Siren's Cove was protected by its king's stronghold, rather than the other way around. From what I could see, the city was more like my hometown of Abbington than what I imagined a bustling capital to be. Smoke billowed out of straw roofs, chickens and more horses squawked and neighed. Families and children and women balancing buckets and baskets milled about.

But the most jaw-dropping view was much closer, out the carriage and to my right. A few miles down from the royal home was the beach.

The docks in Abbington were, at best, a murky, fishy hub for driftwood and pelicans. Boats and ships of all shapes and sizes crowded the harbor, and fishermen with few teeth took up whatever space was left. My siblings and I would walk forty minutes down to take a frigid dip, wandering back at dusk against the shimmering sun melting into the marina, our legs sore and tanned and reeking of brine and trout.

This was something else entirely. The crescent-shaped cove, sheltered by low stone cliffs, was filled with emerald waves rocking against a beach of soft pink sand. A thick rain forest grew beyond the cliffs, filled with spiked trees I had never seen before. A cool breeze mixed with humid air tickled my skin. I wanted to take a bite out of the atmosphere.

"Come on," said Mari, pulling me out of the carriage as soon as it halted. We followed the soldiers toward the castle gates.

I was less pleased to see Princess Amelia than I had anticipated. Her white-blonde hair cascaded over her loose clothing. A single beige band of fabric covered her chest but showed off the taut, tan skin of her belly. A skirt of the same breezy material flowed from low on her hips down to the ground.

She had an incredible body, and the sheer fabric made sure anyone in a five-mile radius knew it. Somewhere between watching her flirt her way into an alliance with an old flame and feeling Kane's tongue in my mouth, I had decided she was my nemesis. Or perhaps something slightly less dramatic. But only slightly.

Next to her stood her father, King Eryx. He had the same pale hair and eyes of bright, warm amber. Like sunflowers—just like his daughter's.

"Welcome, Commander Griffin," Eryx boomed.

Griffin bowed, and the rest of us followed suit.

"Commander." Amelia greeted Griffin warmly. He bowed once more, taking her hand and kissing it.

Eryx looked rather pleased at the interaction.

"Still waiting to take a wife, my dear commander?"

Amelia rolled her eyes with enough venom that even I cowered. But Griffin, cool as ever, didn't even blush. "I have my hands a little full with our current circumstances, Your Majesty."

Eryx gave a warm smile and a sly laugh. "Understood. I think I speak for all when I say we are grateful for your dedication. Once we have defeated the Amber bastards, I assure you my lovely Amelia will still be here, waiting. As always."

I nearly went cross-eyed with the urge to roll my eyes. I didn't particularly care for Amelia, but I didn't like her father offering her up like cattle, either.

"She may be tricky, but I wager the title of Prince of Peridot sweetens the pot?" His wet cackle turned into a cough, and Griffin's bland smile never met his eyes.

I spotted Mari out of the corner of my eye, with a pinched look on her face. Without any more pleasantries—if that's what we could call Eryx's tactless offering—we were ushered inside the airy palace and Griffin followed Eryx into another hallway.

The princess acknowledged neither Mari nor I at all before disappearing.

"She's annoying, right?" Mari said under her breath.

"You have no idea."

WE WERE EACH SHOWN TO OUR OWN ROOM FOR THE OPEN-ended duration of our stay. I couldn't help my theatrical gawk at the warm expanse of teakwood floors and the canopied bed upon entering. The breeze from the huge windows overlooking the glimmering turquoise bay flitted through my hair. A single exotic bird with wings of bright scarlet perched on the windowsill.

I stretched out against the soft, white cotton bedsheets and hummed in relief. No more inns, no more sweltering heat. Maybe I'd finally get a good night's sleep.

But I couldn't rest yet. I'd promised Mari three books and I intended to keep said promise. Plus, I was excited to see the Peridot library. Shadowhold's library was exquisite, and that was just an army stronghold. This was a palace in the Peridot capital of Siren's Cove. Maybe their library was in a lagoon.

I made my way through the castle. Every inch was adorned with either vines, cushions, or delicate beadwork. I asked one of the servants who was dusting a canvas chaise for directions to the library. It was strange, having been a villager in a small town my whole life, then a prisoner just a few months ago, and now a guest of royalty.

The sound of the waves crashing in Siren's Bay followed me everywhere I went, like a welcome lullaby. I pushed open the bamboo doors to the library and passed a few shirtless Peridot soldiers clad in armored pants and helmets. Their torsos and forearms were covered in intricately patterned tattoos that matched their long spears.

The library was simple, filled with colorful books and scrolls, and had a warm hearth at the center of the room surrounded by white cushions. But the cozy fireplace and its few huddled readers weren't the room's highlight—it was the sprawling balcony that looked out onto the pristine bay. Calm, crystalline waters washed over the shore. To the left were at least fifteen massive ships with the green Peridot symbol imprinted on their sails. The sun hung low in the sky, reflecting off the waves in sparkling rays.

I didn't know how I had gone twenty years without seeing an ocean like this, or how I would ever go another day without it again. Glittering sunshine, colors and textures and waves—I could barely believe it was real. Something about being at the edge of the continent felt at once both freeing and completely frightening. Frightening, and yet my all-too-familiar panic was nowhere to be found.

Pulling myself away from the view was like untangling a vine from its post. I finally made my way over to the section marked "Lore" and pulled three books: one on Fae mythology, one grimoire, and one about various types of hybrid creatures and their diets. I knew my girl.

Plus, after everything Kane had told me, I wanted to learn more about the Faeries as well. If he was somehow to beat his father, he needed all the information he could get. I tried not to think about the odds of him defeating the last living full-blooded Fae when he had lost so terribly a mere fifty years ago.

On my way out I doubled back to the section marked "Horti-culture" and grabbed a book entitled *Evendell Flora by Kingdom*. That one was just for me.

I dropped the books outside Mari's room, remembering that she was going to nap before dinner, and returned to my room. A knock at my door had me back up before I had even crawled fully under the silken sheets for a nap of my own.

"Come in."

Princess Amelia strolled inside and sat down on the bed. I scram-bled to politely sit beside her, then tried to bow. It wasn't pretty.

She gave me a pitying glance. "No need for . . . whatever that is. I brought you clothes for tonight's dinner." She handed me a simi-lar dress to what she was wearing. Very sheer, pale blue fabric. It looked like it wouldn't cover much of anything. "The tragically dark and heavy clothes of Onyx won't suit you here."

"Thank you, Your Highness," I said. "I have to ask, does the princess always hand deliver clothing to her guests?" I wasn't sure what made me so snarky. I didn't trust this woman. I trusted her even less when she was being kind to me.

She offered a prim smile that didn't reach her eyes.

"I know you think I am your enemy, Arwen. That I am trying to bed your king, or take him from you, or whatever little problems you concern yourself with. It could not be further from the truth. In fact, I want to offer you some advice. Woman to woman."

Like a child being scolded, I stared down at my interwoven fingers. I didn't dare bring up that I knew she had already bedded the king many times. I wasn't sure who that discussion would be more unpleasant for, her or me. She dipped an elongated finger adorned with jewels under my chin and tilted my face up to hers.

"Kane Ravenwood has not been wholly truthful with you."

I blinked twice.

"I urge you not to lead with your heart," she continued, "but rather with your mind and spirit. You seem a bright young woman. Do not be easily fooled by his allure."

Before I could tell her I was more privy to his secrets than she thought, she got up and left the room, gently closing the door behind her.

I clamped my lips together as irritation flickered inside me.

She couldn't have been more wrong. Up until a few days ago, I would have agreed wholeheartedly. But he had finally let me in—shared his darkest secrets with me, as I had with him. Maybe Amelia was jealous, or maybe she was genuinely trying to help. Either way, it didn't matter. I had no idea when or if I would see him again, and as long as we were apart, I wouldn't let my faith in him waver.

I looked at the slips of fabric the princess had referred to as *clothing*. I wasn't as slender as she was and wasn't eager to have so much of my body on display. I undressed completely and slipped the blue fabric on. The wisps of shimmering sheerness looped around my neck and waist at a low angle, leaving my midriff exposed, before pooling on the floor like melted cream. It was less fabric than I had ever worn outside of my own bedroom.

I looked in the mirror anticipating mortification but felt a surge of power waft over me in its place; I actually looked quite lovely.

I tucked my hair up atop my head and secured it with a black ribbon. You could take the girl out of Onyx, but you couldn't take Onyx out of the—

My door creaked open and I turned, expecting Mari or Amelia once more.

Instead, I came face-to-face with a dazed Kane.

"Fuck," he grunted.

I was so shocked to see him, I was even less eloquent. "Huh?"

Kane cleared his throat. "Hello," he said, flushing. "You look so—I mean, very—hello." His brows knitted inward as if even he didn't know what was coming out of his mouth.

He was here.

In Peridot.

Alive, and happy to see me. I felt my cheeks warm. "Very hello to you, too." I pulled him through the doorway and into my room, lifting on my toes to press a single kiss against his cheek. He had shaved, and his smooth jaw was hot under my lips.

"When did you arrive?" I asked, not recognizing the rasp in my voice.

His hands grasped my hips firmly, but he held me at a distance. "Moments ago. I need to show you something."

My face fell. "Right now?"

Kane looked like he could break solid rock with his teeth. "If you can believe it, yes."

He grasped my hand and pulled me down the wooden stairs into the great hall. The room smelled of freshly grilled fish and citrus fruit. My stomach rumbled. We were surrounded by Peridot nobles and commanders, and I thought absently that I should probably let go of the king's hand.

But then I saw them, and all other thoughts disappeared from my mind.

26

Only slightly worse for wear and in garnet clothes I couldn't have imagined any of them wearing were my family. My mother, Leigh, and Ryder were seated at a wooden table with Griffin and Mari, laughing and eating. My face crumpled and I couldn't control the tears that spilled down.

I ran to them, throwing myself at Leigh first.

"What the—" But when she realized it was me, she squealed. Her little arms wrapping around me only made me cry harder. Later, I would take the time to inspect every finger and every toe and prove to myself that she was really all right.

"I missed you so much. And I love you, but I can't breathe!"

I released her, but only to get a good look at her face. She was thinner than when I last saw her, but she was beaming at me, and her expression lit up her sunken cheeks.

I looked to Ryder next, as he hustled over and scooped me into his arms.

When he let me go, he appraised my sheer outfit with a grimace. "You look deranged."

I laughed through my blurry eyes and held him tighter. "Thank you." I pulled back but kept my voice low. "You kept them safe."

"Of course I did. What did *you* do?"

"It's a very long story."

Then I made my way over to my mother. She didn't look quite as good as Leigh and Ryder. The months had aged her, and she seemed frail and tired. I crouched down and held her in my arms.

"I can't believe it. I thought I might never see you again," she breathed.

My heart rose in my chest like the sun after a storm. Bright and shining and clear. I held her even tighter. "I know," I said. "I'm so sorry."

We stayed like that for I don't know how long. When my back began to ache, I let go and took a seat at the table.

I searched for Kane, only to find him stalking out of the hall with Amelia and Eryx. I ran after them, joy and disbelief making me bold.

"Hey! Wait!" I caught up to him and yanked on his shirt, wiping my eyes with my other hand. "Where are you going?"

Amelia gazed at me with cynical interest next to her father, but I couldn't be bothered. Not tonight. Not when Kane was looking at me with such affection, my cheeks began to hurt from all the smiling.

"I thought you might want to be alone with them. I have some things to do here before I leave."

"We do have a war to strategize on, Lady Arwen," Amelia said, condescension dripping from her voice and even, stony features.

"Oh, of course." I turned back to Kane. "Thank you—I'll never be able to say it enough—for reuniting us."

"I told you I would," he said, eyes shining.

"How did you get here so quickly? From Garnet?"

His head cocked to the side as if he was preparing to answer my question with another question.

"Dragon?" I asked, as if it was completely normal to me.

He smiled a bit. "Yes." Then, leaning away from our hosts, "I'm not sure who was more thrilled, your mother or the little one."

"And Ryder?"

"I think he vomited."

I loosed a too-loud laugh, and Kane's eyes crinkled at my joy.

"When do you leave?" I asked.

He shifted back toward Eryx. "Tomorrow morning."

"Right," I said. "Well, even busy kings who are waging wars have to eat. Want to join us? Would probably be the shock of my mother's life." I grinned up at him.

His usual wolflike charm was gone tonight, but he didn't seem sad, either. Maybe resigned, which made sense. I understood the severity of the situation. But nothing could take the joy of seeing my family away from me right now.

He glanced at Amelia and Eryx, their faces twin masks of irritation. Then his eyes flitted over to the candlelit table that held my family, Mari, and his commander.

"Sure," he said.

⸻ ❧ ⸻

DINNER WAS FASCINATING.

I had given my mother the burrowroot concoction I brewed on our journey here, and while she wasn't thrilled with the taste, her face had brightened just over the course of our dinner.

Despite my family's initial unease at the dark king's presence, Kane was on his best behavior, and they softened to him one by one. Leigh first, of course—the girl was gutsy. Then Mother, who had many questions for Kane. *"What does it feel like to carry the burden of a kingdom on your lone shoulders?"* *"Do the deaths you have caused weigh on you daily?"* Not quite leisurely dinnertime conversation. I tried to convey my displeasure through relentless eye contact.

At least her approach was better than Ryder's. He had watched us return to the table with a strange look in his eye and hadn't let up since we sat down. He interrupted my mother's next question for Kane with one of his own. "So, King Ravenwood," he asked, bread roll in hand, "how did you end up befriending my sister?" I shot him a dirty glare. I did not care for the emphasis he put on "befriending."

Kane gave him that signature wolfish grin. I turned about eight shades of red in anticipation. "She offered to be the healer in my keep in return for the coin you stole. You might owe her your thanks."

Now it was Ryder's turn to redden. "Your Majesty, it was a simple life-or-death scenario. You would have done the same for your family, would you not?"

"I have no family, so I wouldn't know," Kane said offhandedly. A twinge of sadness echoed in my heart at his words. He must have seen my facial expression, as he added, "But I'll take your word for it."

"Bleeding Stones," Ryder muttered under his breath, shrinking away.

"Language!" Mother hissed at him.

I couldn't help my smile. I had even missed her ridiculous prudishness.

Mari, too, had lots of questions. Mostly about Abbington and what misconceptions people had about Onyx. Leigh loved her immediately. The two of them were like two halves of a comedy act—finishing each other's sentences and laughing maniacally at things nobody else at the table found funny.

"That actually brings me to another thought," Mari said to my mother. "What was the—"

"You're making the woman choke on her swordfish. Let her eat in peace." Griffin's tone was pleasant enough, but Mari shot him a withering glare.

"I'm so sorry, Commander. I forgot how good you are at making conversation. Do you want to compliment her hair?" asked Mari.

A laugh spasmed out of me and I almost spewed papaya all over the table. I grabbed Kane's arm beside me in between fits of giggles. Kane bit down a laugh at my hysterics. Out of the corner of my eye, I saw Ryder quirk a brow at the moment between us. I quickly extricated my hand from the king's sleeve.

"Don't worry about it, Red. I think she likes being interviewed. Don't you, Mam?" said Ryder.

My mother smiled and started to speak, but Griffin interrupted. "I don't know, *Red*, I think the kid's just being kind."

Mari scoffed, and Ryder grinned at Griffin, but it didn't reach his eyes. "If I'm a kid, what does that make you, Commander?"

"A man," Griffin said into his food, already bored by the exchange.

"Could've fooled me," Ryder chirped, sending Mari and me into another fit of laughter.

I looked to my left and saw Kane and Leigh deep in conversation. She was explaining something to him with animated expressions and complex hand gestures. Kane, to his credit, was following intently, chin resting on his fist and nodding along to her story.

I took in this strange group before me and felt as though my heart might burst. It was better than I could ever have imagined, having all of them together.

When dinner ended and we were all full to the brim, rum and carbs coating our stomachs, I rounded to my mother's chair to help her stand. To my disbelief, she stood up easily.

"Mother!" I said, not even trying to hide my shock.

She moved slowly at first, then found her footing and walked like she used to. Slow, but deliberate. Elegant, even. Leigh and Ryder watched with awe. I felt more tears prick at my eyes. Tonight had to be some kind of happy-crying record.

"Arwen . . . I don't have words."

"Me neither. How do you feel?"

"Better. My mind feels less foggy."

"So, it wasn't the fever talking," Kane said.

I whipped to him behind me, his eyes like stars.

"No," I whispered. What I had done in the woods that night was unbelievably stupid. But nothing could have been more worth it than the look on my mother's face tonight.

"What's he talking about?" my mother asked, brow raised.

"Nothing. Let me walk you to your room for the night." I turned to Kane, but he read my thoughts.

"I'll come see you before I leave. Enjoy your family tonight."

I nodded in thanks.

Halfway up the stairs, my mother turned to me. "So, you're sleeping with a king. That's new!"

"Mother!" I gasped, but I was unable to hide my grin.

She laughed. "I'm only teasing. But he is clearly very, very fond of you."

I felt the familiar tug in my heart. "We are absolutely doing nothing of the sort." I linked her arm in mine as we rounded the torchlit hall. "But I'm fond of him, too. He has been kind to me since I've been at Onyx. Despite everything going on, everything at stake. Well—" I thought better of my phrasing. "His version of kind."

My mother clucked, patting my hand. "He seems very thoughtful, under all those layers of brooding." Now it was my turn to laugh. Kane would love that.

"It wasn't an easy few months, but there were a few silver linings. You would adore the flowers in the Shadowhold gardens. They are the strangest colors I have ever seen."

She gave me a half smile before going still just a few steps from her room. "Arwen, when Ryder went back for you and saw the . . . the blood, we thought the worst. I could scarcely sleep knowing we had let you turn back." She took my hand into hers. "But I am so, so proud of you, Arwen."

I squeezed her hand tightly, my brows knitting inward. "What for?"

"When the king found us in Garnet, he told us what you did for Ryder. For all of us. How many you had healed in the Onyx Kingdom outpost. I had no idea where you had gone. If you were still alive. But part of me knew all along you would be just fine on your own. That maybe it was necessary. I fear I sheltered you too much. I just know how dark a place this world can be."

My thoughts flashed to Bert, the wolfbeast, Halden's lies. "I'm grateful. Had I known what was out there, I might never have given myself the chance to be brave."

My mother shook her head and pulled me into her arms. "I'm so lucky to have you as my daughter. The world is a better place seen through your eyes."

It felt like home, resting my head against her shoulder and feeling her soothing hands on my back. "If anything, I get it from you," I mumbled into her.

"My kind girl. Don't let anyone take that from you. The shining light you have within."

I nodded into the crook between her neck and shoulder, the nighttime buzzing of crickets and cicadas like a cocoon for our embrace. With everything that was unfolding—understanding I would likely not see Kane again for months if not years, the brewing conflict with a Fae king—I hadn't realized how much I just needed my mother. I never wanted to let go.

She squeezed me harder and said, "I think tomorrow I'm going to swim in the bay. What do you think of that?"

A single tear slipped down my cheek onto her dress. "I think that sounds wonderful. I'll join you."

27

I WAITED UP UNTIL I COULDN'T KEEP MY HEAVY EYES OPEN a moment longer. The candles I lit for Kane's visit had long since puddled, swallowing their wicks whole and drowning the room in shades of blue and black. I had hoped Kane would come see me before he left in the morning, but he hadn't yet, and I steeled myself against the nagging hurt. I wasn't a child. He was a king heading into a greater war than I had ever known, and the worst was yet to come.

He had more important things to do than say goodbye to his . . . to me.

I wasn't sure what I was to him.

We definitely weren't lovers, but we were more than friends.

I slipped into my nightdress and crawled under the covers. Sleep was a welcome drug, pulling me under a fog of rest and away from emotionally complicated thoughts.

I woke to the familiar smell of woody fir, and surprise gave way to warmth, unfurling inside me as I buried my face in Kane's chest.

He was here—in my bed.

I nuzzled even closer.

We had never really cuddled before, except maybe when I was dying—which, of what I could recall, wasn't all that romantic. I took a moment to enjoy his strong hands around my back, pressing me to him.

"You feel good," I murmured.

He hummed his response against my ear and ran a gentle hand down my back. My nipples pebbled at his touch, my breasts becoming tight and full against the silky fabric of my nightdress.

When his finger brushed my tailbone I shivered, and a dark chuckle rumbled from his chest. I pulled back slightly and looked up at him. His body felt languid against mine, but he was breathing as heavily as I was, desire filling his eyes like endless pools.

"I thought you weren't coming," I said.

"I wouldn't have missed this for anything." He brushed a few hairs away from my face and ran his hand up my bare thigh, his touch rough and warm and setting me on fire. I wanted to devour him—to feel him everywhere. I had wanted this for so, so long, every minute we were both still fully clothed was a tragedy.

And his extraordinary gentleness was killing me.

My eyes focused on his full lips, and I parted mine, breathless.

He leaned in as his hand ran lazily up and down my thigh, pushing my nightdress up ever so slightly. His mouth was close—

So close—

But when his fingers grazed my hip bone, he pulled back, jaw rigid and pupils flaring.

"What is it?" I breathed.

"You're . . . not wearing anything under your nightdress."

I flushed, my face somehow going hotter than it already was. "No."

"Why not?"

A laugh slipped out at his confusion. "I don't usually sleep in them. I don't know. I can put some on?"

He barked out one dark, cruel laugh and then rolled onto his back with a deep, pained sigh, and a forearm draped across his eyes.

"Are you all right?" I asked, breathless, and confused by the shift in his energy.

"Not by any stretch of the imagination. In fact, I'm losing my mind a bit."

I slunk closer to him, my breathing still uneven, and planted a single, soft kiss on his warm neck. Balsam and leather filled my senses, and I released a soft hum against his skin.

A groan, guttural and raw, fell from him and he stood, climbing off the bed altogether.

I sat up, raising an eyebrow in silent question. "Do you really not want this?" I asked, slightly sheepish.

"You know I do," he said through clenched teeth. "More than I've ever wanted anything."

"So you wouldn't prefer I sleep with someone else?"

I was only kidding, but he stalked closer, eyes blazing. He looked like he wanted to crush mountains.

I bit my tongue.

"Arwen, you aren't—" He fought for the words, though they looked like they physically pained him to say. "You aren't *mine*. You don't belong to me. You can spend your time with whoever you please. All I hope is that they treat you with the respect you deserve, and I will try every single day not to think of ripping out their still-beating hearts."

I tried to hide my smile. I loved imagining Kane jealous. It was twisted, but his barely contained fury sent a thrill through me.

Silly king—as if there could be anyone else.

"Have you ever thought about it?"

He raised a brow. "Of you with another man? I'd rather gouge my eyes out."

I laughed out loud. "No, of what it would be like. Between us . . ."

"Ah, of course." His voice had dropped to a low growl.

It was the most profoundly erotic sound I'd ever heard.

He stalked closer to me. "Ever since that day we rode back from the woods together, I have thought of little else. Each night I rub myself raw thinking of your long legs, perfect breasts, and gorgeous laugh." He lifted one single strand of my hair and rubbed it between his fingers. "I imagine you on top of me and come apart faster than I care to admit."

I was panting now, resisting the urge to bring my hand between my legs and release the tension building up inside me. He must have read the wanton desire in my eyes because he sighed, thick and heavy, released my hair from his fingertips, and paced over to the chair across the room.

He looked miserable. And so tired.

"Arwen, I came to say goodbye." He said it like he was convincing himself, not me.

"I know."

"And that"—he gestured to the bed behind me—"would not be a very fair goodbye."

I huffed, crossing my arms. "Don't be so condescending. I'm an adult woman. I can make those decisions for myself."

He paused, running a hand through his hair. "I meant for me. I'm a selfish bastard, remember? Having you, and then . . . leaving you. It would kill me."

"Oh," I said, a little dumbly. "Maybe it doesn't have to be goodbye?"

"Our deal is done. You're safe now, you have your family. Your mother is healing. It's all I could have hoped for you. I can give you enough coin to live a long and healthy life with them here. All I would do is put you in danger."

I knew he was right. My family and I could have a real life here in Siren's Cove—a happy one. I could picture it in my mind with perfect clarity—Leigh's chickens and cows; Mother, finally healthy, cooking and dancing in the kitchen like she used to. Ryder would continue his woodwork. I would still heal, but maybe I'd open a tropical flower shop, too, one day. Maybe Kane would visit every few years. We could share nights just like these, tangled together under clandestine moonlight until he left before sunrise, his kingdom calling him back. Until one day I built a life with someone new. Someone else . . .

How could I want more than that? More than safety for myself and my family?

But I did.

I wanted him. All of him. All the time. Preferably forever. The reality of my feelings for him hit me with the force of a tidal wave, nearly knocking the wind out of me.

"Our deal," I repeated his words. "Why did you have me stay? It wasn't just to heal your soldiers or pay off a debt. Was it just to keep me around?"

Kane rubbed his eyes. "Doesn't matter now." He stood to leave. I felt a wave of unrelenting panic. Was this the last moment I was ever going to have with him? It couldn't end like this.

I rose from the bed and raced to stand in front of him before he reached the door, my heart thundering in my ears.

"Don't leave," I whispered.

His eyes were punishing. "Arwen, we can't."

But he made no move to push past me, so I stood on my tiptoes and took his face in my hands, gently.

"I know you said I'm not *yours*. But . . . I want to be." I swallowed hard. "*I want to be yours*, Kane."

His eyes simmered with heat and anguish.

Before I could protest even further, he caught my surprised lips in his.

Groaning into my mouth, he physically stumbled toward me, as if the relief of our kiss had made his legs weak. I stifled a moan and wrapped my arms around his broad shoulders, feeling the soft hair at the nape of his neck. His breathing was harsh and ragged as he sucked my bottom lip into his mouth, savage and restless and hungry.

Finally, finally, *finally*—

His hands, the ones that had been so gentle, teasing along my thigh in bed, were now grasping at my entire body. It was making me hot and needy, knowing his fingers were so close to all the places I wanted them.

And his taste, his mouth—like sweet whiskey and mint from the earth—it was more than overwhelming. All-consuming. This was nothing like his soft, chaste kiss in the gardens. That had been searching, careful, cautious. This was—

He ran a single finger across my pointed nipple, producing a soft hiss from me that turned into a shudder as his finger worked its way down, brushing right up against my waistline, but no lower.

More, please—

I tugged at his shirt. I needed to feel his skin, to taste it. Breaking our kiss, he ripped the linen over his head in one swift motion. I ogled him shamelessly, the breath punching out of me. Even in the moonlight, his chiseled, tan skin glowed.

"You're beautiful," I murmured. I wasn't even ashamed. It was true.

"You're one to talk." He stared at me in reverence before his eyes turned wholly feral. Gripping my ass, he hoisted me up, capturing my mouth in a savage kiss and slamming us into the wall beside the bed, careful to cradle the back of my head in his hand. Immediately I felt his length against my core, hard like solid rock and pressing angrily through his pants. I clawed at his back, his neck, his jaw, fingers roaming with minds of their own.

But still, I needed more.

I wanted to be compressed between his body and the cool wallpaper behind me. Pressed like one of the flowers in my books under his delicious weight. I was needy and aching, grinding myself against him like a cat in heat.

He released my lips and trailed a line of feather-soft kisses down the column of my throat, and my fingers tangled in his silky hair, eliciting a pleasant growl from him. The noise made my breasts pinch and ache, and I ground my hips into his impressive length, wrapping my legs around him even tighter. He slipped one strap of my nightdress down and bit at my shoulder.

"More," I begged.

"Don't tempt me," he purred against my collarbone, nibbling

and biting until he reached my breast over the silken fabric. He pulled back and traced a reverent finger down the scar on my chest.

"This is healing very quickly."

"That happens with me sometimes," I breathed, but Kane was lost in his own thoughts.

"I thought"—his voice cracked, and my heart stumbled over a beat—"I'd lost you. I couldn't eat. Sleep. Move." A sad smile tugged at his lips. "Shave." He considered me with something akin to awe. "I did not want to live in a world without you in it."

I felt the energy in the room shift at his words. We had danced around the chemistry and emotion between us for so long that admitting our feelings felt unthinkable. His eyes shone like stars and for a moment all I could hear was our ragged breathing.

But he saved me the words that lodged in my throat by placing a single kiss along my new scar, so carefully I could have cried. His lips traced down my chest, along the silk of my nightdress, until his mouth circled my pointed nipple over the silky fabric. His teeth were sharp yet gentle around the sensitive bud, and I mewled out a wild-sounding noise.

"That's it," he said, grasping my other breast with his hand and softly massaging it. I tipped my head back, nearly going cross-eyed at the sensation, and bit down on my lip, trying not to make any more silly noises. The throb between my legs was teetering on pain.

He brought my mouth back down to his and carried us to the bed, laying me down and climbing on top of me. He tried to slow our kisses, worship each angle of my jaw, my neck, but I kissed him with a fiercer desire than I had ever felt, needy and wanton and desperate, likely bruising his lips.

Emboldened by my searing want, I looped a leg over his waist and rolled us until I was straddling him. He sighed into my mouth and wrapped two large hands around my waist. He was so big, his thumbs nearly touched under my belly button. One hand came up to cup my breast and rub my nipple lightly, and I whimpered on top of him.

I felt alight like a flickering flame.

"You're not making it very easy for me to savor you, bird," he joked, voice husky and eyes wild.

Ignoring him, I trailed light kisses down his naked chest, basking in his salty, sweet skin.

He tasted like pure moonlight—dark and sensual and all too tempting.

When I reached his waistband and my hands grasped for the laces of his pants, Kane groaned. The noise made my thighs clench.

But his hands snapped to mine, stopping them. "Fine. No savoring."

Before I could argue, he brought me back up to him with a wicked grin, and tucked me into his chest, my back pressed flush against his front. He slid one hand under me, around my stomach, holding me to him. When his other hand slipped beneath the silky fabric and found the soft skin of my breast, we both arched farther toward each other.

Kane swore and pressed his mouth to my neck. "You're even better than I ever could have thought. All those months, thinking I'd never get to be with you—it was the worst torture I could've imagined. I want to bury my mouth in between your pretty thighs."

His words were unraveling me. I was soaking wet and rocking against him rhythmically. I needed his hand lower.

A positively filthy idea crossed my mind.

"You know," I managed to breathe, "you aren't the only one with indecent thoughts from that horseback ride together."

Kane stilled behind me before releasing a shaky exhale. His hand still held my breast under my nightdress, and I rocked myself against his length, making myself whimper with need.

"You are forbidden from not finishing that thought."

Humor played at my lips and I moved against him again. He grunted—a brutal and depraved noise—and moved his hand to slide my nightdress up.

"Do you remember when you barged in, and I was in the tub?"

He laughed lightly. "I could never forget. You were so cute wielding that candlestick." He traced lazy circles on my hip while he licked and sucked at my neck. "Being that close to you, knowing your body was naked and glistening . . . It was agony," he whispered, pulling the fabric of my dress all the way up to my stomach.

"Well," I said, breathless. "I had been touching myself before you barged in. I had actually been right about to come."

He snarled in satisfaction at my words and thrust his hips into my ass.

I loved how powerful I felt in his arms.

"Please, do not stop." His voice was hardly more than a whisper. He pushed my legs apart and took his time tracing across my inner thighs, stilling when he felt the wetness that had pooled there. "Oh, fuck. So wet for me. What were you thinking of that day, my pretty bird?"

"You," I breathed.

That seemed to be enough to push him over the edge. He turned me to face him and kissed me roughly, his tongue exploring my mouth slow and hard. As if, if he didn't kiss me more deeply, he would drown. Like I was oxygen. He finally traced his fingers lightly over the single spot I had been aching for, and stars clouded my vision. His light strokes were making me shudder and clench.

He exhaled through our kiss, and it came out like a choke. But his fingers were unrelenting—teasing and massaging, playing me like an instrument and making me sing. I was so close, and he hadn't even—

Finally, he let one finger slip inside me, and I cried out just a little as his thumb continued to circle. We both sighed at the sensation, and I kissed him harder, my hands roaming his chest as he thrust his finger in and out of me.

Slow, controlled strokes, so tight, so full—

"Can you take more?" he asked, and I released a low hum of need.

Yes, yes, please, yes. More.

When he slipped a second finger inside me, I writhed on his hand and shuddered out a moan as he filled me further—plunged his fingers into me, wrung each breath and sigh from my lips.

"Arwen," he growled. It was nearly my undoing. Keening and bucking, I gave myself over to him, impatiently waiting to be gifted the release I craved.

The boom of cannons shook us violently from our intimacy. I looked up at Kane, and he hopped from the bed over to the window lightning fast.

"Get dressed," he choked out. "Now."

Flustered and with still-shaking knees, I climbed off the bed. I had a feeling he wasn't talking about putting on the blue Peridot number, so I scrambled for my leathers and slipped my nightdress off, the silk puddling at my feet. Laces flew between my fingers as another cannon rocked the fortress.

He crossed the room and threw his shirt on, his expression sharper and blacker than I'd ever seen it.

I knew before I even asked. "What's happening?"

"The castle is under attack."

Then came the screams.

28

Explosions rocked the room like a ship on a tormented sea. Shouts of fear echoed from the hallway as flecks of dust and debris rained down from the ceiling.

"Come on," Kane said. "Stay close to me."

I followed him out into the dim hallway, air shallow in my lungs. Onyx guards were waiting outside my door for their king, and they pulled us through the wreckage.

I could hardly breathe, let alone move. I needed to get to my family.

"We have to—"

"I know," he shouted over the panicked cries surrounding us. "They're around this corner."

Flickering lights swung with the blasts, casting grotesque shadows on the hall. I could only catch glimpses of servants and nobles alike scrambling from room to room. The calming smell of coconut and ocean salt was at odds with the fear coursing through my veins.

This never should have happened here.

A belated horror hit me, tearing my hand from Kane's and up to my mouth. The guards behind us stopped abruptly, slamming into one another.

"Are you hurt?" Kane took my face in his hands, searching for the source of my gasp.

"I did this," I said, unable to move.

"What are you talking about?"

"I told Halden that your banquet was with King Eryx. That you were hoping to make an alliance."

I had essentially condemned all these people to death. The enormity of my mistake—

Kane shook his head.

"Listen to me. You are not at fault. The fault is of the men behind the cannons. We need to keep moving."

I knew he was right. We had to find my family. But the guilt was all-consuming. As I looked at the terrified faces, it sank deeper into my bones. The ashy scent of smoke wafted toward us. Out through the windows, the spiky trees were lit with flames. A piercing scream beside me nearly popped my eardrum.

"We have to help these people," I said as we ran through the shaking corridor.

"We will."

"How does Amber have such manpower? To light the whole castle on fire? It's not possible."

"They don't. Garnet does."

"Can we stop the cannons?"

Kane looked like murder. "It's not the cannons I'm worried about. It's the salamanders."

I broke our stride and redirected to the nearest window, looking for the first time at what was lighting the forest ablaze. Massive fanged lizards crawled across the beach. With their long necks they looked like snakes, but hefty legs moved them forward like lizards, each with claws that could rip a person to shreds like wet paper. Manned by Garnet and Amber soldiers alike, they made their way toward the castle. With each exhale, a rope of fire sprayed the ground in front of them, charring everything in its path.

Unfaltering Peridot soldiers were stationed around the perimeter, but their spears were no match for the slithering, flame-throwing creatures. More hot, dancing fireballs flew past the Peridot men and toward the castle's exterior.

That's what was shaking the castle—the blasts from the salamanders. We were being trapped and roasted. Burned alive.

Bleeding Stones," I whispered. Kane grabbed my hand and pulled me onward.

We ran as fast as we could toward the other rooms. We got to Ryder's first. Kane rapped on the door.

"Open up, it's us!"

When we didn't hear anything, alarm flooded my senses.

"Open it. Now!" I urged.

Kane slammed his body into the wooden door with more strength than I had ever seen someone exert. Fae strength. The door popped clean off its hinges and fell flat on the floor with a thud.

Inside, my mother and Ryder were huddled up behind the armoire.

"Thank the Stones," I said, rushing over. "Why didn't you answer?" When I got a good look at my mother's tear-streaked face, panic expanded in my chest. "What's wrong?"

"Leigh isn't in her room," she said.

I turned to Ryder.

"We'll find her, but she's not on this floor." He seemed calm, but I knew my brother. His too-wide eyes gave away his dread.

Kane put his hand on my shoulder and gave a slight squeeze. "We need to get everyone to the throne room. It's where you will all be safest. We will not leave here without the little one." He looked at my mother. "I swear it."

We made our way there at a breakneck speed. I was amazed at how well Mother could move. After all these years, there had been a cure for her.

The throne room was heavily guarded by Peridot soldiers. As soon as we approached, they opened the doors for Kane. Inside we found King Eryx, Princess Amelia, and all the other dignitaries, Peridot and Onyx alike. Commanders, generals, and lieutenants moved around the room in a frenzied dance, barking orders at soldiers and guards. Everyone was shouting over one another. My head was swimming.

Where in the Stones was Leigh?

Mari was sitting in a corner, knees up against her chest, while Griffin talked to a Peridot commander a few feet away.

I ran to her and dropped down to the floor.

"Oh, Holy Stones, you're all right!" She wrapped me in her arms. I inhaled the cinnamon scent of her and tried not to cry. If I started now, I'd never be able to stop.

Next to Griffin stood a broad shape I recognized instantly—Barney, uniform still a bit tight, a pillar of stillness. I nodded and he returned the gesture back to me, worry shadowing his expression.

I just needed a sword, and I could go track my sister down. A longsword glinted on the makeshift table that had clearly been shuffled in here minutes ago and was piled high with maps and lanterns and weaponry.

Before I could stand and make my way over to it, King Eryx's voice boomed through the room to Kane. "It is as we feared. Garnet and Amber have joined Lazarus. They will take the kingdom before daybreak."

I had seen the attack with my own eyes mere moments ago. And still, genuine fear—pure and all-consuming—clouded my vision.

His wrinkled general was next to speak. "The only way out is the caves below. That's how we can get to the beach." He turned to Kane and his Onyx men. "The fortress at Siren's Cove is built atop an elaborate expanse of caves that border the bay. Our ships are tethered where the stone cliffs meet the sand, and the caves are the fastest way out."

"Way out? We aren't going to stay and fight?" Princess Amelia asked.

King Eryx shot her a brutal glare. "We do not have the blade. It is not worth fighting Lazarus without it. We cannot win."

"We can't make for the beach, they're stationed there," said a lanky Peridot soldier.

"Well, that's where our ships are. We'll never get everyone out via horse or on foot. The palms that surround the castle are on fire," said the general.

"How did they get through the bay?" Amelia raged at them. "Where were our guards?"

"Your highness," the lanky man tried, "they sank each of our guard ships. Lit all the watchtowers aflame. It was more firepower than we ever could have anticipated."

It was Fae lighte—that was how. And Amelia knew it.

Even if Peridot had had months to prepare rather than minutes, they were no match for Garnet, Amber, *and* Lazarus.

Amelia glared at Eryx with disdain. "These are our people, Father. Our sole purpose on this continent is to keep them safe."

Eryx only turned to Kane. "Do whatever you need to do, but Amelia and I will be on our ship within the next hour. I won't stay to see my only remaining family torched alive."

"Father!"

"Silence, Amelia!" he roared, spittle flying from his reddened face. "It is not up for discussion any longer."

I couldn't listen to this a minute more; I needed to find Leigh.

I stood, heart in my throat, ignoring Mari's objections.

Kane's incensed silver eyes met mine immediately.

"Griffin," Kane interjected, before Amelia could protest further. "Go with Eryx, Amelia, and their men. Take everyone you can with you. Get them to the ships. I'll find Leigh and meet you there."

"You are my king. I am not leaving you behind." Griffin's light green eyes hardened. For the briefest moment, they dipped down to Mari before shooting back to Kane.

"You will do as I say," Kane insisted before turning to the rest of his guards in the throne room. "You all will. Nobody is to come with me. Now go."

"Well, I'm coming with you," I said, following him out and grabbing the longsword from the table beside me.

He barked out a dark laugh. "Absolutely not."

"You'll never find her without me. I know her better than anyone."

My mother held tightly to Ryder, who let the debate unfold in silence.

Kane considered me, his eyes burning like the fires that surrounded us. "No, Arwen. If something were to happen to you . . ."

"You won't let it." I looked down at the sword in my hand. "And neither will I."

Without giving him a moment to argue, I pulled my mother, Ryder, and Mari into quick embraces. "Stick with Griffin. Get to the ships. We'll be right behind you." And then I pushed my way out of the throne room, Kane following closely.

"Where should we start?" Kane asked, dodging a toppled statue.

I couldn't let myself believe that someone had taken her, or worse. I pushed the thought from my mind. "If she fled, she would have gone high up. She's a sneaky climber."

We hurried up a thin spiral staircase toward the thatched roof of the fortress.

"Leigh!" I called out. Kane echoed my cries. We looked through the floors, each room, each nook. Long minutes passed with no sign of her. There was nothing but destruction and despair and death.

The castle had started to fill with smoke. I coughed and rubbed at my eyes as we dug through a slowly crumbling parlor room.

I felt Kane watching me.

"Don't even say it."

"You should get to the ships. I'll take you there and double back for her."

"No—"

A charred plank of wood dislodged above us and fell with shocking speed. I jumped out of the way and grasped at my heart, willing air into my lungs, then coughing hard. Not air, then, but smoke.

"Arwen!" he roared. "You can't save her or anyone else if you are dead."

I closed my eyes and tried not to let my face crumple. I could not break down right now. I just wanted to hold her in my arms and know she was all right. *Please,* I begged the Stones. *Please, not Leigh.*

"Let's just try the stables. She loves animals. Maybe she tried to escape on horseback?" I said.

"No," he growled. "You cannot leave the castle walls. It's swarming with soldiers and salamanders out there."

"I'm going whether you come with me or not. I think I'm a lot safer with a Fae such as you than alone. Don't you think?"

He ran a beleaguered hand through his hair. Ash had coated both our heads and it rained down onto the floor beneath us. He must have agreed with me because he gave one curt nod and took my hand, and we ran toward the back of the castle.

The balmy night was filled with a cacophony of anguish and damage. Amber, Peridot, Onyx, and Garnet soldiers crowded the courtyard like ants on spilled honey. We ran for the hills that marked the stables, and I tried not to think of all the other people who were looking for—and losing—their families, too. And how it was my fault.

Once the structure was in view, I sprinted.

"Arwen!" Kane's voice rang out through the night air, but I moved as fast as my feet would carry me. The area was clear of soldiers, of people in general. It was too quiet.

I looked in each stall, under every gate.

The stables were empty.

"Where are all the horses?" I breathed. Kane caught up to me, catching his breath, and looked around.

"Perhaps the stable hand freed them when he saw the fire."

"No, I did," came a small voice from the corner.

The relief was so intense it nearly knocked the wind out of me.

I choked back a sob. Leigh popped her head up over a haystack and ran into my arms, shaking with emotion. I tried to hold myself together for her, but blubbering tears slipped down either side of my face.

"What were you doing out here?" I wiped the tears from my face and stroked her honey hair back.

"I couldn't sleep. I was looking for the dragon."

The sound of footsteps sent shivers up my spine and across my neck.

"Come," I whispered, pulling Leigh behind a wooden stall. Kane slipped behind the one across from us.

A lone soldier in Amber armor strolled through the path between the stalls. I squeezed my eyes shut and held Leigh to my chest, quieting the breath in my lungs.

"Halden!" Leigh gasped, dashing from my arms and throwing herself at him.

29

BLEEDING STONES.

Halden held Leigh at arm's length, disbelief in his eyes. "Leigh? What are you doing here?"

She stammered, her voice drowned out by the sound of the bloodbath coming from the castle. Too quickly he put the pieces together and scanned the stable for my face. There was no hiding now. I emerged from the stall.

"Arwen." His face hardened. Leigh looked from him to me, and her face fell. She had always been too perceptive.

Inching her way back, she stood behind me.

I knew I'd have to beg. "Please. Just let us leave."

He shook his head, as if he was dreading this as much as I was. "Why didn't you meet me? It was because of him—"

"Halden—"

"He's here, isn't he?"

"No," I lied. I knew as soon as it fell from my mouth that it wasn't convincing. I had gotten better, but not good enough to fool someone who had known me all my life.

Halden's eyes were almost forlorn. "He'd never leave you."

My stomach twisted, threatening to surge up my throat. Halden inhaled once and stalked toward me, and I drew my sword. Leigh stifled a gasp.

"You're right," came Kane's cold, velvety voice from the darkness. "Clever kid." Kane stepped out slowly, palms up and open to Halden.

No, no, *no*.

I couldn't let Halden take him back to Lazarus. Halden reached for his sword, but Kane shook his head. "I don't want to fight you."

I held my sword tightly. "I am begging you, Halden. Nobody would know. Just let us go."

"I can't do that."

I couldn't tell in the shadows if he felt any remorse.

"Then take me," Kane said. "Let them go. I'll go to my father willingly."

My body shuddered, but I kept my mouth shut. I tried to tell myself Kane would be fine—he was Fae.

Halden shifted on his feet—an excruciating pause, and then, "I can't do that, either."

Kane nodded, a horrifying resolve crossing his face. "So, he knows."

"Knows what?" I asked. My voice sounded shrill and not my own. Leigh shifted behind me.

Before either could answer me, Kane launched himself at Halden with a growl. They flew violently into the bales of hay behind us. Leigh shrieked and I took off running, dragging her with me. But as we rounded out of the stables, I stopped short, whipping Leigh into my hip bone.

A herd of soldiers was walking past, headed for the castle, now a towering bonfire amid the palms. Leigh peered up at me, more fear than I had ever seen shining in her eyes.

"Shh," I said, my lips already cracking from the now-dry air. We held still as they passed us, not even daring to breathe.

Leigh squeezed her eyes shut.

When we were out of their eyeshot, I inched us back toward the stables.

It was even worse inside.

Halden's battalion had found him, and Kane was on his knees, held down by six Amber soldiers.

I could hear my heart break in my eardrums as I beheld his beaten face. Halden was behind me before I could think, and he grasped my arms, forcing my sword to clatter on the ground. Leigh screamed as two soldiers pulled her from me.

"No!" I cried.

"I never thought our last embrace would be like this," Halden said against my neck. Acid churned in my stomach.

"How can you do this? What happened to you?"

"I don't know, guess you never—"

Fueled by pure rage, and zero interest in hearing the rest of that sentence, I smashed the back of my head into his nose with all the strength I had.

A satisfying crunch reverberated through my skull, and I dug the heel of my boot into his instep. Halden let out a strangled squeal, releasing me, and I lunged for my sword.

He groaned and grasped at his face as a faucet of blood let loose, spilling between his fingers.

And I relished it. Every last drop.

I pulled my sword from the ground and hurtled toward the guard that held Kane's right arm, dodging the other men who dove to catch me. I swung my sword at the lone man wrestling with Kane's arm, forcing him to either release Kane and duck, or lose his head.

With wide eyes he chose the former and freed Kane's hand for a mere split second to dodge my strike.

Two more guards found me, grasping at my hair, my arms, my waist, and taking me down to the dusty hay of the stable floor.

But it was all Kane needed.

I whimpered, a knee in my back crushing my windpipe, as I watched Kane, with only one free hand, take out the rest of the men that held him down, easily and with ferocious delight. Snapping, crunching, and squelching rang through the wooden barn, and when I wrestled free for the briefest moment, all I could see was a heap of unconscious Amber bodies.

Kane pulled the two men off me effortlessly and threw them each into the walls behind us with two stomach-turning thuds. I plunged my sword into a third soldier's thigh and ran for Halden.

"Arwen—" he pleaded from the ground.

I kicked my ashy boot into his temple hard enough to knock him out. Blood roared in my ears. I never wanted to hear him say my name again.

Kane got to Leigh before me, and the two men that held her let go instantly, backing away from his hulking, terrifying form.

"Smart," he seethed, and scooped Leigh up in his arms. "Very smart." Then, to me, "Come on."

I regarded Halden's unconscious body with one last look and ran after Kane.

We raced for the castle, but—

It . . . was gone.

My throat constricted as I inhaled pure ash and hacked a cough.

The entire fortress was ablaze and crumbling. A billowing black fog of smoke and ash like a thundercloud amid the rolling hills. The crackle of wood echoed through the night.

But we didn't have time to stare.

Two salamanders crawled toward us menacingly, Garnet soldiers atop them, guiding them in our direction.

"This way," Kane bit out.

Sweating, coughing—I peeked back behind us.

A mistake.

Another herd of soldiers, these in Amber uniforms, were headed for us from behind the stables, marching with purpose and flanked by at least fifty more. They must have seen us as soon as we left Halden and his men. We were stuck.

A sob choked out of me.

I knew we needed to keep moving, but there was nowhere to go. *Shit, shit, shit.*

Kane looked up at the night sky with something like acceptance. He released a long exhale.

"I'm sorry" was all he said.

With one hand still holding Leigh to him and another pressed outward toward the soldiers, he closed his eyes.

It was hard to see in the dark, and the billowing clouds of smoke had blotted out any moonlight that might have illuminated the scene before me. Still, I watched as a single pitch-black tendril of shadow, as if with a mind of its own, wove through the army marching toward us. It splintered off into vines of black ribbon, silently, and every single soldier in front of him was smothered by the dark, twisted specters. Agonized cries for mercy pierced through the night but Kane didn't relent. He focused harder, conjuring darkness and thorns and shadow and dust. Choking, sputtering, the men fell one by one. Kane didn't move a single muscle, but his jaw was steel, his eyes ruthless and blazing.

My blood turned to ice, my throat closing with a strangled gasp. I knew what he was. I knew what he must have been capable of.

Still, nothing could have prepared me for the monstrousness of his predatory, fatal power—the instantaneous death of so many men.

I backed away instinctively.

"Run," he bit out, dropping Leigh to the ground, so he could use both his hands. "Make it to the beach."

I knew what he was. I had accepted it.

But the vicious, thorned wisps had sprouted from the very earth and destroyed—no, decimated and decayed—each man. One moment, alive, enraged, ready to kill—the next, a pile of ash carried on a wind.

It was enough to seize the air from my lungs and turn my stomach to sloshing water.

"Go!" he roared at us.

I had to move. *We* had to move.

I whirled, taking Leigh's hand, and did as he said—running as much away from him as toward the hope of safety. The salamanders still blocked our path back toward the castle, and thus the caves to the beach, but a second wave of inky blackness descended on the salamanders in front of us, drowning them in a suffocating tidal wave of shadow. The creatures spat out fire in retaliation and I ducked, shielding Leigh in my arms, but it never reached us. Instead, the fire turned to ash midair and rained down on the grassy hills like sickly snow, lit by moonlight and darkness and death.

We kept running, past the smoke billowing out of the burnt castle and toward the beach.

Amber and Garnet soldiers were everywhere, reveling in the screams as they dragged pleading souls out of the armory and the smithy. Blood pooled in the dirt and grass in little puddles, our feet splashing in them like it was a rainy day.

We dodged through shrieking people and burning structures, past warring soldiers, sword fights, and gore I would never be able to strip from my mind, let alone Leigh's.

Upon passing a dismembered corpse, I whispered to her to close her eyes. But I knew she wouldn't.

The Fae king had done this. Had destroyed this peaceful capital of earth and flowers and salt water. Reduced it to a bloody, burnt husk.

He had to die.

He had to, for what he had done.

Kane would make sure of it.

Finally, we made it to the stone outcropping that sheltered the beach.

"Follow me," I whispered to Leigh, heart in my throat, as we trudged through the caves surrounding the cove. Our feet were cold, ankles itchy with salt water and rough sand. Only the sound of crashing waves and faint battle cries penetrated the still caves. That and our ragged, desperate breaths.

Through the end of one cavern, I could just make out the beach. Soldiers warred on the sands, the now abrasive sound of metal on metal like a violent chorus rattling in my skull. On the far edge of the cove the enemy had built an encampment of sorts, surrounded by cannon and fire-breathing beasts.

If we could make it past that we could reach the fully rigged ships, where they were anchored in the shallower water near the cliffs. Except—only ships with Amber's leafy emblem filled Siren's Bay. Where were Peridot's?

"They must have sunk the others," said Kane. I nearly smacked my head on the stone behind me in my shock.

Where had he come from?

The instinct to wrap my arms around him and rejoice in his safety was tempered by the memory of his strange power. I took a step back. Leigh seemed to feel the same, sliding behind me ever so slightly.

"You're afraid of me," he said, face dark. It wasn't a question, but I still couldn't fathom a response. He swallowed hard. "We'll have to take one of their ships."

"What about everyone else?"

"I'm sure that's what they're thinking, too." *If they made it this far.* He didn't have to say it.

I squinted into the darkness. The moon was a pale, glimmering reflection in the ocean waves and a strange contrast to the blood-shed on the sand before us. Out of the corner of my eye I noticed movement near the sea.

Not the chaos of battle, but an anchor floating out of the ocean, moving of its own accord.

"There." I gestured to Kane. "That's got to be Mari."

He quirked a brow at me. "The redhead's a witch?"

Ugh. Now was not the time for this conversation. "Yes, and Briar Creighton's amulet isn't in your study anymore. Also, we almost killed your pet strix."

The shock on Kane's face would have brought me great delight at any other time. "You what?" He shook his head. "Acorn? He'd never hurt anyone."

I wanted very badly to tell him a thing or two about keeping secrets, but getting to safety had to come first. Lessons on hypocrisy later.

He dragged a hand down his face. "Briar's amulet doesn't contain her magic. That's just a myth."

"So what is it?"

"A rather lovely and expensive piece of jewelry."

My eyes went wide. "So all the magic Mari's done . . ."

"That's all her." His voice echoed against the cave walls as he reached down to scoop up Leigh. "All right, come on. Let's go."

But she flinched away.

I stepped in front of her. "I've got her."

Kane's jaw hardened, but his eyes were focused. "Fine. I'll be behind you."

I took a deep breath that tasted like the ocean, and felt the wet grit under my boots.

"One more thing," he said, his voice soft. "Keep your head clear. Both of you. No thoughts in or out."

Queasy suspicion pooled in my stomach. "Why?"

"I'm not sure if he's here, but if he is, Lazarus can enter your mind. Don't give him the ammunition to find you."

Wonderful. I trembled with panic and fear and fury.

We just had to make it to the ship.

I carried Leigh in my arms and moved slowly, ducking behind rocks and cliffs and branches. We drew closer to the barracks of armed men in silver armor I hadn't seen before. Dread curled low in my stomach.

I cleared my mind.

Clouds, empty space. Nothing. Nobody. Silence.

We were so close. A few yards ahead, a flash of red hair tucked behind a palm tree filled my heart with hope. Just a few more steps . . .

"Going somewhere?" A voice like silk laced with something far more deadly spoke to us with peculiar calm.

30

IN THE DARK, THE SILVER SOLDIERS THAT SURROUNDED us looked like mythical giants, looming above us on horseback. I pulled Leigh close to me and tried to ignore how her shaking limbs were tearing my heart to bits.

Before I could draw my sword, my arms were pulled behind me by one of the silver-clad men, and I fought, kicking and thrashing in the violet darkness and the uneven sand, to hold on to Leigh.

"Don't you lay a single fucking hand on her," Kane spat at the soldiers behind me, but they dropped him to his knees with a flurry of punches, and I winced and gagged at the cracking sounds.

Leigh was wrenched from my arms, wriggling and screaming, and both of us were held down by more and more and more soldiers in the icy silver armor. Desperately, hopelessly outnumbered.

An older, shockingly handsome man stalked forward in the sand and stared down at us. That same carved jaw, cheekbones that could cut glass, and slate-gray eyes—the resemblance was impossible to deny. Deep in my soul, I knew. I knew exactly who he was.

My vision blurred.

The man turned to Kane, who spat blood onto the sand. "No letters? No visit? If I didn't know better, I'd think you didn't miss me at all."

Horror dripped down my spine like the blood on Kane's chin.

Lazarus Ravenwood. The Fae king.

Destroyer of us all.

Kane stared at his father but said nothing.

Fury bloomed in my heart, in my stomach, replacing the icy coating of shock and fear. Molten and unrelenting rage heated my blood as I strained against the Fae soldier that held me back.

If Kane didn't kill this man, I would.

An angry sun mirrored my blooming hate as it began to crest over the dark sea behind us. The rays illuminated Kane's eyes, and for the first time, I saw genuine fear in them. His hands were shaking, and he schooled them into fists by his sides. A fog of dread so crushing I could hardly think of anything else filled my mind.

Lazarus turned his attention toward me. His cropped gray hair, smooth tanned skin, clothing that rippled and glimmered with fabrics not of this realm. He was tall, like his son, but older, leaner. Clearly he was ancient, but his face only gave away a refined, mature beauty. Chiseled and charming and aged like a fine wine. But his eyes . . . they were depthless. Hollow.

Striding toward me, he lifted a single finger toward my face and ran it down my cheek. My stomach roiled and Leigh whimpered at my side.

I was going to *rip* this man's skin from his bones.

"Feisty, aren't we? You don't even know me."

"Do not touch her," Kane said, each word more pointed than the last.

"Always so temperamental," Lazarus said to his son, chiding. "It's not my fault you fell for my assassin."

His what?

I forced my brow to unfurrow, but not quickly enough.

"Not so honest with your lady friend, my boy?"

I went still as death.

Assassin? How were there *more* lies? *More* I didn't understand?

No. It couldn't be. He was lying—trying to tear us apart.

Still, I couldn't bring myself to look at Kane.

"Good thinking, lady friend. Your first instinct was the right one."

I needed to shut my brain up. "Stop that," I hissed.

The Fae king turned to Kane once more.

"I see the appeal, son. She's magnificent. After all these years of searching, she's just as I always imagined she would be."

My stomach sank like a stone in a deep sea. *What did that mean?*

Kane lunged toward him with lethal intent, but Fae soldiers pushed him back down to his knees.

"Stop!" I moved toward them, but more soldiers swarmed me, pulling my hands and arms backward, holding my head still.

I thrashed and gnawed, trying with all my might to move even a single muscle, but they were stronger than anything I had ever felt. Their arms and hands were like steel bands around me. Lazarus just smiled and assessed my trapped form.

His eyes swept over me, predatory and rife with curiosity.

"If you harm so much as one single hair on her head," Kane snarled from the sand, "I will reduce you to fucking ash. I spared your life once. I will not do it again."

Lazarus couldn't have been less interested in Kane's threat.

"Is that how you remember it, son?" he asked, turning to one of his men, who handed him something I couldn't make out.

I strained to see what he held, and then all the air left my lungs in a strangled gasp.

A silver dagger glinted in his hands.

Kane thrashed—*thrashed* against the men behind him. Horror ripped through me. I couldn't look into his eyes. I didn't want to see his fear. I—

"My son never told you of the seer's prophecy? Color me shocked," the king said, approaching me slowly, as if I were a rabid animal. "You must know that's the only use he had for you. A tool to beat his old man, once and for all."

I shook my head from the soldier's hold and turned to Kane. "What is he talking about? What else haven't you told me?" Pure fear rang through my voice. It was a wail. A cry. A plea.

"I'm sorry, Arwen. I'm so sorry—"

I shook my head as if I could rattle any of this information into place. Nothing anyone was saying made sense. Sobs and panic were welling up in me, betrayal burning my cheeks. The Fae king closed his eyes and recited the prophecy from memory.

> *"A world of lighte blessed across the Stones,*
> *A king doomed to fall at the hands of his second son.*
> *A city turned to ash and bones,*
> *The fallen star will mean war has once again begun.*
> *The final Fae of full-blood born at last,*

Will find the Blade of the Sun inside her heart.
Father and child will meet again in war a half century past,
And with the rise of the phoenix will the final battle start.
A king who can only meet his end at her hands,
A girl who knows what she must choose,
A sacrifice made to save both troubled lands;
Without it, an entire realm will lose.
A tragedy for both full Fae, as each shall fall,
Alas, it is the price to pay to save them all."

Humor danced in his eyes. "Kind of miserable, isn't it? 'Each shall fall'? Pity. I think we could have been great friends."

I could barely formulate a thought. My mind was reeling, stomach turning. I—

He had lied to me. After everything.

The prophecy—

Cold calm coated my veins as finally, *finally* I understood with perfect clarity. The one thing Kane had never told me, had always continued to shroud in mystery, to dismiss, to hide.

The single reason Bert had brought me to Shadowhold. Why Kane had kept me there.

The powers I had never understood—

But Kane had.

I was destined to end this man before me. The Fae king.

Because *I* was the last full-blooded Fae.

And I was fated to die.

Lazarus lifted his silver dagger toward me. "It will all be over soon, Arwen. Try not to struggle."

I thrashed against the men who held Leigh and me. Her sobs shredded me from the inside out.

"No!" Kane roared.

A blast of dark billowing power erupted from the ground and shoved the Fae soldiers off Kane with the force of a crackling storm. The silver-clad men scrambled for him, but none of their own powers—not rivers of fire nor violet light nor shimmering mirrors—were a match for his poison-black shadows. Kane slipped from their clutches and launched himself at his father with sheer, unending venom.

Deadly black smoke unfurled from his hands, rippled off his back like wings, and nearly reached the Fae king.

Nearly.

But Lazarus spun, and with a wave of his hand a single stake of solid ice appeared from thin air and lodged into Kane's chest, forcing his legs to buckle and slamming him to the sand with a hideous groan.

"Kane!" I screamed, my voice not my own.

He moaned in agony, sticky dark blood spilling out through his hands as he tried and failed to pull the ice from his sternum. I crawled and pulled against my captors, sobbing too hard to scream. My power twitched in my fingers; I could heal him, I could save him, I could—

But I couldn't move an inch. Couldn't even look at him when the Fae soldier behind me forced my head away from Kane and to face Lazarus.

I didn't want Leigh to see this. I shook my head, unable to think, unable to breathe—

"Please," I begged.

"Arwen . . ." Kane groaned from the darkness, bathed in his own blood, soldiers on him once again. His eyes filled with unending, utter rage. And agony.

And sorrow.

So much sorrow it was cleaving me in two.

His hands reached toward me, but he was held down by too many, and bleeding. *Bleeding* out, ribbons of blood—

Lazarus was in front of me now with the glittering silver dagger. I braced myself for the inevitable searing pain.

A sharp gust of wind and the sound of sparks on metal knocked me off my feet, and I toppled backward onto Leigh and the soldiers who held us.

I clamped down on the relief—

Free. We were free.

When I sat up, my vision still blurred from the force, Kane was gone.

In his place on the sand, beside three *eviscerated* soldiers who were just moments ago holding him down . . .

Was the dragon from the very first night I was flown to Onyx. My heart froze solid.

All sleek black lines and glistening scales— it seemed ridiculous I hadn't known all along. Kane in his dragon form was the same: a mind-bendingly beautiful, terrifying creature of wicked power.

Then, without a beat, Lazarus shifted as well.

The power of his transformation forced sand into my eyes, and I coughed against the biting taste of lighte on my tongue, shielding Leigh in my arms.

Lazarus's shifted form was a gruesome, gray-scaled wyvern. Larger than Kane's dragon by more than half, and twice as frightening. While Kane's shifted self still retained some warmth, some humanity, Lazarus was all monster. Nothing but cold, unfeeling violence.

The pointed ridges down his long back and across a swiping

tail glinted in the cresting white sun, and a ragged pink scar sailed along his scaled rib cage. Rows of teeth shone like stalagmites in a crowded, treacherous cave. Bright red eyes like fresh blood shot to me only once before he lunged toward Kane. His claws slashed through the air as he took Kane's dragon form in his jaws by the neck and shot into the sky.

I squinted up at the early light above the battle-torn beach. Like a horrific domino effect, a handful of the Fae soldiers around us shifted as well and shot upward after the two of them.

Sphinxes, hydras, harpies.

All Fae mercenaries as Kane had told me, taking off after their king.

Kane didn't have a chance.

A hideous and bewildering celestial battle waged above us among the stars that mingled with early, pale light, but I didn't wait to see what might happen next.

I grabbed for my sword and swung at the soldiers that surrounded Leigh and me. I knew we were outnumbered. Still, I had to try.

"Stay with me," I barked at Leigh, as I drove my blade into a Fae soldier's neck.

I parried and blocked, moved through soldier after soldier.

But something wasn't right.

Why had nobody so much as touched me?

I wasn't that good. These were Fae soldiers, supposedly the deadliest men ever to have existed, and they were trained for battle.

"What are you doing?" Leigh asked, her voice small.

"I was taught to wield a sword. It's a long story."

"I'm not talking about that."

Then I saw it.

The sand below our feet as we moved was dented inward. Each soldier that attempted to touch us was blasted back by a glass-thin protective burst of light.

"That can't be me," I said, but my voice was softer than a whisper. *The final Fae of full-blood born at last.* Images of the warm glow and strength I felt when I fought the wolfbeast flooded my mind. "But let's not stick around to find out."

I sheathed my sword and raced for the ship, carrying Leigh in my arms. The golden arc around us was a second sun to the bare blue light on the beach giving way to morning.

"What about the king?" Leigh screamed as we bowled over soldiers of every creed and kingdom.

"Which one?"

"Your king!" she cried.

"Leave him." At the thought of Kane, a thundercloud of fury settled over me. He had lied to me from the very first moment we met.

Used me.

If he lived, I was going to choke the life out of him myself.

Upon reaching the ship, Leigh ran up the gangway.

There they were.

My mother and Ryder, their faces bathed in relief.

Leigh fell into their arms and a tiny part of my shattered heart healed.

"Thank the Stones," said my mother, holding Leigh to her chest.

The deck was strewn with fallen Amber bodies--Griffin and Eryx must have taken the ship from them while we were held by Lazarus. A hum of triumph sailed through me at their success.

But Peridot and Onyx soldiers were barely keeping Lazarus's

men from boarding the ship. Amelia and Mari helped to untangle ropes and unfurl sails as swords clanged and voices bellowed. The fiery roars in my ears signaled the salamanders were coming.

Our steel was going to be no match for a firefight.

"You have to go, now!" I called to the Onyx soldier captaining the ship. The sun was just rising over the sea, and we were losing the cover of darkness we would need to sail away and not be followed. I helped a young Peridot man clad in armored pants and tattoos hoist the anchor aboard. Griffin gave the signal to the captain, the vessel creaked into motion, and I sprinted back down the gangway, ignoring the pleas of my family.

No matter how much their voices crushed my heart.

Ripped it in two.

I had to help, to do something. I scrambled down into the shallow water, planted my feet in the sand beside the other Onyx warriors, and raised my sword.

Two clawed feet landed beside me.

I swung the metal in my hands to attack but recognized the sea glass eyes immediately.

"A griffin? Really?"

The hulking, feathered beast nodded. "My parents weren't very creative."

Griffin moved first, taking out rows of soldiers with his deadly wingspan and ripping heads clean off with his lionlike teeth. Blood splattered my face, but I didn't care. If anything, I relished it. Looking at the carnage, the bodies, the slumped carcasses of scaled beasts—what they had done to the peaceful city of Siren's Cove.

I was going to kill *each and every one* of them.

I parried and stabbed, but moving in the shallow water slowed me down and I heaved with the force of swinging my blade against stronger fighters. Above us, I heard the roar of Kane's dragon form as he lit the soldiers that fought us with fire, the gray wyvern following in close pursuit. The smell of charred flesh threatened to bring my stomach's contents onto the sandy bank beneath us. No amount of time spent in an infirmary had desensitized me to scorched human remains.

Still, the hordes kept coming.

I jabbed and grunted, narrowly dodging blades and flames and fists. I was grateful for the pale light. I didn't want to see how red the ocean water we moved through had turned. A Garnet soldier came at me and slammed his blade against mine. I blocked and spun but he slipped through, and I barely caught Barney out of the corner of my eye as he sliced through the soldier's chest before the man impaled me.

"Thank you," I breathed.

He slammed me down into the shallow water in response, covering my body with his.

"Hey!"

"You have to get on the ship, Lady Arwen."

"We can't leave these people to die," I grunted under his weight.

"We don't have a choice."

I knew Barney was right.

They had too many men. And beasts. And Fae. They weren't even using any light—their swords and arrows and cannon were enough to decimate half of Siren's Cove. Barney rolled off me and whistled at the sky, and not a minute later gnarled talons picked Barney and me from the sand and carried us over the sea and onto the moving ship. Wind assaulted my face, and we landed with a

...ud, the force of Griffin's wings sending some of the Peridot soldiers aboard running for the galleys.

I looked back to the shore. Some soldiers still clashed calf-deep
in the bay, but most of our enemies looked to be retreating. For a
moment, I wondered with childlike optimism if they would simply
let us go. If being ripped from my home, then the keep, and now
this palace, losing my oldest friend, and destroying whatever might
have been with Kane might just be enough loss for a lifetime.

Instead, I watched in silent horror as the salamanders lit enemy
arrows alight and a fiery rain of piercing metal hailed down onto
our ship. Everyone on the ship ran for cover. Ryder and I lunged
for Leigh and Mother and moved to get under the deck.

We toppled into the captain's quarters with a thud.

I sucked in a great lungful of musty cabin air.

"Thank fuck," said Ryder, checking to make sure he was in one
piece. Once he was sure no limbs had been lost, he flattened out
against the floor to sip in gulps of air.

"Bleeding Stones," exhaled Leigh, untangling herself from me.

I waited for my mother's admonishment against our foul language.

Surely even near death wouldn't stop her automatic reprimand—

But it never came.

The darkest chill—pure dread—barely tickled my neck.

I turned around, sitting up from the worn wood beneath me.

My mother was still lying on the ground, an arrow lodged in
her heart.

"No!" I shrieked.

No, no, no, no, no—

I gathered her into my arms, shaking and screaming, my pulse
too loud in my ears, shuddering—

"Arwen, you can fix this, right?" Ryder scrambled to the other side of my mother. "Mam, Mam! Stay with us."

"Mother?" Leigh grasped her tightly and my heart stopped beating altogether.

I knew as soon as I held her. My stomach turned and my vision blurred, and I couldn't breathe. I couldn't *breathe*.

My abilities had never worked on my mother.

I tried anyway, pressing my palms into her blood-drenched blouse. I poured all the energy I had into her. Like Dagan taught me, I thought of the sky and air and atmosphere. Tried to pull everything around me into myself like sucking in a final breath. My pulse thrummed, my body ached, my head pounded, and I waited. Waited for her tendons, muscles, and flesh, at my power's urging, to stitch themselves back together around the arrow. My nerves vibrated and my jaw clenched at the effort, but the blood continued to pour out in rivulets, and nothing happened.

"I am so, so sorry. I can't– I've never--" I sobbed.

"Arwen," she said, her voice a whisper. "I know."

I cried harder, unable to find strength or courage or hope. Her wound was too great. Ryder's face was crumpling. He held Leigh tight, but she had gone deathly pale and still, the tears welling in her eyes the only sign of her horror.

"I did this. It's all my fault," I wept.

"No. No, Arwen." She swallowed a wet cough. "I have always known what you are and loved you just the same."

Confusion and shock warred inside my reeling, spinning mind.

How could she have known? The ask died in my throat as she coughed again.

She had so little time left.

"I am proud of you, Arwen. I always have been, and always

will be. Wherever I am." I buried my face in her neck. There was no pain, no suffering greater than the looks on Leigh's and Ryder's faces.

"My beautiful babies," she whispered. "Take care of each other. There will be—"

She went limp before she could finish her last words.

Then it was only the sound of our weeping.

My mother was dead.

I had failed her completely.

The sun was peeking through a pastel, clouded sky. The choppy water rocked below us, a calm rhythmic melody.

And my mother was dead.

I could not endure this. I wasn't strong enough.

Ryder's crumpled face heaved over her still body as Leigh just stared in shock. Her simple tears and uneven breaths were the only signs she was even conscious. I wanted to reach for them both. To hold them close to me. Tell them it would be all right. But I could barely even think, let alone speak.

Let alone lie.

Without feeling my legs bend beneath me, I stood. My heart was a dull thump, my mind clear. I might have heard Ryder behind me. Calling to me. But there was no way to tell for sure.

I left the captain's quarters in a daze and stood at the stern of the ship, facing the shore. Arrows still rained down on the deck, missing those who were ducking for cover, but none pierced my skin. Garnet's and Amber's ships followed us in the uneven waters. The salamanders were retreating from the beach, leaving the remains of the carnage behind them. Husks of armor, discarded weapons, sand mottled by blood. The dark skies above were filled with purple clouds amid a morning that promised rain. Sky-bound creatures fought, talons and scales clashing among the mist.

A pure, white-hot rage was consuming me. Filling me from my feet to my palms. I vibrated with fury and sorrow.

But not fear.

A torrent of raw, brutal power unleashed from my soul, spilling from my eyes, palms, and heart. I could feel it flowing from me like a dam breaking open. I screamed, unable to control it, my lungs burning with exertion.

White light and a gusting wind as sharp as blades cut across the sea and decimated the soldiers. Amber and Garnet, battalions on the shore and ships at sea alike, lit up in golden, hot shimmering light. Their screams were my fuel. Their suffering my spirit. And I drank and drank and drank.

Raising my arms to the sky, I pulled from the air around me. The rain-tinged ether, the lightning, the clouds. They filled my veins and lungs and eyes. I brought the remaining ghastly winged creatures above me down into the sea one by one until the salt water turned red and the waves churned with their blood. I felt the horror radiate from those around me on the deck. I heard screams, even from those I loved.

But I was powerless to stop it.

I thought of all the innocent citizens of Siren's Cove. Dead, wounded, without homes. The injustice of it all.

I thought of Leigh and Ryder, without a mother. The horrors they had to witness all for kingly greed. The nights of nightmares and days spent crying that stretched ahead of them.

I thought of Powell. The sickly smell of his clothing. The tight, confined space of his shed. The agony of each lash, both his belt nd his words. All that his abuse had cost me. A sheltered, pitiful life.

I thought of my mother. The sweet children she had raised almost entirely alone. The small life she had lived. Her lifelong pain and suffering. Her one shot at health, squandered. How her own daughter, blessed with the gift of healing, had never been able to heal her. And the undignified, excruciating, arbitrary way in which she had died.

And then, I thought of myself. Every exploitation, manipulation, blow, insult. Everything that had shaped my childhood and these past few years. A life wasted in fear, hiding from what was outside, terrified of being alone yet always feeling lonely. Betrayal from the only person who had shown me what anything else could feel like. A prophecy that promised my death.

I finally had a profound understanding of my purpose in this world, and it was to die.

I wailed and purged—

Sputtering the pain outward as it bled from my fingers, my heart, my mouth—

Power shuddered through me, decimating, destroying, unending. I screamed my suffering into the skies and brought down a merciless hail of fire on the enemy soldiers.

The world was too cruel.

Nobody deserved to live to see another day.

I would annihilate them all.

I would—

"You showed extraordinary bravery when you had no hope it would save you."

"What you call fear is indeed power, and you can wield it for good."

"*I did not want to live in a world without you in it.*"

"*You are a bright light, Arwen.*"

"*I have always known what you are and loved you just the same.*"

I collapsed on the deck in a heap, sobbing and gasping for breath.

31

A COOL COMPRESS SAT ON MY FOREHEAD. THE ANGRY morning sun beat down on my shoulders and prickled my skin.

"There she is," said a soft, familiar voice. My eyes were heavy with sleep and sorrow. I blinked up at Mari's kind, somber face, her mass of red curls looming above me. I sat up slowly, head pounding, and realized we were still on the deck of the ship. By the sun's place in the sky, I guessed I had been out for hours.

I turned to look at the sea, letting the salt spray across my face. Peridot was long behind us. There was no land for miles.

I had—

I couldn't even think of it. What I had done.

What I had lost.

"Nobody is following us," I said instead.

"After your . . . episode"—she paused as if trying to get her wording right—"there was nobody left *to* follow us. None of King Ravenwood's witches from the capital are here, so I found a spell to cloak the ship. When they gather their armies back together, at least we'll be untraceable."

I nodded, numb.

I was not going to ask about Kane. Whether he was on this ship or—

"So," she said, removing the cool compress and soaking it again. "You're a Faerie. You could have told me, you know." I could hear the hurt in her voice.

"She didn't know."

I looked up, squinting into direct sunlight. The voice belonged to Ryder, who had Leigh by the hand. She was stone-faced.

I had never seen her expression so cold.

"How are you a true Fae, and neither of us are? We had the same mother," he asked. He, too, was graver than I had ever seen him before. That endless light that shone inside him regardless of circumstance was gone.

"I don't know," I said. It came out like a plea.

I stood up with Mari's help and walked toward him steadily. When I knew neither would flinch, I wrapped them in a hug.

We stayed like that for a long while.

Even though we had different fathers, I had never felt like they were my half-siblings.

I had never known my father, and my mother had never spoken of him in my childhood. At last, I had pried it out of her just two years ago. She told me she had met a man from another kingdom, which one she couldn't recall, in a tavern outside of Abbington.

She was drowning her sorrows over the recent loss of her own mother, and he had lifted her spirits and taken her dancing. The next morning, she woke up in his cottage and he was gone.

She never saw him again.

I hated to think of my father that way, so I didn't think of him much at all.

Even as I racked my brain, I knew it wasn't possible that the man could have been responsible for what I was.

I was the last *full-blooded* Fae. Both my parents had to be *full-blooded* Fae. Which meant either my mother had hidden her Fae nature from us our whole lives, or she wasn't really my mother.

My siblings were now my only living family, the closest people I had left, and odds were, I wasn't related to either of them at all. That, coupled with the gaping hole deep in my heart at the loss of my mother and the realization that she wasn't really the woman who had given birth to me, was enough to break whatever spirit I had left.

Despite our embrace, I had never felt so far away from them, and we had just spent months apart. I hated what I now knew I was, so foreign and removed I hardly felt like myself.

But most of all, I hated Kane. I wasn't sure where he was—I told myself I didn't care if he had survived the battle with his father.

Why should I?

I pulled away from my siblings and looked out across the too-bright deck. A few soldiers were tending to the wounded, but it seemed most everyone else had gone below.

The stomps of petite footsteps from the captain's quarters echoed across the deck, breaking me from my somber thoughts.

"Ghastly cowards, that's what we are!"

I spun to see Amelia, Eryx, Griffin, and Barney make their way onto the deck in succession.

No Kane.

I couldn't tell if it was grief or fear or relief that twisted my stomach.

Each of their gazes lingered on me, Amelia's as cold as ice, King Eryx's conveying vague interest, Barney's sympathetic, Griffin's unreadable as always. A flicker of shame sparked deep in my chest at their prying eyes, but I was too numb, too exhausted to really feel it.

"Amelia, we had no choice." King Eryx turned back to his daughter. "We had to *survive*."

Amelia whirled to face him. "We left our people to suffer." She practically spat the words.

"We got some out on the other ships, they—"

"*I* got them out. You just ran like a—"

"More importantly"—he enunciated right over her—"we lived to fight another day."

"And where will we go now? Just keep running?" she asked, bitterness coating her voice.

King Eryx looked to Griffin, but he didn't respond. Instead, Griffin turned to the bow of the ship.

Like a dark and vengeful demon of death, Kane stepped out from the shadows.

"We sail for the Kingdom of Citrine."

He was alive.

I thought I heard my heart crack open.

He looked wrecked. Gashes covered his arms and neck, one eye was blackened and sealed shut, and his lip was split. A chest wound was haphazardly wrapped under his open, billowing shirt, but bright red blood was seeping through the makeshift bandages.

Kane's focus landed on me immediately. His eyes flickered with concern.

I pulled my gaze from his and settled it on the briny, bottomless water across from me.

"We have no way of sending ravens to let them know we are coming, King Ravenwood," Eryx said to him.

"We'll just have to hope they welcome us with open arms."

A dark laugh barked out of Griffin at the sentiment. "They won't."

"I know," Kane said with lethal calm.

He passed the group of them and approached me tentatively. When I couldn't avoid his eyes anymore, I turned to him.

"How are you, bird?" His face was a mask of regret, but his voice was like a spirit—for an instant relieving, even pleasurable, before turning bitter on my tongue.

"Don't speak to me," I said. Even if this wasn't all his fault, I was so emotionally destroyed it had to fall on someone. He seemed more deserving than most.

Ryder stepped in front of me protectively, arms folded.

"Give us a moment, Ryder." Kane really did look brutal.

Ryder looked to me, and I shook my head vehemently. I didn't want to be anywhere near the man.

"I don't think so, Your Majesty," Ryder said with as much courtesy as he could muster. Kane paused, then nodded his understanding.

"I am so sorry for your loss," Kane said to all three of us. Leigh wouldn't even look him in the eye.

He walked toward the left side of the deck. I looked at Ryder and then to Mari. Neither met my eyes. I knew what they were thinking. I had to talk to him eventually. The ship was only so big.

"Let's go inside. I need some food," Mari said. Ryder followed her, looking back at me once.

I kissed Leigh on the head and pulled together what little strength I had left. "I'll be right behind you."

Griffin, Eryx, Amelia, and the rest of the guards and soldiers on deck had moved to the bow of the ship to continue their argument.

Maybe they sensed the onslaught of tension between Kane and me and didn't want to be anywhere near us. I wouldn't blame them. Besides a few stragglers, Kane and I were the only two left on this side. I met him where he stood, the wind battering his hair. He was closing his eyes to the sun.

Sensing my presence, he turned to me, but I could only stare at the ocean below us. The briny smell of kelp and salt fit my stormy mood. We stood in silence, listening to the waves crash against the ship for far too long.

"I'm the last full-blooded Fae," I stated.

He stilled, but answered me. "Yes."

My heart thumped violently. I knew it was true, but it still shook my very bones to hear him say it.

"Griffin is Fae, too."

"He is."

My cheeks burned. Griffin, Dagan, Amelia—how many had known what I was before I did?

"And you're both Fae that can shift," I said. "You're the dragon that flew me to Shadowhold that first night?"

"Yes," he said, and faced the churning sea.

"And the Blade of the Sun? From the prophecy?"

He turned toward me. His eyes awash with . . . was it misery? Searing regret? But he hid it as quickly as I had noticed and tensed his jaw.

"It's what Halden wanted that had already been stolen from my vault years ago—the only weapon that can kill Lazarus, when wielded by you." He swallowed hard. "He likely came to Shadowhold ooking to murder Fae defectors, but somehow heard the blade was in my possession. Truth is, it could be anywhere."

My heartbeat pounded in my ears. "I thought it was 'in my heart'? That's what the prophecy said."

"Most scholars I've consulted think that's not to be interpreted literally. But let's not discuss it with Amelia. She's all too game to cut you open and check." The look in his eyes was murderous, and I could tell he wasn't joking.

"So, I'm a true Fae, like you said." The words still felt insane to me. "How does a halfling like you have lighte?"

"I'm not a halfling. Halflings are just mortals with trace ancestral amounts of Fae lineage. It's barely noticeable if you don't know what to look for. Often, they're strikingly beautiful, very strong, or live unnaturally long lives. There are only two kinds of Faeries. Fae—Griffin, myself, all the soldiers, all those trapped in the Fae Realm. We all have some mortal lineage from millennia of crossbreeding. The other kind are true Fae, or full-blooded Fae—only you, and Lazarus."

"But how? I was born in Abbington, my mother was mortal." I was babbling. "My siblings are all—"

"We aren't sure."

Horror struck me. "Could you and I be . . . related?"

A grim smile crossed his face. "No, bird. You were born long after the last full-blooded Fae female passed on. Your birth is—well, it's a miracle. One even my father doesn't understand."

"So Halden . . . his mission wasn't just to hunt down any Fae. He had been looking for . . ."

"For you, yes. The Fae from the prophecy."

Horror struck me like a slap.

Halden.

Halden.

He would have killed me in those stables.

Kane stepped closer and I braced myself. "Arwen, I am so, so sorry. For everything. All that I kept from you. For letting him find you." The pained grimace on his face told me what he knew could have happened on the beach had he not shifted in time.

My lungs tightened. The air trapped inside of them burned. I reminded myself to exhale. "Maybe I should have known all along," I said. "I never understood my abilities, or why they would dissipate after I used too much." I thought of the night I couldn't heal myself after helping the chimera. "Dagan. Did you ask him to train me?"

"As a young man, he was my kingsguard for many years in the Fae Realm until the rebellion. When we came to Onyx, he retired. But there is nobody better on the continent to train you, both with your sword and your lighte."

The way Dagan had known about my abilities, and where I could draw power from. He, too, had lied to me. Anger and humiliation and hopelessness warred inside me. How had I been so blind all along? Amelia had been right. I had been such a fool.

"You told me you had never lied to me. You promised you had told me *everything*." I couldn't help turning to face him. I studied his slate-gray eyes as they welled with anguish. "I deserved to know, Kane."

He looked a moment away from breaking. He reached for me but thought better of it and tucked his hand back into his pocket. "I couldn't risk anyone else knowing. Anyone having another reason to hurt you. Lazarus's entire army has been looking for the last full-blooded Fae who could spell his death for nearly a century."

"*Bullshit*. You needed to use me as a weapon. You knew if you told me all of this—what defeating Lazarus meant for me, for my . . ." I swallowed. "My fate—that I would never help you achieve your vengeance."

The word was bitter on my tongue. Kane had the audacity to look shaken but said nothing.

Hatred funneled through me. He would not see me cry.

I tucked my shaking hands into fists and turned away.

"How long did you know what I was before I did?" I asked, my voice rough and low.

He ran a hand through his hair. "Bert realized you were who we had been looking for the night you healed Barney. When I flew you to my keep, there was a light in you that couldn't be anything but Fae." I remembered the ride. The strange connection I had felt with him in his dragon form.

"For almost a hundred years I have woken up each morning with one thought. Just one. Find the last full-blooded Fae. Fulfill the prophecy. Kill my father. I lost the people who meant the most to me at his hand. So did Dagan and Griffin. The day we rallied against him, I let them down and we all suffered for it."

My heart skipped two beats. Dagan's family? Lazarus was the one who killed them?

"If I don't finish what we started, none of their sacrifices are worth anything. Still to this day, millions live enslaved in a waste-land because of him. You thought you knew what a cruel king looked like, but you have no idea, Arwen. None. Every mortal on this continent will die a senseless death if he isn't stopped.

"And yet, even knowing all of that. That day we raced"—a sor-rowful smile crossed his face—"I was so enchanted by you. I had never met anyone like you. The night you were attacked"—I faced him, unable to look away any longer—"I knew I couldn't go through with it. Not even for the good of all of Evendell. I brought you and your family here to live the rest of your lives in safety."

My heart was shattering.

"Do you hear me?" Unable to hold himself back a minute longer, Kane finally reached a frantic hand toward me. "I was willing to sacrifice the entire world to keep you alive!"

"Don't touch me." I pulled away and turned back to the relentless ocean beneath us. Despite my promise to myself, a single tear slipped down my cheek.

"I tried to take the choice away from you, and for that I am sorry. But I will die before I let him have you. You have to know that."

Power rippled off him in waves at his oath. But I wasn't afraid of him. I was afraid of myself. I was afraid to die. Afraid to live. Afraid of the power that roiled inside me. A thick fog of despair invaded every sense—suffocating me. Trapping me within this new reality.

Because of *him*.

I could have lived my whole life and never known of my fate. I wouldn't have had to die.

But now I knew I was the only one who could kill Lazarus, and if he died, I would as well. It was all information I could have gone my whole life without.

And now, there was no other choice.

"I will help you end this war. We can find the Blade of the Sun, and I'll plunge it through his heart. We will save all of the people Lazarus intends to kill, save the Fae Realm, avenge those you lost, Dagan, Griffin, everyone. We'll finish what you started, Kane."

"No," he said, his voice breaking. "I refuse to lose you. I—"

"It's not your choice."

"Arwen—"

"You've made enough choices for me."

A bluster blew his hair across his chiseled face—vulnerable in a way I had never seen before. I almost folded into him. *Almost.*

But instead, I stepped back.

And took a deep breath of salt water– and rain-soaked air.

"Maybe before, I would have caved. Forgiven you out of fear of being alone. Done whatever you told me I should. I would have felt that I needed you, especially knowing what horrors were to come. But now . . . You lied to me. Used me. You—" I steeled myself. "I can't be with you like that, Kane. Not anymore."

"Please," he said. It was almost a whisper.

I shook my head. I was breaking, twisting apart. My mother was gone, the man I—

It didn't matter now.

He wiped his eyes. "As you wish." And with that, he crossed the deck and slipped below to the galley.

I turned my attention back to the waves ahead of me. The rough blue water was a tempo I couldn't follow, chaotic and choppy— swaying in a strange dance under the ship's bow. The sight was more beautiful than I had realized.

I had been wrong before. It was not a cruel world.

Or it was, but it was also wonderful.

I had seen more beauty, joy, and hope in the past few months than I'd thought existed. And there was so much more out there. There were so many people, so much love, and so much possibility. I couldn't let it be snuffed out by one man, Fae or otherwise.

I could do this, for Evendell. For my family. For Mari. For all the innocent Fae and mortals alike. I could find this blade. Fight this battle alongside the man who had thoroughly shattered my heart. I could be strong.

It was a world I had to save, even if I wouldn't live to see it.

*Turn the page for an exclusive look
at Kane and Arwen's first meeting
from his perspective.*

KANE

Five Months Earlier

I HATED THIS KINGDOM. EVERY INCH OF IT.

Saccharine nutmeg coated my tongue and the back of my throat every time I inhaled. There was too much corn, too many fallen bronze leaves crunching underfoot. The taverns here only served one ale, a stout brewed with apple and cinnamon that was so sweet it made your teeth ache.

My fangs prickled along my jaw at the thought.

I'd wanted to leave the Amber Kingdom hours ago, but Bert had insisted on getting Barney medical assistance in the nearby town of Abbington, and since he'd just lost his general, I gave him an hour.

It was my fault our men were being hunted in the first place.

When my father's face materialized in my mind, I dove downward, closer to the autumn trees below, wings outstretched against the early evening air, and tried to let the wind whistling against my scales calm the boiling in my blood.

I knew it was a waste of lighte to shift like this. I wasn't flying the battalion back to my kingdom for another hour, possibly longer if Bert found an infirmary for Barney. But seeing yet another murdered member of my army spurred more fury, more pent-up restlessness inside me than I knew how to handle.

Not long now. I just need the girl—

The mantra wasn't doing much to soothe me these days. Perhaps because I'd been saying it for twenty years.

Ever since the night of the fallen star.

The moment replayed in my mind's eye as clear as if I'd seen it through a looking glass. Two decades ago, I'd shot out of a deep sleep like a man possessed, sweating and gasping, clutching at my chest like my heart had been broken in two. I staggered out onto the balcony, icy air cutting at my face, just in time to see it—a lustrous, bright white star descending behind the mountains, like a drop of iridescent paint slipping down a night-black canvas.

The words of the prophecy had rung through my still-sleep-addled mind—*the fallen star will mean war has once again begun.*

I'd been like an eager child then, naive as I waited impatiently for the promise of blood and battle. For the last full-blooded Fae, expecting her to show up at my castle gates any minute. *Here I am! Sacrifice me!*

But nothing had happened.

Just an inexplicable feeling I was saddled with, that something infinitesimal had shifted within the fabric of our world.

And while we waited twenty years for some fated Fae girl, I was forced to investigate the deaths of more and more of my high-ranking officers. Each one killed by a mercenary sent by my father. To kill me, to taunt me, to distract me. I wasn't sure.

Tonight's executioner had been especially monstrous. That bastard must've shifted into something with horns, given the gaping holes that perforated the murdered general's lungs and throat. Perhaps claws, too. Barney's gut was practically shredded.

The flash of his entrails spilling onto the damp Amber soil turned my own stomach.

Barney was a good man. I almost cared.

And speaking of—

At the sight of my battalion walking through the glade below, I plunged downward. Cool evening air stung my snout as I sailed before landing with ease. The thud of my weight on the ground sent dirt and debris up in puffs around me like smoke.

And when the dust settled—

There she was.

Like a glowing ember in the dark, beckoning to me.

Pale moonlight dripped along her jaw and delicate nose, her full, round lips. Her worried brow and tangled, chestnut hair. Wide olive eyes fell to mine, shining and unreadable. Pulling me toward her as if—

"Healed the oaf," Lieutenant Bert said, low but not a whisper. Liquored breath stung my nostrils and pulled my attention from the girl's sorrowful face. Beside us, soldiers heaved a half-conscious Barney onto my back. His gut had been wrapped in bandages, seeping with red like wine through a tablecloth.

"Think he'll be fine."

My lips curled into a snarl.

The lieutenant was a decent leader and a skilled swordsman, but Gods, I hated the man. He was a sniveling suck-up.

"But I have something even better for you, my king. I've never seen such healing. What she did for Barney—it wasn't witch magic. It poured from her fingers like nectar. I think she might be what you've been looking for."

As the rest of the men climbed atop my outstretched wings, I studied the girl once more.

Graceful face. Dainty collarbone and shoulders. Flushed cheeks—

Actually, upon closer inspection, she looked . . . awful.

Still so, so beautiful, of course. Beauty such as hers couldn't be marred by fear, or dirt, or blood. But she was covered in all three from head to toe.

And she wasn't wearing much. Perhaps she was a courtesan? I wouldn't have been surprised. I was sure Amber men would pay buckets of coin to have their way with her.

Regardless of the state she was in, the truth was painfully obvious. So obvious it nearly knocked the breath from my lungs. Most wouldn't have been able to identify a full-blooded Fae off appearance alone, but having grown up with a full-blooded father, it was like seeing a rose among weeds. The lighte inside her was nearly glowing. She could have lit up the entire clearing if she had wanted to.

I almost wept with relief.

After all this time.

She was real.

And she was here.

And she was . . . digging her feet into the ground, whimpering against her restraints, and quivering in fear.

Oh, *from me.*

She was afraid of *me.*

"It's all right, the beast won't hurt you," Barney said from my back, still clutching at his wrapped wound.

His words didn't seem to calm the girl. As she neared me, still whining and resisting like an animal, I tried to look slightly less menacing. I wasn't sure why—I enjoyed being menacing. It was one of the many perks of my dragon form. The looks on people's faces, the way they ran and hid—at least it was an improvement on their bowing. More fitting for a beast, as Barney said.

Finally her swollen, red eyes caught mine. And in them, more grief than I'd seen in years. Glistening doe eyes, like pools of melancholy. They reminded me of the woods outside the palace I grew up in. So much so, I could almost smell my mother's perfume that filled the halls. The feeling was uncanny.

And over in an instant as she climbed onto my back.

"Don't try anything smart, girl."

I rolled my eyes at the solider. It wasn't as if she could escape into the clouds.

"Not really anywhere for me to go," she snipped.

I stifled a laugh.

And then everyone was aboard and I was off, bounding into the night sky, ready to get home. It had been a long night, and I knew--

Her touch almost sent me plummeting into the dirt thousands of feet below us. Despite my enormous dragon form, and the near dozen men piled atop of me, I could feel the singular touch of her fingers on my spine like a white-hot brand. Her dainty fingertips along my back- the sensation shot all the way down into my claws.

And her *pulse*—I could feel it racing through my scales. Like a captured sparrow in a child's sweaty palms, heart pattering so fast its whole body shook with the effort of staying upright. I tried in vain to wriggle free from her grip. It was too personal—feeling her touch and hearing her breathing and knowing the rhythm of her fear.

She was most definitely the full-blooded Fae girl from the prophecy. She couldn't be anything else. It was the only way to explain the bizarre physical reaction I was having to being around her.

I needed a drink.

~✧~

"YOU'RE JOKING."

"I am not. She's here. In the castle."

"After all this time." Griffin shook his head and threw the small leather ball for Acorn, who scampered across the study on all fours, puncturing it between his sharp teeth before it rolled under a mahogany bookcase. As the air hissed out of the ball, his shoulders fell in remorse, his owl-like wings knocking clumsily against the shelves.

I fought a grin. He wasn't a typical pet, and certainly not fit for a mortal king, but the bony, frightful strix had been mine since boyhood, and the Gods themselves couldn't bring me to part with him.

Acorn trotted the deflated ball back to Griffin with an eager squawk.

"What was she doing in Amber?" he asked, tossing the flaccid ball higher this time.

"I have no idea," I mused, downing the rest of my glass and leaning back into the cushions of my velvet chair. The whiskey burned my throat and soothed my racing mind.

"Meanwhile, we just captured a man who hides coin for one of

Rose's largest criminal rings. They're thieves and arms salesmen—
if the Blade of the Sun is being sold anywhere on this side of the
continent, he'll know about it."

The Blade of the Sun contained unimaginable power when
harnessed by Fae, but it was no more than a hunk of metal in the
hands of a mortal. Even a halfling. And yet foolish, greedy men had
sought it for centuries, unaware that they could never truly wield
the thing.

And one of those very fools was in my dungeon as we spoke.
Hope unfurled in my gut—I was having quite the night. "Excellent.
Let's get him on the rack."

Griffin's brow furrowed as he lounged back into the charcoal
couch, ignoring Acorn as he nudged the ball forward. "He'll die
before we get him to talk. The man's run the crime capital of the
continent for fifteen years. He's trained to withstand everything
but death."

I set the icy mug down and ran a hand over my face in thought.
It wasn't ideal, but I could work with it. I'd just have to get the felon
to open up some other way. Maybe to a peer—

A fellow prisoner.

Someone he could commiserate with. Brag to. They always
wanted to brag. Perhaps we could bribe some other asshole chained
up in our dungeon to ask the right questions and report back.

But the girl. She would be down there.

"I'll just go talk to him myself."

Griffin cocked his head at me as I moved through the study
door into my quarters, pulling off my silver rings and grabbing an
old hunting fur from the depths of my wardrobe.

"Well, not myself, exactly," I called back toward him. "Back in
a bit."

I was off before he could object. Barreling into the hallway, past my guards, and down the stone steps of my keep. It was late, and the castle was silent save for a few guards, who bowed with each opened door.

A real lead on the blade, the last full-blooded Fae in my possession, and all I could think of was seeing her again. Just getting one more look at her. It was the thrill of finally finding her after all these years. Of knowing I would finally end my father's life, and free all of Lumera.

It had to be.

"My king." The young guard on duty outside the dungeon door greeted me with a reverent bow.

"Not tonight, Toole. I'm just another prisoner this evening, got it?"

"Sure, Your Majesty, I understand, of course." Toole's steadfast nod melted into a wince. "But . . . I actually do not understand."

I stifled a sigh. I needed to get down there. She was likely minutes away if not locked inside already. "Which cell holds the man Griffin brought in from Rose?"

"Seventeen, my king."

"And is cell sixteen open?"

"Yes, but—"

"Good. Now, force me down there, and throw me in." I didn't have time for Toole's confusion.

"My king—"

"Now." When venom crept into my voice, Toole did as I said, and we made our way down the spiral stairs.

The dungeon's air was so thick, I could taste the must and mildew.

"Rot in there, you piece of filth!" Toole threw me into the cell with theatrical flair. I appreciated the commitment, despite his wooden performance. Toole snuck me an eager smile on his way back through the passageway and I tried not to grimace.

The cell wasn't terrible. Frankly, the gray stone, dim lantern light, and drip of murky water fit my dark, damp soul quite nicely. Griffin would have mocked me for my self-pity, but it was true. I belonged somewhere just like this. I even appreciated the spider's fine work in the corner, its web like dainty, macabre décor.

I scanned the passage. No Fae girl. Not yet, at least. But in the cell next to me was the man from Rose, snoring in a lump in the corner. Perhaps I could find a pebble to chuck at him.

"No, wait! I can't go in there."

Ah. Right on time—

I leaned forward to peer out into the shadowy corridor.

"I'm not going to harm you. It's just a place to lay your head until the lieutenant decides what to do with you." Barney's voice.

"I just can't be locked in. Please. Where do the healers stay?"

A laugh slipped out of me. The enchanting Fae was a bit entitled.

Vulgar hoots and hollers filled the dungeon, bouncing off the walls and floor as Barney walked her through and tossed the girl unceremoniously into the cell next to mine.

"Show me your tits, sweetheart! I've been down here for ages!"

"Spread them legs for me, girl!"

Sick satisfaction worked its way through me knowing I had chained these animals up and they wouldn't see daylight again.

"Wait!" the girl yelled after Barney, sobbing and panting.

She was being a little dramatic. How old was she? Twenty, if the fallen star had indicated her birth. She sank down in the corner and brought her knees to her chest, shaking in earnest, her breaths coming in uneven bursts. What was wrong with her? Surely she had to have some power she could use. In fact, I was surprised she hadn't used her lighte yet. For the last full-blooded Fae, she wasn't putting up much of a fight at all.

Perhaps she didn't know of her own power. Of the prophecy, of her Fae origins—it wasn't as if the Amber Kingdom had a robust Fae population to educate her. The race was practically nonexistent here in Evendell.

I let my head fall back against the stone behind me.

If that was the case, how was I going to get her to fight for us? How would I tell her she was destined to die?

The girl's strangled, muffled gasps rang through my cell. She really wasn't breathing now. I peered closer.

It seemed like she was panicking. Like my brother, Yale, used to.

Dagan used to soothe him through deep breathing, but I preferred another way. All Yale ever really needed was a distraction. To take his mind off his body and focus on something else.

But that was unrelated.

I wasn't going to help her.

She was just anxious. She'd be fine.

It wasn't the right time.

I only had one shot at convincing her to fight Lazarus. I had to position myself and our plan flawlessly. And I needed to get information out of the slumbering half-wit in the other cell. That was more important. I had only wanted to observe the girl; I wasn't going to talk to her, regardless of how miserable she looked. How hard it was for her to breathe. How many tears were splattering on the ground beneath her. How rushed her breaths sounded, how scared, how agonizingly frightened.

Don't talk to her, don't talk to her, don't—

"Bleeding Stones," she cursed under her breath.

"Quite the mouth on you," I hummed.

Damn it.

The girl snapped her head up, chocolatey brown hair falling over her face and sticking to her tear-streaked cheeks. She was still inhaling air as if paid by the breath. But now she also looked embarrassed.

"Sorry," she muttered.

"It's just . . . a little dramatic, don't you think?"

What are you doing? Leave her alone.

Her brows knit inward and she dropped the hand that was pressed firmly to her chest as if to slow her beating heart. "I said I was sorry, what more do you want?"

A laugh that was more surprise than anything else tripped out of me and I leaned forward, intrigued. So the little hummingbird had claws. "Some peace and quiet from your weeping would be nice."

"I'm done now," she conceded, drawing in a long, slow breath and dropping her head back against the damp stone. "It's not every day you get imprisoned." She snapped her head up. "Or . . . maybe it is for you, but—not for me."

The distraction was working. Good. It was a good deed, to help the Fae girl. A payment for all those she would help with her sacrifice. The least I could do, truly.

"I'm just saying, some of us are trying to get some sleep around here. Your theatrics and heaving bosom aren't going to change your situation." I paused, debating the next words that played at my lips. "Though the latter is nice to look at."

"You're disgusting," she breathed, and I swallowed a smirk.

"Someone's feeling brave with these bars between us."

"Not really. Just honest."

Her panic seemed to have subsided. She had wiped her tears with the back of her hand; the air was flowing slowly in and out through her nose. I just needed a better look to be sure.

I rose and felt my stiff bones creak, stretching my hands above my head and nearly scraping the mold from the ceiling. My earlier sentiments about the comfort of the cells had been incorrect. Now I felt like a chicken in a coop.

Walking toward the iron bars that sprouted between our cells, I peered down at the Fae girl. She was very small from this angle. Fragile. Bony. How would a woman like this defeat my father? It didn't seem possible.

I leaned an arm onto the bars and examined her bruised shins and bare feet.

"Are you trying to scare me?" she asked quietly.

Quite literally the opposite. "Something like that."

"Well, you don't. Scare me, that is."

"Such a brave bird," I hummed. And I believed her. Courage might be the only weapon she could wield against him. "Good to hear. Perhaps now I can sleep."

That would be tomorrow's problem. Tonight, the girl would be fine, and I was free to play ally to the thug from Rose. I'd be out of this cell in—

"Your cruelty is a bit cliché."

Why was she so bold? She was practically studying me now. Unable to help myself, I dropped down to a crouch to get a better look at her, too. Her wide olive eyes, framed by long fanned-out lashes, pored over mine. My lips, my chin. Heat rose in my blood.

"Why, because I'm imprisoned?" I asked.

"What?"

I fought a smile as her cheeks turned pink. "The cliché, as you said."

"Yes. Cruel, dark prisoner." She shrugged. "It's done to death."

"You wound me," I mocked. But she was in here, too, was she not? "Couldn't I say the same of you?"

The most adorable, tiny, frustrated pinch furrowed between her brows, but she remained silent. Perhaps she didn't like the fact that despite her assumptions about me, we were locked in the same dungeon. She was a bit naive, this girl. What was ahead of her—bravery aside, she'd need to be savvier. "You'll have to buck up a bit, bird. You're in Onyx now. It's not all mud-colored hair, ruddy cheeks, and squash farmers. Bastards like me are the least of your concern."

"How do you know I'm from Amber?"

Shit. Maybe her farm clothes would give her away. I scanned down her body, and remembered how nearly bare she was. Dirtied white camisole splattered in Barney's blood. Long wool skirt. The girl folded her arms across her chest in modesty, shame coating her cheeks.

Shame?

Was she feeling modest?

Perhaps she wasn't a courtesan at all. In which case—

I clenched my jaw against the irrational anger. "What happened to the rest of your clothing?"

She swallowed hard. "It's a long story."

The thought of anyone abusing this girl was suddenly very upsetting. *Very.* "I've got time."

406 ◆ KATE GOLDEN

"I had to use my blouse to help someone. That's all."

When she shivered and little pebbles broke out across her bare arms, I couldn't help myself. "Are you cold?"

What was I, her mother?

"Yes," she said, honestly. "You aren't?"

"I must be used to it. Here." I pulled off the hunting cloak and folded it through the bars between us. Her eyes widened, and I added hastily, "I can't listen to your teeth chattering a minute longer. It's grating on the nerves."

She took the fur with no snark, no bite, and wrapped it around herself like it was the single nicest item she had ever owned. The girl's eyes nearly rolled back in her head from the warmth as she murmured, "Thank you."

The garment was two sizes too big for her, but she snuggled into it as if it were made for her.

She looked . . . comfortable. Cozy.

As if all the horrors that had delivered her, bloody and bruised, to Bert this evening, and all the horrors that followed, from the back of a spiked beast to the confines of a cell, were manageable as long as she could just be *warm*.

Safe.

And the feeling brewing in my chest at such a sight—

Oh, Gods.

I was fucked.

Acknowledgments

There is no other way to begin this than by thanking my brilliant, supportive, and endlessly patient partner, Jack. On our ten-year-anniversary trip, amid sunburns, whale sightings, and poolside Popsicles, you helped me discover Arwen and Kane's story. You woke up each morning, and instead of hitting the breakfast buffet we both love so much, you let me sit on our balcony and click-clack on my laptop, lost in the Onyx Kingdom, until the midday heat forced me into the pool. And after the trip, you let me pitch story ideas to you, fixed my plot holes, came up with significantly less stupid names for all my cities, and even read my first draft in record time. And then you asked, "When do I get to read book two?" All the while, you never complained that this was not what you signed up for, that this was very much *not* the career I had spent the last seven years building, or that twenty-eight was a little late in life for me to decide I wanted to be a fantasy romance author. I am so grateful for you; there is no way to put it into words. I would brave a hundred Shadow Woods for you.

Along the road to publishing my first novel, there were so many other wonderful, helpful individuals I'd like to thank as well. My creative, imaginative mom, who taught me everything I know about storytelling (and humans in general). My thoughtful beta readers, who convinced me this might be a story worth sharing with others. My brilliant developmental editor, Natalie, who reminded me to take my time and build and build and *build* the tension. My lovely proofreaders, Naomi and Danni, who elevated the entire novel with their sharp eyes. My incredible agents, Taylor, Sam, and Olivia, who brought this story into the big wide world of traditional publishing that I never could have faced alone. My creative genius of an editor at Berkley, Kristine, who I met and within three minutes knew understood this series, these characters, and this world as deeply and with as much enthusiasm as I did. The loyal (and hilarious) TikTok community that so closely followed this book and its release—none of this would have happened without your passion. And lastly, my darling Milo, the best dog a person could ask for. Thanks for sitting beside me for entire weekends while I wrote, and never complaining when I would randomly scream at my computer screen for no reason. You're a real one.

Turn the page for a sneak peek of

A Promise of Peridot

the next book in the Sacred Stones trilogy.

ARWEN

I'M GOING TO BE SICK AGAIN," WARNED RYDER AS HE HUNG his head over the wet steel edge of the boat. Angry droplets of rain pelted us both as I rubbed soothing circles into the damp fabric clinging to his back.

"I'm here," I said as I tried to send lighte into his knotted stomach. I waited, and waited some more, until I couldn't help but tense my fingers against the emptiness I felt where my power should have been, gritting my teeth against the void—

Still nothing.

Ryder retched into the churning sea below us.

For the last ten days following the battle of Siren's Bay, I had healed the entire ship of all their battle wounds without my power. The injuries inflicted by Lazarus's army, burns singed and gashes slashed by lighte and Fae weapons, were more damaging to the Onyx and Peridot soldiers than any mortal steel. It had been the most taxing work I'd ever done.

And all the while, elbow-deep in bandages and sickly, fevered sweat, I tried to grieve.

We had held a small, makeshift funeral for her—the woman I had always thought was my mother. The unscathed soldiers aboard lowered her body into the churning sea beneath us, and I had said a few words, all of which felt flat and foreign in my mouth. Mari sung a hymn. Ryder cried. Leigh didn't look at any of us, and then slunk into our cabin belowdecks before we even finished.

It had been awful.

Kane had asked if he could join us. I believe his words were, *"I'd like to be there for you, if you'll let me."* As if his presence might have somehow made me feel better, instead of infinitely, *infinitely* worse. I hadn't wanted him anywhere near my family. Or, what had been left of them.

Then, the storm came.

A thunderous assault of rain, with waves that sloshed against the ship like battering rams. It raged and raged without letting up our entire journey. Each day, within minutes of stepping out onto the deck for a reprieve from stale cabin air, I was soaked in frigid, briny seawater.

Yesterday the captain had rationed the ship's coal, so now there was no hot water. Already I couldn't stomach any more lukewarm porridge. I looked down at my fingers on Ryder's back. They were eternally pruned, like little sunbaked raisins.

He heaved again, and down the bow a couple feet, a Peridot woman in a thick wool cloak followed suit. Though I was lucky not to suffer from seasickness, the same couldn't be said for the rest of the passengers. The stomach-turning sounds of retching echoed at all hours of the day and night. I offered care to whomever I could, but with diminished lighte, there wasn't much to do.

I hadn't offered any help to Kane, though.

I'd watched him climb a rickety set of stairs with ease a single day after being pierced through the chest by a spear of ice. He'd scaled them two at a time—nimble, strong, lively even.

And yet, he had needed me to heal him so critically that day in the Shadowhold infirmary?

All lies. More and more lies. My head swam with them.

I waited for the instinctual rush of fear to ripple through me when I thought of the fate he'd kept from me all those months. The prophecy that foretold my death at Kane's own father's hands. But I felt nothing.

I had felt nothing for days now.

After a lifetime of too much fear, and tears, and worry—now I couldn't muster anything at all.

With one final dry heave, Ryder slumped down against the bow, his forehead dented by the metal, and sucked in a deep breath. "I think that's the last of it. There's nothing left in my stomach to vomit up." When he stood, his blue eyes were watery from exertion and rain.

I frowned. "A lovely mental image."

His answering smile was weak.

But I had drifted back to another time in my life. A memory of a slow, autumn evening—silent save for the sounds of wind rustling among the weeds outside our house. I'd been sick after eating something rotten—Powell's *leave no scrap behind* mentality at work—and like Ryder and me on this deck, my mother had rubbed my back in steady sweeps, calming me as I purged. I could have healed myself, but chose not to. I liked how it felt to have her comfort me. I liked her hand on my shoulder, her quieting words. Leigh had been born recently, and I think both Ryder and I missed Mother's attention.

It was such a selfish, childish thing to do. To retch for an hour rather than heal my own illness, to not use the power I was lucky enough to have just to keep her by my side in the chilly evening air, away from her new baby, her husband, and her son—to keep her with me.

But it felt so good to be cared for.

And now—

Now I fell asleep every night wondering who the woman even was.

Had she found me on the street one day?

Had someone forced her to raise me?

And if so, where in the world were my real parents? If they were Fae, they were likely living in another realm. A melting world of parched earth and ash, governed by a tyrant—

"Feeling any better?"

My eyes landed on Mari, wandering over wrapped in a thick fur cloak. She'd raided the ship on our first night and somehow found the most fashionable pieces aboard. But even the elegant pelt couldn't hide the way her copper hair clung in wet ringlets to her face or the icy drops that showered her nose and near-blue lips.

At the sight of Mari, Ryder stood two inches taller and pulled his hands from the bow to fold them confidently across his chest. "Right as this rain. Barely even sick." He nodded toward the woman still heaving down the deck. "It's all these other folk I feel sorry for."

"He vomited the entire contents of his stomach out and then some," I said to her.

Ryder glared at me, and Mari gave him a compassionate frown. "Sorry to hear it. This storm is unrelenting."

"Yeah, well—" We sailed over another swell and Ryder turned

pale, clutching at his stomach. "I . . . I am going to go talk to someone about that. Right now." Then he dashed for the other end of the ship and out of eyesight.

Mari lifted a brow at me. "Talk to someone . . . about the storm?"

I shook my head. "He's too proud."

"I think it's sweet that he's embarrassed. Here." She pulled a small bronze vial from her skirts. "Give him this. It's Steel of the Stomach."

"Another potion? Isn't that used for working in a mortuary?" After I'd read the book on Evendell flora from the Peridot library twice, I had started working through Mari's grimoires out of sheer boredom. She didn't have much use for them anymore, anyway. Not now that she had the amulet.

Though Mari's mother had been a witch, she'd died in childbirth, so Mari never learned to wield her magic properly. It wasn't until she stole a necklace that belonged to Briar Creighton, the supposed most powerful witch of all time, that she was able to harness her power—and quite a bit of it. Now she did magic whenever and however she pleased. And the amulet never left her neck.

Mari shrugged, pawing absently at the violet charm as it hung below her collarbone. "I figured it might help him. It was easy to brew."

Kane had told me back at Siren's Cove that the amulet was merely a trinket. Mari wasn't actually pulling any power from Briar or her lineage. All the magic she harnessed with such ease these days was her own.

Every time I tried to tell her the truth, I found a well of apathy where my ethics used to be. I didn't want to lie to her, but—

But I just didn't have the energy.

For anything.

"Have you talked to Kane at all today?" she asked, gripping the slick bow as the ship pitched over another uneasy wave.

I sighed, a long and thorough noise. Another thing I couldn't bring myself to do. "No."

"What if there's another way? Hadn't he said as much?"

She was referencing the last time he and I spoke, after the battle. After my mother's death. After my outburst of power and butchery.

Kane had said he was willing to let the entire continent fall to Lazarus to save me from my death sentence. To help me live my life in peace.

But I didn't want him to.

What kind of "peace" could I find knowing all those who would suffer at Lazarus's hands because I was holed away somewhere hiding from my fate?

I wouldn't do it. I wouldn't be a coward ever again.

"There's nothing he can help me do but run."

Mari pursed her lips. "He knows more about this prophecy than anyone. You could be wrong." She frowned, reaching a hand for my shoulder, before thinking better of it and twining it in her fur cloak. "I know it's unbelievably hard, and I can't imagine being in your shoes, but can you try to have a little hope?"

"I just need off this boat," I said, staring up into the heavy, rumbling storm clouds above.

"I know." She sighed. "This journey has been miserable."

But I wasn't thinking of the rain or the cold or the vomiting. Only of getting Leigh and Ryder safely to Citrine, and myself as far from Kane as possible. Somewhere I could be alone until I was needed. A sacrificial lamb, awaiting slaughter.

So I stayed silent as the rain battered my face, searching my heart for an ache at Mari's empathy, for hope, for even a trill of fear at the thoughts of my future.

But I found nothing.

I missed my mother.

I wanted to go home.

I wanted to sleep for a long, long time.

ABOUT THE AUTHOR

Kate Golden lives in Los Angeles, where she works full-time in the film industry, developing stories with screenwriters and filmmakers. *A Dawn of Onyx* is her debut novel, and the first in the Sacred Stones trilogy. In her free time, she is an avid book reader, movie fanatic, and functioning puzzle addict. An embarrassing LA cliché, she likes to hike, brunch, and go to the flea market with her fiancé and her puppy. You can find her on Instagram at KateGoldenAuthor and on TikTok at Kate_Golden_Author, where she is known to post both spicy and heartbreaking teasers for her upcoming books.

Ready to find
your next great read?

Let us help.

Visit prh.com/nextread